PRIMEVAL

ALSO BY DAVID LYNN GOLEMON

Event
Legend
Ancients
Leviathan

PRIMEVAL

An Event Group Thriller

DAVID LYNN GOLEMON

THOMAS DUNNE BOOKS
ST. MARTIN'S PRESS 🙰 NEW YORK

This is a work of fiction. All of the characters, organizations, and events portrayed in this novel are either products of the author's imagination or are used fictitiously.

THOMAS DUNNE BOOKS.
An imprint of St. Martin's Press.

www.thomasdunnebooks.com
www.stmartins.com

ISBN 978-0-312-58078-0

First Edition: July 2010

10 9 8 7 6 5 4 3 2 1

For Kiera—
My new baby granddaughter, the most valuable jewel in the world!

For my son, Shaune, and daughter-in-law, Tram—
you did real well!

ACKNOWLEDGMENTS

For the Royal Canadian Mounted Police for assistance beyond the call of duty—my many thanks.

For Major Rudolf Anderson, a brave man and U2 pilot who helped save the world in 1962.

PROLOGUE
THE CROSSING

BERINGIA
(EASTERN SIBERIA—WESTERN ALASKA
LAND BRIDGE)
20,000 YEARS BCE

The grass was tall and abundant. The men watched as the herd of giants grazed on the sweet, salt-laden growth close to the edges of the warm seas. The waters lapped at the north and south shores of the narrow spit of land as it traveled eastward toward the new and unknown world where the sun was reborn each day. The land was widening as it traveled east, expanding into a vast plain of tall grass. The giant wall of ice lay to the north and was clearly visible from the vantage point of the lowlands. Soon, that wall would start its slow move south as the ice would return once again to the world of man.

The herd, far larger in stature and strength than the tusked, woolly creatures of their old home to the west, stood their ground, too ignorant to fear man even after one of their old males had succumbed to spear and stone.

The elder of this nomadic tribe suddenly straightened from the day's kill. The evening breeze had brought with it a scent he had come to know well since their trek began more than three months before from the steppes of Asia. It was *They Who Follow*—always within two miles of the band of forty men, women, and children, but never close enough to see or hear. The only evidence of their being near was the massive prints left by their alpha male: Prints so large, that two of his younger hunters could place their feet end to end into the eight-inch-deep depression.

A strong, young hunter stood next to his grandfather and followed his gaze to the west, toward the home they had been forced to leave. There was nothing there for the people except starvation and ravenous creatures driven mad by the same predicament as they themselves. The younger male sniffed the air, but the telltale scent was gone, blown away by the shifting evening winds.

The old man gestured for his grandson to continue the butchering and harvesting of the giant kill. His attention was still focused on the western horizon. He knew that the great man-beast was watching, waiting for the scavenger's chance at their kill. The elder didn't know for sure how many mouths the alpha male fed in its roving clan, but he knew that when he and his grandson backtracked, the carcasses of their kills were always stripped bare of meat, the marrow sucked from the bones.

As the young hunters bundled the meat from the old bull into the tough and woolly outer skin of the tusked one, the old man reached down and stayed his grandson from picking his ration of meat from the tall grass. The elder shook his head, his long hair flying free with the wind. The boy of sixteen looked from the familiar lined and chiseled brown face to the west, and immediately understood. They would leave one of the bundles for *They Who Follow*, an offering of goodwill to a clan of man-beasts that could easily kill them all if that was the path chosen, but had thus far let their small roving band be. Their only offense till now had been that of curiosity. The old man had puzzled over their strange behavior, never having come across this breed of creature in their old homeland, and had come to the conclusion that it may be the beasts only sought the comradeship of beings not far removed from themselves.

The grandson tossed the meat to the grass, nodding his understanding of the elder's intent. He turned to the other men and gestured with his spear that they should move back to their camp before the sun dipped below the hills far to the west. Before moving off, the boy thought a moment, then placed his hand inside the leather pouch draped over his shoulder and brought out his prize for bringing down the woolly beast. The liver, wrapped inside the slippery stomach, lay beside the bundle of meat. The delicacy was an offering of highest honor for the followers of men.

The old man nodded at the boy's offering, then turned and watched the tall grass behind them. He knew the eyes of the giant were on them. He sensed it—felt the presence of the creature that had picked up their trail in the northern reaches of the high country well over a year gone, following and forever watching.

The elder raised his arms to the sky, the sharpened staff crowned with the feathers of the great winged eagle held high as he swept his arms low, indicating the offering to the great creature he knew was watching. Then he moved the staff to the south and the band of hunters moved away, leaving only the bones of their kill and the offering to the great beast.

The giant creature stood over eleven feet tall. Its sheer weight alone was equal to eight of the humans it followed. The massive head had a broad brow, indicating the possibility of it carrying a brain near equal to that of a man's. Its ability to walk upright made the animal quick of foot and steady on uneven terrain. The eyes held the spark of intelligence like no primate before it. The mouth was filled with teeth capable of chewing the harsh grasses, twigs, and bushes of the western continent—being flat and broad—as well as the large, sharp incisors of the meat eater.

The great beast was not usually a scavenger. In its natural element of forest or jungle, its kind excelled at providing for its females and its young. The art of camouflage came naturally to the hairy beast, blending in well no matter the terrain due to its thickness of fur and its ability to vary the crevasse and valleys of that fur, creating many broken lines and never a clean silhouette.

The great creature watched as the old man gestured toward the spot from where he was crouching, hidden from the humans. The creature's brown eyes narrowed as the stick the man held indicated that there was something on the ground. The giant huffed, deep in its throat. The large, thick lips were pursed, as it thought and puzzled something through. Then it relaxed when it saw the old man follow his young away from the spot of their kill. When the humans were far from sight, heading toward the dunes of the southern sea, the beast stood to its full height. Its brown and black hair rustled as it tilted its head. The great beast liked the evening and its coolness. The large hands reached out, touched the tall, sweet grass, and ran its powerful, thick fingers over the tops of the growth. It blinked, sniffed, and looked as if it were enjoying its moment alone in the soft evening of this new world.

Then, like the old man a few moments before, it froze and sniffed the wind. There was a scent it had never smelled before—a heavy musk that was similar to the great cats of the beast's home region, only different somehow. The giant crouched and smelled the air, but as it did, it knew the scent was gone, vanished on the breeze as if it had never been at all.

The creature felt the approach of the three males and six females of its own clan, as they came from the taller grass where they had been hiding from the band of men. The two offspring, the last of their young, ambled out on unsteady legs and watched as one of the largest of the males in the group turned toward them. It eyed the male and female young, then turned around, and smelled the air once more, turning in a slow circle, huffing and sniffing at the air. Satisfied that there was no danger to their young, it grunted and then ambled toward the offering of fresh meat left for them.

As the alpha watched, the second largest male pulled the liver from the grass, tearing at the stomach lining to free it. The young ran for the huge broken skeleton and wrestled with the giant ribs, shaking and pulling as the adults watched. Their eyes were kind, but aware, always aware of their surroundings. The alpha knew the others felt it, too. Something lurked in the gathering darkness around them . . . something that stalked for its sustenance.

The great beast looked to the south once more. The scent had vanished, but not before the giant gleaned which direction it was heading: to the place where the men had chosen to lay for the night.

The alpha grunted several times until the other adults stopped feeding and looked up from their squatting positions. The bundled meat had already been pulled open and the portions given out without any fighting or snarling. They watched as the alpha grunted again, then turned and left. Heading south, its huge strides followed the childish footprints of those of the old man and his people. They knew the alpha had caught the scent of something large and dangerous stalking the unsuspecting men.

The fire was high. The old man kept sending out the younger of the men in groups of four to bring in more wood. For him, the fire pit could not be high or hot enough for the dark night coming. The group of men and women were happy in anticipation of a good meal, one they hadn't shared since the last full moon. Over twenty suns of dried meat, grass, and berries. These items had been mashed into soft dough that hardened after only a few hours of lying in the sun. The promise of cooked meat was what made the group relax, not heeding the old man's worries about what may be lurking in the night around them. The men and women of the clan had faced the creatures of their own world and conquered all, so what could this new land offer that could outfight or outthink them? They knew they were safe around the night fire that all animals, except man, feared.

The elder scratched the side of his face and drew his light coat around him as a wisp of breeze blew in from the sea to their campsite. The coat was old and wearing thin—the small wolf that had provided it had done so in the summer months, so it lacked the fur of a warmer winter coat. The chill in the air was becoming more perceptible every day, but with the promise of heavy fur from the great tusked ones, winter coats and warm shelter should not be a problem.

The old man nodded when his grandson laid three large cooked rib bones beside him. The grease was running thick and hot, and the marrow was bubbling free of the bone—just what his aching stomach needed. As the old one picked up one of the large rib bones, he heard the rustling behind them. As he froze, he could see his grandson had heard it also. He watched the boy's eyes as they traveled along the line of tall grass. In the firelight, the old man could see the grass reflected in the boy's dark eyes as something pushed the heavy vegetation aside with its massive bulk. The heavy and wild smell of a cat hit his nostrils as he dropped the rib bone and reached for his sharpened staff.

The boy turned and was about to shout a warning to the others when the grass parted and the ground trembled slightly as the largest, most fearsome cat the old man had ever seen in the western lands, leaped into the midst of the humans, actually turning in midair just before it landed. Its roar filled the night with horror. The canines of the great cat were the length of a man's forearm and they curled into lethal cutting knives that hung from its gaping upper maw. The cat's eyes glowed with golden heat in the firelight as it swiped at a female, gutting her before the men could react with spear and stone. The seven-hundred-pound cat then turned and roared at the men returning from wood gathering, its twelve-inch claws raking the air.

The old man tried to bring the women and children closer to the fire that the cat so clearly feared. As a girl of ten ran with her mother, the great cat reacted with lightning speed, jumping clear of the spear-toting men and taking the screaming child in its massive jaws. It shook the girl, trying to break the child's back, but she kept screaming, fully aware of her horrible fate. As the men poked and prodded at the giant cat, the women were terrified, screaming at the nightmarish scene. The thick hide of the animal was like hardened leather and the spear points lost all momentum as they pierced the cat's side and shoulders. The cat was starting to become enraged as the men inflicted pain such as it never felt before.

The long-toothed cat was about to leap clear of the huge fire and disappear with the struggling child, when an even louder, defiant bellow of rage filled the night air, freezing not only the panicked men and women, but the cat as well. The growl was deeper than anyone had ever heard. The great beast, seen for the first time in all the weeks of it following them, jumped into the midst of men and cat. The men drew their spear arms back, ready to attack, when the old man started screaming and gestured wildly for them to concentrate on the cat.

The spear-toothed cat crouched low to the ground, defending its meal against the strange creature before its murderous eyes. The giant manlike form bent low to the ground, mimicking the cat's offensive posture. The large brown eyes stared at the girl clutched in the cat's mouth; the child was growing weaker, the air to her small lungs cut off by the smaller teeth of the cat. The giant was trying desperately for an opening, feigning right, and then left—its instinct to save the child outweighing the danger to itself.

The strange creature charged the cat, throwing up sand and dirt as its huge feet tore into the ground for purchase. The cat launched itself at the same moment, the dying child still in its mouth. The weight of the cat struck the giant but it was like two great boulders colliding during an avalanche. They both hit and rolled through the fire, the giant bellowing. The hair-covered creature pounded the cat on the back and sides, making the animal want to spit its meal from its mouth, but through sheer animal menace, it held on. The great creature tried desperately to wrap its powerful arm around the thick neck of the cat as it swiped at its antagonist, leaving three-inch-deep bloody furrows along the giant's back. Then, finally, the creature gained a firm hold on the cat. It grasped with all its strength the cat's neck, bringing bone-crushing power to bear.

The cat finally did as the giant wanted: it screamed, loosening its thick jaws just long enough for the rescuer to pull the child from its maw. It tossed the girl into the sand and rolled with the giant cat into the tall grass. The men rushed forward but the elder held them at bay as the sounds of the fight continued. The roar and screech of the cat and the deep, booming bellows of the giant continued for twenty minutes as the two magnificent animals fought for domination in the tall grasses of the new land, out of sight.

The girl child was barely breathing. The cat's smaller teeth had punctured deep into her chest, and every time the girl child breathed, she exhaled blood. One eye had been lost, and one arm and one leg lay useless and broken in the sand, but the old man thought the child might have a fighting chance to survive.

As suddenly as the night had exploded around them, it became still. The men watched with raised spear and stones at the area where the two frightening creatures had vanished, but there was no sound, no movement. The grandson started to move forward, spear at the ready, but the old man once more held him back. Even if the great creature had survived the awful teeth of the cat, it might be so wounded it would strike out at anything or anyone who came near. No, they would stay near the fire.

The elder watched as the fingernail moon rose into the sky, and in the distance, he thought he could hear the sound of wailing. Humanlike in tenor and woman-sounding, it gave the old man chills as he knew there was anguish etched in those cries.

The man lowered his head. They would move on tomorrow, furthering themselves from their ancient homeland, distancing their hunger, and keeping pace with the easily moving herd. However, for some reason the man could not fathom, he felt the days of *They Who Follow* were at an end. Why the great creature had saved one of their own, he would never know, and now he would think on it no more that night.

As he watched the men build up the fire and the women tend to the injured girl, the old man turned to the west and listened as the sad sound of death continued to fill the night. The strange noise of many large sticks slamming into the ground and the few trees on this small, thin plain joined the wailing. The constant beat sounded as if a herd of creatures ran through the night. Both the thumping and the cries unnerved the group of men.

The clan of giants had lost one more of their kind and was fast dwindling to almost nothing. The beasts, unlike any animal in the world, had an instinct—not unlike that of man—about the inevitability of death. With little hope of finding the new world to the east any better than the barren land they left behind, the giant humanlike animals, the most intelligent creature next to evolutionary man, could soon vanish from the face of the earth. However, the elder was wrong about one thing: The clan of giants was now attached to his band of wanderers, and they would forever seek the companionship and warmth of men.

JULY 16, 1918
EKATERINBURG, RUSSIA

The royal family was allowed out of the confines of the house to enjoy the morning air. Crown Prince Alexei was bundled heavily against the chill, while constantly being attended to and pestered by the family doctor. His father watched from a distance. They were in the large courtyard, and he never liked being far away from the children. He watched two of the Bolshevik guards as they strolled lazily by his four daughters, giving them a quick appreciative glance, then knowing they were being watched by the royal family, the guards continued on their way with a sneer and chuckle as might be expected from the lowborn men they were. Last year at this time, these very same men would have been shot for their arrogance.

Tsar Nicholas II accepted his fate as the last tsar of the great Romanov dynasty—however, he did not have to accept that same disgraced destiny for his children.

He waited by the tall wall, and was tempted to shift his weight from one foot to the other in nervousness, but finally he forced himself into stillness. He looked without turning, catching the small dark eyes of

Commissar Yurovsky watching the family from the ground-floor window of the large farmhouse. The small man was paying particular attention to the tsar, but that was no surprise; the beady ferret eyes of the commissar were forever watching, studying.

Nicholas saw the tall man walking toward him down the garden's lone path. The tsar could tell that the big man also knew the eyes of the commissar were scrutinizing his comings and goings in the courtyard—therefore the large man paused to converse with the girls, nodding as they spoke to him, smiling in the coquettish way they always had. His daughters found the blond-haired Bolshevik irresistible. He was able to put everyone—highborn and lowborn—at ease. It was a talent Nicholas himself had never attained through his many years of rule in Russia.

Finally, the tsar saw Yurovsky turn away from the window and he relaxed—to a point—as he knew there were several other sets of eyes watching from places he could not guess. The large man, Colonel Iosovich Petrov, was respected even among the ruthless guards, largely because they feared *what* he was—a member of the dreaded Cheka, the secret police of the new Communist Party. What the Bolsheviks did not know, however, was the fact that at one time the handsome colonel had been on the payroll of Tsar Nicholas himself.

The large man with the easy gait, standing tall in his knee-high polished boots and splendid green uniform, nodded his greeting to the tsar, half bowing, a simple gesture that the guards saw as mocking the royal, but it was actually a sincere greeting as taught to him by his superiors while he was training in exile with Vladimir Lenin. This did not stop him from moving his blue eyes to the far window, looking for the pinched features of the commissar.

"Young man," the tsar greeted in return. That simple gesture was something new to him—something that should have been incorporated long before his abdication. Small things like that little greeting, employed over his reign, may have been beneficial to his understanding of the classes that were far beneath his station. Creating a road to understanding his own people is exactly where he had failed so miserably.

"Sire," the man said as he straightened his hat, "your family looks well this morning."

Nicholas cleared his throat, raising his gloved hand to his mouth, and then nodded once. "Thank you . . . comrade—uh, that is the proper word these days? Comrade Colonel?"

Petrov smiled. "Yes, but just *Colonel* will do for the time being . . . as in the old days?"

The tsar turned and started walking, the uniformed colonel, without hesitation, walked along casually with him, towering over the smaller Nicholas. They both placed their hands behind their backs. The colonel, without turning to face the tsar, spoke in low tones, saying what he had to say.

"I was only able to get the one girl from Tetrovisk. Your cousin's family, including his daughters, had already left the country from the port of Vladivostok in the east three weeks ago. The one daughter I have was left behind in the local hospital; she was too ill to travel with the rest of her family. She is just recovering from pneumonia. She has fully recovered and I have explained to her the task ahead. On your behalf, she has agreed to cooperate—it must be nice to still have loyalty, even among your lower relatives."

The tsar was quiet, ignoring the thinly veiled reference to his royal nieces and nephews. Instead of commenting, he closed his eyes in an effort to fight back the despair he was suddenly feeling at Petrov's news. He swallowed, then smiled as best he could and forced himself not to look the part of a dejected and desperate father. The news meant that only one of his precious daughters would survive their possible black fate. As ruthless as the plan was—the killing off of relatives to save his own children—was the only hope of having his direct bloodline survive the madness that had swept his country.

"The boy?" he finally asked, looking out of the corner of his eye at the two guards watching from the garden's main gate. He desperately tried to keep from choking up as he waited for the fate of his son to be announced.

"There, I was able to secure you some good news. The British intelligence service was much helpful in getting us the son of your cousin's mistress—the little man even has the same blood type as the crown prince."

"Does he resemble my son?" Nicholas asked through clenched teeth, an almost desperate question.

The tall man smiled and looked over at the guards, and then he lowered his head so his lips could not be seen.

"It was as if I were looking at the bastard son of a mistress of yours . . . Your Highness."

The tsar closed his eyes and fought a desperate battle with his rising anger, as again he had to endure the insults to his royal dignity.

"Apologies . . . very rude of me—yes, the boy looks like Alexei. They could even be twin brothers."

"Only two children? There is no chance of finding any more to match my other daughters?"

The large man stopped and looked at the back of the once powerful tsar.

"Two of your children are guaranteed to survive tonight. That is how you must look at this. Any other way would be foolish, and may cause you to falter at the wrong time, and that could lead to all of them getting killed. Tonight, above all else, you must be braver than your reputation."

Tsar Nicholas stopped suddenly, felt the eyes on him from around the courtyard, and again turned back to face the Bolshevik colonel.

"Tonight?" he asked as his lips and left cheek twitched under his closely trimmed beard.

"A Czech contingent of the White Army is drawing too close. Commissar Yurovsky has his orders. I delivered them myself just this morning. I am sorry—murder is a despicable business."

"Tonight," Nicholas repeated, head turning to look at his family as they admired the flowers lining the broken wall. He looked at his wife and she glanced at him. The tsarina saw the look on her husband's face and turned away, looking at her daughters and only son. When asked a question by one of the girls, she cleared her thoughts and smiled brightly. Nicholas knew his brave Alexandria understood.

"Which of my daughters is to live?"

"The one girl that matched in features, age, and weight is Anastasia."

Nicholas grew silent, only nodding his head as his eyes went to his smiling daughter, and he saw her through the tears that formed. Quick witted and vivacious, Anastasia. *Yes,* he thought, *that is who it was meant to be. She is the one who will carry on in her family's absence.*

"The commissar will wait until close to midnight when most of the miserable souls here and in the village are asleep. Then he will send for you, your family, your family doctor, and even your servants."

"No one is to be spared?"

The large man grew silent. He wanted to ask the tsar how many families had been awakened in the middle of the night by *his own* secret police, to be taken away for questioning and never heard from again. However, what use would there be in that?

"The arrangements are all concluded?" Nicholas asked, his eyes never leaving his family.

"The two children and I will travel overland many days. We will have safe conduct papers signed by Comrade Lenin himself. We will travel to Nalychevo, where a ship is already waiting on the eastern coast."

"The contents of my will are also secured there?"

"The portion of the royal treasury you were able to convert to American gold double eagles, have been successfully smuggled out of Moscow and will arrive three days before us. Your children will be very well cared for—on that, you have my word. Even after my comrades take their half of the bounty, they should be satisfied with dividing six million dollars in American currency."

Nicholas turned and resumed walking, retracing his steps back in the direction of his family. Meanwhile, Petrov held his ground, facing in the opposite direction.

"Noble of you, Comrade Petrov," Nicholas said and then stopped. "Your destination?"

"America is where your royal relatives will receive your children. I cannot tell you more than that."

"Colonel Petrov, if it were still in my power, I would reward you—"

"It is not in your power, however. I will give my accomplices the portion of the treasury reserved for them, and that for your children's upbringing, and that is all. I suspect that the Twins are intact, your people were able to secure them with the gold that will meet us?"

"The Twins are there, both Twins with the weight of forty diamonds. They reside in a gilded and ornate three-lock box."

"Then, indeed, the legend of the Twins of Peter the Great is true? Imagine, twin diamonds the size of ostrich eggs. I fail to see how your family kept them a secret for so long."

Nicholas was not interested in telling the colonel about the great Twins of the tsar's. What matter did the diamonds hold for him now other than payment to the man who would save two of his children?

"When will you take my children from—?"

"That is not your affair. You will be awakened sometime before midnight by your executioners, and your son and daughter will be at your side with the others of your family. Mind that you, your wife, or your daughters show no difference in the treating of these two imposters. If they can accomplish that much, I will hopefully be many kilometers away with—"

"My two children," Nicholas said, cutting him off as he turned to look at Petrov, who nodded his head, half bowed, and then abruptly walked away.

The tsarina greeted Nicholas before he came to his family and took the crook of his arm with both of her white gloved hands. Her wide-brimmed hat was tilted against the freshening breeze and the falsely joyous sun.

"Is there news, Nicky?" she asked.

"Tonight, my love," Nicholas answered with bowed head, his cap hiding his distraught features.

Alexandria's only reaction was a quick twitch of her lips, and then she tried to smile brightly.

"The children . . . our plan?" she asked through the falsity of that smile, swallowing desperately to keep the sob she felt trying to escape from deep inside of her.

"Two."

"Oh, Nicky, no," she moaned.

"My son . . . and Anastasia," he replied with only a brief movement of his lips. "They were the only matches found."

They walked arm in arm to join their children, each silent with his or her own thoughts of the coming horror.

"When?" she asked, opening her umbrella, not trusting herself to allow the scream to escape her lips at the murderous insult to their children.

"Midnight," Nicholas answered, quickly swiping away a tear with his white gloved hand.

At exactly thirty minutes after midnight, Commissar Yurovsky stood over the eleven bodies inside the dank and bare basement. He knelt down and removed the tsar's hand from around the head of the crown prince. He quickly moved his hand away when he saw the boy twitch and draw a quick, shallow breath.

"The heir is still alive," he said angrily as he looked closer at the features of the boy. For a reason the old man could not grasp, Prince Alexei did not look the same. Even with a bullet in the side of his head, he could still make out his features clearly.

Suddenly a guard, one of Petrov's men, whose job it was to make sure all went as planned after the colonel and his young charges left the house, stepped up and fired three quick shots into the upturned face of the crown prince.

Yurovsky was so taken back at the sudden action of the guard that he fell onto his bottom side. He quickly recovered, and then stood and faced the man who had fired his pistol.

"You fool!"

"You said the boy wasn't dead; now he is," the guard replied quickly and sternly to the local communist official, a man that was as despicable an official as any the guard had ever known.

"I wanted to examine him for official reasons!"

The guard looked down. "Dead, four gunshots to the head and face. In your report to Moscow, you can say it was natural causes. In this day of communist glory, what difference would there be . . . Comrade?"

Yurovsky turned and looked at the guard with murderous rage, then quickly stormed out of the basement, threatening to add the guard's name to his report.

The guard smiled, holstering his pistol, and then he gestured for the others to start removing the two servants, the maid, and the doctor. Then he examined the bodies of the four girls and found them quite dead. It had been a close run thing, the girl posing as Anastasia had actually called the tsar "Uncle." Yurovsky, thank the heavens, hadn't heard the girl's remark. He knelt down and then saw that Tsarina Alexandria had somehow managed to reach out and touch her husband's extended hand. *Such devotion*, he thought, *clinging to him even after death.*

Crown Prince Alexei, or the child that posed as the prince, was quite unrecognizable. The girl, Anastasia, wasn't that much of a concern, as the imposter had been shot in the face, a rather cruel way to go for such a pretty child. The guard stood and motioned for the men to take the royal family out.

"The crown prince, and that one," he said pointing to Anastasia, "place them in the last truck; we have orders to burn and bury them separately."

He watched as the last of the Romanov dynasty was removed from the cellar, far from the glamour and royal standing of the grand social gatherings in the cities they had been accustomed to. He shook his head and then pulled his pocket watch from his coat. He had to move quickly because he didn't want his portion of the royal treasury to depart for America without him accompanying it.

EAST OF GLACIER BAY, ALASKA
SEVEN WEEKS LATER

20 September, 1918

As I make this journal entry, it has been two weeks since the cargo vessel, Leonid Comerovski, ran aground south of Glacier Bay. After our initial good luck with surviving the storm at sea, and in acquiring the ten needed wagons from an American prospecting camp, and then securing the needed stores from the wrecked ship, my men—all thirty-five of them—plus seventeen crewmen from the Comerovski, along with the two children, set out heading for the Alaskan capital of Juneau. The crewmen of the vessel were surly at best, and my men had to make an example out of three of the rougher, more aggressive seamen. It seems they were none too pleased in our disposing of their captain and his more loyal men, a necessity due to the fact we needed their food stores. Needless to say, the others fell into line immediately when they gained knowledge on how the new Russian security service operated. The sad fact is, I despise my own men more than the communist sea captain and his crew. I am foolish to believe I can rise above the filth I have covered myself in.

Providence, however, only doles out luck on a begrudging basis. We now find ourselves very much lost, with the American city of Juneau I now believe to be far to our south and west of us. The nights are turning cold and the men are starting to get anxious as to our fate, and now they are not understanding why we didn't seek passage from Glacier Bay to the city of Seattle to the south immediately. I've had to explain to them on more than one occasion, that our transgression in Russia may have been discovered, and that the party's spies could be in hiding in any seacoast settlement waiting on our arrival. Comrade Lenin will have a long memory when it comes to stealing a great deal of the royal treasury, not to mention the two children.

The problem now, besides the fact we are lost and running low of food, are the children. The men want to eliminate the need of caring for them. Not that I am a sentimental man, but if we are caught by the American or Canadian authorities, they would become a valuable bargaining tool as for the reason we are in their countries uninvited. This time, however, even my brothers of the secret police are not buying my goods. I am afraid of losing control of the situation.

The gold and its vast weight, coupled with the harsh terrain, are starting to cause considerable problems with the wagons. They were not constructed for such loads or travel over the rough ground. They are in constant need of repair and I fear we will have to abandon some of them, with the gold, once we exit the mountain pass we now find ourselves.

Postscript: The past few evenings as we settle into camp, we have detected the movement of something, or someone in the night. We do not know if Indians of the great northwestern territories are among us, because whoever they are, they are stealthy and silent for the most part. There is also a knocking of clubs, or sticks, against the trees at night, and unheard of animalistic screams. I must admit to myself, if not to others, it is truly unnerving. If indeed it is Indians, I have never heard of such behavior in any of the adventure novels I have read or other accounts of Indians in the Americas.

Missing pages. Recommence with page 231—

9 October, 1918

Bad news when dawn broke this morning. We saw a wide river to our front. My merry band of cutthroats, as well as I, were so exhausted the night before, we collapsed without noticing the sound of flowing water. I'm afraid—according to the very inaccurate royal map—we were looking at the Stikine River. Far north of where we were supposed to be, meaning we were in the harsh unexplored back country of British Columbia.

As I write this passage, the men are looking at the two children, and what I see in their eyes is sheer madness. Four of the mules from the now empty and abandoned wagons were slaughtered and eaten. I fear for the children because they have become objects of hate and superstition because of our wrongdoing—the men want the children given to them. I fear I may lose control very soon, but I cannot allow these fifty men to do what I know them capable of doing.

10 October, 1918

I must now note that I have made the gravest of errors. While studying the Twins of Peter the Great three nights ago in the dying firelight of our camp, and thinking all but the perimeter guards were asleep, I failed to see one of the men watching me from afar. When I returned to the Twins the next morning, I discovered one on the ground by the wagon, and the other missing from its gilded box. The thief must have dropped the diamond in the night, and then unable to find it in the dark, absconded with the one remaining Twin. The man is now missing, escaping with half of my prize for this fiasco. I am losing hope of surviving this ordeal, but now have only half payment and a growing attachment to the only two people I can trust—the girl and boy. The man I recognized, the thief, was Vasily Serta, one of the more intelligent guards, and a man I had trusted.

Postscript: The screams and the striking of wood has not only continued, but has grown far worse in the last few days. Five men are now missing, joining the thief, vanishing into the night. If they are deserters, that is something I can deal with; however, the alternative is something that scares me far more than freezing or starving to death, as I feel there is something stalking us in the night.

Last remaining page of journal—

2 November, 1918

The wagons have all broken. The men and I have hidden them and the gold in a large cave in the facing of a small plateau, and then covered the openings with tree, rock, and snow. They should never be found by anyone as lost as we. Upon study of this immense cave, we discovered the paintings of primitive man. Strange designs of hunts, of daily living, and of one particular painting of an animal that struck fear into all who saw it in the flickering light of the torches—a beast of huge proportions that walked upright like the hunters it towered over. Why did this ancient depiction frighten me so? Is it the sounds we hear at night? Or the men that we discover gone almost every morning now? Or is it the fact that we all feel the primitive intuition that we are being hunted, stalked, and taken in the night?

The forest around us is impenetrable and the river is starting to choke with ice. True winter has struck early. The men will soon be coming for the children, so I have decided it is better to die here and now, than to contemplate the fate that awaits the sickly boy and the proud young girl. I go with the knowledge that evil things come to evil men, and thus I would be satisfied with that particular outcome, but for the children. Especially the girl. I have become dependent on her bravery and intellect—she is no fool.

After much study of the ancient forest that surrounds us and the very terrain of our travels thus far, I have come to the conclusion that no man has ever passed this way before. At night, the trees crowd in and act as a smothering agent, at least to the hearts and minds of the men. The natural animal noises all cease after the sun goes down with the exception of the strange pounding of wood on wood. I have come to the bizarre conclusion that these are signals of some kind, an intelligence that is making a mockery of the most ruthless men in the world. This is unlike any forest I have ever ventured into.

My belief that there is an intelligent presence in the woods, back beyond the safe glow of our campfires, is persistent and disturbing. I believe myself a brave man, but I am quickly becoming unnerved by an element I do not understand. Annie, as I have come to call the girl, and I have spoken of the strangeness that surrounds us, and we both agree that a feeling of "knowing" has entered our thoughts, even our dreams. Knowing that whatever is out there, has been there for our collective memories to conjure in our waking lives. It's as if we have lived this journey a million years ago, a retained and collective memory of danger in the night suffered by our ancestor. How the men in camp feel about this theory will go unasked, as we have had yet another two men vanish from guard duty the last two nights. With the Stikine River to our south and the woods surrounding us on all sides, we feel trapped. Game has vanished as we hear and see them running in the daytime hours, always in the same direction—away from the river and woods, and always away from our guns.

Finally, the men have started talking about the dark and almost impenetrable forest, and what it is that constantly surrounds our camp at night. The sickening boy has heard the tales the men tell, and is now not

sleeping when the miserable and weak sun goes down beyond the moun-
tains, making him weaker each morning than the day before. In all hon-
esty, I find sleep just as elusive and I fear whatever hunts us is coming
soon.

The large colonel checked the loads in his pistol, and then closed the
hinged breech, snapping the barrel into place, and then he placed it in his
heavy coat. He then walked over to the fire and knelt beside the boy. He
lifted a hand and felt Alexei's forehead. He smiled as he pulled his hand
away, and then pulled the woollen blanket closer to the boy's chin.

"Well, the fever has calmed; you just may make it," Petrov said in a
low voice, looking from the dull eyes of Alexei to the sad eyes of Anastasia. He stood and walked toward the girl who had become a woman in the
short time away from her parents.

Anastasia watched, making sure her brother could not hear, and then
turned to the tall man beside her.

"Colonel, my brother is ill; he shall not recover. We need not be told
things that are mere flights of fancy because it eases your mind to do so.
I am afraid we left our childhoods back at a dreary farmhouse in Russia."

The princess looked around her and saw the stark white faces of the
emaciated men that leaned against the broken wagons and fallen snow-
covered trees. They were down to thirty-four men and they were starving. Anastasia remembered the horrible stories of the dark and forbidden
woods read to her at bedtime, with the absolute worst, *Hansel and Gretel*,
never far from her mind as she looked at the brutal, soulless men watching them.

"No, he shall not die. I believe he is of stronger blood than you know,
young one."

"Once more, Colonel Petrov, he is sick. He is a hemophiliac and is
prone to infection. The finest doctors in the world from France, En-
gland, and America have treated my brother, and declared it so. He also
has developed pneumonia." She looked at the men surrounding the large
fire again, placed the coat's collar up around her neck, and held her small,
delicate hands out toward the warm fire. She turned her head slightly
toward the colonel, framing her beautiful face in the firelight, and then
she looked into the blue eyes of the Bolshevik. "It would be best for us, I
think, if you would place a bullet into both of our heads. We are brave,

like my mother, my father, and my sisters. The fate of the bullet is far more merciful than the fate those men will have for us. It would be a kindness, Colonel."

Petrov swallowed.

"You are far beyond your years for one so—." He caught himself patronizing the girl and knew she would call him on it. "Your imagination is running wild. You will feel better with a hot meal in your stomach."

"We wish to join our mama and papa. We do not fear the reunion, only the manner in which we begin our journey."

"Anastasia, such talk will do no one any good."

The girl ignored the colonel and leaned over the crown prince. When his dark eyes fluttered open, he tried to smile at his sister.

"Papa—he would have been very proud of you," he whispered in his weakened voice. "So tough a girl."

"No, it would be his pride and joy that shone brightly in his eyes. You, Alexei, were his and Mama's entire lives. Why, they would have been so—"

"Colonel, we have come for the children."

Petrov looked up into the face of Geroden—the sergeant—the very guard who had been left behind by Petrov, and the only one in their lost expedition to have actually taken part in the elimination of the Romanovs.

Colonel Petrov raised his left brow and stood. His knee-high boots cracked with cold and stiffness. He smiled as he placed his hat on his head, and then squared it up as if getting ready for an inspection.

"Is that so, Comrade?"

"Yes," answered Geroden. The smaller man then looked away from the children, took Petrov by the elbow, and steered him away from the fire and their young ears. "I have convinced the men that you are not to blame for our . . . situation. I was able to sway them to the idea that the Romanov children have cursed us, making us lose our way." He smiled, showing the four gold teeth in the front of his mouth.

"You know I am originally from the aristocracy myself, so why am I accorded such lenient treatment, Comrade?"

"Because, Iosovich Petrov, you left your family for the ideals of the revolution, just as we."

Petrov laughed loud and heartily—strong, as if he had had a large meal just that evening and was feeling its strength, like a horse full of wild oats.

"The ideals of the revolution. . . . Is that how you and those fools are justifying your avaricious actions of the past months—for the revolution?"

"Comrade, all we want is the children. There is no need for you to—"

"Hypocrites! All of you, hypocrites! You betrayed your revolutionary ideals the moment you heard this plan and did not report it," he said, but ceased his maniacal grin. "Just as I did," he finished with distaste.

The smaller Geroden sneered and gestured behind him. Ten men started forward toward the children. Anastasia placed her hand on the chest of Alexei and closed her eyes in prayer.

Petrov never hesitated as he removed the pistol from his holster and emptied it into the approaching men. Five of the ten dropped into the powdery snow and the others dove to the ground behind the high wall of flames of the campfire. On the first click of the empty chamber, Petrov swung the pistol wildly at the stunned Geroden, striking him cleanly in the face and dropping him. Then he quickly grabbed up the boy and ran into the thick forest, quickly followed by the fast-thinking Anastasia.

Three men rushed forward to assist the bleeding Geroden to his feet. He angrily shoved them away, and spat blood and two of his gold teeth into the freezing snow.

"After them!"

Eight men broke away from the camp and spread out into the thick, ancient forest. The men remaining grabbed their bolt-action rifles and long knives, and went in the opposite direction as the first group. They knew Petrov was a master of deception and a skilled soldier, thus they thought he would try and work his way back to the last four mules and try to make his escape.

Geroden drew his pistol from its holster and angrily pushed away the men who had tried to help him. Then he gestured angrily in the direction where the colonel had vanished. As the three men reached the first line of thick trees, the clacking of wood started once more. Geroden stopped and listened. The noise was far louder than any previous night. As he listened, the cold wind picked up in intensity, but it wasn't the wind that forced a chill to run down his spine; it was the closeness of the strange knocking.

"It's all around us," one of the three men said as he pulled the bolt back on his rifle, chambering a round, never realizing he had just ejected an unfired bullet from the rifle. He flailed the British-made weapon in all directions.

Except for the banging of wood against the trees and the wind in their branches, the forest seemed dead. The sound of the men crashing through the underbrush was becoming fainter as Geroden tried to pierce the night with his eyes. The man in front of him had backed toward the warming fire, still rapidly swinging the rifle toward any sound he heard. Geroden took hold of the man's rifle and stilled it.

"Careful, you fool; you'll shoot one of—"

The horrible scream of a man chilled the blood of Geroden and his hand slid slowly from the barrel of the frightened man's weapon. The screaming went on for three seconds, and then abruptly stopped. The noise of the sticks striking the large and ancient trees continued. They seemed to be drawing closer and were very much louder, doubling the fear that was near to crippling them.

Several of the first group of men came rushing back from the surrounding woods and into the large circle of firelight, backing in as they trained their weapons on the woods behind them.

"Did you see it? Did you see it?" one man yelled at another as even more of the first group backed into the camp, their rifles also pointing into the forest.

Geroden strode quickly to the man that had spoken. He was wide-eyed and terrified.

"Why have you returned?"

The soldier didn't hear the question. He shrugged the sergeant's hand from his sleeve and continued to stare into the woods. The fear of the sergeant had disappeared as something far more dangerous had arrived.

"You," Geroden said, pulling on the arm of another of the frightened men, "what is the matter with you?"

"There is . . . is . . . something out there . . . more than one I think."

"What do you mean *something?*"

Before the man could answer, screams of pain and terror filled the darkened night once more. The men still out in the dark forest started to fire their weapons, making those in the camp stoop low and aim at anything that looked menacing, which of course was everything.

Suddenly, the large fire exploded as a shapeless object flew from the woods and struck. Flames and burning embers shot high into the air as the men saw what had hit: the mangled body of one of their own. His uniform and hair quickly caught fire as the men stood watching in stark terror.

The striking of wood against wood became louder. The beat was not uniform but it seemed as if whatever was out there was herding them together. Then came the first sounds other than the screaming of men, or the strange beating of the trees—a horrendous bellow of something inhuman. Other growls and roars answered the first cry. More men ran in from the trees, from front and back. They were all looking behind them in absolute terror. The night became alive around them, the beating of wood sounding as if it were right at the very trees next to the camp, just out of the large fire's circle of illumination.

"For God's sake, what is out there?" one of the men yelled just as a shot rang out.

Another, then another rifle exploded, and Geroden flinched as the second gunshot went off next to him. All of the men started firing into the woods, striking trees and snow-covered underbrush.

Two more bodies of their comrades were thrown into camp. The first struck a tree, sticking for a moment before flopping lifeless to the snow-covered ground. Then the second landed at Geroden's feet. As he looked up in shock, the giant animals attacked the camp in force.

Geroden had taken aim at a darker-than-night shadow as it traveled from the thickness of one tree to another when warm blood struck him in the face, unnerving the sergeant. He turned and ran, running over one of his own comrades, knocking him into the fire as he tried to escape through the back of the camp. Behind him were the cries and defensive fire of his men. The nightmare of the past few weeks had made its presence known, and the reason man feared the dark forests of the world was made evident as the night became death.

Colonel Petrov held the children close to him as the murderous rage of whatever had been tracking them attacked the men inside the camp. The screams of terror and pain seemed to last all night as men fled, and then were taken down and butchered just as others died, trying in vain to find and to kill the invisible intruders.

"Colonel, what is out here with us?" Anastasia asked, holding her brother hard against the large man's body as they cowered behind two large trees that seemed to grow twisted against one another.

"Satan may have come for us this night," he mumbled as he pointed his pistol into the night. Petrov found himself sliding back into his childhood—the days when he had been forced to pray at the cathedral with his family. The thought and memory made him wish for those times once more, the comfort in the belief of good.

"I'm frightened, Anna," Alexei cried.

Suddenly the screaming stopped. There was one shot, then one more—then silence.

Petrov cocked his pistol and waited, sure that whatever had killed the men, would soon make him and the children their next target.

A crashing came through the woods and Petrov knew he had to try to save the children. If they remained with him, he knew they didn't have a chance. He quickly stood Alexei up and pushed him into the arms of Anastasia. Then came a louder and harried sound of something crashing through the underbrush. While looking into the woods, Petrov reached in, pulled out his journal, made sure the oil cloth covered the leather book, and then thrust it into Anastasia's grasp.

"Take this—you and your brother must run. Hide until morning and then head to the south, down the river as it flows toward the sea. Find other men—they will know what to do. Show them my journal and they will see to it you are reunited with family in America."

"Colonel, I'm scared," Anastasia said as she pulled Alexei to her.

"As I am also, child, now go. God hasn't been with your family of late, but maybe now he will have mercy—now *go!*"

Anastasia pulled Alexei along by the hand and vanished into the trees just as Geroden tripped and stumbled into Petrov. He caught the large colonel's coat sleeve and arrested his fall.

"God . . . oh . . . god, they are coming, Comrade Petrov, they are coming!" he breathed heavily, trying to force the words from his bloody mouth.

Petrov looked at the cowering fool and then, shrugging him away, he placed the pistol against the sergeant's head and pulled the trigger, sending the smaller man crashing to the ground without even a grunt.

When the colonel looked up, he was satisfied that he had done his duty to the children. If they were to die, it would not be by this man's hand.

He swallowed and looked up. He saw the giant looking at him between two large trees. The massive and muscle-bound arm was perched against the two thick trunks. The eyes glowed with an internal fire that cast them in the shade of yellows and reds. The creature could not be any smaller than eleven feet as it watched the Russian. The great head tilted to the right, as if trying to figure out what the man had planned. As the cries of the escaping and frightened children came to Petrov's ears, he saw the giant's eyes narrow and look in the direction where they had vanished. It sniffed the air in all directions and then it grunted deep within its massive chest. The great beast tilted its head, and something akin to a nod made its chin drop to its collarbone. That was when a small rock struck the colonel from behind, dropping him easily.

The beast took two large steps and stood over the two fallen men, and then watched them closely for any sign of movement. When there was none, the giant grunted once more. It easily stepped over the one dead man and the unconscious Petrov, and went in the direction the children had fled. It saw the small prints in the snow as if they were glowing bright green. As the great animal disappeared, blending into the darkness, several of the other giant beasts showed themselves from their hidden places and came forward, dragging Petrov and the dead sergeant away into the night.

Anastasia tried her best to keep Alexei moving. The boy was dead on his feet as they broke through the last of the trees and onto the stony riverbank of the Stikine. The smell of the water made Anastasia pull even harder on Alexei's hand and arm. She thought she could maybe traverse the thicker of the ice flows and get across to safety. It was foolhardy, but she knew it was their only hope of escaping the horror she knew was following them.

Just as they reached the river's edge, she came to a stop. Alexei collapsed against her legs as she cried, "Oh, no . . . no."

The ice had melted during the day at the river's edge, or was so thin she could see the moving water beneath in the moonlight. They would fall through if they tried to escape over the ice. She tried to get Alexei up. He refused. She angrily tossed Petrov's journal away, where it landed on the thin ice, then slid until it hit the water through a large crack ten feet away. The journal lodged against the side of the ice for a moment, and then the swifter current caught it and dragged it under, sending the re-cord of the last of the royal family on a long journey south.

Alexei was still refusing to move, so Anastasia just simply gave in to the boy and slowly sat down beside him on the snow-covered rocks that made up the shores of the Stikine.

"Our journey away from Mama and Papa has come to an end," the young girl said as she placed her hand on the cheek of her little brother. As she did, she saw the giant step from the trees. It stood, watching the children. "It will be nice to see them and our sisters once more, won't it, Alexei?" She made sure the boy's face was covered so that his eyes could not behold that which could not really exist.

"I am sorry I was not stronger for you, Anna," Alexei said in a whis-per, his large eyes looking up and then holding hers. He started to turn away, but Anastasia held his head and made him look at her, most desper-ate that he not see the giant horror that watched them from twenty feet away.

"You are the strongest boy I have ever known. To be as sick as you are, you have done the most amazing thing—you have traveled half the world. Even Colonel Petrov said he would be proud to have you in his combat regiment any day."

"Really?" he said as his eyes slowly closed in exhaustion.

"Yes," she answered. She looked up and saw the beast was now coming toward them, slowly, menacingly. She rubbed her gloved hand along the boy's face and watched their destiny as it came at them, and soon they were surrounded by the only inhabitants of this area of the world for the past twenty thousand years.

Anastasia Romanov closed her eyes and waited.

In the small valley, hidden in a snow-covered covered cave, were four large wagons filled with gold. The bulk of the smuggled treasure of the last tsar and tsarina of Russia would stay hidden for almost a full century until future men of greed found it, and the hidden world of the past would once more run with blood.

The Forest Primeval had not changed for 20,000 years—always hid-ing its secrets well, protecting whatever lived amongst its woods and streams.

In the night came the nocturnal cry of *They Who Follow*, as they, too, waited for their lands to be visited by men from the outside world once more. The woods swallowed them, and they became one with the world that nurtured and protected them.

MCCHORD AIR FORCE BASE WASHINGTON
OCTOBER 7, 1962
OPERATION SOLAR FLARE

Thirty-five armed USAF air police had most of the base maintenance personnel cornered in a giant hangar outfitted for one of McChord's many Globemaster cargo planes. Most of the men had noticed that the M-14 automatic rifles carried by the police unit had their safeties in the off position. But even stranger was the fact that there were thirty U.S. navy flight technicians waiting just inside of the giant hangar door. No explanation had been offered as the men were rounded up and placed inside the hangar. They waited twenty minutes, and then a loud horn sounded.

A U.S. navy officer in class "A" blues and a white saucer cap nodded at the captain in charge of the air police, and he in turn waved his men into action. In thirty seconds, the hangar was cleared of all air force personnel with the exception of the base commander and ten of the air police. They were soon joined by twenty men in civilian attire. The men went straight to some very large crates that had been unloaded thirteen hours earlier after they had been delivered from March Air Reserve Base in California. They quickly started uncrating the shipment.

As the group of base commanders and air police waited, they heard the loud whine of twin jet engines as they spooled down. The roar was loud enough that all inside knew that a beast was demanding entrance to its dark lair. As the giant twin hangar doors started to slide apart, the men inside were blinded by the landing lights of a powerful jet as it barely waited for the doors to open wide enough to fit its extraordinary wing design. The aircraft cleared the doors by mere inches as it made its way inside, flanked on both sides and also front and back by United States Army Special Forces soldiers who had been waiting just off the runway for the arrival. The president of the United States himself had instituted the new concept of the Green Berets, and the group was newly arrived from Fort Bragg, North Carolina, and they trotted inside with the aircraft with their weapons at the ready.

As the technicians and security men watched in silence, the scream of the twin J79-GE-8 jet engines bounced loudly from one corner of the giant hangar to the other. The pilot of the brand-new Navy F-4 Phantom made a fast maneuver with its nose wheel, and made a complete and precise 180-degree turn until it was facing the now closing hangar doors.

The newest and only version of the Navy F-4 was loaded with the new AN/APQ-72 radar, its bulbous nose standing out dramatically from the front end of the fighter. Every technician noted the package the Phantom carried under the centerline hard point. The plastic-covered, steel-framed object was hidden from view, but every man present was aware of what the disguised monster was, and they all had that deep-seeded fear upon seeing it only feet away. They were even aware of what the package and also the very operational name of the mission was called, a name thought up by air force and naval intelligence—Solar Flare. It was a five-hundred-megaton nuclear weapon, and was the most powerful nuclear device ever created. For the moment it was harmless, but its potential as a man-made hell on earth shook them all to their core.

With the brakes finally set and the giant General Electric engines winding down, the cockpit canopy started to rise. The lights from above shone off the Phantom's gleaming dark blue paint scheme, and all present saw that the aircraft had not one identifying marker on its aluminum skin. No navy serial number, no numbers of any kind. The stars and bars had been removed as well as every single etched engraving that would identify the origin of the flight or its manufacturer. As the canopy rose, the navy pilot didn't wait for the ground crew to assist him from his seat. He stood as soon as the large Phantom stopped moving, and was quickly stepping onto the wing. He avoided the ladder that was placed for him and hopped nimbly down from the slick wing. He waved several of the crew away.

"Bathroom!" he called out as he ran in the direction he hoped was appropriate.

A man ran to catch up to the helmeted officer, still dangling his oxygen line and directed him to the right door, and then they both disappeared.

The ground crew from the navy and several of the civilian technicians ran for the Phantom and started removing small plastic covers along the Phantom's wing hard points. The caps hadn't been off more than four seconds when the ground crew rolled up seven experimental fuel pods specially designed for the Phantom. The fiberglass and plastic pods were extremely lightweight and each of six was fifteen feet in length and was capable of carrying a thousand gallons of JP-5 jet fuel. The seventh fuel pod was designed to fit under the Phantom's belly to the rear of Solar Flare, and was only ten feet in length. With every hard point of the fighter filled with fuel pods, the aircraft had not one single defensive or offensive weapon onboard—not counting the strange object hanging hidden under the Phantom. Even the defensive flair and chafe system had been removed. With all of this, the massive twin-engine fighter would have to fight the forces of gravity to even get off the ground.

The pilot soon emerged from the restroom and was met by a navy doctor and medical corpsman. He was directed to a closed-off area where a catheter would be inserted into his bladder for the long flight awaiting him after his next fuel stop. That was where the pods would be fully loaded and the mysterious shroud would be removed from Solar Flare. The next stop for this most secret mission of October 1962, would be Elmendorf Air Force Base, Alaska. At that point, Solar Flare would become active upon the order of President John F. Kennedy, and then Solar Flare would vanish into the night sky, its destination—the Soviet Union, its mission—to advance beyond its fail-safe point and to destroy the top military leadership of not only the Soviet military, but the KGB and the high command of all Russian strategic rocket forces.

As the pilot cleared the medical area, he felt uncomfortable with the attention of everyone as they followed his every move. He didn't know if it was because of the mission he was chosen for or the fact that he just had two feet of plastic line shoved up his penis—he hoped it was the latter.

Commander John C. Phillips, fresh from the Aberdeen Proving Ground in Maryland, was preparing the largest strike package ever issued by the U.S. navy. The weapon was far beyond the scope of detonations delivered by the U.S. Army Air Corps at the end of World War II. An experimental device loaded upon the newest supersonic jet fighter in the American inventory, and with the aircraft loaded with so many secret and technical devices, Phillips knew he was more than likely to blow himself and half of either Washington State or Alaska into oblivion than he was the intended target, the head of the chicken, or as it was officially known—the Soviet high command.

As the commander was approached by two admirals, a general, and three men in civilian suits, he took advantage of the little time he had to wolf down a ham and cheese sandwich and a glass of energy orange drink.

"Commander, your final orders: You will unseal them ten klicks before you cross into Soviet airspace."

Phillips handed one of the flight crew the empty glass and wiped his mouth onto the sleeve of his flight suit. His eyes took in the admiral and didn't flinch.

"And the members of the high command targeted are going to be where they are supposed to be?" he asked, still not reaching for the orders. As he watched the brass before him, the rumor mill was being proven right, and all of the hard work and training was about to be realized if the negotiations in Washington and Moscow failed. Phillips knew he was the only member of the four horsemen of the apocalypse that really counted, and it made his stomach queasy.

"Assets inside the Soviet military apparatus have informed our intelligence services through the French DGSE that everyone from Khrushchev down to his valet will be there. Yelteli is your target, commander."

"And if they're not in Yelteli?" persisted the navy officer.

"They are, buried underneath five hundred feet of reinforced concrete and two hundred of clay, with nothing else but trees protecting them. They didn't think we knew about their little hiding spot, but thanks to the head of French intelligence, we do."

The commander had no doubt that he was carrying the payload to do the job. He knew it would create a crater the size of the meteor hole in the desert in Arizona, only deeper. He was just concerned about his mission being the one to initiate a full nuclear exchange.

"What if the president gets those stupid bastards in Moscow to back down?" he asked, almost, but not quite reaching for the plastic-covered orders.

"He won't," said a man in a black suit.

"Your name, sir?" Phillips asked.

The man remained silent as he looked from the commander to the admiral, and then turned and walked away.

"In that case, Commander, you'll receive the callback—*Genghis*. Are we clear? Everything is explained in your orders. Now, your mission will continue with no further communication from here on out. Your layover at Elmendorf is only fifteen minutes, so you will not even leave the cockpit. After the strike, if you successfully egress from Soviet soil, your training in ice landings will become perfectly clear to you. The coordinates for the ice-pack landing are included. Sorry that couldn't be explained to you during training."

Phillips finally nodded his head and took the offered orders, feeling them under his gloved hands and knowing the impossibility of it, and also knowing full well he would never make it past Soviet defenses after his bird laid its nuclear egg. There would be no ice landing, and he doubted very much if there was even a plan for him to do so.

"Will you gentlemen excuse the commander and me for a moment, please," the small rear admiral asked.

The men surrounding the pilot walked away when asked and didn't bother with protesting the time restraints they were under.

"Listen to me, Commander, the president has been backed into a corner here. Hell, he has Soviet merchants and armed combatants charging to the Cuban quarantine line, and he doesn't think those bastards are going to stop. If they don't, this may be the only chance we have if the Soviets strike in Germany or, God forbid, the U.S. You're the first option for stopping this before it really gets started." The admiral paused for the next words he would speak. "Commander, if you have any doubts, it's worse than we thought in Cuba. At least four sites there are fully operational, and the ranges of the missiles are not what have been reported. They can hit as far away as Seattle."

Phillips didn't respond to the admiral's pep talk because he knew the Soviet military, no matter how much of the command structure he destroyed, would strike back. It was what he would do, and he knew the Russian soldiers and airmen would feel the same.

"Yes, sir," Phillips said as he gave the admiral a salute, crisp and sharp. He didn't wait after he let his hand slip to his side; he stepped away and joined his ground team.

Ten minutes later, under cover of darkness, and no runways lights save for every thousand yards as an aiming point, Operation Solar Flare roared down the McChord runway. As the wheels lifted free of the concrete, Phillips felt a small pop from somewhere in the aircraft as it rose into the sky. Unbeknownst to the highly trained pilot, the restraining bolt holding the nose of Solar Flare to its hard point broke free and tumbled into the woods surrounding Fort Lewis and McChord.

Two hours later, the aircraft passed over the most desolate and unexplored region of British Columbia on its zigzag course in order to avoid the Russian trawlers off the coast toward Elmendorf Air Force Base in Alaska, when the nose of the most secret weapon in the American nuclear arsenal broke free and dropped three feet. Now its center and rear bolts were the only restraints keeping the weapon from tumbling into a large river that wound its way across the northern face of hills and mountains below.

Commander Phillips knew his aerodynamics were shot as the weapon hung, suspended half on and half off its hard points and was pulling the aircraft into a nose-down attitude. The problem started in the planning stages of the operation as the Canadian government knew nothing of the American flyover of their territory and airspace, so the commander was under orders to stay "in the weeds," below the Canadian radar. It was a good plan, but it doomed the mission and Phillips. He just didn't have the altitude to maneuver.

"Snowman, Snowman, this is Arrowhead, mayday, mayday," Phillips called out as calmly as he could as the Phantom rolled hard to the right side. He fought the control stick as hard as he could but knew he was losing the Phantom far more quickly with the heavy load. The design of the extreme aircraft was so radical, it naturally didn't want to stay in the air anyway, and he knew that. "My position is—"

The heavy F-4 Phantom clipped the tree line with its right wing and then Phillips felt his face flush and his heart freeze as the heavy jet fighter, with Solar Flare still attached, slammed into the Stikine River and then bounced three times as it came apart, spreading fire and debris into the desolate reaches of the surrounding woods and finally smashing into pieces against the facing of the small rise that sloped into a barren plateau.

The code name, Operation Solar Flare, would be lost forever, never to be mentioned in the annals of the Cuban Missile Crisis of October 1962, nor would the official histories of the U.S. navy and air force have anything placed into their archives telling the world that the United States was prepared to strike first against the Soviet Union. Even with the massive four-decade search for the lost superweapon, Solar Flare, the cover-up of an event of that magnitude would be kept secret—until fifty years later.

STIKINE RIVER
JULY 1968

L. T. Lattimer was the last of the old miners who had worked the gold-fields from Nome to South Dakota. Like most, Lattimer had spent twenty-four years of his life, his life savings, and a good portion of his family's fortune, and again, like most, had absolutely nothing to show for it. Raised in wealth and educated in ivy, the Boston-born Lattimer knew he could never go home again after such a monumental misjudgment. The burned bridges and a family alienated by his arrogance have assured him of a life of loneliness.

Reduced at times to hiring himself out as a guide to men who used to be his equal in the wealth department, he contracted out for the rich on fishing and hunting expeditions to the many lakes that were fed by the Stikine River.

In between these excursions to the tamer areas of the basin, Lattimer worked his illegal claims and panned, mined, and subsisted on the forested slopes of the valley. Every few months he would strike a small deposit and that was usually just enough to offer a faint glimmer of hope that he was onto what he knew was out there—the mother lode that had supplied the strikes in Nome and the rest of the great Alaskan goldfields. However, as always, the small deposits he had found turned out to be nothing more than that: a deposit, left there by the flowing waters of the Stikine, a mere shadow of the lode that awaited the right man. It was enough, however, to keep the nightmare alive in his heart.

Just recently, he had hired out to a group of graduate students from Stanford University, a subpar institution in his Ivy League mind. Most of the students were studying wildlife that flourished in the Stikine area without the intervention of man; others were there to study the way of the Tlingit Indians. They called themselves anthropologists. They had walked the southern shore of the Stikine for twenty-two days, taking notes, setting up equipment, and listening to loud music half the night. Lattimer suspected they were using drugs, but as long as he was paid, he didn't really care. However, the rock-and-roll music drove him absolutely nuts as he suspected it did also the wildlife they were there to study.

Lattimer was frustrated beyond all measure on this afternoon. He was walking the riverbank with a long-haired and thinly built student everybody called Crazy Charlie Ellenshaw. He was one of the anthropologists that kept him awake at night with his music and social philosophy, but he was a brave sort that had broken away from the others that day out of boredom and followed Lattimer on a quick look-see of the new area. He had even braved the swift current of the Stikine as Lattimer waded across the shallowest spot he could find. Ellenshaw looked as if he were a drowned rat, his crazy long hair was wet and disheveled, but as Lattimer took the boy in, he knew him to be what he called *a gamer.*

"So, after all of these years, you have never found anything worth being here for so long?" Ellenshaw asked as he looked north toward the large face of a plateau. As he observed the small rise before him he tied his crazily arranged hair back with a leather tie.

"Tracer bits and pieces, nothing to scream and jump for, I'll tell you that," Lattimer answered as he reached down and ran his hand through the river gravel at his feet.

Charlie Ellenshaw watched the guide and then he, too, looked down at the gravel. He saw glittering bits of rock and he also reached down and scooped up a small handful that he held out toward the bearded Lattimer.

"There's gold right here."

Lattimer didn't even look back at the graduate student.

"They don't teach much to you Stanford students, do they, boy?" He laughed out loud and then finally turned to face Ellenshaw. "That's pyrite, sonny. Fool's gold; iron sulfide. It's everywhere, and has sent many an idiot off screaming claims of massive strikes. Sorry, son, finding gold's not quite that easy."

Crazy Charlie let the gravel and fool's gold slide from his hand. He then followed Lattimer toward the tree line. As he did, something caught his eye. It was sticking out from under a large rock that looked as if it had been smoothed by a million years of rushing water. Charlie walked over and kicked at the rock, but it didn't move. Then he bent over and rolled the heavy rock away and then saw the crumpled metal underneath. He reached down and picked it up and rolled the shard over. He saw some black numbers standing out against a lighter black paint.

"Hey, I thought men have never been in this area before?" he asked, looking at the back of Lattimer.

"I never said no one was ever here. Just that you can count all the fishermen and sportsmen on one hand's all." Lattimer irritatingly looked back at the young student. "Why?"

"Aluminum, and look, there's more right there." Charlie pointed to the ground not far from where Lattimer stood.

"Trash—maybe washed up here from someone north, way north." Still, Lattimer walked over and picked up the metal that lay dull in the sunlight. It was crumpled and looked as if it had been in a fire. As he looked from the twisted aluminum in his hand to the stretch of gravel that made its way to the trees, he saw even more of the garbage that had washed up along that stretch of riverbank. "What in Sam Hill is this?"

The young Ellenshaw dropped the piece of aluminum and looked around. He saw something else farther away and walked over. It was also under a rock, washed by a long-ago flood of the Stikine and buried. He knelt down and felt the material. It was rotted and came off in his hand. Then he lifted the rock, not expecting much, and that was when he saw it. The book was old. Its leather was covered in some sort of material that had aged well, but was now deteriorating to the point he saw the pages through the cracks. He lifted the small book and looked it over. The pages for the most part had vanished over time. Some looked to have been torn out, and some appeared to have just turned to dust. Even the pages that remained were almost illegible because of the ink having been wet, dried out, and then wet again over the many years of being exposed to the elements. He raised the small book to his face and saw that some of the writing looked to be in Cyrillic—Russian.

"Mr. Lattimer, do you read Russian?" he asked as he carefully thumbed through the six remaining pages. "Looks like a journal of some sort."

"Living here, you have to speak a little bit and read at least the basics—I was taught by Helena Petrov down at the fishing camp, 'nough to get by, anyways."

"Yes, we met her and her very large son on the way in. Didn't know she was Russian, though."

"Well, she is. Hates the damn Ruskies, though. I mean, she really hates 'em, even though she's one of them."

Charlie walked over and handed Lattimer the journal. Then he looked around him as a sudden breeze sprang up. As the wind ruffled his drying hair, he felt something strange come over him. It was as if he had instantly stepped back into a world he didn't recognize. It wasn't a feeling or thought that Charlie could explain—it just was. He also knew, or felt, they were being watched.

"Well, I can tell you it belonged to a Russian named Petrov. By the looks of it, he was a colonel of some sort."

"Can you read it?" Ellenshaw asked, still looking around him, finally settling on the trees and the plateau beyond.

"It'll take some studying, but maybe, yeah."

"Are we about finished here?" Charlie asked, feeling uncomfortable.

"Yes, we had better get back to your friends before they get themselves lost out here," Lattimer said as he closed the journal. "Look, uh . . . Charlie?"

"Yeah?" Ellenshaw answered as he kicked at another piece of the black aluminum while turning for the river.

"Let's keep this between you and me. I mean, give me a chance to see what this thing says . . . okay?

"Whatever you say," Ellenshaw said as he continued walking away, looking around at his surroundings nervously.

Lattimer watched the young man wade back into the Stikine. Then he raised his head and looked around him. He had the same thoughts that Ellenshaw had had a moment before: that feeling of being watched. Or was it nervousness at the few words he had read from the journal that he hadn't mentioned to the kid. He turned to follow the grad student across the river, repeating the one word he had read that stood out clearly from the rest of the water-stained passages and one that he kept muttering, the lone word keeping him warm as he crossed the cold waters of the river—
Gold.

While the other graduate students from Stanford sat around the large campfire, the song "Incense and Peppermints" by Strawberry Alarm Clock, wafting through the moonlit night, Charlie Ellenshaw was somewhere else. As he sat on a large rock, he kept taking off his thick glasses, wiping them clean, and then replacing them. The others didn't think much of the quiet Ellenshaw because he always seemed to be somewhere else, and after his return to camp late this afternoon he had virtually been antisocial.

Charles Hindershot Ellenshaw III waved away the leather bag full of cheap wine. The girl who had passed it to him looked at him strangely.

"Charlie, what's with you tonight?" she asked, taking a swallow of the bitter-tasting wine.

Ellenshaw acted as though he didn't hear her as he scanned the woods. They were camped three miles downriver from where he had been this afternoon with L. T. Lattimer. Instead of answering, he stood when he thought he saw something move just inside of the tree line, a darker shadow among many.

"Charlie!" the girl said loudly enough to be heard over "Incense and Peppermints." She quickly handed the Volta bag of wine off to the next person in line. "You're starting to freak me out, man."

Ellenshaw saw that he had been fooled by the wind in the trees. The shadows they cast made it seem as though something was standing near a large tree trunk and every time he tried to focus on the shadow it would slip back behind one of the ancient trees. He had been seeing things like this all night. He swallowed and then finally looked down at the girl.

"You did your thesis on the Tlingit tribe, right?" he asked, about the local Indians that inhabited the Stikine River. As he waited for her answer, he slowly sat back down onto the large rock.

"You know I did, you helped me with the research. You know that thesis as well as I do."

"Not everything. What about their legends of this area, did you find anything . . ."—he paused, almost as if afraid to broach the subject— "strange . . . you know like—"

The girl laughed, making Charlie shrink away.

"You mean the Bigfoot legend?" She tried to stop her chuckle, but between the wine and being stoned she was having a hard time keeping the laughter in check. "Charlie, you kill me. Are you attempting to tell campfire stories to scare me?" She finally got herself under control. "I think that's so cute."

Ellenshaw didn't say anything. He turned away and shook his head. He then looked back at the young student and he was showing no humor in his asking of his next question.

"Are they firm believers in the legend?" he asked.

"Charlie, the Tlingit aren't the only ones that have a Sasquatch legend in their shared history; the Apache as far south as Arizona and Northern Mexico have the same. There has been eyewitness accounts handed down by the plains tribes, too. The Sioux and Northern Cheyenne have their own legends about a large creature that inhabits the highlands of the continent. That doesn't mean that they are grounded in solid fact. Besides, most of the old stories have been cast off by the newer generations of Indians; it's just not politically correct these days. They're trying to be taken seriously."

Charlie was about to retort when he saw their guide, L. T. Lattimer, placing items in his pack on the far side of the campfire. Ellenshaw scratched his head and stood, ignoring the girl when she asked him where he was going. He strode quickly to the old guide.

"Where are you going?" he asked Lattimer.

Placing his old brown fedora on his head, Lattimer looked up and frowned.

"You again?" he asked Charlie as he straightened up, and then shook his head. "Look, most of you kids are staying close to camp tomorrow doing paperwork, so since none of you were going to be much in the way of danger, I thought I would take another look-see at that area we found today. Figured I would start out tonight . . . no sense wasting time."

"It's after midnight."

"Ooohhh," the older man joked as he shrugged into the straps of his backpack. " 'fraid the ghosts in these woods will get me?" Lattimer laughed and then held Charlie motionless with his gray eyes. "Son, I quit being afraid of the boogeyman many years ago."

"Okay, you're a tough guy. But I'm tagging along with you."

Lattimer looked at Charlie as if he had been a bug climbing out of his kitchen cabinet.

"The hell you say."

Charlie turned and ran toward his tent as Lattimer stood there stunned. He quickly returned with his own pack and stood next to the old prospector.

"You got the gold fever, sonny?" he asked.

"This has nothing to do with gold," Charlie said as he squirmed into his pack.

"Ah, I see. You're interested in monsters aren't you?"

"Shall we go, Mr. Lattimer?"

Lattimer looked at the kid and shook his head.

"Well, if you want to make a fool out of yourself, I can't stop you. But if we find any color, don't think you can stake a claim, boy."

Charlie swallowed and looked up at the swaying trees and then quickly back down at Lattimer.

"No, sir, I'm only interested in the boogeyman."

After saying good-bye to the rest of the graduate students, and with the four track tape player belting out "a Double Shot (Of My Baby's Love)," by The Swinging Medallions, Charles Hindershot Ellenshaw III stepped into the woods lining the Stikine River, and he and L. T. Lattimer headed north toward the plateau, which was just visible in the moonlight.

Once they arrived at the site south of the plateau and had crossed the river, Charlie used his large flashlight to pick out the aluminum they had discovered that day. Whatever it was, the pieces were easy to see even though they were covered in black paint due to the river-washed white rocks of the riverbank.

"I don't know, but it looks like all that aluminum trash may lead us in the direction we want to go," Lattimer said as his flashlight picked up the same trail.

Charlie started picking out larger pieces of the strange debris as they entered the tree line. He really didn't know how much he wanted to observe in the three hours leading them to daylight. As he shone his light around, he had noticed the cool breeze had stopped completely and the surrounding woods seemed to become oppressive.

Lattimer was moving fast, making Charlie nervous as he tried to keep up with the prospector. Then Ellenshaw struck something about three hundred yards into the thick woods. He hissed through his teeth as he stumbled back and then looked down, his light picking up what looked like a chair. Charlie angrily kicked out at it, wanting it to be Lattimer for hurrying foolishly through the trees. When his boot struck the chair, it slowly slid over onto its side, almost in slow motion because of the twisted vines that had curled through its base. When it hit, Charlie felt his bowels almost let go. He fell back as the eyeless sockets of a skull stared back at him. He fell backward, his light never leaving the body. He struck the ground and stared at his grisly discovery. The crash helmet was missing its faceplate. The torn oxygen hose dangled away from a rotted rubber mask that had once covered the features of the pilot. The face had a massive crack in the bone that ran from the brows to the jaw, where the lower half was missing.

"Jesus," Ellenshaw said. Then he nearly crapped himself as he heard a crashing noise coming from the woods ahead of him. He braced himself to see the devil incarnate coming for him.

Lattimer came through the last of the trees and shone his light first on Charlie, and then on his discovery still strapped into the ejection seat.

"Well, I thought as much. All that aluminum, and up ahead the rest of the plane is all smashed up against the base of the rise. It's a mess." Lattimer moved the light toward Ellenshaw. "Hey, you alright?" he asked moving to assist the boy to his feet.

"Just didn't expect it, that's all."

"Yeah, it's not something you expect to find on your daily hike in the woods, is it?"

The humor was lost on the young anthropologist. He shook his head and then reached down and rubbed his shin. "How long has it been here, you think?"

"No tellin', quite some time I expect. Look at that flight suit, rotted through in places. And the rubber, it's seen too many hot days and cold winter months to be cracked and falling apart like that."

"Poor guy," Ellenshaw said as he shone the light onto the mangled remains.

"Yeah, but he's long past caring, son. Now let's see what there is to see here."

Charlie swallowed, and then giving the corpse due respect, walked past the ejection seat. His light caught and held on a small spot on the shoulder of the aging flight suit where there was a darker spot than the other areas around it. He could tell there used to be a patch or something there, but it had vanished long ago. He turned and followed Lattimer away from the final resting place of a pilot who had died almost six years before.

Lattimer waited for Ellenshaw this time. He knew that finding the corpse of the long dead pilot had made the boy far more jittery than he had been.

"Now, wait till you see this," he said as Ellenshaw stepped up beside him.

The older man shone his large flashlight onto the wreckage of the downed aircraft. It was in so many pieces that Charlie just assumed it belonged to the dead pilot and the ejection seat. The thickest of the wreckage was imbedded into the base of the plateau, looking like it covered a crevasse of some sort. Lattimer shone the light around the bulk of the smashed aircraft and then smiled. He stepped up and pulled a large section of what had been the plane's fuselage away from the rock. He quickly stepped back when it fell free and hit the soft floor of the forest.

"I'll be goddamned and go to hell. Look at that, son."

Charlie stepped up and saw that the wreckage had been jammed tight into the opening of a cave. It was a broad expanse of darkness beyond. Ellenshaw saw Lattimer as he opened the old journal they had found earlier that day. He studied a small drawing that was sketched on the back of the last page. The old man smiled and slapped at the old leather-bound book, sending one of its rotting pages to the ground. When Charlie reached for the dislodged page, Lattimer placed his large boot on it. When Ellenshaw looked up, he saw the look in Lattimer's eyes that froze him cold. It was as if he was having his pocket picked and had caught the man in the act. Ellenshaw straightened, leaving the handwritten page where it lay. Lattimer never lost that murderous look as he slowly reached down and picked it up. He seemed to relax when he had the page safely in hand.

"Don't want it torn is all," he said by way of explanation. "Now, are you ready to go see what's inside?"

Just as the words escaped Lattimer's mouth, the beating of wood started. It was close and it totally unnerved the young student. He looked around wildly as he thought the noise was right behind him. Then he looked right, then left. The noise was coming from all directions. Ellenshaw never considered himself to be a coward, but the noises he was hearing drove a hard wedge in between what he wanted to be and who he really was.

"Good God, what is that?" Charlie asked, trying hard to keep his nervousness in check.

Lattimer, looking just as astounded as Ellenshaw, only turned and walked toward the opening of the cave.

As Charlie watched the man leave in amazement, he turned and saw a flitting shadow among the trees. The darkness moved again, this time to his right. Whatever the shadow thing was, it was large. It moved from tree to tree. Then Ellenshaw saw what the strange noise was as a dark figure raised something to the sky and then swung it. The object hit the tree with such force that Ellenshaw actually felt it through his boots. The club struck the tree again and then he heard something that chilled him to his bones: the thing in the trees growled. It was a deep, menacing, and primal sound that sent Ellenshaw stumbling backward toward the cave's opening. He backed into the total blackness of the interior and immediately bumped into Lattimer. As he watched the opening, there was no movement, only darkness. Charlie was even afraid to shine the light there for fear of what he would see. As much as the thought of a missing link intrigued him, he didn't care to meet it in all that inky blackness that was prevalent between moon fall and sunrise.

Lattimer moved away deeper into the cave. Charlie turned and started to follow as silence descended from the outside. The beating of wood on wood had ceased, and even that sudden silence was frightening. As Ellenshaw turned, he saw designs on the wall in the glare of his flashlight. The depiction was that of ancient man—hunter gatherers of the last ice age. Ellenshaw had seen many examples of this kind of historical documentation before in a hundred different sites from Colorado to New York. They depicted man for what he was, a skilled hunter of the animal life that inhabited the Stikine River Valley.

As he moved back along the caves wall, the paintings became older looking, and far more faded. The years depicted on the wall must have covered four to five hundred years of prehistoric life. Many scenes of snows and the baking sun, repeated over time, told Charlie that this cave and surrounding area must have been home to a large group of ancients.

As he moved deeper, forgetting all about his terror of a moment before, and losing Lattimer as he moved farther and faster, Charlie began to see paintings of a large animal, always standing away from the hunters, but never too far away from them, either. The beast was humanoid. He saw it was bipedal and was far larger than the small humanoid group. Ellenshaw tilted his head and was sure he saw in the faded paintings that the beast seemed to be watching the activities of the men. Charlie smiled, intrigued by the facts before him that the men and the giant beast seemed to live in a harmonious environment. He ran his fingers over the ancient depiction of the large animal. He quickly pulled his hand away when Lattimer screamed. Ellenshaw turned at the loud noise, then he realized it wasn't fright: It was an exclamation of pure joy. As he approached the bend in the cave, Ellenshaw heard Lattimer as he talked loudly to himself.

"Hell, I don't even have to dig it out! Just pick it up and spend it!"

Ellenshaw saw an amazing sight. Lattimer was standing up in an old, broken-down wagon. He lifted a sack into the air and then allowed its contents to fall out. The gold coins made loud thumping sounds on the wagon's wooden bed. The laughter came flooding through the sound of the thumping noise.

"Look at this, boy! Uuuuunited States gold double eagles—must be a million of 'em!" Lattimer said, letting the empty canvas sack fall to the floor of the wagon with its former contents. He looked up through the flashlight's glare at Ellenshaw. "Okay, okay, you can have some, but I get the mother lode here, boy . . . the mother lovin' lode!"

Charlie didn't know why; he just started backing away. He felt they were no longer alone in the cave. What in the hell was the gold doing this far from civilization? He thought about the possible downed aircraft and its long dead pilot. Could the two be related somehow? As he looked around the strange drawings as he left Lattimer, he saw the shadow of the second wagon farther back. How much gold was there, and why was it here? As he backed away, he saw more wreckage—it was if the pieces were brought into the cave. He saw an oblong container, or what looked like a container, lying against the far wall. He also spied backpacks, canteens, torn and shredded tents, and all manner of camping gear. As strange as it seemed to him, it was if something were collecting the trash from outside and storing it.

"Boy, I got a mission for you."

"Huh?" Charlie said as he found himself staring at the collected pieces of lost humanity lying on the cave's floor.

"If you do it, you'll never want for anything ever again; all I want you to do is take this"—he held up the journal—"and mail it to my father in Boston. He'll know what to do. I've written instructions on the last page by the written map. That will give me the Providence I need. He'll get my lawyers to get the claim filed in Ottawa. I have written my account of finding the cave and doubled the description of this area." Again he looked around wildly. Then he reached out and handed Charlie ten golden double eagles. "I think that will cover the postage," he said as he started to laugh crazily.

Ellenshaw shook his head as he gained his feet. He knew then that the years of loneliness and failure had driven the old man insane, maybe even murderously so.

"I'm going to stay here and get the gold ready to move out, I'll hire some of the locals to help me get it downriver. First, I have to make sure they don't know what it is they're moving."

"Don't be crazy, Mr. Lattimer. Come back now; don't stay here alone," Charlie said as he looked around the cave nervously. "I don't know what's out there, at least I'm not a hundred percent sure, but I don't think they like us being here."

"Son, superstitions don't scare me. I've heard the stories these Indians talk about, they're made to keep the young ones in line and out of the woods at night. Now, you go and take this with you. You kids can find your way back easily enough." Lattimer pressed the journal into Charlie's hands and then his face became a mask of menace. "And you will take care not to spread the word about *my* find, right, boy?"

Ellenshaw didn't answer. He clutched the old journal in his hands and was sure Lattimer would just as easily murder him right there if he failed to give him the answer he wanted to hear.

"Yes, sir, I'll tell no one, and I'll mail the journal to your father."

The excited glee came magically back into Lattimer's facial features. He smiled and slapped Ellenshaw on the back.

"Good luck, son. Get across the river as quick as you can and put some space between you and the north shore, understand?"

Charlie didn't say anything, he just turned and walked as quickly as he could through the darkness, shoving the journal into his shirt as he moved while hoping beyond hope that there wasn't anything out of legend waiting for him outside.

Lattimer looked at the stacked bags of golden double eagles. The American currency would not be hard to pass off without garnering too much attention. He would claim to be an investor in gold and that he had bought up the double eagles years before. He shook his head and then ran his hand over his beard.

He had made several torches and slipped them inside cracks in the cave walls. The flickering light showed the paintings that had captured the attention of that kid, Ellenshaw, and for the first time Lattimer studied them. When he stood and took one of the torches from the wall, he held it to the last of the cave paintings and examined it. As he brought the fire closer to the large slothlike beast, he froze. The grunt was a deep-seeded hollow sound and it had come from behind him. He froze and then closed his eyes as a wild, pungent smell assaulted his nostrils.

When a loud scraping sound struck his ears, he turned in the direction of the cave's opening just as the light from the day was shut out. Someone or something had covered the cave opening. As he started to move toward the front of the cave, he heard the sound of his treasure as the coins slowly slid from one of the many bags. Something behind him had upended one of the sacks and was pouring its contents onto the ground.

He swung the torch toward where he had stacked the thousand bags of double eagles and saw the owner of the many sounds he had heard through the many strange nights in the woods lining the Stikine. The beast was well over ten feet in height and stood with its powerful arms at its sides. As Lattimer watched the empty sack fall from the beast's enormous hand, he saw that the eyes were fixed on him—the yellow glow of the eyes shone brightly in the torchlight and they seemed intelligent. The deep seated orbs moved only slightly when Lattimer brought the flame of the torch higher so he could see more clearly.

"You leave my gold be," Lattimer said beneath his breath, the insanity of his own words making his eyes go wide. He wasn't seeing a magnificent beast standing before him, he was seeing only a thief of a lifetime find.

The great ape grunted and took a step toward Lattimer. The large left arm raised, it was as if the animal was offering something to Lattimer, but the old prospector refused to give the thief any benefit of the doubt. He swung the torch at the large creature and struck its massive hand, making the animal roar in anger. The large muzzle rose into the air and the cave shook with the powerful, voiced exclamation of pain and rage.

Suddenly, before Lattimer knew what was happening, several more of the giant animals appeared in back of the first, and that was when the old man's mind finally snapped. He screamed and went wading into the beasts of that long-told legend, an animal that supposedly died out tens of thousands of years before that summer of 1968. The animals closed in on L. T. Lattimer and soon after, the secret of the Stikine would be left for others to uncover.

They Who Follow waited for mankind to return to the lost valley that had been their home for twenty thousand years.

The graduate students had been frightened when they hadn't seen or heard from Charlie Ellenshaw until he stumbled into their camp in the late afternoon. As much as they questioned him on where he had been, the more Charlie clammed up. He sat on the same rock he had the night before and held the old journal in his hands. He had wrapped it in a handkerchief and wouldn't let anyone near it.

When the others started packing for their return trip downriver, Charlie reluctantly started to help. His silence unnerved the others but they didn't press him as to why Lattimer hadn't rejoined them. Charlie had told them that the old man had continued upriver, searching for his gold.

As the rubber boats shoved away from the shore of the Stikine, all thought of the plane wreckage had escaped Charlie's thoughts; only the vision of the cave's paintings and what they depicted remained. He watched the trees surrounding their camp slide away from view, with only one thought going through his mind: *They* were watching.

PART ONE

WHEN DIAMONDS ARE LEGEND

1

The prestigious one-hundred-year-old Rainier Building had been bought in 1991 and had been completely renovated. The first sixteen floors were quite normal, if expensive, two- and three-bedroom condominiums. The seventeenth and eighteenth floors, however, belonged to just one man, the owner of the property and the person who designed the interior of the building: Valery Serta, the son of a Russian immigrant and heir to the vast fortune left to him upon his father's death in 1962. The family fortune was in the felling of the ancient forests of the great Northwest—forests that filled the pockets of the family Serta since the late twenties and supplied the U.S. markets with rich wood and paper products.

With a twenty-four-hour house staff of twelve, and with a minimum of two on duty at all times, the old man kept them busy with his imperialistic demands. A loner in his old age, the only visitor he took was from his grandson who was now a student at Harvard, and one or two old friends from the logging business. For some reason, that no one who knew him could fathom, Valery Serta never tired of hearing about the destruction of the woods that had covered the area since the dawn of time. He closed his eyes upon hearing the news of another tract of land that had been cleared and raped of the woods that covered it. The enjoyment stemmed from the dark tales his own father had passed onto him, never explaining why the woods and forests of North America held such a bad place in his heart.

The sky outside the Rainier Building was splitting open on this early Tuesday morning. The thunderclap woke the old man and he rolled over to look at the clock on his nightstand. Six thirty. He knew that sleep would not come again once it was so rudely interrupted, so he slowly threw his covers back and sat up. He yawned and felt around in the semi-darkness. His thin, liver-spotted hand hit the glass of water and then he cursed in English as some of it splashed onto the expensive wood. He shook his head and reached for the dentures that he had deposited in the glass the night before. Once that was done, he slowly placed his feet into the slippers that had been perfectly placed by his maids the night before.

As he stood and placed a silken robe over his thinning frame, he stopped and listened; more important, he smelled. Sniffing the air he knew something was amiss. Every morning of his life he started the day with a pot of coffee, six eggs, potatoes, sausage, and toast. However, today there was none of those smells coming from the kitchen, which was situated on the open floor plan just below him on the first floor. He shook his head, angry that his most simple routine of the day was being usurped by people that worked for him. He angrily tied his robe and walked to the door and threw it open. As he approached the railing of the upper floor, he saw that the house was completely silent. The shades were open in the living room and the dull, cloud-laden day filtered in, letting in just enough light that he could see things lying on the floor beneath him.

"What is going on down there?" he asked as he grabbed the railing and tried to focus on the floor below.

Suddenly, a streak of lightning flashed through the twenty-foot-by-ten-foot plate-glass window that looked out over old Downtown Seattle. In that brief flash of illumination, he saw the bodies. Each of the twelve had been tied up and shot in their heads. He instantly saw his two female maids in the center of what could only be described as an execution circle with his employees' feet facing outward. With a yelp of terror, Valery Serta placed his hand over his mouth to keep the scream inside. As he started to back away, the words from the darkness, spoken in Russian, made his hand fall and the scream escaped anyway.

"We figured the view from up here into your living room would allow us to dispense with the threats of violence against you. This way you know we mean business—as your adoptive Americans would say—'from the get-go.'" The last was said in heavily accented English.

Serta turned and saw the man who had spoken was standing in his bedroom doorway. He almost went into shock when he thought that the man must have been in his room the whole time he was sleeping.

"As my partner says, we are here for answers, and we will only ask you one time," said a smaller man who stepped from the large bathroom across the hallway. He was wiping his hands on a towel, which, when finished, he turned and tossed it on the floor. "As you can see, we will not be disturbed for the time being."

"Who are you? What do you want?"

"Now, you see, you are asking questions and wasting our valuable time. Did we not say we killed your staff so you would know we were serious men?"

The old man started shaking.

"Relax, comrade. You have to answer one question and one only, before you join your employees. Until that moment, you have no need of being afraid—you will not be mistreated—unless your answer calls for it." The smaller of the two men stepped closer to Serta. "Why should you answer, you ask?" The small man with the ponytail tied by a leather strip, nodded at the taller man who produced a cell phone and opened it, and then he pushed a single button and then listened. He handed the phone to the old man.

Serta heard a boy crying on the other end of the line. He started shaking even harder than before, enough so that the tall man held the phone for him.

The small man nodded once more. His companion holding the phone spoke a few words in Russian and then closed the cell.

"You recognized the sound of your grandson's voice, Mr. Serta? He sounds as if he is having a hard time at Harvard University. Now, it is totally up to you on how much of a hard time he has in the next few moments. If you refuse to answer our single question correctly, and on the first attempt, we will cut the young man's head off."

Serta looked horrified as the small man pursed his lips, as if the statement he had just made was just as distasteful to say as it was to hear.

The larger man, his hair cut short to this side of cruel, moved Serta into the bedroom and sat him at the foot of the large, ornate bed. The smaller man turned back to the bathroom and emerged a moment later with a glass of water. He offered it to Serta and then sat beside him. The old man shook as he raised the glass to his mouth. He hesitated, and then drank deeply. When he lowered the glass, the smaller man removed the water from his shaking hand. He handed the glass to the large short-haired man.

"There, you have sated your thirst, and I can see you have calmed to an acceptable degree. I believe we are ready to proceed."

The old man looked at the Slavic faces of the men looking at him. They were Russians, not others from the satellite states or provinces—they were Moscow-bred, just as his own father had been.

"Before I ask, I must warn you, so you don't waste time thinking about how we gained our fantastic knowledge. We have several people on our payroll who reside at Lloyd's of London. To be more precise, Lloyd's—North America, based in New York." The man smiled when he saw the face of the old man go slack. "Ah, I can see you have realized your mistake."

"I don't have—"

The small Russian held up his hand so fast that the old man flinched as he thought he was about to be struck. Then he watched as the man's eyes once more went to his friend, who remained standing over Serta. He nodded and once more removed the cell phone and then looked at the withered face of the old man.

"If he has to open that receiver, Mr. Serta, your grandson will have a brief moment of pain and then his head will be removed. Now, as I will state the question, your answer should already be formed in your mind. We know you have one half of the Twins of Peter the Great. Where is it? You became paranoid in your old age and requested an insurance quote on a diamond of rather amazing proportions, one pound eight ounces to be exact. That information was forwarded to our offices. So, we have dispensed with the details and now the question has been asked." The small man slowly removed a large caliber automatic from his coat and then reached into his pocket and removed a short stubby cylinder and started screwing the silencer onto the pistol.

Valery Serta lowered his head and then with a stronger than normal voice, started talking.

"Since 1919, my family has not had to use the diamond for anything other than collateral. It fed my father's ambition without losing the stone.

Yes, over the years I knew that men such as you may track the Twin to my family, so I wanted insurance against that eventuality."

"After today, you will have no such worry. Now, answer the question."

"Floor safe in the shower stall—combination is 18-34-17."

"You have done well. You have followed our instructions, and thus you have saved the life of your grandson—a very noble thing. A thing that people with your family history did not have an abundance of in the early days of the Soviet Union." The small man stood and then placed the silencer up to Serta's temple.

"May I ask a question?" the taller and much more muscular man asked as he replaced the cell phone into his jacket.

"Yes, of course," came the polite answer from his partner.

"Mr. Serta, you wouldn't possibly know the whereabouts of a certain diary belonging to a former associate of your father's, would you?"

"How silly of me, I should have thought to ask myself."

Serta looked up and knew beyond any doubt that these men must be searching for the other missing Twin. Singly, the diamonds were worth a billion dollars on the open market, but placed together as a set, the Twins of Peter the Great would be priceless. He knew he would answer their question, as it would be the only triumph he would have in the few remaining minutes of his life.

"The other Twin was lost with many men, many good men according to my father, somewhere in the Canadian wilderness almost a hundred years ago." Serta said his piece and then closed his eyes.

"Ah, no more knowledge than we had before. But, there was no harm in asking. Now, there is a rumor of a diary with the description of where the diamond was lost. Do you have information on this missing journal?"

"I have never heard of such a thing. If there was a journal, it would have disappeared with the officer it belonged to."

"Ah, you see, you think you have lied well enough to deter us from the truth, but in reality you have told us everything. Whoever said it was an officer who wrote in a journal? I see your father was very observant those many years ago. He knew the officer commanding their small expedition wrote in a journal. Now, did your father happen to take that item when he betrayed his officer and stole the diamond?"

"I know of no journal."

"Ah, I see," the small ponytailed man said, and then nodded at the large one.

He turned and made his way to the bathroom. He looked around and then shook his head. It was the first time that he had ever heard of anyone building a safe in a shower stall. He stepped up to the rounded, clear-glass enclosure, pulled open the door by the gold-plated handle, and looked at the Tuscan tile. He could see no flaws or anything that would indicate a door. He knelt down and felt around the tile edges, still not discerning any area that might reveal a secret hiding place.

The Russian was just getting ready to stand when he saw what he was looking for. Most would have missed it, but the big man had the instincts of a cat. He reached out and allowed his fingers to play over the drain cover. On the outside it looked like a normal trap, but he had noticed there was no caulking around its edges. His fingers played over the stainless-steel surface, and then he pushed down, and then tried to turn it to the left. The cover didn't move. Then he tried to the right, still applying downward pressure, and smiled when the drain cover popped free of the tile.

"Now, this is ingenious," he said under his breath in Russian. The drain cover was actually the dial for the combination safe that was still buried in the tiled shower stall. He turned the facing of the cover and entered the correct numbers that had been covered up by the drain rim. The lights automatically dimmed in the bathroom and the Russian stood. His eyes widened when three floodlights embedded in the ceiling of the bathroom illuminated as the flooring, not in the shower itself, but in the center of the bathroom, behind him, started rising. The floodlights caught the first glimmer of the egg-shaped stone. Then, as the small enclosure rose, the lights struck Peter the Great's most prized possession—one of the Twins. The diamond had been cut in five thousand different places around the circumference of the egg. The effect was such that when the stone was illuminated, blue, pink, and green shafts of light speckled the white walls of the ornate bathroom.

The large Russian was stunned. With all the treasure they had gathered over the years, this was the most amazing sight he had ever beheld. Not standing on ceremony, he reached out and touched the large diamond egg. It was cold to the touch, and he smiled, wondering how something with such fire inside could be so cool. He grasped the egg and removed it from its glass cradle. He went back to the shower, turned the combination lock, and then depressed the drain cover. The cradle for the Twin slowly started its return to obscurity. The lighting from above dimmed and the regular bathroom light came back on.

"Well, are we that much richer, my friend?" the small man asked, his eyes never leaving the old man beside him.

The large man stepped out of the bathroom, and held up the one half of the Twins to show his partner. "Yes, we are, and always will be, two of the richest men in the world."

The old man buried his face in his hands and sobbed. The diamond had been in his family since it was taken by his father in a forest long ago. Now it was in the hands of men who would either sell it on the black market or cut it to pieces.

"Come now, you could never have thought to hold such a magnificent treasure as this without unscrupulous men coming after it, did you? Besides, old man, what we are really after makes this small diamond very insignificant. We are after much more than riches; we are after the future."

The old man looked up, not understanding. Then he realized he wasn't meant to as the small man stood and pulled the trigger.

As the two men started downstairs, the rain outside had started to dwindle to a heavy mist.

"Now that we have the one Twin, the other will be more of a challenge to find without the pages of the journal."

"If the cursed thing even exists; remember the KGB from the old days were expert liars, just as we were," the smaller man said as he buttoned his overcoat. "Our newest ally says he'll take care of that end of things. All we needed to do was seal this end of the trail so no one can figure out where this diamond was originally taken from. Now it's up to our new partner."

"I have to admit, he seems very resourceful."

"By the way," the small one asked as they closed the door and entered the private hallway, "did our man at the airport forward the video disc of our arrival to our friend?"

"Yes, I have done as he has instructed, but why would he want video of us coming into the U.S.?"

"I did not ask; he will inform us when we get in the air. I'm sure he has an excellent reason for it."

Again, the two Russians smiled. Their day had turned out to be full of sunshine, despite the storm that had passed through Seattle that morning.

EVENT GROUP COMPLEX
NELLIS AIR FORCE BASE, NEVADA

The head of the Senate Ways and Means Committee, Senator Lyle P. Casals, knew the feeling of claustrophobia was all in his head. Although it was a fact that he found himself three thousand, two hundred feet underneath the sands of Nellis Air Force Base, he tried desperately to get that little fact to stop entering his mind as he walked alongside the Director of an agency of the federal government he had known nothing about twelve hours ago.

The director of Department 5656, known to the president of the United States and a few others as the Event Group, smiled as the senator from South Dakota wiped his brow with a handkerchief. Niles Compton could not figure out if the man was frightened about the treasures and archaeological finds he had just been shown, or fear that the entire cave system was about to fall on his head. Compton suspected the latter since the bespectacled man kept glancing up at the steel netting that held some of the rock strata in place.

The senator swallowed and then looked up at Director Compton. Niles removed his own glasses and smiled at the Ways and Means representative.

"Astounding is all I can say, Mr. Director. To think that all of this"— the small man gestured around the massive and curving hallways that held no less than one hundred of the largest steel vaults in the complex— "has been kept secret for over a hundred years is completely amazing to me."

Niles nodded his head and looked around and smiled when his eyes locked on Virginia Pollock, his deputy director. The short and balding Compton felt even smaller standing next to Virginia, who was well over six feet tall. Her hair was loose today, and her green eyes expressive as they always were when she was dealing with politicos. Niles was ashamed he used his assistant's looks to assist in swaying support from either the numbers cruncher that now stood before them or even the president. Virginia knew this fact, but to her credit, she never said a thing or complained one bit.

"Some of our artifacts would cause a great uproar in the world if we released to the public the fact that we had them."

"Yes, I understand that. Imagine having the flying saucer from

Roswell in our possession. I always thought it was just a story." The senator lowered his head and swiped at his sweating brow once again.

"You are literally the first American outside of the president to view the vault chambers at this complex, Senator Casals. However, since the damage we sustained last month was so extensive, we couldn't hide the cost from the House. So here we are, you've seen the damage and I hope you understand our reasons for being enough that we can get an appropriation for repairs." Virginia smiled and batted her eyes twice, not blatantly, but she did make sure the senator saw the movement.

"And your advice to the presidents, past and present, has assisted in making policy with foreign governments? I mean, from historical records and finds?"

"Yes, sir. That's our charter as laid down by President Woodrow Wilson. We will assist in guiding our country through the minefield of policy making. Mistakes by us and other nations occur on a repeated level that, by the numbers, is unbelievable. We make the same mistakes over and over again. Even now, we are in the process of recovering an artifact from Chinese territory that will hopefully pave the way for better relations with the heir to power in North Korea. If recovered, we believe it will open inroads to that nation that have never been constructed before."

"How can an artifact do that, as a 'for instance,' that is?"

"Well, Senator, I don't know how well you know your world history, but in Korea in 300 BCE, what was known as the early Common Era, the three largest kingdoms of that nation, Goguryeo, Silla, and Baekje, conquered all the people and land as far as the Chinese border. These three kingdoms came to dominate the peninsula and much of Manchuria. The three kingdoms competed with each other both economically and militarily. The city states of Goguryeo and Baekje were more powerful for much of the era, especially Goguryeo, which defeated massive Chinese invasions. Silla's power gradually extended across Korea and it eventually established the first unified state to cover most of the Korean peninsula by 676, while former Goguryeo general Dae Jo Yeong founded Balhae as the successor to Goguryeo. This was the first truly powerful nation that would lead to the Korea we know today."

"I'm not following, Mr. Compton," Senator Casals said, looking from Niles to Virginia.

Virginia took the senator by the arm and looped hers through his own and walked him alongside one of the larger vaults as two security men followed. Niles looked at his watch and rolled his eyes.

"You see, this General Dae Jo Yeong is to his people what George Washington is to the American people. When the general was only forty-two years old, he was assassinated by the emperor of China, and his body whisked away as a preventative move to keep the general from becoming a martyr. The move failed and he became a symbol for his fledgling nation anyway." Virginia stopped and looked down into the senator's eyes, becoming serious. "His body was never returned by the Chinese."

"I don't follow how this has anything to do with your very secret department, Ms. Pollock."

"Could you imagine the trust that would be garnered by whoever assisted in returning the Korean George Washington to his homeland? I think that would go a long way in assuring a new regime in Korea that we can be trusted, in their estimation of us, not to blow their asses to hell if and when we decide to do it."

"Ah, I see. But do you have the general in your possession?" the senator asked.

"As a matter of fact, we have our security teams there right now negotiating for just that, Senator. We should be hearing from them at anytime," Niles finished for Virginia.

"Which leads nicely to my next inquiry, Director Compton?"

"And that is?"

"Your security department." Senator Casals pulled several sheets of paper from his breast pocket and opened them. "You'll have to excuse me; I took these notes from several personnel files before I left your office. Now, security, oh yes." He looked up at Compton, who was perplexed as to why his security department was being brought into a budget request. "Colonel Jack Collins. I have read his 201 file, and I must say, for someone as experienced as Colonel Collins, to have him standing guard at what amounts to a historical repository is a trite wasteful in my humble opinion, maybe even a bit of overkill. I would think that with all that's going on in the world, the colonel's skills could be better utilized in another arena."

"Colonel Collins is useful in ways that can never be divulged to you, Senator. I'm sure if you had brought this up to the president, he would have informed you that the colonel's record and his achievements are out of bounds."

"Just curious as to why you would need someone with his obvious qualifications in what is really a think tank?" Casals said as he looked from Niles and then at Virginia.

"Jack has done more for the stability of this nation than anyone in either houses, or the other branches of service. I dare say even more than the president," Virginia said, taking offense to the standards the senator thought their group should stand by. "The colonel is capable of getting out of any trouble. He thinks faster on the run than any man I have ever known. If he gets in trouble, he gets out of it. He doesn't fall into traps, Senator; he sees trouble coming and avoids it, which is how he keeps our field teams alive. He is the best at what he does."

The senator removed his glasses and saw that Virginia was beyond passionate about this Colonel Collins.

"So, he basically walks on water and is a survivor of some renown, a man who never finds himself in trouble?"

"That very man and his team are in China at this moment recovering the artifact we just spoke of, Senator. And yes, he and his men are the best at what they do. They always succeed," Niles said proudly.

SHANGHAI, CHINA

The small Chinese man in the white silk suit with the radiant blue shirt and tie, slapped the bound man before him again. With his hands tied behind him in the high-backed chair, there wasn't anything Colonel Jack Collins could do to defend himself. He felt the effeminate hand scrape across his two-day growth of beard but managed to keep his anger in check. Usually he would just wait it out, knowing his second in command would be along to pull his ass out of the fire. But this time he thought there may be a problem with that scenario.

The small, well-dressed Chinese took two steps to his left and then used his backhand to slap the large man sitting to Jack's right across the face. Commander Carl Everett was bound just as snugly as Collins, and couldn't do anything other than hiss his anger through clenched teeth.

"You know, I'm going to slap you into unconsciousness when I get loose," Everett said as he glared at the small man before him.

"You fool, as arrogant as most Americans. You will not be leaving this house. You will tell me where the urn is and just who it is you work for."

Jack smiled as the small man took his place in front of him once again.

"Why is it you think I'm his boss? You've slapped me five or six times more than him. He just might be the one in charge, not me."

The Chinese army officer smiled and then slapped Jack again. "Your friend is too angry to be in charge of anything as important as stealing a national treasure from my government, so that leaves you." The man held his hand out and one of his goons slid a file into it. He smiled again at Jack, and then at Carl, as he opened the file folder.

"Colonel Jack Collins, it says you are an elite special forces operative. I have no listing for current assignment." He turned his attention to Everett. "Captain Carl C. Everett, United States navy, a former SEAL, his current duty station also unknown. I believe you are nothing more than thieves, ordered by your government to embarrass the People's Republic of China. This is why you will not leave here alive, gentlemen. So please, make your death quick and painless, and give us the location of the urn in which the ashes of General Dae Jo Yeong are stored."

Jack glanced over at Everett and shook his head. "Persistent little son of a bitch, isn't he?"

Everett looked away from Jack and stared at the small, menacing man before him.

"Yeah, persistent."

"Look, whoever you are, you may as well get on with what you're going to do, because my two men are long gone out of this country with the urn and the general. They're under orders to get out with the artifact and not look back."

"And your men always follow your orders?"

"They are highly trained and would do their duty above all else. So, do what you have to do," Collins said as he almost had the knot of rope loose enough to get his hands free.

"That's right, pal, our men do as they're told," Everett chimed in as he, too, worked the rope around his own wrists. "They're probably drinking mai tais in Hong Kong by now."

At that moment, the door to the front of the apartment came crashing in. Second Lieutenant Will Mendenhall fell through onto the floor and two men were on him before he could recover. As two of their guards lifted the stunned black officer off the carpeted floor, one of them hit him over the head. Mendenhall staggered but was held upright by the two men.

Collins looked at Everett and angrily shook his head. "Mai tais, huh?"

While two of the guards held Mendenhall to the floor, the man on the left suddenly jerked backward after the initial crash of glass sounded from the side window. The bullet that struck the stunned man had whistled only a foot over Jack's head. Collins reacted without thinking when he saw the first man go down. He rolled to his right, taking the chair with him until it struck the one in which Everett was bound to. They both hit the floor just as a second bullet came through the side window and took the second man in the side of the forehead. He fell hard onto Will and died only inches from his face.

The Chinese interrogator had a brief moment of life and drew the hidden sidearm inside of his white coat. That was as far as his movement went as a third aimed bullet struck him in the chest, splattering blood all over the silk. For insurance, a second round caught the man in the throat, dropping him like a heavy sack of potatoes.

Jack was silent, waiting for what he knew was coming.

"Clear?"

Collins moved his face upward and shouted as loud as he could so there could be no mistake as he didn't want any more bullets flying into the small living room. "Clear!"

"Clear," Mendenhall echoed.

Suddenly, the remaining glass was knocked out of its frame and the curtain at the side window parted. A Glock nine-millimeter with a long silencer appeared. It roamed first to the right and then to the left. Then it remained steady as Lieutenant Jason Ryan gingerly stepped over the windowsill and jumped into the room, his weapon still sweeping the area of the living room.

"You're a little late!" Mendenhall said pushing the dead guard off of him and swiping at the blood that was staining his Hawaiian shirt. "You were supposed to open fire when I broke the door in, I thought these guys were going to blow my brains out!"

Ryan finally stood and ran to the opening of the hallway and aimed the weapon down its length. Satisfied the hallway was empty, he raised the weapon to the ceiling and then turned back into the room.

"Well, the safety was on—"

"And you forgot to chamber a round, didn't you?" Mendenhall said as he got to his feet.

"Yeah, I said you should be the one doing the shooting."

"And who was going to break down the door with one attempt, you? All one hundred and forty pounds of navy officer?" Mendenhall said with a sneer while staring at Ryan.

"Uh, if you wouldn't mind?" Everett said from the floor.

Both Mendenhall and Ryan saw that the full weight of Collins and his chair was on top of Everett, and they both moved quickly to get them upright.

"You two were supposed to be on that damn boat out of here," Jack said as his hands were finally untied.

"Yes, sir, and you were supposed to lose those three and then meet us there," Ryan said in defense.

"Mr. Ryan, we were just about to make our move. You took a chance on letting those guys get their hands on that urn," Carl said as he finally gained his feet, rubbing at the rope impressions on his wrists.

"Excuse me, Captain, but through the crack in those curtains it looked as if you were having a little trouble getting those knots undone. Maybe your basic seamanship is lacking."

Everett stopped rubbing his wrists and fixed the younger naval officer with his cold eyes.

"Keep going, Mr. Ryan, you're already at a year's worth of weekend graveyard shifts at the complex for this little stunt; do you wanna try for two?"

"We just couldn't leave you guys here . . . sir," Mendenhall said.

Jack started to say something but Everett grabbed his arm, silencing his boss and then looking at Will.

"It was his idea," Mendenhall said quickly as he pointed at Ryan.

"Thanks, buddy," Ryan said tossing the rope that had held Collins to his chair into the corner.

"You can both commiserate with each other during your cancellation of leaves for that year that you're pulling weekend midnight duty," Carl finished. Then he looked at Jack. "Damn the military for abolishing hanging."

"I absolutely agree. Now, since Batman and the Boy Wonder came to our rescue, let's get the hell out of China."

Colonel Jack Collins watched as Mendenhall and Ryan were pushed to the front door by an angry Carl Everett. As he started to follow, the smile slowly spread across his face. His two men had finally learned to think out of the box, to adapt to that fluid situation that he always preached about to his security department. Although they disobeyed orders, Jack knew it was a good thing they did because if they hadn't, there would two bodies lying dead in that living room instead of three.

EVENT GROUP COMPLEX
NELLIS AIR FORCE BASE, NEVADA
TWO WEEKS LATER

The director of Department 5656, Director Niles Compton, watched as the presentation was given to him by the historical forensics team. He sat with his shirtsleeves rolled to the elbow and his glasses perched on the end of his nose as he looked over the tops of the lenses. His eyes moved over the assembled department heads who sat around the large conference table situated on level seven.

"So, in conclusion, Director Compton, it is our opinion that when Kim Jong Il passes away, there will be the narrowest of opportunities to approach his successor, most probably his youngest son, Kim Jong-Un, about dropping the disastrous policies of his nation. We had this opportunity when Kim's father died, and the U.S. government missed it by having a hardened Cold War stance against those very policies. The president may be able to move the younger leader to see the terrible actions of his father and grandfather." Professor Geraldine Kinkaid looked at her notes and then up at her director. "Our recommendation is for the president to have a softened position in the initial stages of the North Korean power transfer. Historically speaking, the Korean people have a tendency to listen soon after a leadership change."

Niles Compton nodded his head and then looked around the table. He saw the empty chair where Colonel Jack Collins usually sat at the far end opposite himself. The colonel's initials were on the proposed report as approving the research and the gentler approach to North Korea at the eventual death of Kim Jong Il, although he did enter his own thoughts in regards to a possible coup opportunity coming from Kim's older son, Kim Jong-Chul, who Jack's military experience says may not take the succession rebuke lying down. But with the historical artifact returned to the North Korean people instead of the United States ally in Seoul, the door may be opened for better relations, thanks to Jack and his men.

"This report, if the president uses it, will cause some consternation in certain circles of the federal government," Virginia Pollock said from her seat to the right of Compton. "We have a history of close to seventy years of unrelenting hostility between North Korea and the West. I would like to ask our resident military people their opinion of this report other than what's officially stated. Will our eventual gift to that nation assist in getting us to the peace table, or would the president be wasting his time?"

Captain Carl Everett looked up from his notes. As the number-two man in the security department, it was now up to him to answer for Jack Collins. They had both put in over a hundred hours on the military aspect of extending a helping hand to Korea after the crazy Kim Jong Il passed, and that included the time they put in stealing the previously stolen artifact from the Chinese. Everett stood and opened a file on the table in front of him. The six-foot-five-inch navy SEAL cleared his throat.

"Based purely on our research, and with a small amount of personal opinion interjected, the military has always been adamant about ending this destructive relationship with North Korea as quickly as humanly possible. The drain in resources, men, and material, has the U.S. army and navy at the breaking point. We can no longer afford the cold and sometimes hot war that has existed between the United States and North Korea since the peace accords of 1953. The general public has always believed the Pentagon wanted troops stationed along the demilitarized zone, but the truth of the matter is no military think tank in the world has ever recommended the status-quo along the 38th Parallel." Everett paused a brief moment and looked at the faces around the conference table. "We feel it has always been a knife placed at the throat of a very distrustful and militaristic government who could use our presence there to lash out at the South. As proven by the recent activities by Kim Jong I, we cannot resupply or even support the thirty-six thousand troops already there. They would be used as cannon fodder in the event of an invasion, only until such a time as tactical nuclear weapons release could be authorized by the South, and NATO. We think after the death of Kim, we need to get ahold of this situation as, historically speaking, they will be listening to the West. We need to take advantage of this strategic time, or our attempts at gift giving will look foolish."

Everett sat down. He looked at everyone around the table once more. They seemed to have taken the military view with a mild form of shock. To Everett, that was a common error by civilians as far as their view of the U.S. military went: they always believed military men wanted to fight, when most only wanted peace, but a safe one through strength, making war a last-ditch thing. Civilians order war, not the American military.

"Thank you, Captain, that was enlightening to say the least, and should put a more positive slant to our report to the president along with our idea to pave the way utilizing the return of their thousand-year-old general," Niles said. "I will sign this report and our idea and pass it on to the president as Department 5656's official recommendation on the historical advantage of taking action. Thank you, ladies and gentlemen. If there is nothing else, I think we can—"

"Niles, is there a new time frame for us getting back into field operations?" Virginia Pollock asked, knowing that every department head around the table wanted to know the same thing.

Compton pursed his lips and ran a hand through his balding scalp.

"No, we're still at seventy-five percent as far as personnel goes, and the curtailment of university digs is still in effect for the time being because of the tense international situation. So, no, we will not be fielding any departmental teams for at least one to three months. I'm sorry. For now, recruitment of personnel and training is the order of the day. Get your people up to date on their classroom studies and get some of these kids their degrees—we'll need new supervisors in a lot of departments very soon. We have placated our new friend at Ways and Means, but he'll be watching us pretty close for a while."

With those words from the director, the meeting broke up. Niles could tell the department heads were frustrated about not being able to commence field operations, but there was nothing he could do about it. They needed rebuilding.

"Captain Everett, may I have a moment of your time, please?" Niles said while he stacked his notes and reports.

Everett nodded at Virginia as she walked past, then continued to hold the large door open for Sarah McIntire, the head of the geology division.

"You, too, Lieutenant McIntire. Please take a seat," Niles said as he finally looked up from the conference table. He removed his glasses and tossed them on the tabletop and then sat heavily into his chair while Carl and Sarah sat down toward the middle of the table.

"I would have expected Jack to give the report on the military aspects of our recommendations," Niles said as he rubbed his eyes.

Sarah McIntire chanced a quick look over at Everett, whose eyes remained on the director.

"Well, boss, Jack assigned me to do the historical military portion of the report, so he thought it would be preferable for me to attend the final meeting."

"I see." Niles replaced his glasses and then looked over at Sarah, who was feeling even smaller than her diminutive frame under the glare of the director. She returned his look as a smile that only touched the very corners of Niles's mouth appeared. "How about you, Lieutenant, have you noticed anything out of the ordinary where Colonel Collins is concerned?" The smile remained in place.

Sarah looked from Compton to Everett, and then made a decision. "Yes, sir, I have. Jack's been acting differently about a lot of things, more secretive. Something is on his mind but he won't say what it is."

Niles didn't respond to Sarah's observation.

"And neither one of you knows why Jack went to Langley, Virginia, and then visited the National Archives building in Washington last week?"

Both Sarah and Carl exchanged looks and Niles saw that they really hadn't known Jack had left the complex.

"Do you have any idea where Jack is right now?" he asked looking from Carl to Sarah.

When no answer came to his query, Niles leaned forward in his chair. "Well, he's in the same place he's been every day since his return from China, and frankly, it's worrying me."

LEVEL SEVENTY-SEVEN
(VAULT AREA)

Jack sat inside the large humidified vault and hadn't moved for the past hour. His eyes roamed over the acrylic box that sat high on an aluminum pedestal before him. The brass hoses that ran into the corners of the enclosure were there to feed cool air and humidity into the chamber to keep its contents at a perfect and airless 72 degrees Fahrenheit. On the side of the vault's wall, a recorded description of the artifact ran silently since Jack had lowered the sound on the computer-driven description. On the large high-definition screen that was not being watched by Collins was the historical film record of Amelia Earhart. Before him in the acrylic chamber were the remains of the lost aviatrix. Still dressed in a tattered, age-worn, tan flight suit, her skeletal remains lay silently as Jack watched her from a chair just to the redheaded woman's left side.

The remains of Amelia Earhart had been shown to Jack on his initial day inside the Event Group Complex in order to sell him on the importance of the top-secret agency. Collins had been impressed with the story behind the discovery of her remains on a former Japanese-held island in the Pacific, but had thought that was as far as it had went. Only lately had the tale of her execution been on his mind. The female aviator had been executed by the Japanese military after she had been forced down over one of their Pacific bases before the start of World War II. Accused of being a spy for President Roosevelt, she and her navigator, Fred Noonan, were both beheaded and buried, to be forever lost and assumed dead by misadventure and faulty navigation.

Jack raised his right hand and placed it on the acrylic enclosure. Collins found that he was comforted somehow by being here with Amelia since his trip to Virginia.

The remains of Earhart were due to be shipped out in three days. The body would be placed back in the sands of Howland Island, three thousand yards from the beach, and then a prearranged new finding of her corpse would be perpetrated by the Event Group and the Archaeology Department of Colorado State University. Amelia would finally be given the hero's welcome home she so richly deserved. And that little fact was what was disturbing Jack and why he came down here every day. She would not be recognized for doing what she was ordered by the president of the United States to do: She would not be honored for being an intelligence-gathering agent during the most turbulent time in world history.

There was something strange lying just beneath Jack's irritation at the situation, something he understood and was the basis for what he was about to do. He knew why he was doing it, he just couldn't think of any reason it would make the situation in Langley, Virginia, any easier.

The withered and dried corpse of one of the most famous Americans in history lay silently, unable to explain to the world the predicament of her demise. Collins knew he had that power, but to deliver it to the amazing woman before him, he had to betray a confidence, not only to the Group he worked for, but himself as well, all because there was a situation in his personal life he couldn't control since his visit out east.

Jack reached into his overall pocket and removed a plastic covered piece of paper. By using his Event Group security clearance, and since Department 5656 was an unofficial section of the National Archives, Jack had done some digging, and using his military experience and realizing the propensity of the armed forces of the United States for placing everything in writing, no matter how mundane or top secret, he had recovered a piece of bread crumb in the National Archives. The paper was part of the trail that was left behind when President Franklin Roosevelt had asked that Amelia Earhart purposefully overfly Japanese-held islands in the Pacific under the cover of her around-the-world flight. The letter was from a lowly signals officer in the U.S. navy, and it was an acknowledgment that certain maps were secretly passed to Amelia in Australia moments before her departure for her leg to Hawaii. With her body soon to be placed back for discovery by legitimate sources, the receipt would be found, and with the reporting of today's journalists, the lost adventurer would finally be given her due as an American patriot. This was a situation that was being repeated at this very moment, only in the present times it was with someone he loved very much. That was why he would help Amelia come back home a hero like she should have been hailed all those years ago.

As Collins looked the paper over, he gently removed the yellow flimsy from its protecting plastic. Jack knew it had to be done this way, because the director, Niles Compton, was a stickler for the department not changing, altering, or correcting history in any way through the auspices of the Event Group. He would not have signed on for it.

Just as Jack stood and looked at the mummified remains of Earhart, the hiss of the vault door sounded and he quickly placed the paper back into his pocket. He slowly turned and saw Sarah McIntire standing at the threshold of the thick steel door.

"I think I'm beginning to become jealous," she said as she took in the dark form of Jack who stood motionless under the spotlights of the vault.

"Nah, she's a bit too old for me," he said as he turned back to look at the corpse in the acrylic chamber.

"Yeah, but she's your type. Pushing the envelope like she did, I guess you could say she had balls."

Collins smiled and then turned back to face Sarah.

"I guess you could say she's like someone else I know, actually two someones."

"Jack, what in the hell are you doing here?" Sarah asked, not catching the plural meaning to Jack's strange statement.

Collins didn't answer. He just smiled at the small geologist and shrugged.

"How did you know where I was?" he asked instead of answering her question.

"The director, Jack. He's right outside the vault door, he wants a moment with you. He knows you've been down here nearly every day and he said something about a clandestine trip you made to Langley and then a quick stop at the National Archives in Washington. Why didn't you tell me about it?"

"It's something I have to work out on my own, so you have to sit this one out. Now tell Niles he can come in. He deserves a crack at me."

Sarah swallowed, and then with one last look back at Jack, turned away and stepped from the dimly illuminated vault.

Collins hated not being able to explain something he didn't understand himself. Sarah needed to know all there was about him and his personal life if they were to continue growing closer. His eyes looked up as Niles Compton stepped over the frame of the vault's door. He still had the sleeves of his white shirt rolled up to the elbows and his hands were now in his pants pockets. As usual, Niles looked tired and worn. The spotlights dimly reflected off of his balding head.

"Hello, Colonel."

"Mr. Director," Jack said as he stepped forward.

"Col—" Compton started and then stopped. They had worked together for over three years now, and he knew the formalities between them had to end. "Jack, are you going to tell me what's going on?"

"You have as much tact as a battleship in a pond, Niles."

"I believe you should come right out and say what's on your mind, wouldn't you agree?"

"The world would be a better place. And in answer to your question, I don't know if I can tell you. One side of it is a personal matter, the other professional."

"We"—Niles paused, rethinking his statement—"*I* need you here, Jack. The world's in a mess, the country's not far behind, and to be frank with you, this department's seen better days. Without you the past three years, we would have lost it all here. You have something that's taking your mind off your duties here; I think after all of this time you've earned the right to be trusted."

"Thank you, Niles."

Compton walked up to the acrylic chamber and looked inside. He, like Jack did a few moments ago, placed his hand on the lid and smiled.

"I'm going to miss her when she's gone," Niles said as he looked up and into Jack's blue eyes. "Obviously you will, too."

Collins didn't respond, he just held the eyes of his director. Then he slowly reached into his pocket and brought out the navy department signals receipt and, closing his eyes, he slowly reached out and handed the paper to Niles.

"Ah, the missing signals message from the Archives, I was wondering when you were going to tell me about it."

"You knew?" Jack asked, not really surprised. Then he quickly understood, "Ah, Pete and Europa."

"That damn computer knows more about what the National Archives has in its files than the people who catalog its items. Yes, Pete knew two hours after you left Washington." Niles held the paper out and then looked at it. "We could have talked about this, Jack."

"I don't even know why I did it." It looked like Collins was going to continue, but stopped and just shook his head.

Compton smiled. "I'm not as by-the-book as people think. I've done some pretty stupid things here myself. You know, once, back when we had the intact crypt of Genghis Khan—I think I was a computer room supervisor then—long before Senator Lee gave me the entire department, I cut all surveillance to his vault, put on his hat, and swung his sword around to beat all hell."

Jack had to smile at the picture Compton's memory described. The little balding computer nerd wearing a fur hat and chopping at the air with the sword of a man that came close to conquering three quarters of the globe.

"Well, needless to say, I was caught red-handed by none other than the senator himself as he was giving a tour of the vaults to the director of the General Accounting Office."

"That must have made your day."

Niles smiled at the memory. "Yeah, three weeks of house arrest in my own room on level eight, then a disciplinary letter in my file." Niles turned and looked at Jack, still smiling. "You know what the old man did?"

"I'll bite, Niles, what did he do?"

"The next month he promoted me to the department head of Computer Sciences, and on that day he allowed me to transport the remains of Genghis Khan back to Mongolia and rebury it. That was my very first and *only* real field expedition."

Jack smiled and nodded his head. He didn't really know why the director told him that story, but it placed a far more human face on Niles Compton.

The director nodded his head, lightly patted the acrylic chamber, and then looked at the remains of Amelia Earhart for probably the last time.

"Senator Lee promoted me because he found out on that day that I had an imagination. He said that was a deciding factor in me getting Computer Sciences. He said you need an imagination to be a leader." Niles held Jack's eyes with his own and then continued. "Sometimes I hate history, Jack. It's not fair in a lot of cases." Niles placed the signal message from the navy department on the chambers top and then slid it over toward Collins. "Just hide the orders in a *not-so-obvious* place on her remains."

Collins looked from the letter to his boss. He nodded just once.

"Now, Jack, do you want to fill me in as to why you stopped and visited your sister at the CIA? A sister you never listed as a family member in your file?"

"How in the hell did you know that?"

"I just happen to have a best friend with the title of president of the United States. He wouldn't allow the director at Langley to use one of my people without the courtesy of informing me as to why. I agreed with allowing you to cooperate with them for the simple reason you know what your sister's thoughts are. "

"The director of the CIA told the president?"

"Your sister and the operation she's currently running is the reason for your interest in seeing to it that Amelia here gets her just rewards, isn't that right?"

Jack was astounded at what Niles knew about what was happening in his life. He decided to come clean about his sister and her situation. It took a half an hour, but Jack felt better for doing it.

Niles had listened in silence and then he stood and turned away, and was just about to leave when he turned once more to face Jack.

"Keep me posted on your sister, Jack." Niles smiled. "And by the way, your letter of reprimand regarding the theft of national treasures will be placed in your file also, just like the senator did me." Compton then abruptly turned and stepped over the high threshold of the vault and disappeared into the massive hallway.

Jack Collins smiled for the first time since he heard what his baby sister was up to. Then he slowly and carefully lifted the cover of Earhart's enclosure, and placed the navy signals message and history back into the proper and correct perspective.

MONTREAL, CANADA
TWO DAYS LATER

The rented Audi sat parked as it had for the past two hours in front of the large cast-iron gates that led to one of the most famous structures in Montreal. The estate was as old as Canada itself, and historians claimed it was actually designed by Marquis Louis-Joseph de Montcalm, the commander of all the North American French forces during that country's battle with the British Empire for control of the Americas—the French and Indian War of 1754–1763. The woman sitting in the rented car knew better. She had done her homework and was aware that the estate hadn't been built until five years after the Marquis's death. Her proof was in the CIA archives in Langley, Virginia. The French Canadians perpetrated the rumor to lure tourist dollars into their city.

The man in the driver's seat lowered his binoculars and looked out into the warming spring day.

"You know, we're sticking out like a sore thumb here. I mean, anyone could look out of any one of those two hundred gilded windows and see us."

The dark-haired woman didn't say anything as she silently watched the house that sat a hundred yards up the long drive. Her blue eyes never leaving the stone facade of the mansion. She panned to the right and looked through the window at the city almost ten miles away. There were a few pillars of smoke from the riots but it looked as though the Canadian government had quelled most of the protests and violence concerning the recent push for French speaking independence.

"This place is fast becoming a mess," she mumbled.

"Maybe we should—"

"We'll stay right here." The woman finally afforded the older man a glance. Her features were soft and she spoke to her partner as if she were a teacher instructing a slow student even though his years of service far outweighed her own. "I don't give a damn if they see us, Mr. Evans. They need to know they are being watched and that old sins are not forgiven—at least by the United States."

The man knew the young woman was tired. She had flown into Montreal just six hours before and she was out of sorts. He just hoped the head of the northeast field desk wasn't making an error in judgment. He knew as well as she that the two men inside that house were two of the most ruthless killers that had ever worked for the old KGB. The field operation was made possible only because of an anonymous tip and a package delivered to her desk that had very unexpectedly brought the golden child, the wunderkind of the agency, out from behind her desk at Langley. Tired as she was, Lynn Simpson looked through the man alongside her. He knew from her reputation—an impressive one for someone as young as she was—and realized that she didn't care what he thought. She played her own game and did it very well.

"We have a vehicle approaching from Tenth Street, followed by a van," came a voice over the earpiece in both agents' ears.

"Thank you, unit two, they are expected company," Simpson said into the microphone located just under her jacket collar.

"Who are they?" Evans asked as he looked from the beautiful young woman and then into his rearview mirror.

"CSIS," she said as she removed the field glasses from his hands and looked through them at the house.

"Why would we bring in the Canadian Security Intelligence Service if we're just watching and verifying if that's really them inside? We don't have anything on Deonovich or Sagli, no warrants at least."

"You'll have to excuse me if you weren't informed of everything that comes across my desk, Agent Evans. Right now the Canadian authorities have them entering Canada under false passports and thanks to an anonymous source, we also have them coming into Seattle with those same false papers. Now, can I assume you're armed?"

"In the glove box. Will I need it?" he asked, not liking the way this thing was shaping up.

Agent Lynn Simpson lowered the field glasses, but didn't look at Evans when she handed him the binoculars. Keeping her eyes on the house, she reached for the glove box, opened it, found the Glock nine-millimeter, and then handed it to him.

"You are currently qualified with *that*, I presume?" she asked him with the first touch of a smile to cross her lips that morning. "I'm just kidding, Evans, just keep it close. I couldn't get my weapon into the country."

"Wait, didn't you fly in by a company plane?"

"Commercial," she said as she opened the car door but looked back before she stepped out. "I needed the travel miles."

Evans watched her as she closed the door and then walked to the rear of the rented Audi as the car and van approached. He closed his eyes and cursed, now realizing the assistant director wasn't here under any kind of authorization from the company. He chambered a round into his nine-millimeter, making sure the safety was on, and then threw open his door.

"I know what you're thinking, Evans, and yes, the director of Intelligence knows we're here; she made me contact CSIS to let them know we'd be in country. We'll soon have the company of the head of the Montreal sector of counterintelligence greeting us." She looked over the top of the Audi and shook her head. The older agents were getting so paranoid that someone was going to snatch their pension right out from under them since most refused to take chances any longer.

The Canadian government car stopped and a large man with a balding head stepped out of the passenger's side, smiled at Lynn, and held out his hand.

"Well, I thought your bosses at the Farm were keeping a closer eye on you these days?" the man asked, shaking the hand of the much smaller American woman.

"Hello, Punchy, how are the wife and kids?"

Jonathan "Punchy" Alexander had been trained through the offices of British Intelligence, MI-5, and was one of the best field men Lynn had ever met. He was the man responsible for shutting down the largest terrorist organization on the North American continent two years prior, and held the prison key to over one hundred and twelve enemies of the

West. He was currently Canada's flavor of the month, or year for that matter.

"My kids are all anarchists and the wife is still mean as a snake," he said as he released her small hand. He looked at the pretty American and watched her eyes. "I suspect that most of my kids are downtown protesting with the rest of the crazies about independence from Ottawa. How's your brother? I haven't seen him in years, hell, I haven't even heard about him, and in our game that says something. I hope the U.S. government didn't bury him too deep after his little snit with the army."

"I wouldn't know about that. If he was dead, I'm sure my mother would have said something about it."

Alexander sensed anger behind the bland look that she put on her face as she casually uttered those words and decided to push a little more. He thought, *Maybe I'll get something for my report.*

"Still touchy on the subject of your brother, I see."

She looked straight at the much larger Canadian and tilted her head and raised her left eyebrow.

"Okay, I'll leave it alone." He knew the problems of big brother, little sister because of the career path the latter had chosen. His old friend wasn't happy his baby sis had opted for the intelligence end of things. Alexander cleared his throat and then looked up at the château. "Now, you're not standing in front of Château Laureal because of the early season tourist rate, so what are you doing in the great white north, Agent Simpson?"

"Gregori Deonovich and Dmitri Sagli," she said as she held the Canadian intelligence officer with her stark blue eyes.

All humor and goodwill left his features. He looked at Lynn and then immediately turned toward the giant house and then without looking away from the structure gestured for his men to exit the car and van.

"I take it you were informed of their arrival by a contact from my country who works for you?"

"Let's not get territorial, Punchy, I was informed anonymously and then I immediately called you people."

Alexander unceremoniously removed the field glasses from Agent Evans and raised them to look at the château, allowing Evans a chance to glare at the larger man.

"You're sure it's those murderous bastards?"

"They didn't even bother to disguise themselves coming through the airport. It was like they wanted to be seen."

Alexander lowered the glasses and fixed Lynn with a look.

"You know, they knew you would be called in any event. Of all the people in the world, they would want to confront you."

"Am I missing something here?" Evans asked.

"Yes. If I know your boss, you've missed everything. The two men of Slavic origin inside of that house have a file on them in every Western intelligence service and those files are over a foot thick. And somewhere in those reports you will find a reference to your Ms. Simpson. She's dogged them since the time she was first assigned to the desk she now occupies. Altogether these two Russians have killed five American, six British, one New Zealander, three Germans, and two Canadian intelligence people, and that's all *after* their time at the KGB ended."

"So what have they been doing since?" Evans asked looking from Alexander to Lynn.

"Don't you brief your field people?" Alexander asked, sparing Lynn a cold look. "They are the joint heads of the largest organized crime syndicate in Russia. That's what KGB retirement means nowadays. The last I heard, they were expanding into the Ukraine and Kazakhstan, which is why I'm so concerned about them coming here where they don't own the intelligence agencies or the police. Besides, with all of this rioting going on and with a major coup in the offing if things don't calm down, them being here makes a mess, just a larger mess." Alexander raised the glasses again and watched the house. "May I assume that your FBI and even your own director don't know that you and your boys are in Canada?"

"My immediate boss thought we could take care of this on our own, Punchy, without bringing both of our agency heads in on it; the legalities involved would have taken too much time. With what's happening here we thought a low profile was best. Look, Sagli and Deonovich are here for a reason, and no matter what that reason is, them being in that château uninvited is what we call, in the States, probable cause."

"I came across an obscure report generated by your NSA that says these two maniacs may have finally pushed the Russians into acting against them. It seems they were alerted to certain illegal activities by someone in the American intelligence community, and this person may have actually forwarded incriminating evidence of murder to the Russian authorities. Them being here may be the end result of that report so they may finally be on the run. Do you know who may have sent the Russians that report, Agent Simpson?"

Lynn held Alexander's gaze for a moment and then nodded toward the château. "Now tell me, Punchy, what is in that monstrosity of a house that would make them risk coming to the one continent where they would immediately skip trial and be unceremoniously hanged if caught?"

The glasses came down again and Alexander took in a deep breath, knowing it was exactly as he thought—Lynn had forwarded the report to the authorities in Moscow.

"Nothing new, antiques for the tourists to ooh and ah over. Maybe . . . Fuquay?" he called out to the small group of men he had brought along.

"Yes, sir," said the man in a heavy French Canadian accent. He stepped away from the group of ten Canadian agents and slung an automatic rifle over his shoulder.

"Wasn't there something about an exhibition on historical gold mining stopping off at the château?"

"Actually, we did receive a detailed report on the security for the exhibit. Nothing substantial so we didn't become involved. It's just some old mining equipment, letters home to wives from miners, that sort of thing. Turn-of-the-century items."

"You're kidding? Why would those two killers have interest in that?" Lynn asked.

Alexander nodded for the man to return to the A-Team of Canadians.

"They shouldn't be interested in anything that we've heard of in there. And that in itself is enough to worry me."

Lynn turned and leaned into the rental car, retrieved a file, and handed it to Alexander. "This was sent to us by our Seattle field office—they 'borrowed' it from the Seattle PD."

Alexander opened the file and the first thing he saw was a crime scene photo of an old man stretched out on a bed. A hole had been punched through his head on the man's right side. The bed he was lying on was soaked through with blood. Alexander turned the page and looked at the second, far more disturbing image taken by the Seattle police department showing twelve individuals, tied and gagged. Each one had been shot execution style and placed in a circle, feet pointed outward.

"The circle of victims proves beyond a doubt that Deonovich and Sagli did this. That circle thing is definitely their calling card. Head to head, that's the way they always leave their victims, symbolizes complete-ness, or so our psych people tell us."

"And this third photo?" Alexander asked, as he flipped the page and saw a clear shot of Sagli and Deonovich. The long ponytail of Sagli and the distinctive crew-cut hair of Deonovich were visible, and the size dif-ference between the two was clear as Deonovich towered over the smaller Sagli.

"That was taken at Sea-Tac Airport and sent to me by that anony-mous source I mentioned. We assume it was taken upon their arrival in country."

"This anonymous source is quite disturbing to say the least," Alexan-der said as his eyes went from the picture and fixed on Lynn.

"It could be anyone: FBI, even the Seattle PD. It's not like these two aren't camera shy—every law enforcement agency on the planet knows about them."

Punchy Alexander closed the file and tossed it on the trunk of Lynn's rental car. The large man pursed his lips and then lowered his head in thought.

"My hackles are rising, Agent Simpson." He held up a hand when she started to say something. "This is squirrelly. They know they are vulner-able when they travel. And you receive this photo out of the clear blue? Surely, you and your area director suspect that this may be a setup? I mean, this location, it's so far from everything, and out in the open like this. No, this isn't right and your boss should have known it."

"Why would they do that?" she asked pointing to the first picture of the dead Serta. "They murdered an old man in Seattle, this Valery Serta, obviously of Russian descent, and killed his entire house staff, for what? They're ruthless killers, Punchy, but that just isn't their style."

"And you're an expert at avoiding the obvious. But let me say this, it doesn't really matter, they're here and they're not leaving Canadian soil." He turned and got the attention of his agents. "You men deploy by twos, all with strength of cover positions, and get me more men in here. Get the descriptions of Deonovich and Sagli to every man, and do not hesi-tate to use deadly force if positive identification is made."

"Punchy, the agency would like them alive if possible; they have a lot to answer for," Lynn said as she followed Alexander to the trunk of his car.

"Look, Agent Simpson," he said, getting very official. "I like you, and I damn well have the deepest respect for your family, but you're well out of your territory and on foreign soil, your higher management people don't even know you're here, just your assistant director of Intelligence— if you want to keep it that way, let me handle this. If not, get back into your car and either get to the airport or to the American consulate."

"You know these two guys are mine, Punchy. I have case files on them all the way back to 1978."

"Yes, I know, and they also know." Alexander let out a breath, calming himself. "They know as much about you as you do them. You're in danger by even showing up here. And you put the operation in danger as much as you put yourself at risk. You should have done all of this by phone from Langley." He saw a look of frustration flicker across her face. "Okay, don't give me that look, your brother always tried that crap on me, and believe me, little girl, you're not him. You and your team, even the two you have watching us right now, are to observe only."

"Listen—"

Lynn never finished her protest. The château disintegrated in an explosion that was powerful enough from a hundred yards away to implode the windshields on the two cars and van. They were all knocked from their feet as the pressure wave hit them. As the fireball and debris moved high into the air, Lynn, Evans, and Alexander scrambled on hands and knees to get to the far side of the rental car. Soon, stone, mortar, and burning wood started striking around them. Men and their equipment were sprawled over the roadway as debris from the massive mansion rained down. Amid the din and chaos, they heard the first crackle of automatic weapons fire.

"What in the hell?" Evans asked covering his head just as several bullets slammed into the Audi's rear quarter panel.

It was then that Lynn heard it: the harsh whine of a Bell Ranger helicopter as it came in low over the street. The van suddenly erupted with a crumpling sound coupled with fire and wind, sending Alexander into the Americans, as they were all three pushed from cover by the blast from the exploding van. The automatic weapons fire continued from both open doorways of the attack chopper as the assassins inside took careful and deadly aim at the thirteen prone people on the ground. Lynn rolled out from under Alexander and looked up just as several pieces of burning wood and debris struck the single rotor blade of the Ranger high above her. The rotors shook off the assault and danger and kept shooting down at them. Lynn realized whatever happened at the château was secondary to what she now knew was a murder raid. The Russians knew they were there and they were out to kill them.

"We need to—"

Alexander had just come to his knee and drawn his weapon when one bullet nicked his shoulder and he was thrown backward. Lynn saw Punchy hit his head hard on the pavement. Evans yelped; she was then splattered with his blood. Without really thinking about it, she reached out, grabbed the Glock nine-millimeter, and then quickly rolled until the large curb that lined the street stopped her momentum. Above all of the noise she thought she heard the sound of approaching sirens.

"Bastards!" she yelled as she took quick aim and then fired up into the belly of the Bell Ranger. The small slugs punched holes into the aluminum bottom but had no effect. She quickly emptied the Glock and all she had to show for it was to add new venting to the helicopter's flooring.

The CSIS men were succumbing quickly to the murderous fire from above just as two Montreal police cruisers skidded to a stop behind the burning van. Lynn tried in vain to warn the patrolmen off as the two jumped from their respective cars, but she couldn't be heard over the gunfire. The two police officers never knew what hit them as slugs slammed into their bodies and riddled them with holes.

Lynn screamed into the microphone that was still attached to her coat collar, screaming for cover fire from her observation team based at the far end of the street. That was when she realized the fire from on high had stopped and she could only hear the sound of the hovering helicopter. As she looked up through the smoke and flying dust, the Ranger moved off slowly. She then knew that the whining turbine sound had not left with it. Her eyes moved to the rear of the departing assault helicopter and that was when she saw another. This one was a French-built Aérospatiale Gazelle attack helicopter. It began a quick decent to the smoking and smashed street.

Lynn came to her knees and started running when she realized the assault wasn't over. As she stumbled past the burning van, the Gazelle swooped in and, with its powerful three bladed rotors, dusted Lynn until she couldn't stand against the force any longer and fell. She tried to stand once more but fell again as the Gazelle came in even lower. As she covered her head, she thought to herself that this was the end, when the Gazelle slammed hard onto the street, the skids missing her head by only five feet. As she rolled over and searched hopelessly for one of the Canadians' fallen weapons, hands grabbed at her. She tried to fight them off, but a blow to her face slowed her reactions down to a crawl.

Lynn Simpson felt the blood flowing freely from a three-inch gash opened on her lower lip as she felt herself being held upright by two sets of hands. Through the noise and her pain, she saw a face come at her from the rush of smoke and dust.

"Predictable, Agent Simpson. Now, if you will come with us, our transportation is waiting."

Lynn gathered herself and spit as far as she could toward the dark-haired Dmitri Sagli. The blood struck the small man's leather coat. He smiled and then with his right hand, backhanded her across the face, making her angrier, but still just as helpless as before.

"You Americans have always been fond of the term, *to kill two birds with one stone*." The former Russian KGB assassin looked about at the dead Canadian agents and smiled. "Now we have managed to kill a whole flock of Canadian geese and catch one American songbird with one stone."

As the Russian watched Lynn being loaded into the waiting Gazelle, he shook his head in wonder at how stupid the West was becoming. They thought everything revolved around dead ideologies dating back to the Cold War, and that was what made their actions predictable. The game had changed for the ex-KGB men and the West just couldn't follow along. It was now all about personal power, not ideology.

As Dmitri Sagli turned for the helicopter, he saw Punchy Alexander move a few feet away from him. He slowly walked up to the prone Canadian agent and placed his foot at the back of his head and then pointed the same automatic weapon he had used to kill Serta in Seattle, he turned and smiled at Lynn Simpson, almost as if making sure she was watching, and then he fired three times into Alexander's back. He then moved off toward the Gazelle, putting the weapon away and buttoning his coat as he did.

As the Gazelle lifted free of the street, it left behind three dead American field officers and eleven Canadians, the largest massacre of Western intelligence personnel in history.

The Bell Ranger soon overtook the French-built helicopter to escort it, and together they both headed toward the border, flying south toward New York.

Assistant Director of Intelligence Nancy Grogan eased herself into one of the two chairs facing the director's desk. Harmon Easterbrook eyed her as she sat and placed a red-bordered file on the desk's edge. Briefly, she looked to her left at Assistant Director of Operations Stan Rosen, and then quickly nodded. Rosen in turn did not grant her the favor of his own greeting. She ignored the snub and listened to the one-way conversation going on in front of her.

"Yes, sir, we'll get a full report of everything we have over to you as soon as we can gather the Intel. Yes, Mr. President, a full accounting."

As the director hung up the phone, he kept his fingers on the handle for the briefest of moments; it was as if he were thinking about his words before he spoke them. He then half smiled, but the humor was lost somewhere between the eyes and the mouth. He looked directly at Grogan.

"Needless to say that was the president. Can you guess what was on his mind this morning?"

"The incident in Montreal would be my guess, and a pretty accurate one I—"

"I was asking Nancy, Stan," Easterbrook said, his eyes never leaving the fifty-two-year-old woman.

"I take full responsibility for what happened. Simpson was there with my full knowledge."

"With three of my field agents, now dead," Stan Rosen said glaring over at his intelligence counterpart.

"Look, if we thought it was anything more than just a sighting, we would have been there in force; as it was, it was an anonymous source that let us know Sagli and Deonovich were in the country. We had nothing other than some grainy photography that it was even them. So, Lynn asked if she could go and investigate. She did it by the book, went through channels and—"

"Got a Canadian CSIS field team wiped out, an American responsible for northeastern American intelligence kidnapped, and three of my people killed."

The assistant director lowered her head for the briefest of moments, but then gathered herself.

"Lynn is the brightest person I have in my entire department. Hell, she's easily my replacement, she outthinks everyone here at the Farm and you know it. This is something more than just Sagli and his buddy being here for theft."

"Explain," Easterbrook said, motioning for Rosen to be quiet.

"We don't even know why they were in Canada. And the mass murder in Seattle? The Seattle authorities are saying a possible motivation was theft, but as of yet they are saying nothing is missing from this Russian's apartment. Now we have Sagli and Deonovich breaking into what amounts to be a museum in Montreal for theft once more? As I said, not their style. There's something more here than we know at the moment."

"It's my understanding that your person has been making life very miserable for Sagli and Deonovich for more than three years, at least since I put her there after her stint in Afghanistan. Hell, she may be responsible for them being on the run; what's worse, they know it's her putting pressure on them from this end. Now, let me know, is this a vengeance thing or something else? Operations has to know so we can treat this accordingly."

The director nodded. "Stan has a valid point," watching Grogan carefully for her reactions.

Grogan turned and fixed her operations counterpart with a raised brow.

"That's right; for once I had someone at that desk who was capable of doing that particular job. Lynn dug her teeth into those two and hung on. They are wanted in this country for the murder of federal agents, including our own. Everywhere they went in Moscow, Minsk, Kiev, and even Kurdistan, she had our people watching them. She was making life miserable by letting their prospective clients and associates be aware their time was drawing to a close. Finally, and this is in my monthly departmental report, she was authorized by me to forward the file to Russian intelligence on their activities. That file included outlays for taking out certain Russian politico's in Moscow who they deemed dangerous to their illegal operations. Evidently, the new Russian president moved on that evidence and sent them scurrying."

"And now your girl wonder is in their hands. Does that make you feel better?" Rosen asked giving back the raised brow look.

"That's uncalled for, Stan. I need you both to work together on this. The Canadian PM just threatened the president with public disclosure. We have to get this thing under some kind of control and get him answers. I want a full court press on this."

"Even though I despise the way this came down, I have to tell you that I think the prime minister is bluffing. His people were there also; what can he say? He doesn't know what his intelligence services are doing? Besides, he has separatist protests and outright riots in Montreal he has to deal with and something like this could only add to his French-speaking provincial problems."

"How is their guy doing?" Easterbrook asked.

"John Alexander is one tough nut. As I told you in numerous reports, he's one of the good guys and the bastard's hard to kill. He'll recover. He was wearing his vest. He's a real pro."

"Good, good. Now—"

"If I know him, he'll want in on whatever it is we do about this. He and Simpson were close. They both spent time with MI-5 in Birmingham on the Al-Qaeda thing. Evidently, he's a close friend of her family."

"If he asks, we'll allow it as a professional courtesy. That's the least we can do," Easterbrook said, nodding that their brief meeting was concluded.

Nancy Grogan cleared her throat. The director looked up and Rosen sat back in his chair.

"You have something else?"

"Lynn Simpson."

"I want her back. If not, I want the men who killed her."

"It's not that, sir. There's a reason why she is as good as she is. Why she's pegged to be a company leader in the near future. It seems to run in her blood."

"Get to the point," Easterbrook ordered.

"Simpson is Lynn's mother's maiden name. Collins is her real name."

Director Easterbrook bit his lower lip and then swiveled his chair to face his large window as he thought. Rosen for his part was lost as to what she was getting at.

"So?" Rosen finally asked.

Grogan shook her head and then turned and looked at the assistant director.

"She's the sister of a very dangerous man, at least he used to be. This Colonel Collins and Punchy Alexander go way back. They were joint heads of a special operations action in Canada. I can't get details on the mission, but it had something to do with recovering a project called Solar Flare. I couldn't get any more details on—,"

"He still is a dangerous man, and there is no such thing as Solar Flare," Easterbrook said, still looking out of his window away from his two assistants. "At least publicly there isn't. It was a search and rescue operation twenty-five years after it was lost. It has no bearing on the action taken in Montreal."

Nancy Grogan caught the drift and knew the subject of this Solar Flare was off limits.

"I thought the army buried Colonel Collins somewhere?" Grogan asked the back of the director's chair.

Easterbrook finally and slowly turned his chair back to face the two. He ran a hand through his completely gray head of hair, and then fixed Nancy with his stern look.

"I hear rumors, and they all say that Colonel Jack Collins is still very much in the mix"—the director picked up the phone—"and if the rumors I hear are true, he won't be very happy about us losing his little sister. Now, excuse me."

"Lynn said she and her brother don't speak that often, that they're not that close," Grogan said.

The director paused with phone in hand and looked at both of his people.

"Do you want to be the one to inform him, if we can even locate him, that is?"

Grogan lowered her eyes and then turned and started to leave.

"I don't get it, who is this Collins, and what is the big deal?" Rosen asked. "He's just a colonel for God's sake."

"From his reputation, he's not only one of the best soldiers this country has ever produced, but also just about the most dangerous man alive—at least he once was," Grogan said as she reached for the door handle.

"This stays in this office," Easterbrook said as he started punching numbers, bypassing his assistant in the outer office, standard procedure when he called the president's private line.

"I don't see the concern here. I think we have bigger problems to deal with than some army colonel," Rosen said as he looked from the director to Grogan. "Come on, he's only one guy, right?"

Grogan turned and caught the attention of the director.

"Look, Collins is a legend, at least in the field."

"I'll bet he's stuck behind a desk somewhere, out of the way, one of those break-glass-in-case-of-war guys; probably just a relic by now."

2

Lynn Simpson wasn't bound or gagged, and had been treated well since the savagery of the early morning. She was now locked in a small room just off the basement of a house. She even knew where she was being held, having recognized the small airfield she had been brought to just outside of McLean, Virginia. She was mere miles away from her own office at Langley, and with the fact they weren't trying to hide their safe house from her was worrisome, because they obviously had no intention of ransoming her back to the company.

Since her arrival, she had been offered lunch, which sat untouched on the small table in the corner. She had drunk the bottled water provided, simply to assist her in holding down the bile in her stomach that rose up every time she remembered the murder of her agents and those of the Canadian contingent right before her eyes.

She hadn't seen the two Russians, Sagli and Deonovich, since she had been led into the room. There were, however, several other brutes that made their presence known. As for why she was here and not dead was something she had yet to figure out.

Lynn paced to the window and stood on her toes to look through the ground-level window. The glass was reinforced with wire, so smashing through it was out of the question—her guards would be on her long before she could push through the wire. She looked around, seeing only cinderblock and concrete. Again she turned to the window and the overcast day outside.

The door suddenly opened and a large man in a tan jacket and white shirt stood looking at her. The black beard hid the fierce features somewhat, but Lynn recognized the large brute as one of the helicopters gunners that had assisted in eliminating the Canadian ground team and her own men at the château. He glanced from Lynn's pretty features to the window and then he smiled, as if saying, "Please try."

The man stepped aside and Sagli stepped through the door alone; Deonovich was not with him. The ponytail was gone and the Russian's dark hair hung free to fall around his shoulders. He carried a small box with him as he closed the door. The large guard took up station beside it and his eyes locked on Lynn. It was as if he really expected her to try something. The Russians must have believed CIA agents all to be James Bond types.

"Ms. Simpson, we finally get a chance to chat. After so many encounters through second, third, and fourth parties, it is truly an honor to finally meet you in person."

Lynn moved away from the wall that held the small window and looked from Sagli over to the guard. She was tempted to take a quick step toward the large man just to see if he would flinch, but decided he might not appreciate that too much. She turned and looked at Sagli, but remained silent. She needed all the information she could get before she did something as stupid as getting herself killed.

"Needless to say, you were an irritant with your constant feed of intelligence to the swine that now occupy the Kremlin. Not that it ever stopped us from conducting our business."

"You'll never leave this country alive," Lynn said as a confident matter of fact as she paced to the only chair in the room and sat down. She picked a small corner of bread from the still full plate and forced herself to eat it.

Sagli saw through her forced bravado and smiled. "We managed rather nicely to come into your country, I think we can manage getting out when the time presents itself. In the meantime, may I show you something?"

Lynn swallowed the piece of bread with as much difficulty as she could ever remember any task. She then shrugged her shoulders.

Sagli opened the small box he was carrying and then looked inside, as if never tiring of gazing at the amazing object. He held it out for Lynn to see. She saw the gleaming diamond that was as big as the largest hen's egg she had ever seen. The ten thousand cuts made on the diamond's surface were as flawless as the stone itself. She forced herself not to react to the most amazing display of geology she would ever see.

"Beautiful, is it not?"

Still she didn't say anything; instead she looked away and tore another piece of bread off and placed it in her mouth. While she did, her mind raced. If this venture into the United States was limited to diamonds, her line of investigation was so far off she almost vomited the bread she had just swallowed.

"It will be difficult to shove it up your ass when you go to prison, won't it?" she said as she swallowed the bread and then reached for the water bottle in front of her.

The Russian reached out and slapped the bottle from her fingertips. His glare was murderous.

"May I remind you, you are not in a position for such false bravado? You will assist us in our quest, or you will die, just as your Canadian colleagues did this morning."

"Just get on with it, you're boring me."

Again, Sagli smiled and then closed the lid to the small box. "The Twins—that is what this is about, Miss Simpson. As you see we have one, we want the other. The Twins of Peter the Great, once a myth and now proven to be a fact. You will assist us in discovering the whereabouts of this diamond's equal."

"I haven't a clue as to what you're talking about."

Sagli held the small box out. The large man by the door took it and then returned to his position by the door.

"We could have taken any hostage we wanted here in the States. However, taking you was just too tempting. You have been what you Americans call a pain in the ass. We knew our picture would lead you right to where we wanted you to be. Now we will get the information we need in exchange for sparing your life."

"Uh-huh, and I'll run for president of the United States next year at this time. My bosses wouldn't give you the time of day."

"Indeed, they may not if they thought that we were not serious in our quest." Sagli nodded over at the large man who nodded and placed the box holding the diamond on the floor. He quickly advanced toward the chair and he went behind Lynn and then without hesitation reached out and grabbed her right hand and slammed it on the table, knocking the now cold meal from its surface. Before Lynn knew exactly what was happening, the man produced a knife and quickly and expertly cut her right index finger off, slicing through skin and bone as effortlessly as a breadstick.

Lynn screamed and then closed her eyes against the pain. For some unknown reason her thoughts quickly turned to her brother, the protector she had known since the time she had been able to remember. She couldn't help it; she let loose with his name in a moment of lost composure.

"Jack!" she cried.

The Russian smiled when the name of her brother was mentioned, and then just as quickly the grin vanished.

"There, now your employers will believe you are in dire peril," Sagli said as he nodded for the man to leave the room with his new proof of life and of Lynn's identity.

Lynn grasped her hand as Sagli reached out and quickly wrapped a handkerchief around the wound and then he ruthlessly bound it tightly. With tears of pain and frustration coursing down both cheeks, she became mad, not only at her complete failure at controlling the pain, but being weak enough to have called out for Jack.

"I'm going to kill that bastard for that," Lynn said between clenched teeth. "Then I'm going to kill you and that worthless partner of yours," she finished far more calmly than she felt.

"We will get what we want from your government, and then you will die, possibly not in that order, but die you will. Either way, the good guys will not win this round, dear Miss Simpson. There will be no one capable of stopping us from finding the other Twin, no American cowboy to come to your rescue."

Lynn's eyes narrowed, knowing that the only man who could come riding to her rescue knew only that she was working on a project that may or may not concern him; thus he was in the dark as to what peril his sister was in, and realizing this, an air of despair settled over her like a dark shroud.

LANGLEY, VIRGINIA

Assistant Director of Intelligence Nancy Grogan had been at her desk going on fifteen hours. Stan Rosen, coming in from a stop at home, poked his head inside of her door after a brief knock. They were both under orders from the director to get a handle on the abduction of Agent Lynn Simpson.

"Anything since I've been out?" he asked, knowing from her tired expression there had been no developments.

"Stan, this makes no sense: Two of the most wanted criminals in the world abduct an American intelligence officer. Where is the plan? They know we won't negotiate her release."

Rosen took a step into the office and removed his horn-rimmed glasses. "You have been in your position, how long? Three months?"

"Four," she said, not in the least bit anxious to be lectured.

"We negotiate with scum on a daily basis around here. The director and the president want your girl freed, and they will be willing to deal with those two pieces of shit to do it. Then we can sweep this thing back across the border where it damn well belongs."

"We have to hear from them first."

"Go home; those files will start blending into each other if you keep going. Get some rest; I'll stay and keep the home fires burning here. The director will have some hard questions tomorrow, and you better be awake enough to have a few answers."

"You're right, at least a nap and a shower," Grogan said as she tossed the thick file about Sagli onto her desk. Then she looked up. "Did the director say anything about contacting Lynn's brother?"

Stan looked at his watch. "Not as of ten o'clock tonight. The president said he wants every piece of intelligence we can gather before addressing that problem."

Nancy Grogan shook her head and stood.

"Call me if anything develops."

"Oh, thank you for not bringing up the fact that it was me that passed on that airport picture of Sagli and Deonovich to you. There was no sense in getting both of us in Dutch with the director."

Grogan stopped gathering her data to take home and looked at Rosen.

"I do have one question; maybe your answer will be payment enough for not mentioning to the director that it was you who gave me the photo."

"Shoot," Rosen said.

"The contact who passed it to you: How did you get someone on the Canadian side to work for you with intelligence knowing? I mean, I should have gotten a report on anyone working with you across the border."

Rosen smiled wide. "We all have our secrets."

Grogan tilted her head and continued to look at her operations counterpart.

"The guy is so small in their government and we pay him so little that he just got lost in the reports, that's all." With a last smile and nod of his head, Stan Rosen left. "I'll let you know if anything happens while you're resting," he called out over his shoulder.

Nancy sat back down in her chair. She looked at her empty doorway and wondered at the fact that Rosen still didn't name his source.

Forty minutes later, Grogan pulled into her driveway at Fort Myer, Maryland. She paused in her car as she noticed that her security lights didn't come on as usual. As she gathered her large bag she knew she had to call the security company first thing in the morning, another headache to deal with. As she took the fifteen steps up her walk to her front door, a voice came out of the darkness. She stopped and without turning, started to reach into her bag.

"Please do not attempt to reach for your weapon, I have instructions that say you are not valuable enough to leave unharmed if you make trouble. You will be quite dead before you turn around, Assistant Director Grogan. We would just choose to go through another spy to deliver our demands."

"Who are you?" she asked as she slowly turned to face the darkness of her front yard. She could see a man, a rather large one, standing just outside of her night vision.

"That is not important. What is of the utmost importance is that you listen. As you know, we have your agent and she is in dire straits at the moment, and in very much discomfort. If you and your agency would like to relieve her of any more pain, and perhaps have her returned, we need one thing from you."

"I need proof that she is alright, otherwise you can go straight to hell. We don't pay criminals for killing our people."

"Proof is forthcoming. Right now you need to return to your agency and gather one piece of information. Six months ago, there was a robbery at the Denver Museum of Natural History. Several valuable pieces were stolen, along with some very valuable papers that were stored in one of these artifacts."

"What does this have to do with—?"

"If you interrupt me once more, we will send your agent back to you in many pieces."

Grogan was silent as she tried desperately to focus on the voice in the dark.

"We want the name of the thief of these artifacts delivered to us. We will recover the property ourselves. This should not be too difficult to obtain for an agency of your renown."

"That could be impossible. The case may be ongoing in Denver and the name could be—"

A small box thumped against her leg and fell to the flagstone walkway.

"Our intentions toward your agent are inside the box. In twenty-four hours you will place an advertisement in the *Washington Post* in the lost-and-found section of that paper. A lost female puppy, a Yorkshire Terrier that goes by the name of Lynn. Please contact—here you will give the name of the thief that we seek, and his address. Once we have recovered what it is we seek, your agent will be returned to you whole, well, minus some weight, but otherwise intact. There will be no interference from the authorities at this thief's location. If you interfere, we will have no choice but to relieve the local civilian population of their lives. We have the manpower and the weaponry to achieve this. Are you clear on your instructions?"

"Yes."

As she waited, she could tell the large man had gone. The air around her grew less heavy as she took a deep breath. She was frightened for the first time in her adult life as she realized these people knew where she lived. That information was classified and a breech such as that was totally out of the realm of possibility.

She reached down slowly and before touching the small box, she tapped it with her toe. It moved easily, meaning there was practically no weight to it. Then she picked it up. If they wanted to kill her, they could have done it quickly and quietly just now in her own front yard, so she gently shook it. There was something loose inside.

"Jesus," she mumbled as she placed her large bag on the walkway and then tore the brown packing tape from the top of the box. As she turned the box toward the weak front-porch light, she almost dropped it.

"Oh, God," she said as she saw the human finger with the red nail polish on it.

CIA—LANGLEY, VIRGINIA

Nancy Grogan was still shaken as she sat beside Stan Rosen in the director's office. On the speaker phone was the forensics lab far beneath the main floors of the complex.

"The fingerprint match has been confirmed as that of Agent Simpson. Blood type is the same as on file and we are currently running a DNA match from a sample she gave two years ago to alleviate any chance of print alteration."

"What are the chances of that?" the director asked as he tossed down the pen he was holding onto his desktop.

"The old KGB had become quite adept at the science, but in this case, we figure it's Agent Simpson's finger. We *can* say that the agent was alive when her finger was amputated."

"Thank you. Please send me the results of the DNA match as soon as you get them."

Director Easterbrook looked from the speaker box to Nancy Grogan's pale face.

"Okay, what have we got on this theft in Denver?"

"Stan Rosen is helping out on that end; he has an operations agent in the Colorado Bureau of Investigation. It was your influence that opened that particular door for Stan. The CBI will hopefully have whatever the local authorities have on the robbery."

The phone buzzed and Easterbrook's secretary came on.

"Sir, Director Grogan has a call from Montreal."

"Put it through."

"This is Grogan," she said leaning forward in her chair.

"If my superiors knew I was making this call, you know what would happen. As it is, they didn't think to bug a hospital phone line."

"Mr. Alexander?" Nancy asked.

"You have my regrets for not being able to better help Agent Simpson."

"This is Director Easterbrook, Mr. Alexander. You have our sincere apologies for this accidental foray onto your turf; I can assure you that this will never—"

"Mr. Director, I have very little time and a very sore shoulder and back. Those bulletproof vests are not all that they are cracked up to be. Now, our people have picked up something that may help you, but this information comes with a warning. We believe Sagli and Deonovich were after two items, one of which they recovered from the château; the other, as you may already know if you have had contact with them, was stolen quite some time ago on your side of the border."

"How were you able to come across this in a burnt-out hulk of a mansion?"

"We may not have all of your resources, but we still have reasonable deductive prowess, Ms. Grogan. The explosive charges were set in a specific room of the château. It housed only one exhibit, the personal artifacts belonging to Jenson P. Lattimer of Boston. This material is what was known on the museum tour as the Lattimer Papers. That coincides with your homicide in Seattle, Washington, of one Valery Serta, a logging magnate. The cause of death was brutal, the details of which you can, get from the Seattle PD. We don't know why he was killed; however, cross-referencing his name in our data banks we came up with these Lattimer Papers and something about the man's father and his arrival into North America sometime after the turn of the century. This information is pretty ordinary and we were able to obtain copies of the brief mention of his name, but the real prize was an incomplete artifact called the Petrov Diary. This diary somehow ended up in the hands of this Lattimer character of Boston, an old blueblood who placed them on exhibit in honor of a long lost uncle."

"You have saved us a lot of valuable time, Mr. Alexander; we are very grateful."

"Ms. Grogan, if this case leads back to Canadian soil, you and your agency are to stay home, I have convinced my superiors to let me handle the case from here. There will be no publicity on this side and I am working totally autonomously."

"Why would you think it will lead them back to your country?" Director Easterbrook asked, showing his anger.

"Because Mr. Easterbrook, the Lattimer Papers referred to a lost treasure in the Canadian wilderness, and we suspect that is what Sagli and Deonovich are after."

An hour later, just moments before Director Easterbrook lifted the phone, it buzzed.

"Sir, the president is on line one," his assistant said from his outer office.

"Yes, sir," he said as he lifted the receiver.

"Harmon, I just read this damn mystery novel you sent over. This has got to be a joke. Are you telling me these two Russians risked their lives to come to a hostile country for the sake of a treasure map?"

"We are still collating data as we speak, Mr. President. We can't be real sure of anything at this point, at least not until we can get a line on who stole that diary from Colorado."

"Well here's a little nugget for you. With the Canadian Prime Minister threatening to go public with our little foray onto Canadian soil, he has cut off the flow of information from his end. You were lucky this Punchy Alexander here has closer ties with us than his agency does."

"Yes, sir, that is the one break we have gotten."

"Now, evidently we have an agent who may or may not be dead. I have a decision to make here, Harmon. I owe her brother a lot. Hell, everyone in this damn country does."

"Maybe I can help you with it if you would allow me to look at this man's file."

"Forget it, no one sees the file on Jack Collins; don't ask again. As it is, he has ties everywhere within our government. Now, I have to get word out to his boss to make sure he doesn't get directly involved any more than his sister already has him. With what Agent Simpson passed along to you, it's obvious we may have to flush a bad guy out of our own cornfield. Until we know what these bastards are up to, I'm going to keep Collins in the dark, no matter what his sister has asked him to do for her. Now you did good, Harmon, by bringing me and Jack's boss onboard with this thing when you did, but the situation has now changed."

"The suspicions Agent Simpson brought to me involved her brother, and I knew Collins worked for you in some capacity. I believe he may know something we don't about his sister's suspicions; we need to contact him and brief—"

"Mr. Easterbrook, it's not just Colonel Collins; he happens to be affiliated with the most brilliant people in the world. If he gets wind of his sister's predicament, believe me, he and his people will become involved. Now, get back to me when you have more; right now I have to make a call."

Across the Potomac River, the president of the United States hung up the phone and shook his head, which was beginning to ache. He reached out and slid over a small laptop computer and used a small key to unlock the lid. He raised the top and then hesitated. He took a breath and then used the cursor. He slid over to the only heading on the left side of the screen. It read 5656 in blue numbers. He clicked on the icon and then waited, knowing that the next face he would see would be that of Director Niles Compton, his friend, and the head of the blackest agency in government—the Event Group.

EVENT GROUP COMPLEX
NELLIS AIR FORCE BASE, NEVADA

The large office had forty 56-inch monitors arrayed around its walls. One monitor, the largest at the center of the far wall was over one hundred inches in diameter. The large desk had four smaller pop-up monitors that comprised the communications link with the rest of the complex, and, of course, the commander-in-chief of the United States. The monitor on the far left illuminated and the seal of the president appeared as a warning to Niles Compton that the president was making a call to the complex.

Niles lay down the proposal by the Nuclear Sciences Division, which recommended the department requisition a new electron microscope to replace an aging device before the restart of operations and field assignments. Compton wrote DENIED on the outer proposal sheet, knowing it would make Assistant Director Virginia Pollock angry as hell, but Niles knew that with all of the repairs to the facility underway, he could not squeeze any more funds out of an already stretched budget; after all, it's not like they could file an insurance claim. Virginia's department for the time being would have to bite it. Niles looked at the laptop screen and waited. Soon, the presidential seal was replaced by a test pattern, and then the face of his old college roommate, the president of the United States, appeared.

"Mr. President," Niles said, growing concerned at the stern look on the president's face. *This isn't going to be a social call.*

"Niles, a problem has developed that concerns one of your people."

"Who?"

"Colonel Collins, I'm afraid."

"Damn it, we really don't need this right now. What's the situation, sir?" he asked.

"When we spoke and allowed Jack in on a certain operation being conducted at CIA, I really didn't know how dangerous the individuals we were dealing really were and so I didn't go into detail about Collins and his sister. What I am about to tell you is classified to the point that you are the only person to be told about it. I do not, I repeat, do not want the colonel to hear about this. At the very least, the situation is touchy—and it could turn deadly. Am I understood, Niles?"

Niles didn't want to commit to answering, but he knew his old friend well enough that if he didn't respond the way he wanted him to, the president would clam up and not tell him what was going on.

"Understood," he finally relented.

"Damn you, Niles, don't you hand me that crap. Say it: You won't tell Collins anything about this."

"No, sir, I won't."

He could see by the president's expression that the answer he gave was ambiguous at best, but his oldest friend pursed his lips and gave in to Niles, knowing the MIT grad could go all day long and not give him the correct answer to his question.

"Okay, smart-ass, but I'll hang you, friends be damned, if you tell Collins."

"So far you haven't told me anything, Mr. President."

"The colonel's sister has been kidnapped. Her field team was ambushed in Canada on the mission I was assured was just a criminal investigation, and she was taken by two very salty characters, Russians—ex-KGB."

"Jesus, and you don't want Jack to know about this? We don't even know why his sister contacted Jack. I figured it was just for advice on something."

"Damn it, Niles, this is a full-blown international incident. I'm not giving you any more details at this time, and you'd better not go digging around with Europa, either, or I'll order the damn thing removed from your complex, is that understood?"

The supercomputer, Europa, had been a gift to the Event Group from the Cray Corporation. The system was remarkable at breaking into other computers and gathering intelligence through backdoor spying, useful in getting information from around the world on university and privately funded archaeological digs. There were only four others like her, one at the NSA, the CIA, the FBI, and the Pentagon.

"Again, your point is understood. However, I want it on record that I protest this order not to inform one of my people about something that affects him directly."

"Noted, Mr. Director," the president said angrily, knowing Niles was trying to get pissy with him. "Follow orders here. You know, and I know, what would happen if the colonel found out. There would be trouble, and frankly, I don't need it at the moment. I have every agency in the country working at getting her back, the Canadians are—" The president stopped, knowing he was giving his friend too much information. "I just wanted to alert you so you can break it to him if the end result is bad."

"Please keep me informed."

"I will," the president answered, his gaze intense.

Niles watched the screen go blank and then he closed the laptop. He replaced his glasses and didn't hesitate a second before picking up the phone to the outer office.

"Have Europa find Colonel Collins and get me his location in the complex."

Niles replaced the phone and then stood. He didn't bother putting on his coat or his tie. He walked to the large double doors and made his way out to his assistant in the outer office to await the location of Colonel Collins.

Jack had to be told immediately; the Event Group owed him that much. Regardless of what the president did to Niles personally for disobeying his order, the colonel would be told, or the talk they had had earlier wouldn't be worth the breath used to say the words.

As Niles waited, he knew he was about to open a tightly sealed can of worms, and that all hell was about to break loose when that seal was broken. He was about to unleash Jack Collins on the world of international crime.

Jack was sitting with Sarah McIntire at the only lounge inside of the Event Group complex, The Ark, named after the Group's most valued artifact. The Ark was situated on level eight, closest to the complex living quarters and was run by retirees from the Group. It was a place where they could all unwind without having to resort to taking the underground tram through gate two into Las Vegas.

Sarah was cognizant of the few off-duty personnel who sat at the bar or tables situated farther away. She was tempted to slide her hand across the small round table and place it over Jack's, but she restrained herself. The full bottle of beer sat untouched in front of the colonel as he continued to stare a hole through the tabletop. Sarah tempted fate and reached out for him, damn military etiquette.

"Did the director have anything useful to say?" she asked as a way of making him at least look up at her.

Instead of answering Sarah, Jack reached out and took her hand and stood, forcing her to do the same. He pulled her along to the far wall and stopped at the old-fashioned jukebox the Group had salvaged from a Philippine bar where the last songs played upon it were those heard the night of December 6, 1941. Jack had added a few of his records from his extensive collection, only because he was the only one in the entire complex who still had forty-five RPM records in his possession. He reached out and punched a few fake ivory numbers. Then he took Sarah by the waist and waited until the song started.

"You never cease to amaze me, Colonel," she said as she recognized the strains of Percy Sledge singing, "When a man loves a woman . . ."

As Jack pulled her close to him, Sarah didn't care who was present—she placed her head against his chest and allowed Jack to hold her tight. She didn't know what was bothering him, but at that moment she only knew he was holding her and that, she figured, was all there was in the world.

When the song finished, Collins leaned down and kissed Sarah, deeply and with a total disregard for where they were. For her part, Sarah almost collapsed into him. Finally, he released her and they walked back to their table. They didn't notice the stunned gazes of the few Group personnel present as they sat down.

Jack took her hand and squeezed it tight, and then he smiled. "Just small talk. You know Niles isn't the warmest person in the world and he struggles when it comes to anything outside of the auspices of the Group. Personal issues aren't his strong suit."

Sarah looked around her; the others inside The Ark were talking amongst themselves and were not paying them any attention. "What?" she asked trying to remember what they had been talking about before his public proclamation of his love for her.

"You wanted to know what the director wanted to talk about; well, it was just small talk."

"Oh, I forgot I even asked."

Jack winked and smiled as he liked doing the unexpected lately where Sarah was concerned.

"Hey, do you know how much I love you?" she asked, a hint of a smile crossing her features.

Collins tilted his head and looked into Sarah's green eyes.

"Oh, I think I do, Short Stuff." He looked around and then leaned in, squeezing her hand even tighter. "You are the most important thing. . . ." He stopped and closed his eyes, leaned back in his chair and released her hand, and then reached for his beer and downed half of it before he looked back at her. "I'm worried about someone. You don't know her, but she's brought a bit of my past up to me that I really didn't want to face." He tried to smile but it died on his lips.

Sarah looked down at her empty hand where Jack's had been a moment before and then slid it into her lap. As long as she had known him, she had never seen him at such a loss. His eyes, since having returned from the dead, were haunted, and she could see through his actions that he didn't know why.

"Is it . . . is it another woman?"

Jack saw the hurt in her eyes and immediately reached out for her hand. That look almost killed him as he now knew his words made her think that it was an old lover from his past.

"Oh, no, no, nothing like that."

Sarah started to say something when she noticed a figure walk out of the darkness.

"We have company," she said in a low voice as she quickly swiped a tear away, momentarily relieved by his words.

Jack turned and saw Compton slowly walk up to their table.

"Are you stalking me, Niles?" he asked as he turned back to his beer.

Niles tried miserably to smile, but it seemed it went the way of all smiles lately; a brief appearance and then gone.

"Jack, you have a minute?"

"I'll go and see what Carl and the others are doing on their day off, it has to be more exciting than anything here," Sarah said as she pushed back her chair.

Niles looked around the dark interior of the bar, and then at Sarah, and then he placed a hand on the top of Jack's shoulder as he came to a quick decision.

"No, Lieutenant, I think you should stay."

McIntire was caught off guard. She hoped the director didn't pick this moment in time to bring up regulations about the fraternization between personnel. She didn't think Jack, at least at the moment, would be too receptive to the reprimand.

"Please sit," Niles said as he came around and pulled out a chair. As he sat, the bartender brought over a small glass filled with ice and amber liquid and placed it in front of Compton.

"I didn't think you were a drinking man, Mr. Director," Sarah said in amazement.

Niles looked into Jack's blue eyes as he took a deep drink of the whiskey. Then he grimaced and then placed the glass down in front of him and then finally looked at Sarah.

"There may be a few things that our head of security doesn't know around here."

Jack half smiled. "Maybe even more than just a few, Mr. Director."

"Oh, I don't expect you to be that good at your job. I may still have secrets you know nothing about."

"Niles," Jack said as he tore at a napkin, tossing the pieces onto the table, "you're drinking one-hundred-year-old Kentucky bourbon. The brand is an obscure make named Delahey's. The bartenders keep two bottles underneath the bar for the rare times you come in here when no one is around, usually around closing time. You never drink while you're on the clock and you keep one bottle of that particular bourbon in your private quarters when there are personnel present at The Ark. You use it more in a medicinal capacity than you do for the whiskey's effects. You're not a drinker in the loosest term of the word, but you do use it to sleep, or when you have something unpleasant to say to someone."

Niles looked from Jack to Sarah, who sat quietly, listening to the exchange.

"I take that back, I guess you do know everything." Niles grew quiet as he slid his empty glass away from him. "Unpleasant. Yes," he said looking at the melting ice in the glass. "You know, I don't know anything about you, Colonel, other than what's in your damned file." He looked at Collins. "For instance, the little sister we discussed earlier."

Sarah wanted to allow her mouth to fall open, but managed just barely to keep it closed as she watched Jack. He made no move other than to keep tossing the torn napkin in its small pieces onto the tabletop.

Collins smiled as he looked from Niles and then fixed Sarah with his deep, blue eyes. For her part, McIntire just tilted her head, waiting.

"Lynn."

"Excuse me?" Sarah said.

"My sister's name is Lynn," Jack repeated.

"Jack's sister works for a sister agency," Compton said to Sarah. He was hoping the colonel would open up a little more with Sarah present. He felt bad for doing things this way, but with what he had to say to Jack, he had nothing to lose.

Collins, for his part, said nothing. Instead, he reached out and swallowed what remained of his beer. Then, instead of looking directly at Niles or Sarah, he remained silent as he stared at the table.

"Jack, I just spoke to the president, and I don't know how to say this, I've never been good at delivering bad news." Niles watched as Jack balled what was left of the napkin up into his hand, closing his fingers slowly until they formed a fist. "The CIA has reported her missing."

Collins remained silent as he closed his eyes.

"I really don't know what's happening here, Colonel. The president doesn't really have a firm grasp of it, either. That is why he ordered me to keep silent about this. He owes you, and that's why I was informed, but he wants you kept out of the loop for now, so the CIA and the other agencies can get a handle on her abduction. Now, does this have anything to do with what it was you stopped by to see your sister about in Langley?"

Jack held the director's eyes firmly with his own as he leaned forward in his chair.

"Give me everything, Niles," he said, ignoring Niles question.

Compton swallowed, not liking the cold, hard look that came over Jack's features.

"There was an ambush in Montreal; a team of CSIS agents, along with some U.S. personnel were shot up, and your sister Lynn was taken. It seems the perpetrators are using her as leverage of some kind for getting information. The only reason I know that much is because, before coming to you, I had Pete correlate with Europa on any recent shooting incident involving Canada."

Jack held Niles in his vision for a moment longer, then slowly stood, sliding his chair away from the table. "Thank you for not obeying your orders, Niles. I won't forget it. Now, I need some time to think."

Niles just nodded his head once as Jack quickly turned to leave. He looked at Sarah and nodded his head for her to follow. Then Compton held his hand up and the bartender, a retired navy motorman, came forward and poured him another drink. He was about to say something to the director, when Niles held his hand up, palm facing outward, indicating the man should leave. Compton stared at the glass before lifting it and staring at the liquid inside. He drained the glass, without a grimace this time. He placed it on the table and then slowly stood and walked toward the bar. He went to the waitress station and then reached over and then under the bar and brought out the secure phone. He punched a number into the handset and then waited.

"Captain Everett," came the voice.

"Captain, Colonel Collins will soon be breaking into the Europa clean room for some illegal activity."

"Sir?" Everett said on the other end of the phone.

"I need you to assist Colonel Collins in any capacity he chooses. He will undoubtedly explain the situation to you. Now listen closely, Captain. He is to be allowed access to anything he wants inside the complex, but if he attempts to leave the reservation without my express authorization, you are to detain him and then notify me, is that clear?"

"Not at all," Carl said, more than just a little confused.

"Good, just do I as I say. It may be better to stay in the dark as long as you can on this one."

Niles hung up the phone and took a deep breath, then settled onto a bar stool.

He had decided to break precedent and stay at The Ark for a while; after all it wasn't every day you could take a presidential order and toss it right out the window. He smiled a grim little smile and waved the bartender over, pointing at his empty glass.

"Another?" the bartender asked.

"Yes, and leave the bottle."

3

Special Agent Thomas Banks watched from an FBI van parked across the street. The house, obviously built pre–World War II, was one of those large four-bedroom monstrosities with a waist-high wraparound porch that was supported by wooden columns placed on a stone foundation. The ancient screens covering the windows were darkened from too many summers and not enough cleaning. The houses around the suspect house were lighted and visibly occupied by families who still clung to the illusion that Elysian Park was a safe neighborhood; an illusion that should have vanished in the area's heyday just after the Korean War.

Banks and his three-man observation team had been called in to observe and assist the Los Angeles police department with the arrest of Juan Caesar Chavez, a man currently under suspicion for a little-known crime he may or may not have committed at the Denver Museum of Natural History six months before. A partial fingerprint was found on a door frame leading out of the area where the display for *The Gold Rush*, was being exhibited—old maps, letters and implements used in the early days of the Alaskan rush for riches. Although a small theft in stature, the works taken were valuable to collectors around the world for their historical significance. The police agencies of Denver and Los Angeles knew Juan Caesar Chavez to be adept at theft, and in the past had targeted well-respected collections far outside of his stature, and that meant the FBI and other authorities suspected he was well financed by another party. Chavez had a small group of burglars and second-story men on his payroll, and as a leading suspect in the case, was about to receive a big surprise.

Special Agent Banks watched as the SWAT team made their way around the house, covering every exit. He adjusted his binoculars and saw that the upper-floor team was already in position. He raised the cell phone to his ear.

"Who do I have on the line?" he asked.

"Agent Banks, you have the FBI director and assistant director of Intelligence, CIA—Nancy Grogan. Go ahead," said his dispatch located in the federal building in downtown Los Angeles.

Jesus, Banks thought, *why was Chavez important enough to have some of the top echelons of intelligence and law enforcement as audio witnesses?*

"Director, Banks here, the SWAT team is just about to move, any last instructions?"

"Special Agent Banks, as soon as the arrest is complete, you are to take charge of the suspect and escort him to the federal building. Once there, a team of our colleagues from Langley will handle the interrogation. An American intelligence officer's life is at stake in all of this, and time is the important factor here. The suspect may have to be handed over to another party outside of law enforcement. Is that understood?"

"Yes, sir, my men are standing by to take charge of the suspect as soon as the arrest is made." Banks held the binoculars to his eyes once more as he saw movement. "The assault element is moving in now, sir . . . hold on."

Outside the small windowed van, several flash-bang grenades broke through windows and then exploded, as simultaneously, using ropes, the upper-story unit swung into the upstairs rooms. At the same time, two six-man teams entered through the front and back doors. Lights shone throughout the interior of the house as the SWAT team made their sweep. Banks gripped the binoculars tighter as he waited, satisfied at not hearing any shots. He never liked using local police agencies, but the FBI HRT team was not available for another two hours, and someone in Washington wanted this bad guy very badly; enough so that the directors of two agencies called in favors from the LAPD.

Suddenly it was over. The lights inside the house started coming on and Banks could see the silhouettes of several of the black-clad SWAT members mulling about. Then, as he watched closely, a small man in Levis and a white T-shirt was led out in cuffs. The FBI agent could see that the SWAT team was taking no chances with this man as he was cuffed both at his wrists, behind his back, and his ankles. He was being carried out of the house with a black hood over his head. Banks smiled, *This poor bastard didn't know what had hit him.*

He laid his glasses down and then raised a small microphone. "Okay, B-team, move in and take custody of the suspect, make sure you Miranda the poor bastard, don't leave it to the LAPD." There were two clicks in answer to Banks's call.

Again, Agent Banks raised the cell phone. "Sir, the suspect is in custody and we are now in the process of concluding the arrest."

"Good. Now, Assistant Director Grogan, CIA, has requested that you have the LAPD SWAT unit accompany you to the federal building. We will not take any chances with the suspect; they need answers from him and time is a factor. Is that clear, Banks?"

"Crystal, Director."

Ten minutes later, the chain of custody was transferred to the FBI from the LAPD. Chavez, although shaken, was defiant and angry at what he was being put through, and was totally confused as to why he was under FBI arrest.

As the SWAT unit stood down, they climbed into two large black vans. One would be placed in front of, and the other in the rear of, the white FBI van. As the teams loaded, Agent Banks looked over the suspect being held between two of his agents. He nodded for a third agent to do as he was instructed earlier. Chavez looked relieved when the ankle restraints were removed.

"That, Mr. Chavez, is a courtesy. I expect cooperation from you. If you behave, my agents will reciprocate. Is that clear?"

"Hey look, man, I don't deserve any treatment at all. You have the wrong guy. I buy and sell needed goods on the open market."

"Mr. Chavez, please, save it for your defense attorney. We have some questions that need to be answered, so I suggest you cooperate, and maybe these small charges might disappear."

With that small announcement, Chavez allowed the two agents holding him to escort him to the van. He had seen the light as the ambiguous offer had been extended; he wasn't dumb, and as a career criminal, he knew when it was time to be a model citizen. The rear doors of the van opened and he stepped inside with his special agent bodyguard beside him.

Agent Banks radioed that they were ready to move as he climbed into the passenger seat of the van, the small convoy moved out of Elysian Park heading for downtown L.A.

As the three vans pulled out and the smaller units of the LAPD started wrapping up the area, no one really noticed the small helicopter as it buzzed past the scene. They assumed it was an LAPD air unit.

That opinion would soon change.

The plan of egress from the arrest site was for the convoy of SWAT vans and the lone FBI unit to make their way down Solano Avenue, and from there make the connection to Highway 110, and then finally to Interstate 5.

As they pulled to a stop at the light, the crowd noise from Dodger Stadium erupted above them in Chavez Ravine. The lights of the beautiful stadium lit the roadway ahead of them.

"Any relation?" the larger of the two FBI field agents asked the handcuffed man beside him.

"Huh?" Chavez asked.

"You know, Chavez Ravine, where the Dodgers play, any relation to you?"

"Man, what are you talking about?"

"Alright, knock it off," Agent Banks said from the front of the van.

The agent smirked as he turned away from the prisoner.

At that moment, several things happened at once. The leading SWAT van to the front started moving forward from the now green light on Solano Avenue; at the same time as the white FBI vehicle started to follow, a streak of blazing white light shot through the air just past the large windshield of following agents. The rocket-propelled grenade struck the rear doors of the leading black van, exploding its sides outward. Banks flinched in shock as SWAT team members were blown through the front windshield of their transport.

Before anyone could react, another RPG flew straight and true into the now exposed interior of the lead vehicle, exploding and bulging the sides even further outward and crumpling the disabled unit until it no longer looked like a van at all. Flames then exploded out and up as the horrible sound finally penetrated Banks's eardrums. He tried to lift his handheld radio but stopped when another explosion from the rear threw him forward in his seat. He would have been thrown through the windshield if it hadn't been for his seatbelt. Although he was saved, he had the breath knocked out of him. So he started slapping at the driver to throw the van into reverse. The flames billowing from the SWAT van behind them were framed in the driver's side mirrors. Men could be seen jumping out, and as they did, they were being struck by small arms fire from the yards around them. All around them, families who'd been out in their front yards enjoying a warm summer evening started to run in a panic—a very small and deadly war had just erupted right in front of them.

"Move, move, move!" one of the agents said from the back as he reached out and threw the prisoner Chavez to the floor of the van.

Just before the driver threw the van in reverse, a SWAT sergeant from the trailing van pounded on the rear window, pleading to be let in; just as the other agent reached out to open the door it was rattled by several bullets. As he recoiled, he saw the SWAT sergeant's head fly forward until it struck the window with a loud thump, breaking the safety glass. As the shocked FBI agents watched, the LAPD officer slowly slid away from the window.

"Go, goddamn it, they're killing everyone!" screamed the agent as loud as he could, his foot placed firmly onto Chavez's back.

The van finally started moving backward, screeching the tires and burning rubber. There were several sickening bumps as they made their way in reverse back up toward the stadium.

"All units, all units," Banks screamed into the handheld radio, "we have officers down, Elysian Park, Solano Avenue, we're taking heavy gunfire from an unknown number of assailants and are moving toward the stadium! We need air support and backup now!"

Banks didn't wait for the dispatcher to respond, he pulled his nine-millimeter handgun free of his shoulder holster as the van traveled in reverse. He saw the burning SWAT unit slide by and noticed belatedly that several of the SWAT team had gotten free of the flaming wreckage and were in the process of firing into the night at unseen targets that were keeping them pinned down. As he started to turn toward the back, checking on the safety of their prisoner, one of the rear tires of the van exploded, sending the vehicle sliding into several cars parked along Solano Avenue. The van spun and then stalled. Before Banks could do anything, fifteen small-caliber rounds slammed into the windshield, shattering it and striking the driver and himself. As the two bodies jumped from the impact of the rounds, a small detonation knocked the others into a daze. The rear doors were snatched open and before the two agents in the back realized what was happening, three men were inside.

"This one," one of the attackers said pointing to Chavez. At the same moment, he raised his handgun and the masked man quickly fired into the stunned agents—two bullets apiece.

When Chavez was taken out of the van, he was bleeding from a cut on his forehead and had a steady flow of blood coming from his ears. He tried to scream, but nothing came out of his mouth, or if it did, there was so much noise even he couldn't hear it. As fifteen men surrounded the van, a small Bell helicopter suddenly appeared out of the darkness, its black paint reflecting the burning vehicles on the street. It flared seconds before touching the roadway, the twin skids clanking loudly on the warm macadam. Chavez was taken to, and then thrown into, the helicopter. As the small Bell lifted free of Solano Avenue, sirens were heard approaching from Dodger Stadium above and then from below in Elysian Park.

As stunned neighbors watched, the fifteen-man assault team calmly returned to six cars. They then removed their black hoods once inside. They slowly drove away, past the three bullet-riddled and burning vans.

In all, the assault and kidnap of the thief known as Juan Caesar Chavez, took no more than two minutes and eleven seconds. The Russians had proven they were still among the most efficient killers in history.

UPLAND, CALIFORNIA

After the short, hedgehopping flight from Los Angeles, the helicopter had set down just inside the small baseball stadium at Upland High School. The transfer of Chavez to a waiting vehicle outside the ballpark was made quickly and efficiently by men who had worked for Sagli and Deonovich for nearly twenty years. The rest of the assault element split into three groups, one remaining with Chavez, one heading north to Vancouver, and the last heading back to Virginia. Chavez was taken to a safe house on Mountain Avenue.

Chavez was blindfolded and led to a room at the back of the large five-bedroom house. As California basements weren't much the trend, the large master suite would have to do. The windows had been sealed with aluminum foil and the house sat far enough back from the road as to be virtually soundproof through distance. They had the whole San Gabriel Mountains as a sound break from any screaming that may come from the house.

The thief was put in a large chair and his blindfold was removed. One of his Russian captors, a small man with beady little eyes and a well-manicured beard stepped forward as Chavez blinked in the bright lights being shone upon his shaking body. The Russian removed the handcuffs and then smiled at the even smaller Chavez. He then patted him on the shoulder.

"Don't worry, my friend; a few answers for my employer and you will soon be set free."

Chavez didn't relax one bit at the reassurance. Even though no names had been exchanged, he knew who it was that was holding him. Sagli and Deonovich were widely known in criminal circles for their ability to find and acquire matchless antiquity and were also known to have the steely nerves to go after whole collections at a time. Jewels, icons, paintings, sculpture—the two Russian mobsters had taken them all, sometimes quietly, sometimes the hard way. They were especially good at the hard way as his former employer had warned him on many occasions and as he'd just witnessed.

The bedroom door opened and a large man with severely short cropped hair stepped inside the room. Through the glaring lights, Chavez saw that he was eating a hamburger. The wrapper held snug around the buns, he stepped up to his prisoner, taking a bite of the large burger. The man wore a black T-shirt under a black sport coat. In all aspects, he looked like any other Southern California business man, except for the eyes. The large brown eyes held not one ounce of humanity as he took in the sight of Chavez sitting before him. He took one last bite of the yellow-wrapped hamburger and then handed it to the man who had spoken a moment before. Then he pulled a handkerchief from his breast pocket and slowly wiped his mouth.

"Dispose of this garbage," he said as he was relieved of his burden. He looked down and then leaned into the face of Chavez. "You Americans, no wonder you are becoming a fat country, a man cannot find a decent meal in all of Los Angeles." He smiled. "Fast food is a fast death in my opinion."

As Chavez swallowed, he saw the man straighten and then he held out his hand. Something was in his outstretched fingers and then before Chavez knew what was happening, a searing pain raked across his right cheek. He screamed out, more because of the pressure and fast motion than the pain, which was slow in coming. However, it did come and along with that pain was a steady flow of blood.

"That was to get your attention," the man said in passable English as he stepped back to admire his handiwork. "Right now, the scar that I have left you could be well taken as a dueling scar across your cheek, my friend; at one point in European history that was known as a badge of honor. If you answer my inquiries, you can skip through your life telling your friends that you received your scar in battle with evil men. Answer me not, and the local county coroner will have a most difficult time sewing you back together so those same friends can view your remains at your funeral."

Chavez opened his eyes against the pain in his cheek. Knowing his skin had been laid open to the bone, he tried desperately to focus on the man standing in front of him with the open straight razor, which now gleamed in the bright lights.

"My name is Gregori Deonovich. My partner and I are in search of something that is in your possession. I speak of the Petrov Diary, or the portions of it that has survived history that is. We understand that it was you who pulled off the robbery at the Denver Museum of Natural History, am I correct?"

"I don't have the diary, it was—"

The flash of the straight razor advertized the split-second warning that Chavez had answered the question the wrong way. The blade struck him just above the right eyebrow, slicing through the thick skin until the razor actually cut into bone. Chavez screamed and grabbed for his face.

Deonovich stepped back and holding out the razor, he flicked twice to get the dripping blood off of it, and then he nodded his head to the right. The smaller man stepped forward and wiped Juan's face, then he made the thief take the small towel and hold it against the two wounds.

"The cost of failure is high; the next time it will be your throat, comrade."

As Chavez pressed the towel to staunch the flow of his blood, he knew he had to answer with the right words.

"The diary was given to the man who set up the theft—a man who paid me and my men for it and a few of the other items."

"The name of your employer?" Deonovich asked as he stepped forward, his face set in a mask of anger.

"At the time he was using the name Ellison, but a few years back he used an alias of Tomlinson; before that another name."

"You are not being very forthcoming," Deonovich said as he raised his right hand to strike Chavez again.

"Wait—wait!"

"Quickly," the Russian said, becoming angrier by the second.

"Listen, my employer, the man who originally wanted the journal, he went missing. He never showed up to give us the payment he owed us . . . so . . . so I burned the journal."

Deonovich wanted to laugh out loud. "You want me to believe you went through all of that trouble to steal this item from a secure museum, and then knowing this journal may lead to a vast treasure, you destroyed it out of anger for not getting paid for the job?"

"How in the hell did I know what the journal said, it was written in Russian."

"Then the journal is destroyed?"

"Yes, so you may as well let me go," Chavez whimpered.

"Yes, we may as well," Deonovich said as he nodded for the small man standing behind Chavez to finish up.

Chavez never really saw the shadow as it fell over him. The next sensation was of cold steel as it sank deep into his throat from behind. The razor severed his airway and his jugular vein in a practiced move perfected in the highlands of Afghanistan many years before.

Deonovich nodded as Chavez fell from the chair. As he lay on the floor, he continued to hold the towel to his face even as he wondered why he was no longer able to move. The large Russian stepped away from the quickly spreading pool of blood and removed the cell phone from his jacket; at the same time he held out his free hand and snapped his fingers. The smaller assassin understood and handed him the cheeseburger he had been given minutes before.

Deonovich took a bite of the burger and waited for the phone to ring on the other side of the country.

"Our friend Mr. Chavez turned out to be most helpful. It seems he was working for an outside contractor when he stole the journal from the Denver Museum. When this mysterious employer never showed to pay Chavez and his crew for the heist, the idiot burned it," Deonovich said with a laugh, almost choking on the cheeseburger. He looked at his right hand and then tossed the greasy burger onto the finally still corpse of the Mexican thief.

"Yes," the Russian said into the phone. "It turns out we wasted a lot of time and killed a few police officers just to confirm the man didn't have what we thought he did. Well, we live and we learn. At least we have closed that end of the loop; now no one besides ourselves can find the area we are seeking. You will pass this along to our associate. Thank you, Dmitri, I'll be back in a few hours."

Deonovich closed his cell phone and then looked at the corpse of Chavez.

"At least no one can follow us using what you have stolen," he snickered and then turned for the door. "Diamonds and gold—such small-minded people. Take his body to the sea and throw him in, then meet us at the Los Angeles Airport, you know where."

Deonovich turned and gave Chavez one last look and smiled. "Yes, they won't follow us from what you may have known."

Deonovich knew they would find the man's body in the next few hours, but that was to be a calling card of sorts warning that they were to be left alone, and Chavez would be a record of their seriousness. There would be shock and anger, but by then he, Sagli and their strike-and-recovery team would be well north of the border, and on the trail of their richest prize yet.

MCLEAN, VIRGINIA

Gregori Sagli closed his cell phone and then eased the basement door open, and saw Lynn Simpson sitting in the dark. She didn't move or respond to the creaking sound of the door opening, nor when it closed. Sagli smiled and then trotted up the stairs. He went to the kitchen table where a few of his men were sitting and eating sandwiches. He reached over and lifted his small briefcase from the end of the table and walked over to the kitchen counter. Opening the combination lock, he lifted the lid and pulled out a large plastic protector that held Xerox copies of the items sent to them by their associate who had planned everything from beginning to end, and thus far, this person had been perfect in that planning.

Sagli looked through the clear plastic at the documents known as the Lattimer Papers and Xerox copies of the pages from a journal once owned by Colonel Iosovich Petrov of the Red Army. The map was clearly seen on the last page as Sagli turned it over. In L. T. Lattimer's own hand, the area was drawn from his eyewitness account of his find.

The copies had been taken from Lattimer's last remaining relative in

Boston by the man who now called Deonovich and Sagli partners. Sagli assumed that the relative had met the same fate as Chavez out in California—at least that was the impression both Russians had when given the orders to find the originals, and for the fact that their new friend didn't seem to be the merciful type, nor did he seem to like loose ends.

Sagli knew they were close to starting on their final journey and he was anxious to get started. What waited was a new beginning for all involved, and a prize that few could ever attain in this jumbled and confusing new world—true power.

LANGLEY, VIRGINIA

The director of the CIA paced in front of his desk, behind the backs of his seated assistant directors. Every word seemed like a dagger into the heart of Nancy Grogan. Even the usually cold-as-ice Stan Rosen was feeling for her.

"Has there been any communication from the Russians?"

"Nothing, sir. We, or I should say, I, have come to the conclusion that they have gotten what they wanted in Los Angeles, so there is no further need to communicate with the agency."

"Fifteen Los Angeles police officers are dead; highly trained SWAT personnel. How in the hell could they have known we were moving on Chavez so soon?"

"I took it upon myself to assist in that matter, sir," Rosen said, half turning in his chair to face his boss. "Sagli and Deonovich have had the police forces of most major cities plugged into their network for a while now, mostly to keep track of international warrants, Interpol requests, things like that. They basically pay for information. My operations people suspect they had a flier out to these moles about anyone suspected in the museum heist in Denver. Once informed, they released a hit team that was either already in the western states or close by."

Nancy Grogan turned in her chair and looked at Rosen, his eyes lowered as he knew he had overstepped his bounds and his department. Grogan wanted to say something about it, but knew he had acted where she hadn't. Her mind was on the lone fact that the two Russians no longer needed Lynn Simpson.

"Stan, you're guessing. I want facts. If there are informants in the

LAPD I want to know who they are, and then I want them brought to justice. I don't believe that any brother officer would be a part of a massacre of their people. Now, what are we doing to find these Russians?" the director asked.

This time Nancy stood and buttoned her blazer. She took a deep breath and turned to face the director.

"The FBI and local law enforcement have been briefed on who they are looking for. I suspect there is going to be fallout about us . . . or me . . . not giving them everything before the raid."

The director pursed his lips and then paced to his desk and sat on it edge.

"The president wants to know what the odds are now that these two maniacs and their organization have what they want, on us getting our agent back."

Nancy Grogan's silence was enough. She swallowed and bent over to pick up her case and then turned and started for the door, she stopped with her right hand poised over the handle.

"She's my agent," she said without turning, "my responsibility."

Rosen cleared his throat and said what everyone was thinking.

"Director, Lynn Simpson is already dead. Sagli and Deonovich would never take the chance of keeping her alive. Remember their file: They executed ten hostages in a Prague antique shop for the simple reason they were late telling them where their third wall safe was located. The last three were shot after that safe was found. Yes, sir, Lynn Simpson is most assuredly dead."

"Then confirm her death, and then bring me those two bastards' heads on a platter!"

EVENT GROUP COMPLEX
NELLIS AIR FORCE BASE, NEVADA

Before Jack had even entered the Europa clean room, Pete Golding and Carl Everett had already begun. Pete looked at Jack, newly clothed in white smock and gloves. He was as miserable having to wear the clean-room attire as Everett was.

"Colonel, Director Compton gave us a short brief, but it didn't give us much to go on. Europa did uncover these details as listed in the Montreal

Police Departments computer. Even now, the Canadians are keeping the information limited, maybe slowing down the filing of their reports for security reasons."

Jack sat in between Everett and Pete, silent as he adjusted the microphone in front of him. The steel door that protected Europa was up and Collins could see the Honda robotic arms as they swung into action placing and removing small discs from racks and placing them into the mainframe.

"Right now, as I understand it at least, your sister is in charge of the northeastern desk at Langley. If you don't mind me asking, Colonel, why would she choose Simpson as her last name?" Pete asked as he started typing commands onto his keyboard.

"That was my mother's maiden name—Simpson."

"I see. The first thing we are checking on is the two names that seem to be popping up in the Canadian reports. Two Russian nationals are believed to have been responsible for the ambush in Montreal. At least those were the names placed on the all-points bulletins coming from Canada to all North American police agencies. Now, since Director Compton notified the captain and myself that we cannot expect cooperation from American intelligence apparatus, we have to use a little bit of stealth in finding what we need, am I correct?"

"At this point in time, Pete, yeah, you're correct. That may change very soon."

Golding saw Jack's eyes as they didn't waver from his own. The look wasn't one of determination as usual, it was a faraway look he had never seen in Collins's eyes before.

"Good. Now, the names of these two men are Dmitri Sagli and Gregori Deonovich. I ran them through Europa and she kicked back this"—Pete gestured at the blue writing scanning across the screen—"as you can see, they have . . . What is the police jargon? Oh yes, quite a rap sheet. Starting with their days in the old KGB, and what they learned of death in the early years of the Soviet war in Afghanistan. I believe that is where they acquired the taste for the more expensive decorations they probably have in their houses. From there, after their exodus from KGB, they quickly graduated to organized crime, financed principally from their thievery in Afghanistan and other war-torn places where Soviet occupation was in bloom."

"What about my sister? What is the correlation between them and her?" Collins asked as he read the blue printed letters on the large screen before them. It was as if he was burning the pictures and the words into his mind.

Carl Everett watched Jack and he knew he was doing exactly that— etching the faces into his brain.

"That is what we are about to attempt to find out. This is going to be tricky: If the president has ordered us to stand down, he may have also ordered the CIA to safeguard an attack on their Cray system from Europa. If that is the case, they will not only be able to track the backdoor entry, but cause a security shutdown, not only at Langley, but here also. Then, I dare say, the cat will be out of the proverbial bag."

"Do it, my authorization, my responsibility," Jack said as he ripped the gloves from his hands and then tossed them on the floor.

Everett removed his also, and instead of protesting, Pete followed suit.

"Okay, Colonel, here we go. Europa, we are going to ask for a protocol 2267 exception to security rule Langley 111-1. Do you understand?"

"Yes, Dr. Golding, bypass security protocol protecting top-secret CIA analysis files, operational files and agency archives. Field agent protection lists are to be excluded under this protocol—is that correct, Doctor?"

"Correct," Pete said looking over at Jack for confirmation. After all, that was the most guarded secret in American intelligence, the identity of undercover field agents across the globe. "Now Europa, you will use my security clearance for this operation, is that understood?"

"Yes, Doctor, clearance number 78987-2343, Department 5656 override."

"Wait a minute, Doc, I said this is my responsibility," Jack said, placing his arm on Golding's.

"Colonel, you may not be thinking as straight as you usually do under the circumstances. If we are caught entering the CIA Cray system, there are going to be arrests made. No matter how secret we are, we are going against a presidential order. It just so happens we are not secret from him. How are you going to help your sister if a bunch of marines come down here and haul you away on presidential orders?"

Jack looked from Golding to Everett, who was sitting silently watching the exchange as Collins removed his hand from Golding's arm and nodded his head.

"That's why Pete gets the big bucks, Jack, he has the ability to step back and look at things logically," Carl said as he turned in his chair and waited for the enquiry to start again.

"Europa, commence a backdoor entry into Cray system 191987—Blue Dahlia—Langley."

"Yes, Doctor," came the calm and ordered reply of Europa in her Marilyn Monroe voice.

The assault on one of the most secure systems in the world was underway. The funny thing was, it was Europa's little brother at CIA, and they were both assembled only days apart. This backdoor mugging was to be a family affair.

It took Europa close to an hour to break into Dahlia's mainframe. She was close to timing out on the attempted break-in when a small backdoor was found in the Langley system that ran out-of-date file subroutine revolving around agency retirement records.

After two and a half hours of skirting the main file location inside of intelligence and operations, they had uncovered the full extent of the ambush in Montreal. Besides confirming their number-one targets, Sagli and Deonovich, Golding, Everett, and Collins were starting to piece together what it was the Russians were looking for: The Lattimer Papers and what was being tagged as the Petrov Diary had been mentioned in no less than seventeen agency filings in the past twenty-four hours, filings the agency had received through their own Cray system, Blue Dahlia, and absconded from the CSIS authorities in Ottawa. That information had been filed inside of Europa for use later in tracking that particular subject matter.

"Okay, gentlemen, here is where it gets tricky, and why." Pete looked at his watch. "I waited until two A.M. to try it. We are going to break into the files of the Intelligence Department, the section where your sister works, Jack. When Europa goes in, she will scan all files using the keywords we have already entered. She will be inside for less than one minute downloading what Miss Simpson's department knows about the event that occurred in Montreal, and about your sister's involvement. During that time, if someone happens to log into the system that is currently being scanned, alarms are going to sound from Virginia to Fort Huachuca in Arizona."

"What will happen then, Pete?" Everett asked.

"That, I really don't know Captain. Dahlia could send a transformer signal through, tracing the program, or send Europa a tapeworm, destroying her completely." Pete patted the console before him and then looked inside Europa's containment room. "But I think she's too smart for that." He smiled. "We've made a few modifications on her in the time she's been here."

"Let's get started."

Pete nodded at Jack.

"Europa, commence scanning the Langley North American Intelligence files."

"Yes, Doctor."

LANGLEY, VIRGINIA

At 2 A.M. in the morning, Nancy Grogan, with fresh new orders from the director himself to stand down for three days, was staring at her computer screen. The file was open on Lynn Simpson. She had read everything she could in that file, trying to find out Lynn's next of kin. She had decided that regardless of what her superiors said, her family, especially her brother, needed to be told about her possible fate, but she found she was loathe to contact the mother of the siblings because she couldn't explain why she needed to find her son Jack. Grogan knew that Lynn had been in contact with her brother. She was the only person at CIA who had that little bit of information. She didn't know how much Lynn had explained to her brother, so she thought it would be helpful to contact him herself if at all possible.

Grogan finally stretched and then started to reach for the monitor's power supply. She still wanted to pack a few things from her office to take home, but she froze when she saw a small and intense flashing icon in the bottom left-hand corner of the screen. USER 5656 LOGGED ON.

"Well, at least they're still working on finding her," Grogan mumbled as she pushed the small button, closing down her monitor.

She stood and found a partially filled box and threw some paperwork from her department inside, then she grabbed the Lynn Simpson personnel file and was tempted to throw it in as well, but she knew that little item would never get through security. As she closed the file, she gently laid it on her desk. The file was a standard "secret" file with SIMPSON, LYNN H typed on its front. Below that was her operations number—1121. This was a series of numbers that all agency personnel had been issued. The number was everything from an employee number, a payroll tag, and Blue Dahlia's computer systems log-in code—the higher the number, the lower the rank and time on the job.

Grogan lifted the cardboard box and then her eyes caught the number on the personnel file once more. 1121. Lynn's number was one of the lower ones since her transfer from operations two years ago. The director of Intelligence let the box slide from her hand as she hurriedly opened her top desk drawer. She found what she was looking for and ran her index finger down the list. It was a directory of log-in numbers for everyone who was authorized to use Blue Dahlia. The numbers ended at 2267.

"Who in the hell is 5656?" she said aloud. As the incredulous thought struck her, she quickly reached for the phone. Someone had hacked what should have been one of the most secure systems in the world. In her haste to punch in security's number, her hand struck Lynn Simpson's file and it fell to the floor, along with Grogan's own notes on Simpson's family. As security answered the phone on the other end, she saw the name Colonel Jack Collins, United States Army, underlined in red ink several times.

"Security, Adamson speaking. Miss Grogan, are you ready to leave the facility?"

Nancy looked up from the file and thought quickly. The rumors of Lynn's brother being very resourceful came flooding through her rapidly thinking brain. She hesitated only a moment.

"Yes, in about fifteen minutes. I'll only be carrying home one box to be inspected."

"Very good, ma'am, I'll have two men standing by for escort to your vehicle."

"Thank you," she said quietly and then hung up the phone.

She knew that what she was doing was very close to committing treason. She also knew that this could have been the way Sagli and Deonovich came across their information on the Los Angeles raid. However, she knew for a fact that Blue Dahlia was as secure as systems can get. The rumor was that only another Blue Ice system could do what was being done, and even Sagli and Deonovich didn't have the funding for that little trick.

As she sat back into her large chair, she flipped on the computer monitor again. The small icon was still flashing in the lower left-hand corner of the screen: *USER 5656 LOGGED ON*. Grogan sat back and watched the green numbers as they glowed in the semidarkness of her office. Then a small smile slowly crept across her features. She knew the log-on numbers had to be an American code for an agency—four numbers, and it seemed Blue Dahlia recognized these call numbers. Her smile broadened as she felt she had an ally somewhere in the world that would help her get Lynn home.

"The mysterious Colonel Jack Collins, I presume," she said just under her breath.

She would give the hacking computer another sixty seconds before she hit the alarm. After all, there was still a small chance it may be someone not so friendly to her government.

EVENT GROUP COMPLEX
NELLIS AIR FORCE BASE, NEVADA

As Europa was scanning agency files at a blinding rate, the phone buzzed and Everett answered it.

"Yes . . . thank you," he said and hung up.

"That was the director's assistant. It seems the man that was kidnapped, this Juan Chavez, was found washed up against the pier pylons in Huntington Beach."

Without saying anything, Jack underlined Chavez's name on the list he was slowly putting together.

"Colonel, I still think investigating that end of things is as viable as it was before this news. Whatever these Russians are up to, they went through this man for some reason, more than likely a link to those papers, or the journal that was stolen."

"Okay, what do you suggest?" Jack asked.

Pete pushed his thick glasses back up to the bridge of his nose and thought.

"The man dealt in stolen goods, antiquities, almost anything of value derived from antiquity."

"Yes, but that could still mean anything," Everett volunteered.

"Captain, the work we do here, the recovery of history, is a very limited field. There are very few people in the world who are truly good at it.

Thieves are not as good as the Group, of course, but they are very adequate when it comes to selling what they steal to private collectors around the world. Our computer is good but there's only so much we can uncover without leaving this room."

"You're suggesting we go into the field, fly to L.A. for a closer look?" Jack asked.

"Well, yes. Look here," Pete said as he stood and pointed at a line of script on the large monitor in front of them. "Yes, here we are. Langley has run this guy Chavez through Dahlia a thousand times, arrest records and such. The man has never divulged his source, who it is that's contracting his services. There wasn't one piece of incriminating evidence to be found in his Elysian Park home. No artwork, no statuary, no antique of any kind. This man sold everything he came into possession of."

"He has to have a buyer," Everett said.

"Not only that, but someone had to fund the world travel the agency uncovered. According to overseas records, this man, Chavez, was worth only two and half million dollars."

Jack looked at Pete and slowly nodded. "In other words, whoever was buying his stuff may have some clue as to what Sagli and Deonovich were seeking and why."

"Exactly, Colonel."

Pete was about to expand on his thoughts when the last line of script was entered onto the Europa main screen from the CIA mainframe. He grew silent as he watched the sentence run its course. Then he slowly removed his glasses and lightly touched Collins on the shoulder.

"Oh, God," was all Pete said.

Jack looked up at what was written on the screen and his heart fell to the bottom of his chest.

"I'm sorry, Jack," Everett said as he closed his eyes and shook his head.

As Europa finally came to a stop, the sentence pronounced their search may be over before it started.

RECOVERED RIGHT INDEX FINGER AT 2230 HOURS, POSITIVELY IDENTIFIED AS THAT SEVERED FROM THE AGENCY EMPLOYEE, SIMPSON, LYNN, H., DNA POSITIVE—FINGERPRINT ANALYSIS—POSITIVE.

"What did they do to her?" Jack asked as his eyes closed and his head sank to his chest.

"Doctor Golding, my entrance into the Blue Dahlia mainframe has been discovered; a trace is currently in process," Europa said calmly.

"Shut down, damn it, shut it down!" Pete said as he stood, pushing his chair back so hard it slammed into the far wall.

"Shutdown complete, trace was lost." Europa said in a calm voice.

Jack hurriedly put his notes in order and stood.

"Colonel?" Pete asked.

"I'm still going to L.A."

"Jack, I guess this is a good time to tell you: The director ordered me to stop you if you tried to leave the complex."

Jack looked from Everett and then to the monitor in front of him, and then returned his determined look to Carl.

"Right, I'll get us a plane," Everett said, shrugging out of his white electrostatic coat.

"Do that, Captain, and alert Mendenhall and Ryan. Tell them their weekend duties are canceled."

Everett watched as Jack left the clean room.

"Doc, correlate what you've recovered; there may be something in there that can help."

Pete Golding watched Everett follow Collins out of the clean room, and then he sat down and almost reached for the phone, but stopped. He almost shouted aloud when the phone startled him when it buzzed. He swallowed and then picked it up.

"Clean room," he said meekly.

"Pete, I just received a call from the White House. The president was informed that we hacked into the CIA mainframe."

"Niles, there's no way they can know that; Europa cut the trace before it took hold."

"Pete, I've had a few drinks here, but even I could figure out who did the hacking if I knew what agencies had the Cray system, and the president, in case you haven't noticed, isn't a fool. Where is Jack?"

"Uh . . . well . . . he and Captain Everett—"

"Have they left the complex?" Niles asked.

"Well, no, they haven't had the time; they just left the clean room."

"Do they have a lead on Jack's sister?"

"Niles, the damn Russians cut that little girl's finger off."

"Do they have a lead?"

"Yes, sir. Los Angeles."

"And they are still inside the complex?"

"Yes, sir," Pete said, feeling like he was betraying Jack and Carl.

There was silence on Niles's end of the phone. Then he finally spoke. "Okay, give them another thirty minutes to clear Nellis, and then issue an order for any Event personnel to detain Captain Everett and Colonel Collins."

"Sir?" Pete asked, not believing Niles was letting them go.

"Hell, you may as well include their little sidekicks in that order, too. Detain Mendenhall and Ryan. No wait," Compton said thinking as fast as Europa. "Get to Lieutenant Mendenhall, pry him away from Ryan and the others, and have him and Sarah McIntire report to me before the colonel can get to him, do it ASAP, Pete, you hear me?"

"But—"

"If Jack thinks there's a chance of him finding his sister, we'll give him the time he needs, but I also know for a fact that everyone from the FBI to Virginia farm boys will be out to stop him from doing so. I need McIntire and Mendenhall in my office; they are not to accompany Collins, Everett, and Ryan."

The phone went dead and Pete just shook his head in wonder.

"It would be nice if someone asked me along for the ride sometime," Pete said to himself.

After Niles hung up, he slowly kicked his shoes off and then lay down on his couch, a place where he had spent most of the last month sleeping, and where he would now try to dream through the dark storm that was about to hit. He pushed his glasses onto his balding head and then closed his eyes. He was wondering just how long it would take Langley to scream bloody murder all the way to the White House about the Group's assault on CIA's Blue Dahlia.

Just as Niles felt the onslaught of whiskey-induced sleep, his assistant stepped into his office and quickly walked to the couch and shook Niles. He came awake like a man falling from a cliff—that unsettling feeling of falling and not being able to stop yourself. Then he opened his eyes and realized he couldn't focus on the face in front of him. His assistant reached out her slim hand and pulled his glasses back down to cover his eyes.

"Sir, the president is on the phone. He says you're not answering your laptop."

Niles laid there, not wanting to move, not wanting to face the man he had disobeyed. He took a deep breath and then slowly sat up on the couch, placing his stocking feet on the floor one at a time.

"Sir, you look horrible. Maybe you should just answer his phone instead of going visual?"

Niles looked his young assistant over. Her name was Linda, and she was reporting more and more for duty since Alice Hamilton was spending more time with Senator Garrison Lee these days, the former director of the Group. Compton figured that the two oldest members of the Event Group deserved all the time they had together; they had after all, earned it.

"I look that bad, huh?"

"Yes, you do," she said.

"Well, your training progresses, young lady. I think I'll follow your advice. Hand me the phone."

She reached out and pulled the phone over from the small table next to the couch. She lifted the receiver.

"Mr. President, we have located Director Compton."

There was silence on the other end of the phone line when Niles placed the receiver to his ear.

"Compton," he said with a mouth full of cotton.

"I warned you, Mr. Director, CIA reported a backdoor hack of their Dahlia system. May I assume it was your people?"

"You may not assume it was my people," Niles said with as much indignity as he could conjure up.

"Okay, then you're telling me it was NSA, the FBI, or the boys at the Pentagon? They're the only ones other than your Europa who has that capability. And believe me, I know what that nervous bastard Pete Golding is capable of, I've seen him work: He can twist that damn Cray system to do backflips if he wanted."

"I resent that, Mr. President, just because Pete's—well, anyway, I resent the accusation."

"Just so you know, I have ordered the arrest of Colonel Collins and anyone in his security department that tries to fly out of Nellis, which I highly expect they'll try. For Christ's sake, Niles, as a friend, I asked you not to tell him. I wanted to let this thing play out a while. As it looks, we'll never know the real reason for his sister's reasoning for talking to her brother."

"And as a friend, I told you what you wanted to hear. Would you want to be kept in the dark about your sister? No, you wouldn't. And that man has done more for this country than anyone you or I have ever known, I think—"

"Don't think, damn it. We may have serious problems here, his sister may have been getting close to something and Director Easterbrook has stuck his neck out to assist her. And don't ask because we really don't know yet. Look, Collins has already screwed the pooch here, he's made a big mistake, he and his buddy, Everett, filed an advanced flight plan to Los Angeles out of Nellis. Hell, it took the FBI all of two minutes to get that information. And they have at least two agents at every dirt airstrip for fifty miles, too. Listen, Niles, Jack Collins is too close, and I don't want to lose him along with his sister—that's what *I* owe him, at least until we get a handle on what his sister was working on. So, let the FBI catch and detain him."

"I know that, but I am not going to keep that man in the dark even if his sister is already dead. If she is, can you think of anybody else in this world who you would want to track the bastards down that killed her?"

"No, but consider yourself under house arrest Mr. Director, you little bastard. I should just fly out there right now and hang you."

"Excuse me, but I'm a little drunk and I'm going to go back to sleep."

"You do that!"

Niles winced as the phone was hung up.

"Is the president mad?" Linda asked.

"Yes, very mad," he said as a smile crossed his lips. "He's going to catch Jack at the base before he enters his aircraft," he said as his eyes started to close and the smile was drifting but still present. "But I think I may have gotten a step on him. When McIntire and Mendenhall get here, give them this," he said as he handed her a folded piece of paper.

"Is there anything else we can do to help the colonel, sir?" the young assistant asked.

Niles didn't answer her question as he had fallen asleep with the phone still clutched in his hand and the smile still on his lips.

Jack, Carl, and Jason Ryan stepped from the tram that led to Gate Two just beneath the Gold City Pawnshop, the clandestine entryway for all Event Group personnel. They were dressed in civilian attire and had identification that indicated they were Los Angeles police detectives, and L.A. County sherriff's officers. As they took the elevator up, Jack looked at his watch.

"Mendenhall was nowhere to be found?" Collins asked the small naval aviator.

"No, sir, he left his security badge in the security office, I couldn't get a track on him through Europa."

"Damn," Jack said as the elevator doors slid open. The view ahead was the dusty and very dingy back storeroom of the Gold City Pawnshop.

They were met by Lance Corporal Jess Harrison, a black marine from Compton, California. The young corporal had the duty at Gate Two.

"Sir, this just came through from the director's office," he said handing Collins a flimsy.

"What's the word, Jack?" Everett asked as he walked over to the arms locker and used his security code to open it. The corporal watched Everett with a wary eye.

"Oh, effective in," Jack again looked at his watch, "exactly five minutes, the director has ordered us detained."

"Do you agree with the wording Corporal?" Jack asked his gate security officer.

The marine looked around from watching Everett removed three nine-millimeter automatic pistols and their holsters from the arms locker, along with three clips of ammunition apiece. He also looked at his watch.

"Yes, sir. In five minutes, I am to detain you," the lance corporal said, still watching Everett.

Everett handed Jack a holstered weapon along with Ryan. "Let's not hang around for that five minutes so our young friend here doesn't have to do his duty."

The three men left the back storage area and into the back office of the pawnshop.

"Sir, Air Police, and what looks like the FBI is crawling all over Nellis looking for you guys," the corporal said as he buzzed them through the secured office and past the armed army private that had his finger close to the trigger of a submachine gun clipped underneath his desk.

"I would be worried if that was where we were going, Corporal." Jack stopped and turned to face his men. "Watch the place for us. If you can't find Lieutenant Mendenhall after we leave, you're in charge of security. I imagine you'll have orders to lock down the complex."

"Yes, sir. Good luck Colonel."

Jack didn't answer, but Everett slapped the young marine on the back as they left the back office and then a minute later the Gold City Pawnshop.

They didn't use one of the three department vehicles sitting in the alley beside the pawnshop; instead, Ryan used his irritatingly loud whistle to flag a cab. With temperatures hovering around 108 degrees, they quickly climbed in and Collins ordered the driver to take them to McLaren Airport where there was a C-21, a U.S. air force variant of the Learjet 35, stashed in a hangar on the military side of McLaren, a hangar complex the gamblers and vacationers never knew existed.

The cab pulled into the far drive that led out onto the taxing tarmac after Jack had shown his fake Los Angeles Police Department ID. As the cab approached the aluminum hangar, the hackles rose on the colonel's neck.

"The agency and the FBI may have outthought me on this one."

"I feel it, too, they're here," Everett said.

"Jesus, we can't shoot it out with our own people, Colonel," Ryan said, pulling the Hawaiian shirt from his chest, having been stuck there with the sweat that was pouring from his body.

"Stop here," Jack said as he tossed the driver two twenties as he climbed from the backseat.

He removed the nine-millimeter from his holster and made sure the safety was on. He looked at Everett and Ryan, making them do the same.

"No accidents—no one gets hurt, if it comes to them stopping us, give me time to do what I have to do, then you two surrender. Am I clear on this?"

Everett looked into Jack's blue eyes and nodded once. Then he looked at Ryan.

"Hell, Colonel, I want to give up now. I'm allergic to the Feds."

"Good boy, Lieutenant."

Carl and Ryan fell into step behind Collins as he made his way to a line of employee cars parked outside of the private hangars that flanked the two military enclosures on the north side of the airport. As they moved, they kept their heads down. Ryan almost let loose a scream as they passed one of the private hangar doors that started rising with a loud whine. They hurried past before the opening could reveal them sneaking by.

Behind them from the hangar they heard a loud piston engine fire up, then a second, but they kept moving as quickly as they could toward the military doors now only ten feet away. Once they got to the personnel door of the first hangar, Jack reached out and took the handle. To their rear, the loud engine noise continued as the aircraft slowly taxied out from the privately leased hangar. Jack ignored the plane behind him and pulled open the personnel door of the military hangar and quickly stepped inside.

Collins, though very tempted, refused to pull his gun. He gestured for Everett to make his way to the far side of the C-21. The plane sat there gleaming in the bright sunlight streaming through two overhead skylights far above. There was no guard on duty and no mechanics evident. Collins shook his head as he saw Everett disappear around the rear-mounted engines just under the tail.

Ryan was the first to the door just forward of the wing. He looked back at Collins and grimaced, shaking his head. Jack nodded once as Everett came back around the front of the plane and shook his head from side to side.

"No one, Jack," he said, barely above a whisper.

"Okay, Lieutenant, open it up."

Ryan popped the stainless-steel guard and the handle popped free and the folding steps deployed as he stepped to the side. As he did, Collins went up the staircase in two steps, Everett followed and then Ryan. Once inside the small aircraft, Jack allowed his eyes to adjust to the dimness of the interior.

"Okay, Ryan, get to your preflight and let's get the hell out of here," Everett said.

Just as Ryan started to move, Jack took him by the shoulder and shook his head.

"Forget it, we have company."

Just then, the cockpit door opened and first one agent, then another came through, and unlike Collins and his two men, they had their handguns drawn. As they watched the agents come toward them, the aft restroom door opened and another two agents came out.

"Goddamn sneaky little bastards," Everett said, even though he knew through his SEAL training he could take at least the two from the back, because against all of the FBI training the two agents went through, they were too close to their targets. When he conveyed this to Jack with his eyes, Collins shook his head.

"Colonel Collins, you and your men are to be detained on a national security matter. Please remove your weapons and place them on the floor of the aircraft."

Jack, Ryan, and Everett did as they were ordered just as the loud aircraft leaving its hangar outside became close to unbearable. The two agents at the front of the aisle slowly came on as Jack watched for some kind of an opening, one that would ensure no one got hurt—well, not too hurt anyway. As the first FBI agent reached down and collected the handguns, he remained low so the three men could still be covered by the man to their front and the two behind. One of the latter slipped past and went down the stairs.

"Okay, Colonel, we want no trouble. We'll take you into our field office and from there, your people, whoever they are, can have you back. No booking, no cuffs, okay? We'll call it a professional courtesy, and that comes from the highest source," the lead agent said, his gun never wavering from the three men. "Now, Agent Williams is waiting for you at the bottom of the stairs. Please, let's be nice," the first man said loudly, trying to be heard over the idling engine noise of the plane just outside the hangar.

Jack could see no way out of this without using deadly force and these men didn't deserve anything close to that. They were fellow Americans doing their job. Collins nodded for Everett and Ryan to start down.

Finally, as Jack made his way down the steps backward, he was suddenly and harshly pulled down and onto his back, knocking the wind from him. On his way down he saw Ryan and then Everett hop over the small cable that was used as a handhold on the stairs, he never saw them hit the concrete. Around him all was a blur as someone shot forward and pushed the stairs back up into the aircraft's fuselage. He heard shots, then he was being pulled to his feet. Another single shot rang out.

As Jack regained his breath and his senses, he saw the man who had taken the single shot was Will Mendenhall. He watched as the black army lieutenant reached up and pulled on the door's handle; when he was satisfied that the handle had been damaged enough to jam the door for a good while, he turned and smiled.

"I think we better go," Will hurriedly said over his shoulder as he ran for the door, jumping over FBI Agent Williams who was writhing on the floor with plastic wire-ties on his hands and ankles. His weapon lay beside him with the slide back and the ammunition clip removed. Collins shook off the hands that helped him to his feet and then noticed who it was. Sarah smiled up at him.

"Compliments of Director Compton. He said you didn't stand a chance getting out of the desert."

Sarah pursed her lips in a pretend kiss and then ruthlessly shoved Jack toward the door and then through it and into the sunlight and the unbearable noise of the desert airport. When he looked up, he couldn't believe his eyes. Sitting there only a few feet away, with a blue-and-white shining paint scheme, had to be the oldest seaplane he had ever seen. It was a Grumman G-21A Goose, a twin-engine plane that predated World War II. It was loud and noisy and with its twin landing gear sticking out of its boat-shaped hull, it looked like the most ungainly aircraft he had ever seen. The Grumman was beautiful and was well maintained. The Goose was designed during the heyday of the flying boats in the late 1930s and a good number of them were still active at air shows around the world. This was the aircraft that had started up inside the hangar they had passed by on the way in.

"Jesus, Colonel, look at this," Ryan said as he pointed to the glassed-in cockpit.

"Unbelievable," was all Collins could say as he saw the small arm of a woman hanging out of the side cockpit window, waving them forward, insisting they hurry.

"Is that Alice?" Everett said as he took off toward the cabin door.

"It belongs to Alice and Senator Lee. Niles thought it was the only thing we could use to get out of here; after all, the FBI and CIA would be waiting for us at any airport we wanted to land, but they can't cover every waterfront in L.A.," Sarah shouted as they bounded up and into the ancient seaplane.

Once inside, the old Grumman's engines were goosed and she started to roll. Alice Hamilton, all eighty-seven years young, complete with leather helmet, headset, and flying gloves, threw the two throttles forward and the plywood and aluminum-framed flying boat sped toward the runway as Jack came into the small cockpit and sat next to Alice, and shook his head.

"You didn't think Earhart was the only aviatrix this country turned out, did you?" Alice said when she saw the disbelief on the colonel's face.

"What in the hell are you doing?" Jack yelled over the sound of the screaming props.

"Evidently rescuing you," Alice answered with a smile as she reached down and started pumping the handle that brought the old Grumman's flaps to the down position. When she looked over and saw Collins frowning, she smiled as the huge wheels left the airport runaway.

"Okay, Niles knew you would be caught if you tried to use a Group aircraft, then he knew even if you did, you would have to land at an airfield where any number of federal people would be waiting for you, so, he knew Garrison bought me this little toy back in 1955 for my birthday, thus, here we are—now hang on!"

Jack was thrown back in his seat as the Grumman shot into the sky at an angle Collins never thought a plane that old could achieve.

As he buckled himself in, he heard the shouts and grunts from the passenger area of the seaplane.

"This isn't good!" Ryan screamed as eighty-seven-year-old Alice Hamilton threw the plane into a steep banking maneuver, heading for Los Angeles.

Director Niles Compton of Department 5656—the Event Group—was rarely, if ever, outthought by anyone in the world.

4

The chartered Boeing 737 was above the state of Colorado heading north. Leased through a third party, the federal authorities had no idea their murderous quarry was heading out of the country.

Sagli leaned forward in his chair and placed his glass of water on the table. Deonovich looked around at the thirty-five men seated around the aircraft.

"I am curious as to why we cannot dispose of our guest—she is too dangerous to keep around," Deonovich asked Sagli, taking a large swallow of water from an iced glass; he then turned and eyed his partner.

"I asked the same question and was told she may be an asset later when we arrive at our destination. She is to be kept healthy at all costs."

"Have you thought that maybe we have placed too much confidence in our new ally?" Deonovich asked, raising the glass vodka and draining it.

Sagli frowned. "That is enough drinking; we have very serious days ahead. I do not need you half comatose."

Deonovich raised his brows and eyed his partner.

"You have not answered my question."

Sagli hated talking about the plan to Deonovich as the large man had a hard time grasping the intricacies of the plan. He could tolerate his small peccadilloes such as his penchant for inflicting pain upon others, but when he tried to question their new partner, it made them both look foolish. After all, the intelligence information this man had delivered to them over the last five years had all been dead-on accurate. The man had proven his reliability and his plan was almost foolproof.

"Look, old friend, when he came to us, I myself was suspicious, but since I have come to know him, I find that his penchant for planning and his eye for detail far exceed the people who trained us in the old days. He is a cold warrior, and we are committed to his plan." He eyed Deonovich closely. "Now, no more drinking."

Lynn Simpson looked up from her seat, handcuffs on her ankles and wrists. The duct tape was itching beyond all belief as she looked up and into the dark eyes of Sagli. She never even flinched when he raised the silenced pistol and pointed it at her right eye. Lynn had figured a long time ago she had been living on borrowed time, so she had mentally prepared herself. She closed her eyes and then said a silent good-bye to her mother and then to Jack.

"I just want to ask you a question," Sagli said as he reached out and gently pulled the duct tape from her mouth. Then, placing the silenced weapon on the seat beside Lynn, he undid her handcuffs.

Lynn opened her eyes at the question and the relief she felt when the cuffs were removed. She glanced at the silenced handgun beside her on the seat, and then she looked from it to Sagli, who was actually smiling, daring her to take it. Instead of taking up the challenge, Lynn rubbed her wrists, taking care not to strike her injured hand.

"The Canadian agent, this Alexander fellow—in your opinion, what are his capabilities?" Sagli asked, finally picking up the handgun and removing temptation from her thoughts.

"Go to hell," Lynn said with a hint of her own smile touching her lips. "You mean what *were* his capabilities."

"No, I mean, what *are* his capabilities. It seems our Canadian spy survived the assault. Now what can you tell me?"

Lynn remained silent as the thought of Punchy Alexander flashed through her mind. She could hardly believe he lived after her witnessing him getting executed by Sagli.

"I suggest you look down at your hands, Miss Simpson, count your fingers and then in five minutes I will ask you to do it again. I guarantee you will not come up with the same number as before. The only reason you are alive is for the fact that this Alexander just may get lucky and get a track on us," Sagli bluffed as he just wanted more information on Alexander. "I am skeptical at best, but if he does I believe you may still be a handsome bargaining chip."

Lynn was down to seven fingers and two thumbs. Her older brother would have said she was still way ahead in the game, but she wasn't her brother and she wasn't as brave as Jack.

"If Punchy Alexander is after you, I hope you're going to a very deep hole in the earth and pull the dirt in after you, because he can be relentless—the second most relentless man I have ever known."

Sagli smiled broadly. "As a matter of fact, we are going someplace much better, Miss Simpson, a place where the most recent maps were made over a quarter of a century ago; a forgotten place right in your own backyard." He gave a slight nod of his head. "And yes, we will pull the dirt in after us, and also over you."

LOS ANGELES, CALIFORNIA

The twin-engine Grumman Goose was flying as low as Alice felt comfortable with in the growing darkness. She manipulated the throttles that she could barely reach on the upper console, firewalling the engines to raise the agile seaplane over hills, and then cutting power to slide the aircraft nimbly into a valley. Jack really didn't know how she could see anything.

"Colonel, it's time you went into the cabin with the others. When you get back there, ask Lieutenant Ryan to come up here, please."

Jack was hesitant about unsnapping his seatbelt, but finally managed enough courage when Alice brought the seaplane into level flight.

Nervous eyes watched Jack as he stumbled his way from the cockpit and into the passenger area. Everett was sitting next to Sarah, and Ryan was sitting across from them. Mendenhall was nowhere to be seen.

"Where's Will?" Collins asked as he slammed into the seat in front of Ryan.

Jason Ryan pointed to the back of the plane with an outstretched thumb, then he grabbed for the life vest he had found under his seat when Alice sent the Grumman down into a shallow dive.

"He's . . . he's in that little closet back there. I think it's the head, but I think it's too small to have a toilet," Ryan finally said. "He doesn't feel too good."

"Can't say as I blame him," Jack said as he snapped his seatbelt. "Ryan, report to Alice up front."

The small naval officer looked taken back for the briefest moment.

"Go on, Lieutenant, she's waiting."

"Yes, sir," Jason said as he nervously popped his own belt loose. At that moment the door to the restroom opened just as Alice pulled up to avoid a small hill just outside of Riverside, California. Before anyone could see Mendenhall clearly, he ducked back inside and slammed the door.

Ryan made his way up front and pulled the curtain aside and stepped into the small cockpit. He hurriedly slammed down into the copilot's seat and fumbled with the seatbelt until he finally managed to get it locked.

"Not like flying F-14 Tomcats is it, Mr. Ryan?" Alice asked with a smirk, managing a quick glance over to her right.

"No, ma'am, not at all."

"Listen, I need you to watch what I'm doing, because you're going to have to take the controls in a minute. I suspect we may have to do some evading."

"Take the controls?" he said as he pulled the belt tighter. "But this thing has propellers, and frankly, ma'am, I don't see any controls, just a steering wheel—I think."

"Yes, it does have propellers, young man. It's called real flying. Now, take the wheel, don't worry, she's real responsive. Use your rudder and stabilizers for up and down, and don't worry about the wing flaps, got it?"

"Why not worry about the wing flaps?" he asked as he took the half-moon wheel in front of him.

"Because we won't use them in flight—stabilizers, tail and engine acceleration and deceleration, that's all. Now, I need to find us a good place to land this thing where we won't bring every policeman in two counties down on us." She let go of the wheel and pulled a map from an oversize front pocket of her coveralls.

"Ma'am, don't take this the wrong way, but you're one crazy . . ."—he stopped and looked quickly at her smiling face—"lady."

"Good choice of words, Mr. Ryan," she said as she unfolded the map, while the former fighter jock tried desperately to see out of the half-oval windows to his front.

"I think here would be the best place." Alice held the map out so Ryan could take a glance, but he was so intent on keeping the plane in the air, that he only looked for a split second and then turned back.

Ryan was getting a quick feel for the ancient Grumman and his vision was picking up far more than he should have been able to, thanks to the advanced windscreen installed in the plane that picked up ambient light and made seeing easier in the darkness. As he turned slightly to avoid a string of power lines on the far side of Upland, he knew he liked flying the old seaplane.

Alice reached out and turned a knob on the aluminum control panel. As Ryan watched a small green illuminated grid appeared on the windscreen, the copilot's side of the window showed the foothills to the right, and on the left side in front of Alice, the Chino Valley spread out as far as the glass allowed. Ryan was shocked at the modern hologram being projected onto the windscreens.

"A little gift from Pete Golding," she said when she saw the amazed look on Ryan's face. "He flew with me and the senator once, and decided we needed some upgrading—poor man almost had a nervous breakdown."

"I can't imagine why," Ryan said with a sheepish grin.

As Ryan flew toward Los Angeles, popping up over Kellogg Hill and then down over West Covina, he knew to hug the hills to his right side. Alice stretched her arms out and then flexed her fingers before she slowly placed the flying gloves onto her small hands once more. Then she reached beneath her seat and pulled out a small cylindrical object that resembled the casing for a small kitchen clock. She ran a cord to the console and then plugged the device into a small socket. When its face lit up, she slid it into an open space in the console.

"There," she said smiling, "now we have radar."

Ryan looked from the hologram in front of him to the avoidance radar on the console.

"If you don't mind my asking, why weren't you using that all along?" Ryan asked incredulously.

"Because, young man, I like to fly once in a while. Now we're heading into a place where buildings can pop up out of nowhere." She looked over at him after adjusting the radar sweep speed. "Pete was really the nervous type; he insisted we have a radar. He's a real wimp."

Ryan was amazed. Alice was either the bravest woman he'd ever met, or she had gone over the edge and into the bleakness of senility.

"Okay, Mr. Ryan, I'll take it from here. If you don't remember how scared you were during night landings on a carrier, you're about to be reminded."

As Ryan let go of the wheel, his eyes widened when Alice Hamilton pulled back on the throttles and allowed the seaplane to dip far too low to the ground.

"Uh, ma'am, there's nothing down here but houses."

Alice leaned back in her seat and then turned her head and shouted through the curtain.

"Everyone, hold on to your behinds, this is going to be pretty dicey," she called as a moment later the sound of the bathroom door being slammed sounded through the cabin.

Inside the passenger area, Sarah touched Carl on the arm and, unfastening her seatbelt, she hopped quickly across the small gap between the eight seats and then threw herself onto Jack's lap. She kissed him quickly and then rolled over to the seat beside him.

"I expect you to save me if we crash, you got that?" she said seriously.

"I was just thinking the same thing about you."

Up front, Ryan watched as Alice turned the wheel sharply to the left, at the same time slamming her small foot into the left rudder pedal as hard as she could.

"Pete could have suggested power steering for this thing!" she said, taking a quick look over at Ryan and winking.

The Grumman pitched over onto her left side and the large plane took a nosedive for the ground. Ryan wanted to close his eyes, but he watched the hologram on the windscreen instead. It went from showing greater Los Angeles to the front right, to nothing but houses, bridges, and streets. Then he saw a straight blank area.

"Uh, ma'am, can I ask what it is you're doing?" Ryan said as he reached out and steadied his slide from the seat.

"The report said this Chavez creep lived in Elysian Park, right?"

"I have no idea!" Jason said as the plane drew closer to the ground, the right wing tip almost touching some of the larger houses beneath them.

"Well, I was informed he ran his illegal operations out of there. Now, we can't very well land at LAX or Burbank now, can we? The police are looking for you and your little merry band if I heard right, so that leaves us one place where we can land that won't put us thirty miles from Elysian Park."

"Where is that?"

"Right here—the Los Angeles River."

Ryan wanted to scream that Los Angeles didn't have a river in the remotest and loosest sense of the word. He knew the river to be a concrete canal that ran through L.A. like a winding snake, and at most this time of year it had about an inch of water running right down its center. He also knew there to be bridges every six hundred feet.

"Oh, shit," he said as Alice leveled the seaplane and then in a blur of motion, pulled down the landing-gear lever on her left. She fought with the old-fashioned wheel and then started furiously pumping the wing flaps down as the Grumman's engine screamed power as she hopped over three houses and then over a small bridge. She cut power to the engines and the eerie silence belied the sheer terror of everyone on the plane.

Finally, the large wheels that had popped free of the boatlike body of the plane struck concrete. She bounced once, twice, finally hitting a foot-deep rivulet of water in the center of the river. Alice pumped up the wing flaps to their stops and the plane slowed after rising again into the air. Finally, she bounced down and then the next bridge in line rose up before them only a hundred feet away. Alice calmly started to apply the brakes, squealing and grinding as the seaplane slowed. Now realizing they wouldn't slow in time, Alice Hamilton turned the wheel as sharply as she could to the left while at the same time slamming down on the left rudder pedal once more, turning the Grumman's rear wheel. The large plane skid and then finally turned to the left, finally fishtailing to a stop.

Silence gripped the interior of the plane as Alice quickly looked around after shutting down the hologram. Ryan, for his part, only stared straight ahead. Alice quickly fired up both engines and then taxied back the way they had come until they settled underneath one of L.A.'s old bridges, where she feathered both engines. She took a deep breath and then looked at the white-faced Ryan.

"Well, we're here. Up the road about two miles is Elysian Park. You see Dodger Stadium up there? Well, the park is right below it."

Ryan was still staring straight ahead, not moving.

"I hope you watched what I did, Mr. Ryan, because you're flying my baby out of here since I have to get home."

"Wh . . . what?" he finally asked, still not looking at Alice.

"I said, you're flying my plane out of here. I have to get to LAX and catch a flight home. I left a casserole in the oven and I can't trust Garrison to follow instructions until he sees flames."

"But . . . but . . ."

Alice slapped him on the leg. "Oh, for an old carrier pilot like you, it should be fun." She smiled wide and unsnapped her seatbelt.

From the back there were audible signs of relief as the others started to realize they hadn't crashed. Then the sound of the small bathroom door was heard opening.

"Hey," Mendenhall said with a shaky voice, "that restroom is officially off limits."

Alice looked back at Ryan as they came through the curtain and a questioning look crossed her face as she removed her headset.

"We don't have a bathroom on this plane."

A moment later, Alice stood under the large wing and the left wing float of the plane after checking the undercarriage of the Grumman. She pronounced everything fit as she looked at Jack.

"Colonel, you know I wouldn't abandon you like this if I hadn't the need to keep an eye on that old man. If I could—"

Collins just reached out and pulled Alice to him, and hugged her, cutting off her words.

"Thank you," he whispered in her ear.

Alice hugged him back and then pulled away, locking her eyes with his. "Find your baby sister, Jack, and bring her home," she said, patting him on the chest just over his heart.

Collins nodded and then turned away toward the tall sloping sides of the concrete Los Angeles River.

Alice Hamilton looked over the old seaplane one last time, patting it lovingly on the wing float.

"Take care of her, Lieutenant."

Ryan smiled and gave Alice a salute as he turned and left, following Jack, Carl, and Mendenhall up the slick sides of the river.

Sarah hugged Alice good-bye. "You sure you can get out of here alright?" she asked.

"Honey, if I can climb K-2, I can get my old ass out of here."

"You climbed—"

"You go help Jack, he needs you. And listen to me, I think this is far more than just finding his sister; this may be the reason Jack has been so distant and secretive. Now go, I'll be fine."

Sarah half smiled and then turned and ran after the others. Alice looked over her old airplane one last time.

"You take good care of them," she said and then walked away toward the steep sloping side of the river.

The low rider, a 1961 Chevy Impala, pulled slowly up to the curb and let out a loud whine as the front air shocks and hydraulics were relieved of their pressure, then the rear suspension raised to level out the car as it settled next to the curb in Elysian Park.

Jack climbed from the passenger seat, followed by Sarah. The others piled from the backseat, with Will Mendenhall lagging while he admired the old-fashioned Tuck N' Roll upholstery. Will knew he was home again.

Collins walked up to the driver's side of the car and handed the driver a hundred-dollar bill. The Mexican American driver took it and then looked the colonel over closely. The red bandana covering his short hair was pulled down almost to his eyes.

"You know, jefe, you guys stand out like white corn in an alfalfa field."

"I suspect we do," Jack said as Sarah stepped up beside him.

The driver eyed the small woman for a very noticeable minute. Then he looked at Jack and then to the hundred-dollar bill. "Keep it, my man, buy the lady something nice," he said as he raced his engine and then peeled away from the curb, the music loud enough to feel it through the soles of their feet.

Jack looked around and then down at Sarah. He smiled and then started walking to catch up with Everett who was confirming the street address.

"I think it may be the one covered in police tape, Captain," Mendenhall said as he pointed to the large house on the corner.

"Smart-ass," Carl said as he spied the house ahead. Then Mendenhall caught sight of Everett reaching into his shirt, obviously clicking the safety off of his hidden nine-millimeter.

At ten at night, most families were still out and about. Lights were on and televisions could be seen flickering through shaded windows. Looking down into Elysian Park, Collins could see kids still hanging out in large numbers, and far up in Chavez Ravine, a Dodger game was just starting. As he took in the Chavez house, yellow police tape was pulled from column to column on the wraparound porch and was crisscrossed at the front door. He looked around to see if anyone was watching. When he saw only an old battered Ford pickup across the street from the house, he walked up the small slope of grass and bounded up the six wide front steps.

Sarah, Mendenhall, and Jason Ryan followed Collins onto the front porch. Everett held position at the base of the front steps, looking outward from the front yard. It seemed no one cared about the house where the thief Chavez used to live.

"Jack?" Carl said after a moment of time.

"Yeah, I feel it, too," Collins said backing away from the door.

"Feel what," Sarah whispered, not feeling at all comfortable.

"Someone's watching us," Jack said backing away from the door. Then Ryan leaned over the side of the porch and shook his head.

"Police cruiser—empty," he said, knowing they had been too hasty to climb the porch.

Suddenly the door opened, pulling away the yellow police tape that was stuck to the outside. Jack and the others placed hands on their hidden weapons.

"Don't shoot," a voice from the dark said. "There were two L.A. police officers here, they're cuffed at the moment and sitting in the living room, unharmed."

Jack shook his head and watched as the front door opened all the way.

"Damn, you're still a sneaky old bastard," Collins said, relaxing.

As the door opened fully, the dim streetlamps that lined the sidewalk showed a large bear of a man as he stepped into the frame of the door.

"At least I don't go bounding up the front steps without reconnoitering first."

"Damn, Punchy, it's good to see you," Jack said as he held out his hand. "There was a rumor you were dead."

Alexander shook Jack's hand and then grimaced and grabbed his chest and then gestured forward with his wounded shoulder. "If it wasn't for the body armor I had on, I would be, my friend. As it is, those two Russian bastards were so intent on taking your little sister they didn't linger to do the job right."

"I always thought you hated wearing armor. You always said your chest and big belly was enough to stop any bullet made." Jack eyed his old friend closely.

"Yeah, well, getting old will make you feel closer to the afterlife than you would think," Alexander answered, not noticing the closeness of which Jack was eyeing him.

"Everyone, this is Jonathan Alexander, the head of the Montreal sector of CSIS, the Canadian Intelligence Service."

"If you're Jack's people, Punchy will do."

"You were there, at the ambush?" Sarah asked.

"Yes, young lady, I was there."

Jack stepped around Punchy and entered the Chavez home. He immediately saw the two policemen sitting against the far wall of the living room. They were, as Punchy had said, unhurt. Collins eased the nine-millimeter into his waistband and then turned as the others entered the entrance hall, followed finally by Everett who eased the door closed.

"Nice touch, Punchy," Jack said, looking away from the two L.A. policemen.

Alexander cleared his throat. "I hate to burst your bubble about my being a sneaky bastard, but they were like that when I arrived."

Their eyes met and Jack raised his brows. "Is that right?"

"Trussed up pretty as a picture, just like you see them now," Punchy said and then quickly saw the look on Jack's face. "Don't worry; I checked the rest of the house. Whoever cuffed them isn't here."

"Punchy, why in the hell are you here?" Collins asked.

"You know why: It's not only my job, but I happen to like Lynn, almost as much as you."

"What in the hell happened out there, Punchy?" Collins asked as he slowly stepped from the living room into the kitchen.

"It was a setup. Lynn was anonymously contacted and she showed up in my yard. Evidently, only her direct boss knew she was coming to Canada. I guess they wanted to make a mark by bagging Sagli and Deonovich on their own. You know how kids are, they just don't know how to play the game," he said looking at Ryan and Mendenhall. "No offense."

Ryan looked at Will and they both just shrugged.

"Do you think Lynn is still alive?"

"You know me, Jack, forever an optimist. That's why I'm here and willing to breach my orders."

"Thanks, Punchy."

"Look, those two coppers in there are going to be relieved soon. If the LAPD overlooked anything here, we better get to looking for it." Alexander watched Collins closely, wondering if he was still as sharp as he once was. "If not, I have to get back to Montreal."

Jack nodded and silently pointed at Will and Everett, then used his thumb to point toward the basement. He silently ordered Sarah and Ryan to take the kitchen and living room. Then he nodded toward the wooden staircase for him and Punchy Alexander to check out.

On the way up the stairs, Jack slowly pulled the nine-millimeter from his waistband and knew Alexander was doing the same three steps behind him.

"You got the report on the man that Sagli and Deonovich murdered in Seattle?" Punchy asked as he gained the landing outside of a long hallway. He pointed his weapon left as Jack was doing the same to the right.

"The Russian-American, Serta?"

"Yeah, we don't know the reasoning for it yet, just a bunch of rumors." Alexander eased the bathroom door open and easily flipped on the light switch. The shiny tile and wood was clean but he could see where the police had tossed the closet as towels and washrags were strewn about on the floor and even in the bathtub.

"Rumors such as . . . ?" Jack asked as he eased the first bedroom door open with his right foot and then quickly stepped inside. He moved the handgun from side to side. He relaxed when he saw the mattress to the king-size bed had been thrown free of the box spring and had even been cut into. *Pretty thorough*, he thought.

"Some fantastic tale that this old man in Seattle inherited one of the Twins of Peter the Great."

Jack looked back into the hallway just as Alexander eased the second bedroom door open.

"Twins?" Jack asked, now feeling that they were on a wasted mission to the Chavez house. He pushed the last bedroom door open and peered inside the already tossed and torn-apart room.

"Diamonds. Legend has it that Peter the Great had made a gift of twin diamonds the size of—hell, I don't know, lemons or something. Well, this lumber magnate supposedly was in possession of one of them."

"I've never heard of anything like that," Collins said as he dejectedly placed the handgun back into his pants. He also wondered why nothing was mentioned in Europa's investigation about these diamonds.

"Well, they supposedly disappeared around the time of the Russian revolution, along with everything else of value, including the tzar and tzarina."

"Well, we know where they went, don't we?" Jack said.

Alexander watched as Collins shook his head and started down the stairs. When he joined him at the bottom, they saw Sarah and Ryan throwing a few of the items still remaining in the coat closet out into the hallway. Sarah straightened and then looked at Jack, and shook her head.

"This is going nowhere fast. What in the hell was I thinking, that this asshole would leave a note behind telling us who his employer was?"

Sarah took his arm and squeezed it. Ryan was also aware the colonel was just grasping at straws, trying out anything for a single lead.

Punchy Alexander slapped Jack on the back and then walked passed. "Don't worry, Jack, we'll turn a rock over soon enough and find out where she's at."

They heard footsteps running up the stairs from the basement. Will Mendenhall soon opened the door and then with his breathing coming in short gasps, said, "Colonel, Captain Everett says you've got to take a look at this."

Jack immediately went to the door and followed Will down the long flight of two different stairs. When they reached the bottom, he saw Everett standing in the middle of a dirt floor with his hands on his hips and staring at one of the outer walls. Collins felt the others behind him as they stopped; he held up a hand when he saw that Carl was thinking something out.

"Number one, the percentage of basements in Southern California is so low I don't even want to think about it," Everett said without turning away from the far wall. "I lived here, in a house just like this in Oxnard. Pre–World War II, stone, just like a million others. Hell, that was the bulk of cheap building material back then, no brick, just rocks."

Jack moved his eyes from Everett's back where he was just staring at the walls, to the open and broken bits of crates, old cardboard boxes, broken furniture, and moldy old clothes. He felt Ryan stir behind him, getting ready to ask the captain a question, but again, Collins held his hand up, wanting Carl to think through what he was tossing about in his head.

"How many tons of rock went into building this house—fifteen or twenty, maybe even thirty?"

"Captain, I don't see one rock down here."

Everett finally turned and looked at Ryan. "That's the point, flyboy, the basement isn't constructed of the same material as the house, which means it was—"

"Recently added," Collins finished for him.

Carl smiled. "Not only that, Jack, look over here." Everett moved forward and pointed at the dirt that made up the floor of the giant basement.

Where most of the dirt was rough, full of footprints from the police investigation, there was a spot about the width of the entire rear wall that was perfectly smooth, as if the entire width had been artificially dragged smooth.

"Remember our antiquities thief in New York, Westchester County, and his remarkable basement?"

Jack smiled at Everett and then walked quickly to the far wall and started looking. Everett, Sarah, Ryan, and Mendenhall did the same, remembering the amazing basement that another antiquities thief had built using a false floor and winding stairway.

"Without sounding downright stupid, may I ask what it is you are looking for?" Alexander asked, placing his hands on his hips as the others started feeling around the walls.

"A switch, or a release of some kind," Sarah said as she went to her knees and started feeling around the bottom of the drywall.

Suddenly, the room grew quiet as they all felt it at the same time, Jack, Punchy, and Everett just a split second before the others. They all three turned as fast as they could and then stopped dead in their tracks when they saw the three men with automatic weapons aimed directly at them. The men were Caucasian and were all very well dressed. Their suits were expensive and their weapons, Israeli Uzi submachine guns, were even more so. The man in the middle of the three shook his head negative and with his eyes, ordered their weapons to be removed without uttering a single word.

As the seven people complied, they heard slow, methodical footsteps descending the stairs. One step at a time, and it seemed to go on forever. Finally, a well-polished shoe appeared, and then the other. A tall blond man stepped down onto the dirt floor. In the bare-bulb light of the basement, Jack and the other members of the Event Group could not hide the shock they felt at seeing the tall, immaculately dressed man standing before them. He wore a white shirt and was wearing a plain pair of black slacks, but his identity was unmistakable.

"How many of your nine lives do you have left, Henri?" Collins asked, keeping his hands at his side.

Colonel Henri Farbeaux, archcriminal and a decade-long enemy of the Event Group, stood arrogantly before them. He slowly placed a hand in his right pocket and then shook his head. The last thing the Event Group knew about the former French colonel was that he had been supposedly swallowed up by the Ross Ice Shelf as it cracked apart and sank into the Ross Sea three months before.

"It's not the lives, Colonel, it's the man. I just happen to know when to bet one of those lives; sometimes as you can see, that wager pays off."

Sarah stepped forward from where she had been looking for the switch that would open the wall. She was actually happy to see Henri alive; after all, it had been the Frenchman who had saved her, Senator Lee, Alice Hamilton, and the kids from the *Leviathan*, inside the cave known as Ice Palace.

"Little Sarah, how nice it is to see you again, and the fact that you made it home alive is something that makes me smile."

"Thank you, Colonel. Tell me, how in the hell did you survive?"

"We will save that for another time, my dear. For the moment, I must ask how it comes to be that the Event Group is in the basement of one of my acquisitions people."

Jack shook his head, really smiling for the first time. "Damn Henri, it is a small world, isn't it? But when I think about it, the illegal antiquities community is so small and tight, this was probably inevitable."

"I'll ask again, Colonel, why are you here, and where is my employee?" Farbeaux took a step forward, his right hand coming free of his pocket.

"Chavez is dead. They found his body washed up under the pier at Huntington Beach this morning." Jack watched for a reaction.

Farbeaux lowered his head in thought and half turned to his men and whispered something. Two of the men spread out so they could cover the group better. Jack heard the ominous clicks of their weapons being removed from their safe positions. Henri Farbeaux then turned to face Collins.

"The murder of my man doesn't sound like you, Colonel Collins; it's not your style," Farbeaux said, taking a step toward Jack.

"No, but it is your style, Henri. What did this Chavez do for you that could get him murdered?"

"That is what I am here to find out. I'll start by asking you once more, why you are here?"

"Henri, we need to know what this man Chavez removed from the Denver Museum of Natural History for you," Sarah asked before Jack could pull her back behind him.

"First, who murdered my man?" Henri asked, focusing his considerable personality on Sarah.

"Two ruthless bastards, Gregori Deonovich and Dmitri Sagli," Sarah said quickly.

Collins half turned and looked at Sarah, making her wish she hadn't said anything.

"The names are not unfamiliar to me. They are a little beneath my standards for a working relationship, but I have heard of them."

"That I find hard to believe," Collins said, making Farbeaux look up and into his eyes. "Nothing is really beneath your standards, are they, Henri?"

Farbeaux remained quiet for a moment, eyeing Jack, and then turning his attention to the others. He stepped forward and moved between Collins and Punchy Alexander, who was totally confused as to who it was that had them cornered like rats inside the basement. He walked to the far wall and stood in the left-hand corner. He placed his right hand up against an ordinary piece of Sheetrock. When he finally removed his hand, the wall started to slide outward. He watched for a reaction as the Event Group watched the space widen into the walled and excavated entrance.

"Elysian Park was once riddled with dry underground riverbeds. We built this wall when we used to store stolen goods down here. Imagine our surprise when the excavation we were doing opened up into a natural storage facility. I believe this is what you were looking for?"

Farbeaux stepped aside and saw their reaction to the immense wealth of antique Queen Anne and Hawthorne furniture, a veritable art gallery of paintings and even rows upon rows of glass cases filled with stamp, coin, and paper-currency collections. Also there were row upon row of books—thousands of them.

"This is just one of my many storage facilities. All of it awaiting my soon-to-be-realized retirement."

Jack turned and looked at Henri. His smile was genuine, at least until he noticed Collins staring at him.

"No judgments today, Colonel Collins; you of all people will not sit in judgment of me. I would trade all of this and all of the others just like it, for one more day with my wife. So don't give me any indignant looks, *not today*."

"What are you planning, Henri?" Sarah asked after she had ceased admiring one of Farbeaux's many caches of merchandise. After the question, she saw the eyes of the man and the hate reflected in them as he looked at Jack.

"You have once again placed me in a harsh situation, little Sarah. I cannot let you go, and I cannot allow you to hurt this operation more so than what has already happened."

"Colonel Farbeaux, do you have the Lattimer Papers, or a Russian journal penned by a colonel named Petrov?" Jack asked, once more pulling Sarah to his side.

"Worthless. They were destroyed soon after they were contracted for, on my orders. They were a hoax."

The Frenchman watched as Collins visibly deflated, making him curious as to why it visibly affected the American.

"I will have to ask you to wait inside of the storage room until I can figure out—until I can make a few arrangements. So, please, all of you," Henri gestured for them to step inside of the large room. Sarah kept looking back, unable to believe what Henri may be contemplating. She thought she may have learned something about Farbeaux in the time they had spent imprisoned on *Leviathan*, but as she watched his eyes, Jack pulled her along. She could see the depth of the coldness that haunted them.

"I am truly sorry, but once more your agency was someplace it should not have been." Farbeaux reached out and placed his hand in the same spot. The door started to pull back into the wall. Jack locked eyes with the French colonel and they met like two thunderheads inside of a small valley.

Sarah bit her lower lip as the wall was only two feet from closing. She suddenly made a decision and pulled free of Jack's grip and quickly squeezed through the wall before the outside world was shut out.

"Damn it!" Collins shouted as the room went dark.

"Is she nuts, Jack?" Punchy Alexander asked.

Collins was quiet as he turned away and leaned against the cool dirt of the expanded cave.

Everett stepped up to Alexander, barely seeing his silhouette in the darkness.

"No, not nuts, but Sarah's just like Jack, and that pisses him off to no end."

The three men turned with raised weapons as Sarah came bounding out of the hidden room just as the wall slammed home. She saw she was about to be shot and she skidded to a halt on the dirt floor. Farbeaux, who had already started for the wooden staircase, saw what was about to happen.

"No!"

The three men didn't shoot, but kept their weapons trained on her as Sarah looked from the muzzles pointed at her to the Frenchman standing on the bottom step.

"Brave little Sarah, you could have been shot." He stepped down and made the man closest to him lower his weapon. He gestured with his right hand for the others to do the same. "I see you are no better at following orders than you were before."

"Please, Henri, I need to explain why we're here."

"I want no reasoning from you or Colonel Collins. You are in the wrong place at the wrong time, and I have too many valuable items in that room to lose to your Group, or the authorities. I'm sorry. I have other places I need to be at the moment."

Sarah watched as Farbeaux turned his back and started back toward the stairs.

"You know we wouldn't ask for your help if it was for any of us. We need that diary or anything else that may lead to Sagli and Deonovich, we don't care about that damn room or what's in it."

Farbeaux turned and tilted his head in Sarah's direction. He remained silent and she decided he would hear her out.

"It's Jack's sister, his little sister. She's been kidnapped by those two maniacs, for what reason, we don't know."

"I would suspect that Colonel Collins's personality may run in the family and that has led to this young lady's downfall."

Whatever the Frenchman had been going through since she last saw him, Sarah could see that his eyes were still distant, meaning to her that the death of his wife down in the Amazon basin was still not far from the surface.

"We are tracking them and this may be our only shot, Henri. You wouldn't want a young woman to get brutalized by these bastards by withholding something that may help her."

"I noticed you have the head of the Montreal division of CSIS with you. Why is he here?"

"He was with Jack's sister when she was taken." Sarah thought something through very quickly. "How did you know Mr. Alexander was Canadian, and the head of his intelligence division?"

Farbeaux didn't comment, he just started to turn toward the steps again.

"They cut off her finger just to prove to her employers what they are capable of."

"Who is her employer?" he asked without turning back.

"She's agency."

Farbeaux started to laugh, but there was a serious lack of real humor coming from the eerie sound. Even his three men looked at each other with smiles. Henri started up the stairs.

"Place young Sarah back with her friends until I decide how to dispense with this problem." He started up the stairs. "You have been a most helpful friend, Sarah."

"What if it was Danielle that was taken and you needed Jack to help find her?" she blurted out as one of the three men took her by the arm.

Farbeaux only hesitated briefly on the stairs leading up into the house, then he continued on. "Follow my orders and place her in the storage room."

My God, Sarah thought, *he's really going to kill us all.*

The wall was opened only partially and Sarah was thrown back into the storage room. She fell to the floor and Jack, Everett, and Alexander were there to help her up.

"You go ahead and try something like that again, Lieutenant, and I'll have your ass!" Collins hissed.

"That was very stupid, young lady," Punchy said as he swatted some of the dirt from Sarah.

Everett walked toward the back of the room when he heard Ryan and Mendenhall coming back toward the front.

"Well?" Carl asked, when he saw their darkened outlines.

"Nothing. A solid wall of concrete—it would take dynamite to get through it, and then about three days of digging," Ryan answered.

"How's Sarah?" Mendenhall asked.

"I guess Farbeaux wasn't in the negotiating mood."

Up toward the large sliding wall, Jack took Sarah by the arm and steered her away from the others.

"Well?"

"He's not listening, Jack. He hasn't changed his attitude toward us. He still blames us for Danielle's death."

"You mean me."

"It really doesn't matter; *all* of us are his problem at the moment."

Collins squeezed her arm and then pulled her to him and looked at her in the darkness. "Thanks for trying anyway, Short Stuff."

"So what are we going to use to defend ourselves when that door opens and those Froggies open fire on us with those automatic weapons?" Mendenhall asked from the rear of the storage room.

"Well, we have a whole bunch of books to throw at them," Everett said.

"Great," Ryan and Will offered at the same time.

Ten minutes later, the wall fronting the storage room separated. It only traveled four feet before it stopped.

"Colonel Collins, and only Colonel Collins, step through the opening please," Henri said from outside in the basement.

Sarah pulled on Jack's arm and he could see her now that a dim light filtered into the room as she shook her head.

"No, make him come in and get us all, you stay put, Jack," she said, the pleading evident in her words and Collins could tell she was close to crying.

"Listen," he said in a low voice, "Farbeaux's a lot of things, Short Stuff, but I don't think he's capable of cold-blooded murder." He smiled. "At least not here, and not now."

Sarah still tried to pull Jack back as he stepped through the opening.

Jack saw the lighted room beyond and the only man standing there was Henri Farbeaux. Collins stood and watched the Frenchman. His men were nowhere to be seen. Henri just stood in the center of the room waiting with his right hand in his pants pocket.

"Young Sarah should be a defense lawyer, she has quite a talent for lost causes." Farbeaux took a few steps toward Collins. "For whatever good it may do you, Colonel, I will assist in your endeavor to recover your sister. I make no promises, the task will be arduous and difficult, but between myself and a mutual friend of ours, I think I know where it is your Russian friends are going.

"You may tell the others they may come out now, if you accept my offer of help."

In answer, Jack turned and stuck his head through the opening and told them all to come out of the storage room.

Farbeaux smiled and looked at each face in turn and then faced Collins once again.

"So, Colonel, our destinies have been placed on hold once more. You can be certain that it was only my friend Sarah and that horrible rebuke I saw in her wonderful eyes that made me change that destiny for you tonight. As for us, we must leave this place; I have transport waiting outside, the local police will be sending their relief very soon."

"Colonel Farbeaux, I've studied you more than any adversary I've come up against, and I can't figure out why are you doing this? It's not for Sarah, and it surely isn't to help me find my sister."

"Ah, you do know me, Jack. I do have one demand—I want the Twins of Peter the Great, when this little expedition is over of course."

"Oh, of course, even though earlier you said they didn't exist."

Henri walked forward and stepped into the storage room and went to one of the first bookshelves and retrieved a small leather-bound book. He blew some dust off of it and then went back to face Collins. Farbeaux only hunched his shoulders, but kept the smile.

"The Petrov Journal and the Lattimer Papers, Colonel," he said as he held the items and then gave them to the American.

"They weren't destroyed—Chavez actually gave his life to protect them?" Jack asked as he took the journal.

"He took a chance that the men who killed him would have more mercy on him than—"

"You?" Jack said, finishing Farbeaux's sentence.

"Exactly," Henri said, smiling.

"Okay, Henri, but after I get my sister back, and you have these diamonds that don't exist, we do have unfinished business."

"Agreed, Colonel," Farbeaux said as he stared right back at Jack.

"Now, you mentioned someone else who knew the destination of the Russians?"

"Ah, yes. Turn to the back page of the journal, next to the map; there is a name there I think you and your friends might be familiar with. He was the man responsible for delivering the journal and notes to Lattimer's family back in 1968. He was a student then, but he was there when Lattimer found what he was looking for. I had planned on asking him myself for his assistance in the near future, but maybe now would be a good time since he knows exactly where to look, and as you say, time is of the upmost importance."

Jack opened the old journal. Seeing the written Russian script, he thumbed carefully through the dried and yellowed pages until he came across the last page. On it was a detailed drawing of the area that had been discovered by L. T. Lattimer, but with no coordinates it would take someone familiar with the landmarks, such as the drawing of the plateau and bends in the river. Under the small diagram was a name. Jack read it and he knew the others saw the wonder of that name cross his facial features.

"What's the name, Jack?" Sarah asked.

Collins handed the journal over to Sarah and the others stepped up to see the name as she held it out in front of her. They had to read the sentence that Lattimer had written to his family. Jack, for his part, turned, unbelieving toward the staircase and sat down on the bottom step. Sarah read as the others looked on. The name was of one of the Group's very own professors.

I, Lawrence Thurgood Lattimer, hereby declare this journal as my personal property and the description listed as my claim to the property

described herein. It is thus forwarded to my next of kin, Archibald Lattimer of Boston, Massachusetts. I hereby sign this article as true and
unyielding this date of July 23, 1968.

L. T. Lattimer, Esq.

Witnessed this day by: Charles Hindershot Ellenshaw III

Stanford University

5

EVENT GROUP COMPLEX
NELLIS AIR FORCE BASE, NEVADA
FOUR HOURS LATER

Will Mendenhall and Sarah McIntire were chosen to drive as quickly as
possible to Nevada to enquire as to Charles Hindershot Ellenshaw III's
current disposition. Jason Ryan and Captain Everett had been assigned
the task of standing by and guarding the old Grumman seaplane under
the small bridge on the L.A. River because Jack figured they may have to
leave quickly if the agency or the FBI found them out. Ryan assured Jack
that he could not only fly the seaplane, but evade anyone looking for them.
When asked how, Jason just smiled and said, "That's navy stuff, Colonel."

Collins, Farbeaux, and Punchy Alexander were holed up inside an old
and tired Motel 6 where they would pore over the Petrov Diary and the
Lattimer note, hoping to get a good fix on where they would find Sagli
and Deonovich—and Lynn. Hopefully, they wouldn't have to drag Doc
Ellenshaw with them if he could pinpoint on a map for Sarah and Mendenhall just where to start looking for the site, a problem because Collins
had counted no less than six small plateaus along the Stikine River that
resembled the Lattimer description.

Punchy Alexander had told Jack that he would return to Montreal and
meet them at the Stikine. He said he had some ground to cover to keep
the prime minister happy. However, it was Farbeaux who suggested it
would be a very bad idea to split up at that point for security reasons. He
figured if one person was caught, they all would eventually succumb to

the authorities. And after Jack thought about it and saw the seriousness of the Frenchman, he agreed. Punchy would take the full ride with the Event Group.

"Tell me, Colonel, how it is that the two of you are so close?" Henri asked Jack while Alexander was in the bathroom adjusting the wrap he was wearing for his bruised ribs.

Jack looked at Farbeaux and saw the man was waiting with a stern look on his face. "I met Punchy in 1989, a joint recovery operation conducted by the British SAS and Delta units in Vancouver, British Columbia."

"May I ask what it was that this joint operation was to recover?"

Jack smiled as he saw the seriousness of Henri's demeanor.

"You may indeed ask, Henri."

"You Americans are becoming very private with your secrets Colonel, almost as good as—"

"The French?" Jack said, anticipating the self-made pat on the back from Farbeaux.

The tall man from Bordeaux looked from Collins toward the bathroom as the door opened and Alexander came through and rejoined them. Henri just looked back at Jack and winked.

EVENT GROUP COMPLEX
NELLIS AIR FORCE BASE, NEVADA

Sarah and Will, who was dozing in his chair next to her, waited inside Niles Compton's office while the director was on the phone trying to seek out the whereabouts of Professor Ellenshaw, after they had explained why they needed to find him.

As she waited beside the dozing Mendenhall, Sarah looked over at two of Jack's security men as they waited for Director Compton just inside of his door.

"Do you have to follow the director everywhere?" she asked the lance corporal who looked entirely uncomfortable doing his job.

"Yes, sir, the director's own orders," he said as he cleared his throat. "He's acting on the president's directive, ma'am."

Sarah was amazed that Niles could just simply stay at the base; instead, he was doing as his friend, the president said: He was under house arrest for having let Jack leave the complex.

"Well, I hope you don't shoot him if tries to escape," she said half jokingly.

The black lance corporal looked hurt and he was taken back.

"I resent that, ma'am."

"Just kidding, Corporal," Sarah said, knowing Jack's people, no matter what happened outside in the real world, every one of them, was loyal
to the colonel, and to their main boss, the director of Department 5656.
They would never allow anything to happen to Niles.

Sarah smiled, trying to apologize for her bad joke, when Niles stood
from his desk and then pointed at Sarah, indicating that she should follow him. She nudged Will who came awake with a start and then realized
they were on the move once again.

"Come on you two, keep up." Niles said to his two guards, "Follow me."

"Where are we going?" Sarah asked as she tried to keep up with Niles
as he hurried to the elevator.

"Down into the dungeon."

Seventeen levels beneath the main science labs of the facility, a small cor-
don of laboratories occupied the lowest level of the science department,
just above the first level of artifact vaults. Director Compton had offered
better facilities for the department currently occupying these spaces, but
the department head refused to move his people. He said they felt far
more comfortable away from the maddening crowd. And to be honest,
Niles knew the department still wasn't well received by the rest of the sciences, no matter how many Group accommodations it had received and
how many times Compton stepped in to protect some of these strange, but
very dedicated people.

The Cryptozoology Department was chaired by the now famous
Charles Hindershot Ellenshaw III, the eccentric but brilliant
paleontologist/anthropologist, formerly of Stanford and then Yale universities, until his beliefs drove him away from mainstream science.

Before Niles, Sarah, Will, and the two security men stepped from the
elevator, the loudness of the music blaring from the hallway caught their
attention although the elevator doors were still closed.

"Is Doc Ellenshaw having a party," Sarah looked at her watch, "at
twelve thirty in the morning?"

"Not that I need to explain Professor Ellenshaw to you, but he does his best work alone, and late at night. He says it gives him the freedom to use Europa and other department's equipment without interference from the other supervisors and department heads." Niles looked over at Sarah. "And yes, he has my permission."

The elevator doors had opened to a semidarkened and curving hallway. The heavy beat of the '60s song "I was so much older then, I'm younger than that now," by the Byrds, slammed into the group. Niles smiled and shook his head.

"You two remain here. I promise not to escape through the bowels of the complex," Niles said as he gestured for the two guards to remain.

"Disobeying orders?" Sarah asked.

"Well, sometimes there are certain things security should overlook; Charlie's labs are one of them."

As the song grew louder, the smell of the corridor changed. Sarah looked at Will and he smiled and made a fake frown. As Niles came to the steel door guarding the domain of the Crypto Department, he turned to face Sarah and Mendenhall.

"I know you work for Jack, but I am giving you a direct order: What you see, and whatever else you may come across, is confidential, Lieutenant, understand?"

"I see nothing, Doctor Compton," Will answered.

Niles continued to stare at him.

"And smell nothing," he finished.

Sarah smiled at Will's dilemma.

"Very well," Niles said as he opened the door.

Charles Hindershot Ellenshaw III was sitting at a lab table examining a small skull of an animal that had existed no less than a thousand years before. The dodo bird, once thought to be extinct, was now believed to be alive and well and living in the deep forested areas of northern Germany. Charlie was intrigued and wanted to help out if he could in confirming it. However, the field team freeze Niles had instituted had made his trip to Europe impossible, and he was miffed about it.

"Charlie!" Niles screamed at the door.

Ellenshaw raised his head, his white mane of hair flowing in every direction. His glasses were perched on his forehead and acted as a headband to keep the long hair from getting in his face. The fifty-eight-year-old professor looked around, and when he didn't see anything out of the ordinary, he returned to examining the remains of the dodo.

Niles, frustrated, walked over to the stereo against the near wall and shut down the Byrds. Ellenshaw almost fell from the tall chair in which he was sitting. He looked around wildly, then he saw Compton and the others as they stared at him from a few feet away through the blue-tinted light he had glowing from a large light fixture from above.

"Ah, Niles, Sarah, what a surprise," he said looking from Compton and McIntire, and then he finally caught sight of Will. "And Lieutenant Mendenhall," he said through his teeth as he quickly waved away some of the leftover smoke hovering about his head.

"Professor," Mendenhall said, wanting to laugh at Ellenshaw at his attempt to hide his illegal activities.

"Ah, Miss McIntire, there was a rumor you and the lieutenant here, were, ahh, on the run."

"We are, Charlie. How are you?" she asked with her smile broadening; now knowing why Niles insisted Will's security men and colleagues stay behind.

"Alright, Charlie, Colonel Collins has sent these two to ask you a few questions," Niles said.

"Professor, I need you to think on this after I ask you the question, think hard on anything you can remember, okay?"

"Why, I will try my best."

"Professor, where were you in the summer of 1968?"

As Sarah watched, a faraway look came into Ellenshaw's eyes.

Ellenshaw turned to face Niles as a clear memory of another old song, "Incense and Peppermints," swirled through his head.

"The summer of 1968," Charlie said, but didn't continue.

"Doctor, were you in Canada?" Sarah prompted.

Ellenshaw smiled and then looked at Sarah and Mendenhall.

"We all looked at it as a chance to get away from Stanford and the troubling times in the country back then. A summer retreat to study the Tlingit Indians of the northern country. They lived along the Stikine, it's a river that—"

"We know, Professor, please continue."

"We thought it would be nothing more than research during the day, and one big party at night—you know, forget about the war and protests, assassinations. It was also a real chance at doing some significant anthropological work in the daylight hours."

"Tell us what happened up there, Charlie." Niles watched his old friend's eyes. He was looking even paler than usual in the blue light, and he could see that Charlie was not going to a place he liked very much. He slowly sat down in his chair. Ellenshaw then turned and half smiled at Niles.

"Sorry," he looked back down at his hands.

"We have a time issue here, Charlie," Niles prompted once more.

"That summer was dry; animals of all kinds were coming down from the high country north of the Stikine just to find water. One night while we were sitting around the campfire telling stories and generally having a good time, we started hearing the most terrifying sounds emanating from the deep forest around us. It was like fifty men out in the darkness hitting the trees with baseball bats, truly frightening to some, but I was intrigued as this was a way our prehistoric brethren communicated at night a very long time ago. However, it seemed I was the *only* one that found the disturbance interesting."

Sarah and Will saw that whatever Charlie had witnessed that long ago summer was still with him, and they could tell every word he uttered was the truth.

Ellenshaw related the rest of the story of that summer, starting with his small foray up the Stikine River with their guide, L. T. Lattimer, finding the cave and the wagons, the collected camping gear, and then recounting his encounter with the animal that invaded his dreams every year since that long-ago summer in Canada. The story ended with him paddling down that same river and never seeing Lattimer again.

"What were they?" Mendenhall asked when Charlie paused to wipe his brow.

"Huh?" Ellenshaw asked, not realizing he had stopped talking.

"Those things in the woods?" Mendenhall asked, his eyes never once leaving Ellenshaw.

"I don't know, name them whatever you want, apes, the missing link . . ." He looked from face to face. "Bigfoot, Sasquatch, whatever, I don't care what they're known by, but they were there."

Sarah, Will, and Niles were silent as Charlie placed his glasses back on. Will and Sarah were watching Charlie with wide eyes that wouldn't move away if a bomb had gone off in the large lab.

"You came across the journal with Lattimer's declaration in it, didn't you?" Ellenshaw asked, his brilliant mind figuring out the reasoning of their questions faster than they could have ever thought.

"Yes, Professor," Sarah answered as she took Charlie's shoulder and smiled at him. "Could you show us precisely on the map where this place was that you and Lattimer found this cave?"

"Oh, my, no. I would have to be there, I just couldn't point it out to you."

"You have to try, Charlie. Jack's sister is up there somewhere, and you're the only one that's been there."

"You know, that summer was the reason I dropped my pursuit of anthropology?"

"I didn't know that, Charlie," Niles said, knowing Ellenshaw was going to say what he had to say no matter what.

"Yes, that animal has been with me for thirty-one years. But yet, I have always refused to allow myself the chance to investigate it. It's like I know it's real and my searching once more for it would only attract attention to a species that seems to be doing very well without us. Besides, that Lattimer character always scared the hell out of me, that man was clearly deranged."

"Charlie, we need . . ."

Ellenshaw suddenly stood from his chair. He shook his head.

"I need to go. I have to go, for the colonel's sister, and for me. For me," he said, almost as if he were begging.

Sarah looked from Ellenshaw to the face of a worried Niles Compton. He took a deep breath and saw the hope in the professor's eyes.

"Okay, Charlie. But the priority is Jack's sister, nothing else. Find your Bigfoot if you can, but assist the colonel first."

Ellenshaw could only nod his head. He looked thankfully from Compton to Sarah and then to Mendenhall.

"Thank you."

Mendenhall watched the professor for a moment and then turned away and mumbled to himself. "This is great. First, killer Russians, and now another myth that couldn't possibly have existed an hour ago, and they are both going to try and take a bite out of my ass."

Sarah just patted Mendenhall on the back nodding her head.

"And don't forget about having a Frenchman along who wants to kill all of us, and then there's half the U.S. government trying to hunt us down."

"Yeah," Will said, looking off into space. "Who needs the monster in the woods? We may not even make it to where we're going."

"See, it's all in the way you prioritize things."

PART TWO
THE VALLEY OF CHULIMANTAN

6

With maps of British Columbia and Alaska tacked to every piece of exposed wall inside of the small hotel room, Collins, Alexander, and Farbeaux compared the description of an area along the Stikine River taken from L. T. Lattimer's letter home on the back of the last page of the Petrov journal.

"I don't know Jack, how many times has the Stikine changed its course, even if only by feet after a hundred years?" Punchy asked. "I think if I returned to Ottawa, I may be able to get a better handle on this. Someone in our interior department may have something to offer.

Jack stepped back from the large map and looked at Alexander. "You know better than anyone that if we went to any branch of any government with this, not only would we be arrested, they would fill those areas with so many Mounties and bureaucratic red tape, Lynn would surely be killed."

"Damn. Sorry, Jack, maybe I need some sleep."

Jack nodded and then looked at his old friend. "We'll have time to rest on our way up to your backyard."

Farbeaux sat at the small table and sipped a large cup of coffee, grimacing at the horrible taste. He turned the pages of the Petrov journal easily, and even as he did he felt the brittleness of the paper.

"Beside the description of the overhanging bluffs and medium-size plateau our Colonel Petrov describes at his last encampment, the exactness of the area leaves much to be desired. Too much has changed."

Jack looked back and saw the Frenchman as he thumbed through the pages. "Lattimer used the journal to discover his gold deposit. Does it say anything about where that strike was made in the papers and letters?"

Farbeaux closed the old diary and then picked up the plastic-covered letter still etched on the last page of the journal. He shook his head and then handed Jack the pile. "I see no reference about his find anywhere, other than he found a wonderful strike."

Jack shook his head. He was beginning to think they would stand a better chance just making their way up to the Stikine and hoping for the best. He figured the Russians couldn't be that inconspicuous in that wilderness area. He became frustrated and slapped the page in his hand against the table, and then sat. He knew he was fooling himself: The Stikine was only the most dense and nearly unexplored region in North America. It could be like finding a needle in the proverbial haystack. In frustration, he started reading Lattimer's announcement again about his find and declaration.

"Why was a Russian colonel even in that part of the world? How could anyone get that lost, especially a trained army officer? And just who in the hell are these 'children' he keeps mentioning?" Alexander asked. "It makes me think this whole book may have been written by a madman. Or, have you even considered the fact that this whole thing is a hoax?"

"I guess we'll ask Sarah what Doc Ellenshaw has to say about it," Collins said as he rubbed his eyes.

Farbeaux was beginning to agree with the Canadian CSIS man. "I believe the man may have been a deserter from the Russian army, after all, they were going through political turmoil at the time, if I remember right it was a little thing called the Russian revolution."

"But run to Alaska, get lost, bury some wagons full of gold, then disappear."

Jack looked at Alexander and then slowly shuffled through the papers again. As he did, he finally found the notation he was looking for. He smiled and then laid the papers down.

"Son of a bitch, it was right there the whole time, and we boy geniuses missed it."

Farbeaux just raised his right eyebrow and took another sip of the bitter coffee. Punchy Alexander turned away from the large maps to look at Jack.

"What did we miss?"

"Here," Jack said as he slid the journal across the table and pointed to the second to the last page. It was notes jotted down by Lattimer. "He said he finally had his strike, hallelujah, he said it was right in front of him the whole time, under a bluff just where the diary said Petrov and his deserters made their last camp. At this site he came across strange-looking aluminum, a hundred yards of it."

"Strike, Jack, not gold-filled wagons, and just because he found a bunch of aluminum cans—I just don't see where any of that helps," Alexander said.

Farbeaux looked from the letter to Alexander who had joined them at the table. He then fixed Jack with his own penetrating eyes. "I think I see what you're saying, Colonel."

"Lattimer didn't find his strike, he found the diary and then he found at least one of the wagons of gold."

"Whoa, that's stretching things, Jack," Punchy said with a shake of his head.

"No, he tells us it was the mother lode, and it wasn't a deposit he found in the river right here." Jack pointed to the dates of the first notes in the upper right-hand corner. The pencil used was faded, but the date was clearly visible: July 22, 1968. "That is the date he wrote his relatives on the back page of the last entry of the journal. Now look here, the last thing he writes is the fact that he was sending Ellenshaw back with the journal and he would take the strike and head back when he had assistance from the local Indians to help load it."

"So?" Alexander asked.

"The date, old friend, on that last letter—July 23, 1968. Now, how can he have a strike, a find of any kind, and have it dug out of the ground, packed, and ready to go in one day, or even two, three, or four?"

"I'll be damned," Alexander said. "Yes, I would say, maybe he found it already smelted and put into coin, maybe American double eagles, just as . . ."

"The diary said," Jack and Henri finished for Punchy.

"Now that is what's called a gold strike," Alexander said smiling. Then the smile faded. "Still doesn't say where along the Stikine to look."

"I think it does," Henri said, shuffling through the letters. "Now, the map that was inside of the journal is worthless, no markings of any value. Except for this." Farbeaux pulled over the last page Jack was holding and then the map with Lattimer's little chicken scratches on its old face. "Here, he says he's sending Charlie Ellenshaw and the grad students back to the camp, and he figured they could find their way back in a matter of two days down river."

"Yes?" Punchy said, but Jack already pieced it together and so he stood and walked over to the map and looked.

"The wording, Mr. Alexander," Henri said. "He mentions the camp; obviously we thought he was saying it was the camp of the graduate students he was hired as guide for. Now, anywhere on the upper Stikine is many more days by boat back to civilization than just a mere two days, not two days journey, so it has to be another camp, perhaps—"

"A fishing camp," Jack said turning to face the two men. "The Tlingit Indian Fishing Camp to be exact." He jabbed a finger at a spot on the large map. "This Wahachapee settlement right here."

"Even if it isn't so, Colonel, I believe it is a good place to start looking," the Frenchman said as he stood, walked into the bathroom, and poured out his coffee. "If young Sarah brings back anything at all from your complex, Colonel, I pray it's real coffee, French roast if possible."

Jack didn't answer the remark, knowing Farbeaux was trying to take his mind off of Lynn if only for a moment. Instead, he just turned and looked at the map once more and studied the legend at the top and its wholly unintentional foreboding message: UNEXPLORED REGION—STIKINE ARCHIPELAGO WILDERNESS.

Two hours later, after Jack had just about worn a path in the dirty carpet from the hotel room's large window and back again to the map, Sarah finally returned from the complex at Nellis. She hugged Jack and through the tenseness of his body, she could tell he was chomping at the bit to get moving.

Jack slowly pushed Sarah away when he saw that standing between her back and the front of Will Mendenhall was none other than Charles Hindershot Ellenshaw III.

"Oh, no, this isn't for you, Doc, sorry," Jack said, eyeing Sarah and Mendenhall with a ferocious glare. "There's enough of us probably going to jail over this."

Charlie, replete with a bright orange hunting vest and green pants and shirt, pushed his glasses back up on his nose and stared at Jack, not moving. He shuffled from one foot to the other.

"It was Niles. He insisted Charlie join our band of outlaws," Sarah said, stepping around Collins, and rolling her eyes at Alexander and Farbeaux.

"Uh . . . Colonel, I think I need to be with you on this trip. To help you get your sister back."

"Colonel, the doc here may have something you need to hear," Mendenhall said, still standing outside of the room, looking almost as nervous as Charlie.

Collins just stared at Will. His eyes told the young lieutenant everything he needed to know.

"Or not," Mendenhall said looking away. "Uh, we brought some supplies and a little equipment . . . I'll go check on it." Will bounded away and then down the stairs without looking back. He had decided to let Sarah battle the colonel on behalf of Ellenshaw.

"Jack, I think you better listen to what Charlie has to say—he knows about the area we're looking for, he can find it and recognize the spot."

Collins finally gave in and stepped aside. "Alright, Doc, you have two minutes to convince me you're worth the weight we have to compensate for on the plane."

Hindershot smiled meekly and stepped into the room. He nodded at Punchy, who only stared at the crazed white-haired professor. Then Charlie saw Farbeaux and stopped dead in his tracks.

"That's right, Professor, strange circumstances call for strange bedfellows," Henri said with a nod of his head. "If I remember right, you're the monster man, correct?"

"I am a crypto zoologist, yes"

"I would have thought you would have had quite enough of your very strange profession down in the Amazon, Doctor," Farbeaux said as he stood and slapped the tall thin man on the back.

"Alright, you can tell your story on the way to the plane," Jack said as he gathered the maps that were pinned to the wall. "If it isn't a good one, you'll have to describe the area as best you can and then hitchhike back to Nellis and tell the director, thanks but no thanks. Am I clear on that, Doc?" Collins said as he quickly folded the maps and shot Ellenshaw another withering look.

"Yes, uh, yes, Colonel, very clear."

"Well, we few, we desperate few, we band of brothers," Henri looked at Sarah and smiled and half bowed, "and sister, shall we head north, and not stop until we fall off the edge of the world."

It was only Charlie that smiled as the others were already leaving. "Actually, I think we only fall off the map, Colonel Farbeaux."

Henri raised his right brow as he gestured for Ellenshaw to go out before him.

"That, my dear Professor Ellenshaw, is just the thing that scares me."

TWO HOURS LATER

Everett and Ryan had been standing beside the seaplane for what seemed to them half the night and now they were only two hours away from dawn.

Everett would glance at his watch and then look up and around the steep incline that held the trickle of water at bay in the L.A. River. The chain-link fence surrounding the river was high, and stopped all but the racers and drug dealers from venturing into the basin. Carl was getting an old and reliable feeling at the back of his neck.

Ryan walked around the right wing float of the Grumman and bent over to check the main landing gear. The tire pressure on that side was low, but there was nothing he could do about it. He remained in his position and acted as if he were checking other areas of the large wheel.

"Captain, I have the feeling we are—"

"Being watched," Everett finished for him. "Stay where you're at for a minute; keep a low silhouette."

Up until this point in time, the large Grumman seaplane had only drawn casual lookers, and they had been lucky thus far that none of them had called the police to ask why there was an antique plane sitting under a bridge in the L.A. River. Everett thanked the heavens that everyone in L.A. kept to themselves: If it didn't affect them, it was none of their business. But now the naval captain was beginning to wonder if their luck had run out.

Against the streetlights from above the river, Everett finally spied the watchers: at least two men, but he knew there were more. He shook his head as he recognized the windbreakers favored by the FBI field offices. *To them*, he thought, *that was plainclothes.*

"We have feds to the left and probably more behind us," he said to Ryan. "Okay, Lieutenant, it's Acting 101 time. I want you to laugh and then go around to the stairs and climb inside; I'll walk to the tail section. When you hear the word, fire this damn thing up."

"Okay, but what about the colonel. Shouldn't we—"

"Gentlemen, this is the FBI. Please stand clear of the aircraft."

Everett closed his eyes, knowing he had been snuck up on from behind.

Two agents came from the dark at the back of the plane. They had weapons drawn and pointed at both he and Ryan. He felt one of the agents remove his Berretta nine-millimeter from the back of his waistband. The other waited for Ryan to straighten up before attempting to take his.

"Your record is indicative of a good sailor, Captain Everett, I would expect you to come quietly. Then we'll take Colonel Collins and the rest when they arrive."

"Look, you know what we're doing; why don't you just turn around and leave," Everett said as he felt the agent's hand checking him for other weapons.

"We're following orders, Captain. If we could let you go, we would. The president says you'll be stepping on a lot of toes, so for now you have to step aside and let our office and the Canadian authorities handle this."

"My friend, since you've read my file, you surely must have read about the man that is in charge here. Do you think this situation will stand?" Carl asked as he finally turned and saw for the first time that the FBI agent was young, possibly too young.

"Our bosses don't like sending us out blind, Captain. We know enough about Colonel Collins that this entire basin is surrounded by fifteen other agents.

Everett looked around. He saw passing headlights on the old bridges in front of them and in back. The one they were under was quiet for the moment, and he suspected there was at least one team of agents up there.

Ryan came out from under the undercarriage with his hands up. He shrugged his shoulders in the false light of the streetlamps above them. "Captain, it's your duty to tell these guys; if you won't, I will."

The agent holding Everett at arm's length looked at Ryan over the large SEAL's shoulders, but refrained from asking what Ryan was talking about.

"Tell us what?" asked the second agent leading Ryan to the front of the plane.

"Listen," Everett said, lowering his hands, and then raising his brows as if to ask if it was alright. The agent nodded but stepped as far back as he could to keep out of range of Carl's long legs and arms. "I'm a nice guy, hell, I know you're only doing your jobs; even Ryan there has his moments of clarity, but the man we work for, he's, well, how do I put this?"

"A prick when mad," Ryan finished for him.

"Thank you, Mr. Ryan. You see, it's not just me, Colonel Collins has his mind set on something and—"

There was a thud and a grunt from above them on the bridge. Then there was a clatter of metal and the sound of something sliding down the steep slope of concrete.

"Never mind," Everett said. "Too late."

The first agent frowned and then relaxed, he still looked around nervously, but then he cowboyed up and tried looking confident.

"Nice try," he said as he reached for his radio. "Two and three, this is one, sit-rep."

There was only static. The agent looked a little different than he had just a second before. "Units two and three, sit-rep," he said just a little too loud, telling Everett and Ryan that he was becoming more than just a little concerned. Carl just grimaced mockingly and shrugged. The agent brought his own weapon up and made sure Everett knew he was covered. Carl just shook his head. That was when they heard footsteps, a lot of them. As they watched, three groups of men were slipping and sliding down the concrete slopes of the river. They were followed by others, and one group had what looked like a white long-haired scarecrow of a man who fell on his butt, but popped right up and kept following the others.

The agent couldn't help it; he turned when he saw the three long parades of men coming down from above. At that moment, Everett easily reached out and took the agent by the wrist and simply twisted the gun from his hand. Ryan wasn't as adept at disarming a man as the captain—he raised his boot into the air, stomped on the agent's right toe, and clipped him on the neck, freeing the gun with Ryan catching it, juggling it and then finally securing the weapon.

"Are we clear down there, Mr. Everett?" a voice called from the dark.

"Clear, Colonel," Everett called out as he ejected the ammunition clip from the nine-millimeter and then the chambered round, he eased the gun back into the agents hand. Jason Ryan did the same.

Finally, out of the darkness marched eight FBI agents, looking mad and very frustrated. One of the men looked at the man Carl had just disarmed and shook his head.

"They were on us before we knew anyone was there."

"You should have remembered your training from Quantico far better than you did," Jack said as he stepped up from behind the agents. "There is no such thing as a secure perimeter in an open civilian area." Collins looked at the agent in charge. "Your men became too complacent with passersby; they were more concerned about being seen than securing any hostiles"—he leaned into the agent—"we, sir, are the hostiles."

Farbeaux, standing next to Sarah and Ellenshaw and still covering three of the agents himself, smiled and knew Collins was the most worthy opponent he had ever come across. It took Jack only moments to smell the ambush as they passed by the bridge, and only another few seconds to figure the plan of taking the agents without anyone getting hurt.

"Colonel, I told them after reading your unclassified army file that we didn't have enough men, but you know how Washington can be." The agent in charge looked down at his feet, and then he shrugged and looked at Collins once more. "Well, you have us, but as one former soldier to another, I'll ask you to reconsider and let others handle this situation. Give over the information you have and let *us* go after the Russians; we have friends up there."

Jack looked at the agent after nodding at Ryan to get the aircraft preflighted. "We have a friend here and I think he even speaks Canadian."

Punchy wanted to laugh, but he figured Jack was only trying to make a point.

"Then, Colonel, we tried." The agent held out his hand. "Good luck, and I hope you get what it is you are going after."

Collins looked at the hand in front of him, and then shook it.

"Oh, this is very touching, but we may want to think about getting the hell out of here, Colonel. The L.A. police may not be so cooperative," Farbeaux said as he waved for Mendenhall to bring the supplies down, as he turned to assist. "In case you have forgotten, we left two of their brethren tied up at the Chavez house."

Jack closed his eyes in frustration. He had forgotten.

"Don't concern yourself, they were found an hour after you left the house," the FBI agent said. "Colonel, I'll give you two hours; after that, I have to tell them you're heading north," he said releasing Jack's hand. Then he smiled, "I believe I overheard north of Toronto if I'm not mistaken."

This time Jack did return the smile, "Yes, Toronto."

Ten minutes later, the FBI agents held flashlights at the bridge that was four hundred feet in front of the idling Grumman. The plane was filled to the brim with men and equipment. Sarah was squeezed into a seat that included two backpacks, one rifle, and Farbeaux. Every time she looked around, she saw that crooked smile of the Frenchman and the bobbing up and down of his brows.

"Don't worry, my little Sarah, you may only have to bear my advances for a very few moments, I don't expect this antique to get off the ground—I don't think she was made to carry this much of a load."

"Thanks, Henri. Between you or the bridge, either way, this is going to suck."

Ryan, with Jack sitting in the copilot's seat next to him, reached up to the overhead console and jammed both throttles all the way to their stops.

"When I say so, Colonel, you pull back on that wheel as far as possible and as hard as you can," Ryan said over the noise of the roaring engines as he released the brakes.

Jack looked very uncomfortable taking the three-quarter steering wheel of the Grumman. He touched it gingerly at first, then grabbed on tightly. "Is it supposed to vibrate this much?" he asked, his eyes wide open and staring at the fast-approaching bridge and the agents holding their flashlights.

"How in the hell should I know, Colonel? I've only flown a propeller-driven trainer three times in my life!" he shouted and then roared with laughter as he pulled back on the wheel, "Now Colonel, *Now!*"

The seaplane bounced once, scattering the agents before it. Then it bounced again.

One of Alice Hamilton's contributions to the upgrade of the old seaplane was to incorporate a flight computer that not only projected a holographic image of the approaching bridge, but also carried the voice trait of the Europa computer back at the Event Group complex. It was she who started warning Ryan of the encroaching danger straight ahead.

"Warning, obstacle detected. Warning, max weight overload. Warning, obstacle detected in aircraft path. Divert! Divert! Divert!" said the sexy female voice just as the Grumman bounced hard off the concrete.

"Are you going to hop over the damn bridge?" Collins asked loudly.

Finally, the nose of the Grumman lifted free of the riverbed and rose. "Come on, old girl, fly, damn it, *fly!*" Ryan screamed while everyone in the back of the plane prayed and waited for the sudden impact that would tell them the bridge was old, but built well.

The Grumman climbed and as it barely screamed over the railing of the overpass, they felt the impact of the rear wheel as it slammed into one of the old streetlamps that lined the bridge. The glass and steel and the seaplanes wheel careened off onto the pavement of the bridge, causing several cars to spin out to avoid the flying debris. Then the seaplane suddenly took a nosedive back into the river, but Ryan quickly compensated with full flaps, pumping furiously at the old hydraulic system. Finally, the plane rose into the night sky, flying barely above the power lines and over houses. Ryan relaxed when he felt the centerline of the plane level off and the weight factor lessen as the Grumman rose. He slowly started to pump the flap handle once more.

"Where to, Colonel?" Ryan asked as he finally got the nerve to take a hand from the wheel and wipe his sweating brow.

"We'll refuel at the mouth of the Columbia River in Oregon, and then we'll push into Vancouver, and just pray the Canadian authorities don't shoot us down. We're not on speaking terms like we are with the FBI."

"Amen to that."

Collins finally made his own body relax as Ryan made his turn north over the Port of Los Angeles. He swallowed and finally spared a thought for his sister, praying she was still alive.

"Hang on, baby girl, just hang on a little bit longer," Jack mumbled to himself as he stared at his reflection in the side window.

The few members of the Event Group had made it out of the first phase of a mission that for the first time had no plan at all, other than to search—and in the case of Jack Collins, to *destroy*, if that search failed.

60 MILES SOUTHEAST OF DEASE LAKE, BRITISH COLUMBIA (THE UPPER STIKINE RIVER BASIN)

Lynn Simpson had to hand it to the two Russians and their small army of employees and guides. They had arranged everything from food and rest stops to refueling areas on the long and arduous helicopter ride from the town of Wrangell, just below the Tongass National Forest in Alaska, to the Stikine River, sixty miles south of Dease Lake, British Columbia. Lynn was surprised that Sagli and Deonovich had been so free with the information about the expedition they were on. She guessed they figured she wouldn't be coming back with them at any rate, so why not allow her full access to their immediate plans.

The four brand-new Sikorsky helicopters skirted the river as low as the trees would allow. They had almost run headlong into a small Bell Ranger of the Royal Canadian Mounted Police an hour before, but the expert pilots on the Russian payroll had avoided them nicely by dipping below the small range of mountains that flanked the Stikine. The helicopters were loaded with men and equipment that had been waiting for them in Seattle, undoubtedly the staging point for every murderous operation since they killed Serta, the lumber magnate a week earlier.

As Lynn watched the Stikine Mountain Range looming before them, she was approached by a man who had been introduced to her as the expedition's doctor: Leonovshki something or other—she couldn't keep all of the names straight, which told her she wasn't doing her job right. If she got out of this mess she had every intention of bringing every one of these bastards to justice. The doctor unceremoniously grabbed her hand and started to unwrap the bandage that covered the area where her index finger used to be. He looked it over, poked the inflamed skin around the wound once or twice, and then grunted his satisfaction. He rewrapped the amputation with a fresh wrapping and then rummaged in his black bag and brought out a syringe.

"Antibiotics," he said as he leaned forward.

"Why bother? I mean, it's not like they're going to let me go after they find what they want."

"I do as I am told, young lady. What my employers plans are, do not concern me; just what they are paying me."

"Spoken like a true mercenary."

The doctor gestured for her to stand up and lower her denim pants that had been supplied to her a day ago. She did, not exposing as much as the young doctor would have liked. He punched the needle home. As she looked around, several of the other killers for hire were admiring the upper portion of her ass.

"In the end, aren't we all just mercenaries? Even you with your agency masters?"

Lynn wasn't about to get into a philosophical debate with the doctor, so she just buttoned her pants and then sat down, staring at the others until they turned away. The doctor reached up and pulled down a plastic bag and handed it to her.

"I believe this should be about your size. The days are still warm here, but the nights can get cold."

Lynn opened the clear bag and pulled out an expensive, bright yellow down jacket. She looked back at the doctor and frowned.

"This would make for a good target in the woods."

The doctor ignored the comment and walked away, using the tied-down equipment to steady himself as the helicopter rose and dove over the trees below.

Lynn placed the jacket beside her and watched as the large helicopter started to descend after smoothing out. They were near some sort of small settlement that looked almost deserted. She spied a few small fishing boats, not more than fifteen feet in length as the helicopter she was riding in circled the settlement. The pilot finally sat the transport down in a small clearing about three hundred yards from the thick forest that lined the base of the mountains. As she watched, the other helicopters did the same, spacing themselves far apart as their wheels touched down on the rocky soil.

Lynn didn't move and was soon approached by Dmitri Sagli. He was wearing expensive hiking boots, denim jeans, and a bright red shirt. He looked ridiculously like a lumberjack of old. He even had suspenders on. She couldn't help but smile, although she hid it behind her hand.

"We are at the Wahachapee Fishing Camp. It is small and is populated by Tlingit Indians. If you make one attempt at either escape, or to relay your predicament to the locals, we will not only shoot you, but everyone here, children included. Do you understand?"

"I've understood you since you first opened your foul mouth in Virginia."

"Then you do understand—it won't be us killing these people, but you." Sagli turned and made his way to the lowering stairs as his ten men started unloading the supplies and equipment.

Lynn shook her head and then grabbed the coat she had been given and followed Sagli out of the helicopter. As she stepped onto the rocky soil, she was amazed at the raw beauty of the area. With the mountains behind and in front of them and the river coursing through the center, the spot was an ideal location for nature lovers. However, as she saw that the area was void of people, her enthusiasm quickly diminished.

A hundred yards to her front, she saw Deonovich and Sagli speaking together in hushed tones, not once sparing her a look. As her eyes scanned the area, she saw what looked like a small general store, perhaps there to sell bait to the local Indian population. Next to the three-story market, there was a large icehouse and its chilling tower. A small warehouse was at its base and several of the local men were standing on the dock, watching the newcomers as they unloaded. The men were of various ages: some had the long hair of the young native, while other older men wore their hair short. Their skin was copper toned from living and working in the open and, like all fishermen, had the honest look of laborers. She saw an old woman coming from the river carrying two baskets filled with fish—the heavy Indian woman looked her way and then quickly in the direction of the two Russians. It was as if she didn't even notice all of the equipment being off loaded from the four helicopters.

Good for you, Lynn thought to herself, *the less curious these locals are, the more likely they will survive the murderous group that was invading their tranquil home.*

"Sikorsky S-76s—four of them—now these are some fishermen that know how to travel."

Lynn was startled as the voice came from behind her. She turned and saw a young woman, maybe sixteen years old, as she placed a hand on the sleek light blue side of the tail boom of the helicopter she had ridden in. Lynn looked back at Sagli and Deonovich, but they were busy supervising the unloading of their equipment. She turned back to face the pretty girl in the dark green overalls and the black shirt. Lynn could see the twin braids that coursed down her back and she had a face as bright as sunshine, setting off her raven black hair. She was surprised to see a Caucasian girl among so many native Canadians.

"I see you know your aircraft," Lynn said as she approached the young girl.

"Sure, we see a lot of nice and very expensive things here; you know, rich doctors and such when they hire out for fishing and hunting guides. I also attend college at Washington State, so I do have an idea how the rest of the world lives and plays." The girl saw the confusion her statement caused the stranger. "I was homeschooled by my grandmother and then I started college early. It wasn't as tough as people make out."

Lynn smiled and then looked around her, surprised at the emptiness of the fishing camp.

"I didn't mean to be condescending, you just didn't look like a student . . . I mean . . . uh, hell, I don't know what I mean."

The girl removed her hand from the aluminum skin of the Sikorsky and looked at Lynn, examining her.

"You don't look like you're much of a fisherman or hunter."

"Touché," Lynn said with a smile as she saw the girls eyes shift from her to the large group of men placing crates and bags along the shore of the river. When she looked back at Lynn, the girl had a curious look on her face, and then it vanished as quickly as it had appeared.

"So, do your parents operate this settlement?"

"My parents are dead. I live with my grandmother, and yes, this is all hers, everything from a mile up the mountains to the water that flows in the river—bought and paid for many years ago. My family buys fish from the few groups of Tlingit Indians left in this area. We freeze them and sell them down south in Vancouver and Juneau."

"I'm sorry about your parents."

The girl smiled. "Why would you be sorry? I never knew them, my mother died giving birth to me and my father was killed a few years after that. I'm afraid all I have are pictures." Her smile broadened. "Would you like to see them?"

Lynn couldn't resist, she liked the young girl immediately. She knew she could be no more than sixteen years old, but she said she was in college already. That would made her something special in Lynn's mind. Plus, her smile was infectious.

"Yes I would," she said quickly. "I would also like to meet the grandmother of a girl smart enough to attend college at such a young age." Lynn watched for a reaction, as maybe there was some way she could get the message through to these people not to interfere with their new visitors. She didn't trust the word of Sagli not to hurt and kill to get what it was they came for—or to cover up that fact.

"My name is Marla Petrovich."

"I'm Lynn. Nice to meet you, Marla."

As Lynn turned to follow the girl, she could not help but notice the attention Marla paid to the lined-up supplies and equipment. It was if she were examining the reasoning behind some of the more exotic of it. Her eyes lingered the longest on four large tarp-covered pieces. To the girl's credit, she kept quiet as she bounded past Sagli and Deonovich.

Sagli watched Lynn and the girl for a moment, and then said a last word to Deonovich and then he followed Lynn and the girl as they walked toward the small two-story store, his eyes never leaving the two women.

Sagli's large partner watched as the three disappeared into the wooden-framed store. At that moment a breeze sprang up and moved the rotors of the four helicopters. Deonovich turned away from the dust that the wind had kicked up, and as he did, he thought he heard the far-off sound of a tree falling. When he looked up after the sudden wind had died down, he stared as far as he could across the river. It seemed as if something had moved there, but the darkness of the woods and the long shadows the giant trees cast made seeing anything impossible. As he turned away, he suddenly knew what the feeling was that he had when looking across the fast-moving river—he felt he was being watched.

As Lynn went through the old door, she was amazed to see that the store was far more modern than she ever would have suspected from the old wooden structure from the outside. There were new advertisements for Coors, Molson, Moosehead, and Budweiser brands of beers. There were up-to-date displays of all brands of fishing equipment and even had a rental counter for those items. The floor was not made out of wood, but was a bright and shiny linoleum that was beige in color. The shelves were clean and dusted and full of canned goods, and even had a quaint sign hanging from the ceiling that said AIR TIGHTS. The store even had a dairy department that carried fresh milk and eggs.

"Well, this is it, the last stop of humanity before reaching the wilds of the Stikine," Marla said as she gestured for Lynn to follow her around the large counter situated at the right of the aisles.

Lynn felt Sagli step into the store and eye his surroundings with suspicion. He allowed himself to relax when he saw there were no apparent customers inside the large store. Lynn could see that he adjusted something under his open coat, obviously warning her that he was armed.

"I have most of my pictures upstairs, but there are a few which Grandmother keeps here. We call it our ghost wall." Marla smiled as she pointed at an old black-and-white picture of two people. One was a large blond man and the other was a smallish woman who had obvious Indian blood in her, and was beautiful. The large man, at least six foot four or five, had his arm around the small woman who was a good foot and a half shorter than the man. "These are my parents; Grandmother says that my mom was actually pregnant with me when this was taken."

"Your mother was a beautiful woman," Lynn said turning and smiling at the obviously proud girl.

"What did your father do for a living—run this store?" Sagli asked as he stepped up to the counter and removed his pair of work gloves.

"Her father was a guide. No man in the world knew this area better than my Eric; he was raised along the Stikine and never left her waters."

Lynn and Sagli both turned to see an old woman come out of a back room wiping her hands on a dish towel. She eyed the strangers with an arched brow. She was dressed in a large pair of denim pants and wore a bright red-and-black wool shirt. Her hair was pulled back into a bun and she looked spry for a woman in her early eighties.

"Oh, hello," Lynn said as she stepped out from behind the counter.

"You folks lookin' for a guide? We usually get advance notice of fishermen headin' our way by the Mounties down at Jackson's Bluff."

"We flew in from Juneau," Sagli said, eyeing the old woman.

"From Alaska, but you are Russian, right?" the heavyset woman said as she gained the counter, and stepped behind it, looking at her granddaughter.

"Grandmother, this is Lynn. Lynn, this is my grandmother Helena, and—I don't know your name," she said turning to Sagli.

The Russian didn't say anything, he looked at Lynn and then put his gloves back on.

"So, I take it you are traveling up the Stikine?" the grandmother asked.

Lynn was about to answer when Sagli slapped one glove against the other. "We will be doing some exploring and sightseeing."

"Sightseeing? Along the Stikine?" the woman said with a smile and a raised brow.

"You'll have to excuse Grandmother, she gets in these moods," Marla said as she came from around the counter. "But she's only concerned; the Stikine can be a very dangerous place if you don't know what you're doing or exactly where you are going. The river can be calm one minute, and with just a small thunderstorm up north, can become a raging torrent the next."

"We are well equipped for any contingency, young woman," Sagli announced.

"Many a fool has gone into the forest, the mountains, and the Stikine Valley well equipped, and we would find some of that fine equipment floating back down a week or two later," the grandmother said as she unlocked the cash register. "Now, is there anything we can help you with before you go?"

Sagli eyed both the young girl and the old woman, then he took Lynn by the arm and pulled her toward the door. Lynn tried to look back, but the Russian kept a steady pressure on her by squeezing her arm so that she knew there would be no more conversation exchanged.

After the two left the store, Marla turned to her grandmother, who was watching the activity outside with interest.

"You don't like that man, do you?" she asked.

Without turning to face the girl, the old woman said, "Russian."

"Grandmother, we do have Russian in our blood. You said it yourself: There are so many Russians in this area of Canada, you can't throw a rock without hitting one."

The old woman just looked at her granddaughter and then smiled. "Come now, help me with the baking. You need to earn your keep before you go back to school."

The girl shook her head and then headed for the back, but the old woman stayed and watched as the newcomers inflated giant Zodiac rubber boats, eight of them in all. Then she watched as the helicopters lifted off and then disappeared over the giant trees. All the while, the Russian who had been in the store watched her through the window.

"Goddamn Russians," was all she said.

Before she turned away, she noticed the face of the smallish woman looking at her. There was something in her stance from that distance that told her that there was trouble. Then the old woman's eyes went to the men loading the supplies onto the boat and she couldn't help but notice the plastic-wrapped items being stored at the bottom of each boat. She knew what they were loading, and they weren't your standard hunting rifles—they were automatic weapons.

She eased herself away from the window and went into a back room just outside of the kitchen. There was an ancient rolltop desk with all the stores financials laid out on its top, and above that on the desk's upper most reaches, was a large radio. She picked up the old-fashioned microphone and then hit the transmit button.

"Charlie, do you have your ears on down there?" she said into the mike and then waited.

"RCMP, Jackson's Bluff," came the answer through the wall-mounted speaker.

"Charlie Kemp, is that you?"

"Helena, how's things up to the camp, eh?"

"Charlie, I think we may need a few of your Mounties up this way. We have visitors, and I don't think they're here for the fishing."

7

TWENTY-SEVEN MILES NORTH OF WAHACHAPEE
FISHING CAMP
THE STIKINE RIVER

Lynn watched as the first four large Zodiacs pulled onto the rocky shoreline of the river. She had been surprised they had traveled as far as they had after the sun had set as the river was one large twisting and turning roller-coaster ride since they started out from the fishing camp. As the men piled out of the huge rubber craft and their two hundred horse-power Evenrude engines were shut down, Lynn was cognizant of how quiet the woods were around them. The sound of the fast-flowing Stikine helped with masking the sounds of the men unloading equipment, but she could tell that when all was said and done, the wilderness would let you hear for miles around.

As she stood at the rear of the boat, her wrist was grabbed by Dmitri Sagli. He held a Remington .306 hunting rifle with a twelve-power scope in his other hand. His eyes met hers, and then darted away, scanning the area around their landing site.

"I will post no guard on you," he said, finally turning back to look at her. His eyes turned silver in the light of the rising moon. "This area is inaccessible; escaping would only hurry the process of your demise, so once we have made camp, think about what I have said. You may stand a small chance with us, but against a hungry bear, or a pack of wolves, you'll will have no chance at all." He let go of her wrist and then started walking away to the area he had chosen to make camp just inside of the tree line. "We will wait for my partner to join us with the last two boats. We will be here for at least twelve hours; use that time to rest—it will be the last chance you have before we push on to our destination."

Lynn rubbed her wrist and then looked around. She had not noticed before, but Deonovich and several of his mercenaries were also nowhere to be seen; as a matter of fact, she hadn't seen him since they left the fishing village.

Lynn stepped free of the Zodiac and started up the shoreline. She looked at the ancient and very foreboding trees that lined the Stikine, and shivered. She had been in wilderness areas before, but she could never remember being in a place where she felt as though she were an entire world away from civilization. As she looked skyward, she swore she could see every star in the universe as they twinkled and winked far above her. It was like looking at an incoming tide of luminescent water as it rushed to shore.

The men were quick and efficient at setting up large five-man tents. As they worked, Lynn could see that they all shouldered automatic rifles and all kept a wary eye on the river. They also watched the very tree line that held their small camp safely hidden. As they set the last of the tent poles and made their ropes tight, Lynn saw several boxes of large caliber ammunition. *What were these men preparing for, a Canadian Mountie's full-scale invasion—or maybe something else?*

"Lions and tigers and bears, oh my," she said under her breath nervously, trying to take her mind off the pain in her hand.

It was two hours later and Lynn had been supplied with a tin plate with rich beef stew almost overflowing the rim. She had discovered she had been near starvation. She had greedily shoveled the food into her mouth as the Russian mercenaries watched her with large smiles, shaking their heads. After she had eaten, she was shown to a small two-person tent and told that was where she would sleep. Not trusting the men she was currently keeping company with, Lynn silently pulled a small fallen branch into the tent with her. Once inside, she saw that an electric lantern had been placed in with her. She turned it on and saw a brand-new sleeping bag and a large bottle of drinking water, and beside it were three painkillers.

Lynn grimaced as she placed the small tree branch over her knee and tried to break it. The leafy branch was still too green to snap cleanly. She redoubled her effort and was rewarded with a snap. It didn't break through all the way, but she knew it would work out. She bent and twisted the branch until it broke and then she pulled, slicing the limb into two separate pieces, with one end sharper than the other. She smiled and tossed the blunt end away, keeping the small jabbing spear and poking at the air with it. At least she could poke someone's eye out with it if she were attacked in her lonely nylon-built domain.

Now that she was armed, she pulled out of her jacket, it being warm enough outside to make the night at least comfortable. She lay down on the sleeping bag and listened to the little spits of laughter coming from the men outside of her tent as she swallowed the three painkillers. Listening to the men, it was as though these bastards were on a vacation. She shook her head and closed her eyes.

An hour later she awoke to the strangest noise she had ever heard in the field. It seemed as though it came from miles away. As she sat up, she heard men as they unzipped their tents and stepped out, also questioning what it was they were hearing. She didn't understand the Russian language, but knew that the sound unnerved the men.

Lynn stood and cautiously approached the tent's flap and slowly slid the zipper down. She saw men standing around one dwindling fire pit. The soft glow showed her that they were, indeed, looking to the north, far past where the Stikine turned at a sharp angle. As she cocked her head to listen, the men were shushed to silence by Sagli as he stepped from his own large well-appointed tent. He was bare-chested but held the .306 at the ready; he went as far as to pull the bolt back and chamber a round.

The noise dwindled, and then picked up in intensity. It sounded like several people slamming large sticks against the trunks of trees. The sound echoed down through the river valley of the Stikine, bringing with it a set of cold chills, the likes of which Lynn had never had before.

As suddenly as the strange banging had started, it stopped, and the dark world around them became silent once more. Lynn saw Sagli lower his weapon and then gesture for the others to get back to sleep or to take up their guard stations once more. Sagli looked up at the giant trees as they swayed in the slight wind that had sprung up. As he turned away after slinging his rifle around his shoulder, he saw Lynn as she looked out of her tent flap. He smiled, with not one inch of it actually reaching anything other than his lips. Did he know something about the strange noise and wasn't offering an explanation, or was he as taken back as the others had been, herself included?

"Beavers slapping their tales against the water," he said as he passed.

Lynn decided to brave a comment from the small safety of her flimsy nylon fort.

"Sounds like wishful thinking."

Sagli stopped for a moment and faced her.

"Does it really matter? Anything out there would be doomed to challenge this group of men—now get to sleep, you will have a hard day tomorrow."

Lynn watched Sagli disappear into his tent and then his light go out. Just as she was starting to zip up her own flap, she looked once more into the darkness.

"Beavers, my ass," she said, and then gave out a slight shiver.

Around the camp the night grew still once more, and little did the Russians know that their presence in the valley of the Stikine had just been announced.

The few Russians on guard continued their watch, but now they listened far more closely than before. Most of the veterans of war-torn Chechnya and other embattled places felt as though they were once more in hostile countryside as their survival senses became active, and they knew as all old soldiers knew. They were being watched.

TEN MILES OFF THE COAST OF PUGET SOUND, WASHINGTON STATE

As the drone of the large twin-engine Grumman thrummed in Jack's ears, his thoughts turned to his sister, where they never drifted very far away from. He was having a hard time recalling her face. He knew that happened from time to time with others in his life, so he knew he had to think of Lynn in context. Recalling her childhood was the easiest. Her smiling face as he pushed his seven-year-old sister down the hill outside of their parents' house, trying desperately to teach her the balance she needed to, as in her words, ride a big person's bike. He remembered being so proud that she kept her balance all the way down the minislope, and then the sheer horror he felt when she wobbled, and then dumped the bike moments before striking the picket fence that lined their front yard. He smiled at the memory. She had bounced up and wanted to go again.

"Colonel, you awake?"

Jack tuned his head, losing the smile and the memory at the same instant. "Yeah, Lieutenant, what's up?"

Ryan could see Jack's face in the soft green glow of the mapped-out hologram on the split windscreen. He looked tired, and thought seriously about not asking him.

"Uh, you think you can take over for a while? I have to rest my eyes for an hour or so. During our twelve-hour layover at the Columbia River, I didn't get much sleep."

Jack sat up straight in his seat with a worried look on his dark features.

"Don't worry, Alice installed one really nice autopilot; she'll fly herself. You shouldn't have to do anything but monitor the threat board right in front of you, but we're flying low enough that we shouldn't be picked up by anything outside of a seagull with Doppler radar."

"Okay, Ryan, don't you go far, and if I call, don't drag your ass getting back here."

"Yes, sir." Ryan undid his safety harness, and half stood beneath the overhang of the flight controls.

"Tell me, Ryan, does it feel good to be flying again?" Jack asked as he looked at the twin steering wheels of the Y-shaped yoke in front of him as they moved up and down, and left and right on their own.

"Yes it does, boss, we have an old saying in the navy: Just don't take the sky away from me."

Jack smiled at the look on Jason's face. He nodded and then gestured for Ryan to get some rest.

"So, my little Sarah, since my left leg has gone completely to sleep from your nonweight, take my mind away from it and tell me about your Colonel Collins, and his little sister."

Sarah shook her head. She was tired, but the constant bumping of the ancient plane kept her from relaxing, so she and Farbeaux had kept a steady chatter going since refueling in Oregon.

"Henri, you may not believe this, but until yesterday, I didn't know Jack had a sister."

"Would you two be quiet for a while? That damn Frenchman's voice has a worse tone to it than those ancient piston engines," Everett said from the tight seat across the aisle. He had an old fedora that he had relieved from Henri's secret basement pushed down over his eyes.

"Sorry," Sarah said as Jason Ryan squeezed through the small opening separating the cockpit from the cabin. She watched him as he looked around, and then finding no seat to sit in, started to lie down on a pile of supplies.

"No, Jason, here, take my place," she said as she stood and removed herself from Farbeaux's leg. "Believe me, it's more comfortable than that mountain of camping stuff; that is if you don't mind Henri hitting on you."

"Touché, my dear, touché!" Farbeaux said as she stood.

"Jesus, can you people take it outside?" Everett said.

"Here, here," agreed Charlie Ellenshaw, who had his head propped up against Punchy Alexander's large chest, who in turn had one leg draped over Will Mendenhall's lap and two rolled-up sleeping bags.

Sarah apologized and picked her way around the crowded cabin and headed for the cockpit.

"You better keep your hands to yourself; I heard what you Frenchmen are capable of," Ryan said as he sat hard onto Henri's leg.

"Oh, you haven't heard the half of it, Lieutenant, believe me," the Frenchman said angrily as Jason crushed his leg.

Sarah poked her head through the small curtain that separated the cabin and cockpit. The four-foot entryway was something a hobbit would have a hard time going through, but Sarah figured she and Ryan would have no trouble.

"Mind some company," she asked, "it's a tad crowded back there."

Jack didn't turn to face Sarah and acted as though he was still reading the hologram readout on the windscreen.

"Hi, babe. No, sit down, silence in here would no doubt be preferable to Farbeaux's chatting you up."

Sarah squeezed into the pilot's seat and looked around. The hologram with its see-through detail cast a green and blue glow on her features. She chanced a look at Jack and attempted a smile.

"Anyone trailing us?" she asked just for conversation.

"We had a close one just south of Seattle, but Ryan ducked into a valley just below Mount Rainier, he lost them pretty fast."

Sarah waited for more, but she saw that Jack wasn't going to add anything to his answer. She swallowed and then turned her head to the left, a large cloud slid by, almost luminous in its while veil because of the moon. She closed her eyes at her own reflection.

"Jack?"

Jack was reaching over and was turning the small knob on the overhead console that automatically adjusted the altitude because he had seen on the readout that the old Grumman had drifted up by about ten feet. When he was satisfied, he looked over at Sarah and half smiled.

"Tell me you love me," she said, her eyes boring into his.

The look on Jack's face wasn't exactly what she had been hoping for. He bit his lower lip, and then after a second, as though the slight frown had never been there at all, he actually smiled. "You know I love you, and one of the reasons I fell in love with you was your confidence in yourself. You, of all the women I have ever known, didn't need reassurance on a constant basis. You knew how I felt."

"You surely don't have a clue about women, Colonel Collins," she said, still holding his blue eyes with her own.

Jack chuckled and then nodded. "Okay, I love you, and I hope that makes up for all the other times I wanted to say it, but couldn't."

Sarah smiled and batted her eyelashes, which Jack saw and shook his head.

WAHACHAPEE FISHING CAMP
STIKINE RIVER, BRITISH COLUMBIA

Helena Petrovich waited silently on the long, covered porch of the store. She had been awakened early by the signals throughout the night by the Chulimantan. The constant hitting of the trees and the unrhythmic beat made her toss and turn. It had been almost twelve years since they had heard the beating of the clubs so close to the camp, and she asked herself why they had ventured this far down from the north. It was causing her a sleepless night.

The beating had stopped about an hour before the sun rose and its rays started reflecting off of the moving Stikine. She had gone into the store an hour before and told Marla it was almost time to get the frozen bait for the Tlingit Indians to start their day fishing. She heard the girl moving around in the back of the store as she sat in her large rocker and listened to the sound of the many fishermen as they walked through the woods on the beaten-down path of a hundred years that wound its way down from the hills and mountains that surrounded the small fishing camp.

She waved and nodded her morning greeting to those that raised their hands to Helena. They were surprised to see her out so early, as she usually was inside getting their bait for the morning fishing. Several of the older Indians knew exactly why she was out that morning—they had also heard the constant thumping of wood on wood throughout the night, and they, as she, had gotten very little sleep.

"Thanks for the help!" Marla said as she kicked the front door open with her arms full of the white butcher's paper-wrapped bait. Sixteen packages for eight boats.

"I'm sorry, sweetheart—I just didn't feel up to facing that stinky mess this mornin'."

"Oh, but it's okay for me to?" Marla asked as she made her way down the wooden steps.

The old woman didn't answer as she watched her granddaughter move her small frame toward the river and the waiting fishermen. She smiled to herself as Marla handed out the mornings bait, and laughed and joked with the old Indians, and fended off the sly smiles of the younger ones. After her arms were empty, Marla adjusted the knitted cap she wore and then waved at the fishermen as they shoved off from shore, starting their small engines as they headed up or down river. Marla started back to the store, then she paused a moment and turned toward the tree line. She stopped completely in her tracks, and the old woman could see the girl was sensing something. Marla was so in tune to the river and woods, nothing could escape her knowing that something was different. Helena wondered if the girl had heard the Chulimantan the same as herself during the night.

"What is it?" the old woman called from the porch, standing and letting the rocker sway back and forth by itself.

Marla looked at her grandmother, and then back at the woods to her left. Then she smiled and shrugged her shoulders. "Nothing I guess—just thought I—oh, never mind."

Helena watched as Marla started walking back to the store. Her eyes went to the woods where the girl had been looking. She, too, was feeling something—she couldn't put a handle on that particular cup, but she knew something was indeed watching from the woods.

Suddenly Marla stopped and listened, and then she clapped her hands as she heard a familiar sound coming from a distance. The old woman now seemed to relax somewhat as the same sound finally reached her ears.

"You didn't tell me Charlie Kemp was coming, Grandmother!" Marla shouted and clapped once more.

Helena shook her head and smiled. Marla loved the visits by the Mounties, especially Kemp. The RCMP sergeant always took her up in the Bell Ranger helicopter and then afterward supplied her with all of the gossip coming out of Vancouver and Seattle. Charlie was only about seven years older than Marla, and every time the girl returned to school, he would almost wilt and fall from the vine. The relationship was innocent enough, at least on Marla's side of the river, but Helena knew Charlie had a schoolboy crush that would only be called off by time and distance.

Marla put her hand to her brow and blocked out the rise of the morning sun when she finally spied the red and white helicopter as it shot low over the trees with a loud whine of its engine. On the sides of the Bell Jet

Ranger were the gold-painted crown of the Canadian government, and on the tail boom read RCMP.

As the Ranger set down in almost the same spot as the Russians helicopters the day before, Marla ran to the door and pulled it open. She screamed aloud, she was so happy at seeing Charlie Kemp. The young sergeant didn't even wait for the turning blades to stop before he had thrown off his headset and jumped from the pilot's seat, and then smiling and yelling himself, picked the young girl up and twirled her around.

As Helena watched from the porch railing, she smiled, and then saw that Charlie wasn't alone. She was stunned to see the commander of the RCMP station at Jackson's Bluff, Captain Dar Wilcox, climb from the backseat, and he also had Corporal Winnie Johnstone in tow. Three men in all—that meant they had taken Helena's call very serious indeed.

"Well, well, Captain Dar, why do we have the pleasure of having the commander of the northern territory to our humble camp?" Helena asked as she moved to the opening in the porch where she waited at the top of the wooden steps.

Dar Wilcox removed his green bush hat and looked around the camp. He had a serious look on his tanned face.

"Damn, did those Indians already start their day?" he asked as he wiped a bit of sweat from his brow.

"Just missed them, why?" she asked as the captain bound up the stairs and put his arm around the old woman and hugged her to him.

"Well, with that call of yours, I don't want anyone running into these fellas until we can find them and check out just what their story is, aay?" He looked around and then finally down at the old woman. "Just how in the hell are ya, Helena?"

"Tolerable, Dar, just tolerable, I've been enjoying Marla's company lately."

Wilcox looked down at Charlie and Marla, who were laughing as they approached the store with Corporal Winnie Johnstone in tow.

"Looks like you're not the only one enjoying her company," he said as he finally released her. "You did good calling us. Speaking of which, Winnie, get in there and let the base know we arrived alive, and we'll keep in contact from time to time."

"You plan on staying a while, Dar?" the old woman asked as the other mountie stepped onto the porch.

"Yeah, maybe a day or two. Figure after we find out what those Russian boys are doin,' we might throw a line into the river and see what we can take back home with us."

"That's good, Dar, real good. I know how hard you Mounties work," Helena said with a jab in the captain's rib cage.

"You better watch it, us Canucks don't take to joking about our work!" he said as everyone laughed.

As they entered the store, several dark shadows moved from the deeper parts of the surrounding woods and finally made their presence known to the sun and river.

Captain Darwood Wilcox sipped his coffee while leaning against the store's long counter. He smiled as the blond-haired and blue-eyed Charlie Kemp showed Marla the magazines he had brought her. *Hell*, the captain thought, *the damn things are only two months old.* He shook his head and then shouted into the back room.

"Well, Winnie, did you get ahold of them?"

Winnie Johnstone stepped from the back room, followed by Helena. The old lady shook her head.

"Yes, Captain, told them we may be a few days up here and that we'd call in if there was trouble."

"Dar, I don't believe you're taking this thing as seriously as you should. These fellas . . . well, let's just say they didn't look like the salt of the earth."

Wilcox sat the coffee cup on the counter and smiled at the old woman. "Ah, you worry like a mother hen, prob'ly poachers is the most we're lookin' at here. If they're as heavily armed as you say, we'll observe only, and then call in the big boys. We overfly 'em with the Ranger and let them know the Mounties are still here."

"Oh, great, you'll overfly 'em with that old rickety Bell Ranger while they have brand-new Sikorskys parked around here," Marla said as she finally tore herself away from Charlie, who in turn watched her walk away appreciatively.

"Oh, I think we can handle them, don't you, Charlie?" Wilcox asked, frowning at the way he was looking at the young girl.

"I can outfly anyone or anything in the northern territory," he said as he finally stopped looking at Marla's butt.

"Cap'n, we have company here, you better look at these old boys," Winnie said as he stood at the large plate-glass window.

Captain Wilcox turned and walked the few paces to the window. He immediately saw six men standing by the RCMP helicopter, and then his face went flush as one of the men opened the pilot's side door and reached into the chopper. He reappeared a moment later and gently closed the door.

"What in the hell do them fellas think they're doin', they can't—Winnie, go tell them to get away from government property."

The corporal looked back at the captain. "Cap, have you seen what those boys are carryin'?"

Wilcox saw immediately what his man was talking about. What he hadn't noticed in his cursory look at the men was that each one was holding an automatic rifle. He counted three AK-47s and three automatic weapons the likes of which he had never seen before. They were all dressed in camouflaged green and black fatigues, just like the ones he and his men were wearing. Then he gasped and straightened as one of the men emptied a full magazine into the engine compartment of the Ranger. The holes appeared in the housing as if by magic.

Helena grabbed Marla by the shoulders and pulled her to the side of the counter.

"You get up to Warriors Peak, and you stay there until you hear from me that it's okay to come home. You hear me?"

Marla was staring at her grandmother with wide eyes. She could only nod her head that she understood, as her eyes flicked from Helena to Charlie and Winnie as they unholstered their nine-millimeter weapons from their belts. Then she saw Captain Wilcox do the same.

"Charlie, go with Marla, make sure she's clear out the door before this mess gets too ugly, then get in the back and call Jackson's Bluff and tell them that we have a situation up here."

Charlie was rooted to the spot of floor he was on and didn't make a move to follow the captain's orders.

"Charlie! Move, goddamn it!"

Finally, his paralysis broke as he ran for Marla and then they both quickly disappeared.

"Helena, you skedaddle, too, you're too big a target."

Wilcox flinched when he heard the old woman as she chambered a round in her twelve-gauge shotgun.

"You shove it up your ass, Dar Wilcox. This is my property and I don't plan on seein' it shot to pieces."

The captain shook his head as he took a deep breath. On his way to the door he tried to figure out just what in the hell he was going to say to the largest armed force he had seen in the territory since the Canadian army held maneuvers in this area over ten years ago. He didn't like the feeling of his shaking as he opened the front doors and stepped out onto the porch.

"You men," he shouted as he took what he hoped was a stance of authority in front of the six heavily armed men who stood in a straight line facing the store, "you're in violation of Canadian law for illegal automatic weapons and destruction of government property."

He watched the men as they made no move. They acted as though he hadn't said a word. Then he felt Winnie step out on the porch and take a position beside him.

"Damn it, boy, I wanted you to stay in the store. The less they know the better."

"I have a feeling these boys wouldn't care if there was a Canadian regiment in there with us, Cap."

Wilcox knew the corporal was right: these men were killers and he was just lying to himself if he thought otherwise. He felt foolish for what he had said to the men already . . . like they would just lay down those horrible-looking weapons and come quietly.

One of the camouflaged men stepped forward of the others. He brought the AK-47 up and rested the wood stock on his hip. He was now only about a dozen yards from the storefront.

"The man and woman who left the store through the back way are now in our custody. Your radio has already been destroyed, both in your helicopter and the aerial for the store. There will be no magical rescue for you. Lay down your weapons, and only what needs to be done will be done."

Wilcox knew immediately that Helena was right, the man spoke with a thick Russian accent. His dull expression told the Mountie that this man had been through this, or something very similar before. The man's eyes never once moved, as the others behind him also stood motionless.

"We have men on the way here, we're not alone," the corporal said as he held his small nine-millimeter outward with both hands, still pointed low, but pointed forward nonetheless.

The man in front of the line half turned and spoke in Russian. Before Wilcox knew what was happening and even before he could react with a scream of warning, one of the men quickly raised a rifle and with blinding speed fired one shot. The round hit Corporal Winnie Johnstone in the forehead and threw him backward one step until his momentum slammed him against the wooden wall of the front of the store where he slumped and then fell over dead.

"I will not ask again," the man said.

"My God, my God . . ." Wilcox said as he lowered his weapon to his side.

The man in front of the line of killers frowned once more and then shook his head. He then quickly gestured at someone Wilcox could not see. As he watched, Charlie and Marla were led from around the back of the store, in between it and the icehouse. Marla looked angry as a seventh man held her arm and with the other pushed Charlie out in front of them. Without hesitation, the man who had spoken, raised his AK-47 and fired a three-round burst into the chest of Charlie Kemp, who just stared as if he were dumbfounded by his sudden death. He finally went to his knees and then to the ground face first.

"Ah!" Wilcox screamed at the same time as Marla.

Charlie managed to roll onto his back and look up as the man holding Marla pulled her by the hair. The man with the AK-47, its barrel still smoking stepped up to Charlie and raised the weapon one last time and fired one round into his face. Then he turned away with no expression and looked at Wilcox.

"I said, drop your weapon. You see what happens when I am forced to give an order twice."

Wilcox tossed the nine-millimeter out onto the gravel. Then he didn't know what to do, raise his hands or keep them lowered.

"Thank you," the large crew-cut Russian said and raised the AK-47 one last time and fired another three round burst into Wilcox from twelve feet away. One of the rounds hit the plate-glass window and it shattered. Helena screamed and then rushed out onto the porch. She saw Dar Wilcox and tossed her shotgun away as she went to his side. The captain of Jackson's Bluff RCMP Station 12 was dead as she kneeled beside him.

The leader of the group gestured for the man holding Marla to take her to the old woman.

"Finish this business and let's get back to camp, we have wasted enough time here."

The man smiled and then started pulling Marla toward the store.

"Wait," the man said as he held up a hand. Then he cocked his head to the right as if he were listening for something. "Throw both of them in the freezer and then come back out here."

The man stood with a struggling Marla squirming in his grasp waiting for an explanation.

"Move, you fool, we have company."

As the men listened, they heard the sound of an aircraft as it approached from beyond the bend in the river. The leader, Gregori Deonovich, saw something that made him blink. An old-fashioned seaplane, the likes of which he had not seen since he was a child came around the bend in the Stikine, its large wings tilting so far over that it looked in danger of hitting the rushing river only thirty feet below it.

"Take them inside. We may need them if something unexpected comes of this."

The man ran, dragging Marla with him and then he gathered up the old woman with surprising strength.

Without shouting one order, Deonovich sent his men scattering. They immediately took up firing positions but he knew they had moved too late as the Grumman seaplane fell lower to the river—he couldn't believe his bad luck, the plane was going to land at the fishing camp. He actually saw the man piloting the old craft wave a greeting, and then lower it as fast as he had raised it.

"Bring that aircraft down!" he shouted.

Suddenly, five automatic weapons opened fire on Alice Hamilton's antique Grumman, and as they emptied magazines into the plywood frame, the Russians became more than happy as they saw large pieces of wood flying off the seaplane as it started falling for the river below.

Deonovich smiled as he knew the plane couldn't maintain its integrity with the large caliber rounds slamming into it.

"Sorry, my friends, this is the wrong day to come and fish this end of the river."

Ryan released the autopilot with little fear. He had disengaged the new system Alice had installed several times during their long flight just to get a better feel for the ancient Grumman. Will Mendenhall, suffering from a severe backache and stiff neck from his rotten sleep in the cabin, had gratefully spelled Collins to keep Ryan company on the last leg of the flight into the fishing camp.

"Well, here we go, hang on back there," Ryan called out as he reduced power to the two Pratt & Whitney engines. The Grumman started to ease itself from the sky as Jason watched out of his side window at the approaching Stikine River far below.

"Damn, that has to be the most twisted river I've ever seen. You sure you can land this thing without cracking up?"

"Come on, man, when a navy pilot can't land on water, something's wrong, wouldn't you think?" Ryan said, smiling as he pumped down the hydraulic wing flaps while using his other hand to turn the large rudder. "It's not like we're coming into a hot LZ or anything."

"Hey, I thought you only landed on carriers. Have you ever landed in the water before?"

"No, in the navy we call that crashing," he said as he again looked out of the side window and saw some men on the riverbank below. He raised a gloved hand and waved, and then he saw what those men were carrying and dropped his hand. As the Grumman made its shallow dive, there were several loud thumping noises.

"What in the hell was that?" Will yelled over the loud engines.

"Take evasive action, Ryan, we're taking ground fire!"

Mendenhall heard the call from the rear cabin and knew it was Captain Everett who had shouted, but at first he couldn't comprehend what he said.

"Did he say . . . ?"

Before Will could get the whole question out of his mouth, heavier caliber rounds slammed into the windscreen, and then he heard some more pinging and whacks coming from the two engines above.

Ryan struggled to add power to the two engines and started pumping the flaps back as the seaplane started to rise back into the air. He managed a look out of the side window, a single bullet passed through the glass and just missed his head, but it did tear the twin throttle controls on the upper control panel out of his grip as they both sheared off and went flying into Mendenhall. The engines were now at full power and unless Ryan cut the fuel off, they would crash into the trees or the river at full speed.

Ryan cursed and tried to look through the shattered glass. What he could make out was several men down below up on the riverbank kneeling and firing into the seaplane.

"We have men on the ground, a dozen feet from the river," he shouted for the benefit of the colonel and the others in the back.

Jack and Everett beat everyone into action as thirty holes stitched themselves through the plywood hull of the flying boat. Three would have hit Sarah if she hadn't had two rolled-up sleeping bags piled in front of her; still, the powerful rounds knocked the wind out of her as goose down went flying in all directions.

Collins started throwing camping gear everywhere as Everett joined him, unceremoniously throwing Charlie Ellenshaw into the small aisle. The Grumman lurched and went almost upside down and then righted itself, throwing Jack and Everett off their feet. Jack stood and grabbed the first M-16 from the plastic container that had been buried under the rest of the gear. He threw the short-barreled M-16 over his head, not caring if it hit anyone. Sarah, finally getting her wind back into her lungs, ducked as an arm shot out and took the airborne automatic weapon. As she turned, she saw Henri Farbeaux holding the weapon and then throwing himself over three folded tents as he quickly smashed out one of the small round portholes that lined the side of the aircraft.

"Here, Punchy," Jack shouted as he threw him another M-16. "I expect you remember how to use one of these," Collins said as he reached for another just as a red hot round tore through his jacket at the shoulder.

"If I don't, I better remember damn quick," Alexander said as he didn't bother to smash out one of the portholes, but instead sent several 5.62 millimeter rounds through the glass before throwing himself prone and opening up at anything along the fast moving riverbank.

Everett took a weapon and slammed home a magazine. "Jack, I don't think someone down there is all that impressed with Alice's plane."

Collins heard a loud creak and then a bang as one of the engines froze up. When he looked up, he could actually see the holes in the upper cabin where engine parts had blasted through the wood.

"We're hit!" came a shout from the cockpit.

"Ryan really has a way of stating the obvious," Collins said as he started slamming the butt plate of the M-16 against the thin marine plywood hull. It only took about six hits before he had a hole large enough for he and Everett to fire from.

"Alright, give 'em hell," Everett screamed above the damaged engines.

Deonovich was satisfied when he saw the starboard engine of the sea-plane burst into flames just as the rising Grumman went flying past at a hundred feet and climbing. The Russian saw large chunks of wood ca-reen into the air as his men continued to pour accurate fire into the old wood of the plane. Then his expression quickly changed as something caught his eye. He knew he must be imagining the sight he was witness-ing: The ancient aircraft was actually returning fire. That observation was quickly punctuated and verified by thirty rounds striking the rocks and gravel of the riverbank. Two of his men screamed in shock and fell back-ward onto the ground, two holes each in their chests.

Deonovich decided that retreating to a covered position was probably the healthiest choice he could make in the next few seconds as the aircraft continued a withering return fire at their antagonists. Whoever these people were, they surely were not your ordinary fishermen.

Ryan was struggling with the dying plane. The river ahead looked shal-low in too many places and the bends in the Stikine looked to be too close together for a straight in landing.

"Goddamn it, there's no place to set this bitch down!" he said through clenched teeth as the wheel assembly started shaking in his hands. "We have to turn around and land in the deepest part of the river in front of the fishing camp."

"Hey, buddy, I don't know if you noticed or not, but there seemed to be some not-so-nice people back there shooting bullets at us!" Menden-hall said, feeling really out of place without a weapon; so he did the next best thing—he pulled his seat harness as tight as he could.

"Colonel, I have to come back around, I suggest you clear those people from the beach!"

Collins didn't answer, he knew Ryan had to do what he had to do and didn't bother the navy pilot with what he really wanted to scream out—*Are you nuts!* Instead, he reached down and tossed everyone fresh magazines.

Everyone in the cabin was tossed to the left side of the plane as Ryan turned the Grumman for everything the old girl was worth. The one remaining engine screamed at full power as the other burned through its wing mounts. The smell of burning wood and its smoke started to fill the cabin and the cockpit. Still, the old seaplane responded as Ryan completed the turn just as the colonel and the others opened up again on the approaching beach.

Ryan knew a catastrophic failure was only a second away when he heard the loud crack of the wing header just above them.

"Oh, shit!" Mendenhall yelled as he heard the same horrifying crack. "That didn't sound good at all."

Ryan pushed the wheel all the way forward, bleeding off altitude as fast as he could, even threatening to bury the Grumman's nose into the river below. They were being raked by machine-gun fire but not at as heavy a volume as before thanks to Collins and the others. However, Ryan knew that was the least of their problems at the moment.

The seaplane flared out, nose up just as its right-side wing float was shot free. It fell off and struck the water and then bounced up into the fire-damaged wing, creasing it along the line of bolts that held it together with the fuselage. The old plywood structure was not meant to sustain that much damage or debris impact, and so, just as the boatlike prow of the seaplane hit the river, the right-side wing let go, shearing off at the cockpit. The seaplane hit and spun in the water, the left-side float hit and dug into the fast-moving river and, even though the Grumman was traveling in the same direction as its southern flow, the float dug in and then tore free, but before it did, it was like sticking a ball bat into a large fan—the plane spun, tearing off the remaining wing and smashing the fuselage into two pieces. As quickly as they had hit the water, the old collector's item was in pieces.

As Deonovich saw the destruction before him, he stood from behind the tree where he had taken cover. He shook his head at the tenacity of whoever was inside of the destroyed plane. It had been surprising that his antagonists had put up such a quick and terrible defense. He looked around and saw that three of his men were down and one other was injured.

"Remarkable," he mumbled as he stepped toward the Stikine to watch the debris of the seaplane as it started its run down river. "Utterly remarkable."

As the Grumman rolled over onto its back, the tail section and most of the cabin sped by the cockpit in an out-of-control rush down the Stikine.

Inside the cabin, Collins had had the M-16 he was holding smash into his shoulder as he was firing, coming near to separating it. As the water rushed inside, he saw Sarah as she fell from what had been the cabin's floor. In a flash, he saw the Frenchman grab her and then they both vanished in the rush of water. Collins knew that Sarah could be in no better hands other than his own.

"Charlie!" Everett shouted.

Collins looked around as the cabin slid completely under the rushing water. He still held the M-16 in his right hand as he used his feet to push off of a shattered rib strut. He felt the river grab him as soon as he was free of the cabin. He felt another, and then another person slam into him as he fought to get to the surface.

"Goddamn it, those bastards are still shooting at us!" Everett shouted as he surfaced, and then his words were cut short when he swallowed a mouth full of water.

Jack felt the rocky bottom of the river and tried to gain what balance he could. He felt a strong arm pull him fully back into the water. It was Punchy Alexander; he had both hands free and was pulling Jack as close to shore as he could get. All around them, geysers of water were shooting skyward as bullets from upriver struck all around them.

"Did anyone get Charlie out?" Jack shouted.

"Hell, I don't know, but if we don't get to the bank we're going to get our asses shot off," Alexander screamed.

As Jack and Punchy gained the shore, he heard an M-16 open up somewhere in front of them.

"That damn Frenchman is fast, him and that little girl are giving us cover fire. Now let's go, Jack!"

Jack stumbled as he gained the rocky shoreline and fell, Punchy continued pulling him. "It would help if you got up and used that damn weapon in your hands."

Jack realized he still held the M-16 and quickly rose to his feet just as three rounds narrowly missed his head. He saw Everett start firing from a prone position ten yards away. He quickly aimed at anything that didn't look like a tree upriver and opened fire.

"There's only one left," Henri Farbeaux called from the tree line to Jack's left. "And he's decided to call it quits."

Collins stood and saw a lone man shove a large Zodiac into the water and then jump in. Collins aimed and fired, but the man was too fast as he started the large outboard motor and streaked upriver, bouncing over the rough surface.

"Son of a bitch used his remaining two men as a shield, stupid bastards." Punchy stepped up to Collins and looked him over. "You've got a pretty good gash on your forehead, old friend," he said as he turned and made sure the boatman wasn't making a return trip.

"You all right?" Jack asked Alexander as he wiped blood from a six-inch gash just into his hairline.

"Nothing a seamstress can't mend," he answered with a grimace as he pushed down a large rip in his right pants leg. Blood was soaking through the wet material in a pretty good spread.

"Short Stuff, get over here and see if you can give Punchy a hand before he bleeds to death. Henri, Carl, let's see if we can find the doc, Mendenhall, and Ryan."

"Goddamn it, Jack, we flew right into that one. We must be getting old," Everett said as he pulled the magazine from his weapon and looked in it. It was empty so he tossed it onto the rocky shore. "I'm out, so if that bastard tries again, I have to chuck rocks."

"Well, this is the place for it," Farbeaux said as he and Sarah joined them at the river.

Collins saw Sarah was fine, a little bruised, but intact. Henri was the same except for three large scratches to the left side of his face. He nodded his head at the Frenchman in thanks for pulling Sarah out of the plane.

"I don't give your professor Ellenshaw much of a chance, Colonel," Farbeaux said as he checked the number of rounds in his own weapon.

They all turned at once when they heard someone coming from the tree line.

"Whoa, hold your fire! We didn't survive that magnificent crash just to get shot by our friends!" Ryan said as he, Mendenhall, and none other than Charles Hindershot Ellenshaw the Third held up their hands.

Jack shook his head when he saw his people, happy as hell they had made it through.

"You crashed, Mr. Ryan. So, tell me how in the hell that makes you a friend?" Jack asked, only half jokingly.

"Now, how did you get into the tree line?" Everett asked as he assisted a limping Ellenshaw to the ground, relieving Mendenhall and Ryan of their burden.

"Well, Will and myself took an 'E' ticket ride in what was left of the cockpit, skidding along the water, and then rolling to beat all hell onto the riverbank and then into the forest. Thank God for seatbelts." Ryan kneeled, still shaking from their ordeal.

Mendenhall leaned down and patted Ellenshaw on the back, making a sloppy wet sound as he did.

"As for the doc here, we found him playing dead about a hundred feet away from us." They all looked at Ellenshaw: He had lost his hat, his thick wire-rimmed glasses were bent so out of shape that one earpiece was dangling down the side of his face, and his hair looked at if a bird had started putting a nest in it.

"I most assuredly thought I *was* dead, Lieutenant," Charlie said as he removed his bent glasses and then covered his eyes. "That was a horrendous way to land a plane, I must say."

Jack was grateful everyone was alive. He looked at the river and saw no sign of the wreckage. The Grumman and all of their supplies would wind up in Vancouver by the end of the week. He took a deep breath and looked around. The store looked as if it had taken gunfire—the icehouse next to it was leaking what could only be liquid hydrogen from several gaping gaps in its woodwork. There wasn't any movement or other signs of life from the fishing camp and Jack feared the worse for the people here.

"Well, let's go see what those people were doing here, and if they left anyone alive."

Jack, Everett, and Punchy Alexander moved separately into the open, spread out as far as possible to make sniping at them a singular event. Carl was the first to come to one of the four bodies that lay crumpled on the stony ground nearest the river. Everett rolled the body over on its right side, bending over and retrieving the AK-47 from the man's frozen grasp. He slung the weapon over his right shoulder and then turned and felt the neck for a pulse. The bearded face was frozen in shock and the eyes were wide open. The captain was getting ready to continue on when he saw that one of the bullets that had struck the dead man had hit him in the upper left arm, exposing something colorful underneath. Tearing away some of the material, Carl quickly wiped away the blood from the bullet wound and then exhaled deeply. Just under the hole where the 5.62

millimeter round had entered the arm, there was a tattoo. A red hammer and cycle, the old Soviet state symbol—only this one had a gold lightning bolt running through it. Everett released the arm and then looked around at the other bodies, betting they all had the same markings.

"Jack," Carl called out, halting Collins in his tracks. "Check the upper left arm of that body."

Collins, who had just checked the dead man at his feet for a pulse and then picked up the AK-47 and chambered a new round into its breech, leaned down and tore the camouflage fatigue at the shoulder. The material ripped away revealing a hammer and sickle, complete with a gold lightning bolt.

"What the bloody hell is it?" Punchy asked a few feet away as he kept a wary eye on their surroundings.

"Spetsnaz," Jack said looking around him, more appreciative of the enemy they had faced. "Old school; tattoos are from the old Soviet days."

"What in the hell are Russian commandos doing here?" Alexander asked, becoming even more aware of his surroundings and now feeling far more vulnerable than he had just a second before.

Jack didn't answer Punchy's question; he straightened and then continued toward the general store. He stopped a moment and looked back at Ryan and Mendenhall. They were huddled with the others just inside the tree line. Mendenhall held the only M-16 in the group and was watching the riverbank to their rear. Collins gestured to Ryan and made a trigger movement with his finger, indicating that he should relieve the other two dead men of their weapons. Ryan understood and sprinted from the trees toward the remaining bodies.

Alexander was still thinking about the Spetsnaz and the rumors of their capabilities. As an intelligence officer, he had run up against the newer versions of the commando group, but most Western nations knew them to be a ghost of their former selves, sloppy and inefficient compared to the old fellas from two decades ago. He looked at Jack and saw that the element of the Spetsnaz hadn't made a dent in his hastiness to hurry their group along. He shook his head and followed Collins.

The colonel quickly went straight for the large front steps of the general store, waving as he did for Everett to go left and check the icehouse. Punchy Alexander followed Collins onto the large front porch and then to the left side of the open door as Jack went to the right of the still closed one. They immediately saw two bodies and Punchy recognized the green uniforms. He mouthed the word "Mounties." Collins took a shallow breath, shaking his head at the horrendous murder of more men, and then before his thoughts wandered even more about life's injustices, he quickly reached out and opened the door. A small bell chimed and Collins grimaced: He knew mistakes like that cost men their lives, and he had just made one of the biggest. He looked at Punchy who was standing there smiling and rolling his eyes.

"I told you we were getting too old for this, but then again, I didn't think about that, either."

"For whom the bell tolls," Jack whispered and then before he could think about it, went inside and then quickly to one knee as he scanned the interior of the large store. Alexander followed just a second later taking aim at the higher points of the store.

Collins didn't see any movement as he slowly scanned the area to his front. Then he stood and gestured for Punchy to take the left side of the store, and he would take the right. The counter area is where he would have set up the initial stages of any ambush, so that was the first place he looked. He slowly lay down and then rolled silently toward the closest end. He saw a can of pork and beans lying on the floor that had fallen from a small display case after the glass from the plate-glass window had struck it. Jack closed his eyes as he easily reached the can, not daring to take a breath. He picked up the red and white labeled can and then opened his eyes, and then pulling it back as if it were a grenade, he eased it through the air until it struck the counter at the far end. As it did, he rolled the rest of the way around the far end of the counter and quickly aimed— nothing. Collins stood and shook his head at Punchy, who returned the gesture. Then he turned and looked to where Collins was looking.

Straight ahead was a large steel door of the walk-in freezer or refrigerator. Jack could hear the hum of the motor as it engaged. He also saw there were two clean round holes where two bullets had punched through it. Collins raised the AK-47 and pointed it at the door and advanced. Punchy kept his M-16 pointed at the upper floors of the store where he suspected the owners living quarters to be. It was another great ambush spot.

Jack reached the door and stood to the right side next to the large handle. He reached out and pulled on it.

"If you open that door, we'll kill your man," came a girl's voice.

"Go ahead and kill him, he's not our man." Jack grimaced, hoping beyond measure he had responded the way he should have. "We killed his companions outside."

"I'm not falling for that bullshit, you want him dead. Just try me, you Russian prick!"

Jack looked over at Alexander who was watching from a distance, he shrugged his shoulders, as if saying Jack was on his own on this one.

"Listen, my name is Collins, I am a colonel in the U.S. army. I have a man here from the Canadian authorities and we're looking for an American woman—that's why we're here. Our plane was just shot out of the sky, and it was that man's friends who did it, so I really don't care if you kill the bastard or not."

There was complete and utter silence coming from the refrigerator. Jack glanced over at Alexander and nodded toward the door.

"Ma'am, I am Jonathan Alexander, an agent for CSIS in Quebec. The man is telling the truth. Come out, you won't be harmed, not by us."

"My grandmother is hurt. One of those bastards shot her in the arm," came the voice, and then that was followed by another, more husky, but feminine protest.

"I've hurt myself worse with a kitchen knife."

Jack heard the first voice—that of a much younger person—shush the second. Then he heard the door handle pop, but it still remained closed. Jack took a step to the front and raised the Russian-made weapon. Finally, the door opened and Collins heart raced for a second when he saw a man in the same camouflage fatigues as those outside. He just stood there, his eyes opened, and then just before the colonel fired his weapon, the man simply fell forward.

Jack's eyes moved from the body to a smallish girl holding an older, heavy woman in the center of the large walk-in. "You were bluffing, he was already dead," Jack said as he bent over and made sure the commando was indeed as he looked.

"He was hit almost as soon as he took us in here to murder us; must have been stray bullets," the girl said as she started to assist the old lady out of the cold of the icebox.

Collins, with the aid of Punchy, moved the dead man out of the way to allow the women out. Jack slung his weapon and then went to the other side of the old lady and assisted the girl with the weight.

"That was pretty good, but what if we *were* the bad guys?" Jack asked, looking around the ample bosom of the grandmother to see the young, brazen girl dressed in bloody overalls and a knitted cap.

"I wasn't thinking that far ahead," Marla said as she eased her grandmother into a large desk chair just to the rear of the sales counter.

"Check the register, dear, and see how much those Russian bastards made off with," the old woman said as she held a hand over the bullet wound in her left arm.

The girl rolled her eyes as she reached into the large desk and brought out a first-aid kit. "I don't think they were here to rob us, Grandmother," she said as rummaged through the kit.

"Well, you never know," the old woman said as she grimaced.

"You said you were looking for an American woman?" Marla asked as she found the small packages of alcohol wipes and antibacterial ointment. "Was her name Lynn?" she asked, not looking up.

Jack took a deep breath and then leaned heavily against the counter; he found he had no voice to answer the girl.

Punchy saw Jack's distress and then stepped up and took one of the alcohol wipes from the girl and started cleaning the old woman's wound. It was just a graze, so he wiped and spoke at the same time. "Yes, her name was Lynn. It's his sister."

The girl looked up and into the blue eyes of Jack Collins. "Yes, I can see that you are her brother, you have the same eyes."

"Is she . . . she . . ."

Marla took a deep breath and then handed Punchy a tube of antibacterial cream. "She was fine yesterday when she left with those other Russians."

Jack closed his eyes and then turned away just as the soaking-wet Mendenhall and Ryan, followed by Sarah, Farbeaux, and Doc Ellenshaw, came to the front of the store. Mendenhall and Farbeaux leaned over and was checking the bodies of the two Mounties outside, and Ryan stepped in and leaned over and checked the others.

Sarah saw Jack as he walked around a few of the stacked shelves full of dry and canned goods. She took his arm and stopped him.

"She was here; the Russians took her upriver," he said as he finally looked down at Sarah.

"Then we have a chance of getting her back," she said.

She saw Jack's lips move but didn't hear the one word he kept repeating.

"What? What are you saying, I don't get it," she said questioning his tone and his look.

"He says, my dear Sarah, that his sister is in the hands of what's known to soldiers around the world as, Spetsnaz—specialized killers from the Cold War. Their own bloody government created them and now they don't know what to do with the ones they discharged. The Russian government is terrified of them." Farbeaux looked around at the bodies, "Evidently, they have found gainful employment."

Sarah McIntire turned to face Farbeaux, who was looking at the tattoo he had uncovered from the dead Russian only a few feet away. Farbeaux tilted his head as he stood and nudged the dead Russian with his boot.

"And this new development is unsettling to say the least."

Jack and Sarah both looked at the Frenchman; only Sarah had a question written on her face.

Farbeaux smiled, but there was no humor there. "I dare say the men that are holding your sister are far more aggressive than I was first led to believe." He looked from Sarah to Collins, his smile gone.

"You can leave anytime you want, Colonel," Jack said still staring at him.

Farbeaux tilted his head as if in deep thought. "No, I believe I'll stay a while, and if things get too hot, I can always trade you for me."

Jack turned away and left. Sarah just looked at Henri, shaking her head.

"I know I don't disappoint you, my dear—you know who and what I am."

"That's what gets me, Henri, I know who you are, and you still go lower and lower in my estimation every time you open your mouth."

Farbeaux watched her leave to follow Collins, and then he turned and saw the young girl looking at him from the porch. She had heard the exchange between the three and the look in her eyes told Farbeaux that he hadn't made a friend with the smallish teenager.

Marla watched the Frenchman turn and leave, eyeing the icehouse and going in that direction; she then turned and looked at her Grandmother who was getting her arm wrapped by Alexander. "Has the world gone over the edge?" Marla asked as she shook her head in disgust.

"The world has always been insane, honey; we just isolated ourselves from it."

Punchy straightened after he finished tending to the old woman's wound.

"In case you ladies haven't noticed, you're not isolated anymore." Punchy stepped back and then retrieved his weapon and then looked at the young girl who was angry and staring at him.

"Believe me, Mr. Ottawa, we've noticed."

Jack stood on the porch and surveyed the fishing camp. His eyes roamed over the rock-covered ground and into the tree line. A stiff breeze picked up and made the trees sway against the deep blue sky of the early morning. Everett was busy checking out the icehouse, the small warehouse, and the equipment shed with Jason Ryan. Will Mendenhall and Sarah stood just off the large porch with Charlie Ellenshaw in an attempt to get the soaking-wet, stray-haired professor under some form of control—the man could not stop shaking. Sarah used Charlie as an excuse to give Jack the time to think things out. She looked up from Ellenshaw as Henri Farbeaux stepped from inside the store.

"In case you were thinking about using the radio, Colonel, I regret to inform you that its aerial has been disabled and that dead Russian there placed a bullet into the set before he closeted himself in the icebox. The old woman is fit to be tied."

Collins didn't turn at the sound of Farbeaux's voice. He was still watching the trees around the camp. Then his eyes went to the Bell Jet Ranger sitting a hundred yards from the water's edge. He saw the bullet holes in the engine housing and knew that the commandos would not have left that radio intact after so thorough a job on the camp's equipment. Out of the seven cell phones on his Event personnel, not one was receiving a signal. Jack was finally realizing that his nonplan for getting his sister back had placed a lot of his people in jeopardy.

"I believe I am beginning to know how you think, Colonel Collins; as they say, know one's antagonist and you shall know yourself."

"Word games at this stage of the trip, Henri?" Jack said still hearing the rush of wind through and around the trees, his eyes moving at every twitch of movement.

"Yes, I do play games, except at this very moment, I am not. You, Colonel, are thinking about ordering everyone here to remain, while you, afraid for their safety, and ever the good commander are going to go it alone, as you Americans are fond of saying."

Collins kept his features neutral, but knew the Frenchman was far more intelligent than his file said he was. Director Compton had tried many times to tell him that, but Jack had always figured one way or another, Farbeaux could be outsmarted. He was now learning that little task may not be possible.

"If you attempt to go into this wilderness alone, you will die, and your sister will perish with you. It's that simple, Colonel. And I dare say that I will not get my reward for you playing the hero, and your own people will nod and agree to do what you order them to do, but in the end they will follow you after you have left. So, let's save us some time here, and not even bring that suggestion up."

"If you're going to follow those bastards, everything you need is in that supply shed in the back. All of my son's guide equipment is in there. He had a small arsenal of hunting rifles and ammunition—he stocked up seeing the fact that we don't live right down the street from Walmart."

Jack and Farbeaux had not noticed the old woman and her granddaughter as they stood just inside the door. Punchy was there also, wrapping his right hand with gauze. He acted as though he didn't care to hear what was being discussed.

"I'm thinking that we should use a boat to get down river and get some authorities in on this," Collins said, more of a test for the grandmother than a statement of what he was truly thinking.

"Authorities?" the old woman said with a smirk. "They killed all the authorities north of Jackson's Bluff if you hadn't noticed." Marla placed a hand on her grandmother's arm and tried to get her to calm down. "I don't fancy leaving them Russians to the authorities. You seem like people who have dealt with this sort of thing before; just do what it is that comes naturally to you folks. I want those pigs out of those woods."

"We'll need most of what you have if we are to go north," Farbeaux said before Jack could say anything.

"You can have everything we can spare. While you are gone, I will send some of the boys down river to round up whatever 'authorities' they can find, and get them up here as soon as they can."

Jack nodded at the old woman as she gestured for them to come back inside. "C'mon, we have a hand-drawn map in here that's more accurate than anything you boys have studied, and I think I know where those bastards are heading."

Sarah, Mendenhall, and Charlie saw what was happening, and followed the four people into the store. Jack turned and saw them.

"Start getting enough food for at least five days—move!"

They quickly started following Jack's determined orders.

Collins turned away and saw that Marla had stayed and waited for him.

"My grandmother is determined to give you a fighting chance; she's angry and maybe should stop to think about what it is she is doing. Where you are going, the land is unforgivable. More than a few dozen have gone up the Stikine in just my lifetime and never came back. And that was without people out there that wanted to kill them."

Collins didn't say anything.

Marla held eye contact for a moment, and then stepped aside when she saw the determination in Jack's eyes. She lowered her head and then saw Mendenhall taking several canned goods from the shelf.

"Put those down, you'll have to travel light because we only have two boats in the shed. The freeze-dried stuff is back here, enough to feed an army."

Mendenhall, arms brimming with canned soup, salmon, and chili, looked deflated. He glanced over at Sarah and they both rolled their eyes.

"I could have gone all year without hearing that you carried freeze-dried rations." Mendenhall slowly started placing the delectable canned goods back on the shelf.

"Someday, we have to buy stock in the companies that make that crap," Sarah said as she, too, started placing cans back where she had gotten them.

"I kind of like the freeze-dried food," Charlie Ellenshaw said looking around and pushing his glasses back up to the bridge of his nose as he saw Mendenhall shaking his head.

"Why doesn't that surprise me, Doc?"

"Now, we are here," the old woman said pointing to the fishing camp. "You won't have to cross the river; stay on this side, and you'll end up on the northern Stikine all the way up to where those people may be."

Jack watched as her finger pointed to the rounded bend in the Stikine more than a hundred and twenty miles north of their current location.

"And how do you know that is where they'll be?" Collins asked.

The grandmother turned to face the Frenchman, the American, and the Canadian. "Because that's where that damn L. T. Lattimer said he found his gold—that is what they are after, right?"

"I didn't think Lattimer was that well known," Punchy said as he popped four aspirin into his mouth.

The old woman smiled as she turned fully to face the others. They all could see that at one time in her life, the heavyset jovial lady had been as beautiful as her young granddaughter, but age and time had caught up with her, but to her credit, she looked as if she really didn't care that her looks were gone. She looked around until she saw the thin man she had seen enter the store. Charlie Ellenshaw was looking at a large can of bug repellant, reading the ingredients closely.

"L. T. Lattimer was an arrogant, untrustworthy man who was a cancer to this part of the Stikine, a most unreliable sort. We learned of his possible fate from that tall and soaked drink of water right there," she said pointing from the back room to where Charlie stood.

Ellenshaw scratched his butt and then felt the eyes on him. He turned and saw everyone in the small office looking his way. He turned his head, thinking that someone was behind him, and then he realized it was indeed himself that was the center of attention. He was about to ask what it was he had done, when he saw the old woman. He squint his eyes and then recognition lit his features.

"That's right, you—I remember everything. The way you came back here with the rest of those hippie boys and girls, talking about Lattimer."

Charlie placed the bug repellent down and nervously smiled. "I remember you. You warned us to watch ourselves with Lattimer. I also told you about the animals that lived in that area. You didn't ever deny that anything that remarkable could live there."

Charlie swallowed as the memory of those days returned. He shook his head and felt weak in the knees.

"As I was saying, he knows more about that area than I do."

"Tell me, madam, did anyone ever go back and look for Mr. Lattimer?" Ellenshaw asked, getting himself back under control.

"My boy spent a month looking for L. T. and never found a thing. Never found your monsters, either," she said turning back to Charlie.

Ellenshaw looked down at the floor, still feeling the others looking at him. He knew they weren't believers in his story of what the world called Bigfoot that inhabit this part of the world, but he didn't care, either; he knew what he had experienced that summer in 1968.

"It's okay, boy, you did real good back then just getting the rest of those students out of there, and back down the river, that's more than most would have done. You have nothing to prove to me," she said and when Charlie looked up at her, she winked. That made him feel better and he looked away, embarrassed.

"Come here, Mr. Science, and join us at the map," Jack said, nodding that he agreed with Helena.

The old woman gave Charlie Ellenshaw a crooked smile as he timidly stepped into the small office.

"As I said, the northern Stikine is unkind to fools." She then turned back to the map. "And like I said a minute ago, we have a stash of weapons, mostly hunting stuff that we have found in the woods from time to time. We don't hunt ourselves here as we have always left the wildlife be. But you're welcome to them; it's a small arsenal if the truth be told. A lot of smart-ass doctors and lawyers who wouldn't listen to reason; let's just say they may have come across something that wasn't as sporting as a deer or elk. That's right, my friend, I listen to the tales that the Indians talk about at night same as everyone else."

"So you believe in that hokey crap about Bigfoot?" Alexander asked, looking almost insulted at the stories that Charlie had been spewing all the way up north.

"Thank you," Jack said, cutting off any further comments about what wasn't really important.

"As I said, you are welcome to all those guns and equipment," she said eyeing Punchy Alexander with what amounted to total disdain, "but you listen to me now." She pulled at Jack's sleeve and nodded toward Charlie. "Do not venture into the woods ten to twelve miles north of the Stikine River. Do you hear me? Even if your quarry goes to ground there! Stay out of that area."

She turned and pointed at a spot on the large map of about a thousand square miles.

"What's in there?" Farbeaux asked, more than a little curious, especially since historically speaking, the mother lode of the Alaskan and

Canadian gold rushes had never been discovered—the source of all that gold was still out there somewhere.

"It's wild, young man, more wild than you could ever believe. Just stay out of there. If your Russians go in there, rest assured that they are not coming back."

Jack, knowing that if his sister was in there, there was no way he wasn't going in after her. He looked at the black, hand-printed words embossed over the field of unbroken green that marked the area the old woman had shown them. Jack wrote the words down on his notes: THE CHULIMANTAN PLATEAU.

Not one of the men ever thought to ask the meaning of the Indian name that graced the valley and the rise of the large plateau. Collins heard the admonishment of the old woman, but paid her no mind.

"Don't go north of the Stikine."

8

After the supplies were organized and stacked, they placed them all in front of the porch. Collins then called everyone except Charlie Ellenshaw to the steps. He was inside looking over the map of the Stikine Valley and Plateau with the old woman. The girl, Marla, was watching the group from a distance, making sure their boxes of .306 ammunition was placed in a plastic pouch to keep river water from damaging them. Altogether, the girl and her grandmother had gathered nearly two hundred rounds for the hunting weapons, and another hundred fifty for the 5.62 millimeter automatics.

Everett took up position beside Collins, looking from face to face. The two officers had come to a decision an hour before, and Carl knew their news was not going to be well received. Farbeaux suspected what was coming because he had watched as the naval captain had cut the rations for their journey upriver almost by a quarter, and he had also tossed aside one of the tents.

"Ryan, you and McIntire are staying here."

"The hell you say," Sarah started to protest.

"No, no. You're not leaving us behind," Ryan said as he looked directly at Everett and not at Collins.

"At ease, Mr. Ryan, you'll do as are ordered," Carl said, making sure Sarah understood his anger, also.

"Look, we don't know what else is right here under our noses, and these people have gone through enough; we have to leave someone here in case they have a rerun of what happened today," Jack said, now looking directly at Sarah.

"Colonel, I would bet two months pay that that old woman could kick my ass three ways to Sunday, and the girl is far tougher than my last three bunkmates combined."

"This is not a negotiating session, Mr. Ryan. Will is a soldier; he's trained for what we do. Doc Ellenshaw, well, he's Doc Ellenshaw, and he has his reasons for being there, and we have reasons to take him. Punchy goes where I go and Colonel Farbeaux has his own reasons for being brave. You and McIntire have no reason for being on the river, but you have a big reason for watching out for things here. I want that RCMP chopper fixed if at all possible."

"Wait a minute, you know I'm not qualified on those damn things," Ryan protested.

Jack turned on him. "Damn it, Ryan, you know and I know you can fly one. Fix the damn thing in case we need to beat a hasty retreat out of this place. Do you understand, Mr. Ryan?"

Ryan didn't respond, he figured since he was in civilian dress, Jack didn't rate a salute, so he turned on his heel and reached for a small toolbox and then stormed off toward the damaged helicopter. Sarah meanwhile watched Jack, her eyes never leaving his. He waited for her to continue her argument, but instead she raised her right brow, which told Collins she was about to explode, and then turned and followed Ryan.

"They just hate being left—" Mendenhall started to explain.

"Not now, Lieutenant. Leave it," Jack said and turned on his heel and trotted up the steps. "Captain, organize Colonel Farbeaux, Mr. Alexander, and Mr. Bleeding Heart here, and get that boat loaded. I want to be on the river in thirty."

Everett and the others watched Jack leave and enter the store. Carl shrugged his shoulders and then turned toward the supplies.

"Come on, you bunch of pirates—the wonders of Mother Nature await."

The old woman watched the white-haired Charlie Ellenshaw study the map. He had a small notebook out and was jotting down his own information just as Collins had done earlier.

"Tell me, the acreage here." He was pointing to the northern most section of unexplored territory far above the Stikine. "How much animal life can that section support in your estimation?" Charlie scrunched up his nose and then turned to the old woman. "I mean, vegetation wise, berries, plants, elk, and deer?"

"You're kind of peculiar, aren't you? Hell, even as a youngster you were, all the way back in sixty-eight," she said instead of answering.

"Excuse me, madam?" Ellenshaw said pushing his thick glasses back up on his nose and looking the woman over.

"You didn't exactly grow into what you would call a male specimen in all those years, Charlie, so just what are you doing here? You're not like these others."

"You mean, Colonel Collins and Captain Everett? I think we make a pretty good team."

"You don't usually get out much, do you?" Helena said, nodding as if she wanted Ellenshaw to agree outright.

"I assure you, I am as field qualified as the next man in this group. I could tell you a story or two," Ellenshaw looked around and then caught himself before he broke his secrecy oath. "Just suffice it to say, I've been places and seen things that you wouldn't find in Kansas."

The old woman slapped Charlie on the shoulder, almost knocking the thin scientist into the large map. "Don't take offense, skinny, I was just funnin' ya' is all. Now, you asked about the vegetation and wildlife up in them parts, well, I'll tell you, Hindershot," she said, using Charlie's middle name that made him cringe inside. "There is enough roughage and game up there to support half of the African savanna. Now, why do you ask?"

Charlie quickly wrote down her information. "Oh, no reason, just a scientist curiosity."

"You're as poor a liar as you are at gunplay, Hindershot Ellenshaw. The colonel's lookin' for his sis, and that French fella, well, let's just say he has the look of a man with another agenda, and the others—well, to this old woman's eye, you can tell they would follow that colonel man into hell if they had to, but you, you are here for something else, aren't you?"

"Madam, I assure you, I am only here to assist the colonel in the task of finding his sister."

A stern, motherly look came to the husky woman's countenance.

"You hear me good, Hindershot, don't go lookin' for something you shouldn't be lookin' for; that something could jump right up and bite you and whoever's with you right in your asses. Some places weren't meant for people, and that area you're askin' about is one of them. You were there once; stay by the river, and you just might make it back to your lavatory," she said with not an ounce of humor.

"You mean, laboratory, and I again assure you—"

"Doc, that's enough. Why don't you go help the others load up?"

Charlie turned to see Collins standing by the counter with his hands on his hips; he didn't look happy at all.

"Yes, Colonel."

Jack watched the professor leave and then rubbed his eyes.

"Ma'am, there isn't another phone nearby? A radio?" he asked as he looked at her with his now red eyes.

"No, there's no phone lines this far out. We're on our own until the fishermen come back in two days."

"I'm leaving lieutenants McIntire and Ryan behind to assist just in case."

"Colonel, we've not needed babysitting in our many years here on the Stikine; it's others who need to take care."

"I understand, but, well, the small woman, Miss McIntire . . ."

"She'll be safe here," the old woman said, knowing what he was going to say because of the intense look in his blue eyes. "There is one thing I remember my granddaughter said about some of them Russian's equipment. She said they had what she thought was some kind of electronics, a lot of it, and some heavy firepower, so you best be careful and not run into another ambush."

"Electronics?"

"That's what she said. Anyway, good luck, Colonel. We'll send help upriver as soon as we can," she said, holding her large hand out for the American. "And we'll make sure nothing happens to your two lieutenants."

"Thank you, ma'am." Jack started to turn but was stopped by the woman's powerful grip.

"Mind me here, Colonel Collins, stay out of them woods north of the river. I think maybe you should let them Russian boys look for what they came for, because in the long run, the result will be the same, so get your baby sis out of there and come back and leave them murdering sons-a-bitches to their own devices."

Jack's hand was finally released, thoroughly confused by the large woman's last remarks. As he left the store, he stopped and watched the camp around him. The supplies were almost loaded and he looked up to see Sarah standing at the bottom of a small ladder, holding it steady while her eyes were burning a hole through him. Ryan was busy taking out his frustrations on the engine cowling of the RCMP helicopter.

He shook his head and started down the steps when he saw the breeze bring the trees to life again around the fishing camp. He stopped walking and looked around. He was totally confused as to why the sound and movement of the trees made him uncomfortable—it was primal in nature and it was if he and the others were not only being watched, but that whoever was watching was a danger. He took a step and then felt eyes on him. He stopped and turned and saw the old woman standing in the doorway. She wasn't looking at him. She was also watching the trees, while wiping her hands on her long leather skirt. Her eyes finally looked at Jack, and then she turned away and entered the store, the darkness inside swallowing her up.

THE STIKINE RIVER (THE PLATEAU)

Lynn Simpson stood at the edge of the river and stared at the woods across the way. The late afternoon was still filled with brilliant sunlight as it dappled off the fast-moving Stikine. Her eyes roamed over to ten of the Russians as they uncrated several small devices that had been encased in Styrofoam. Of these, one very large and powerful man loaded a small rifle. It was short, and the barrel was wide and fat. He attached one of the small, round objects they had just uncrated and then attached a short pole to it. He then rammed the pole into the weaponlike device and raised it to his shoulder. He pulled the trigger and there was the sound of a compressed air blast that sent the object hurtling over the Stikine until it disappeared three hundred yards into the trees. The large man continued until six of the rounded objects had been sent across and deep into the far woods at about four hundred yards' separation.

As she watched this strange delivery method of equipment, other men started sitting up a large tent and they began filling it with small consoles that sat upon tables, while others began digging a large pit. Soon, they pieced together a small generator and placed it into the hole. They soon had it covered with large branches cut from the trees, surrounding the camp forming a weatherproof cover for the generator.

That morning they had traveled more than seventy miles upriver, arriving at a large bend that actually started to turn south on the eastern side. Now, instead of crossing onto the north side of the Stikine, the Russian leader, Sagli, had made camp on the southern shore, for what reason Lynn couldn't fathom. Thus far, he had kept his distance from her as he supervised what looked to be their final camping spot.

Lynn became more curious as a large, fifty-foot-tall antennae was raised just outside of the large blue tent where all the sophisticated equipment had been setup. When they had the guy wires in place and taut, the men went about setting up their tents and then after that it actually looked as if they were preparing defensive fire pits around the camp. As she admired the efficiency of the developing base of operations, she saw Sagli with a set of papers. He was looking from them and then surveying the woods around them, even looking up and out across the river a few times. He was deep into thought. That was when Lynn decided to approach the ponytailed Russian.

"Since I am more than likely going to remain behind when you leave here, maybe I can learn what it is you are looking for?"

Sagli didn't even look up from the papers he held in his hands. "These are copies of the Lattimer note and a description of this area as written by a Russian colonel long ago in 1918 that we received from our friend—" Sagli caught himself before he disclosed something he swore never to divulge. "In them, this colonel describes the area where he had left two wagons full of gold. I am now in the process of correlating his description with the area I have chosen to begin the search."

"It would seem to me you would be looking for an area against the plateau and not out in the open like you are, that is if it is gold you are looking for."

"Observant, Ms. Simpson; however, that is not our purpose here." He finally lowered the papers and looked the beautiful woman over. "I have found the landmarks described in the letters, it is right over there across the river. Do you see the rise of the plateau about a mile and a half into the woods?"

"Yes," she said as she held her bandaged hand to her eyes to shield them against the setting sun."

"The three largest veins of limestone running horizontally down its face, that is the only such variant that comes close to what Lattimer and this Russian colonel had described. His find has to be nearby." Sagli looked at Lynn and then seemed to decide something. He reached into his right pants pocket and brought out a small plastic case. He opened it and removed a large gold coin. "Do you know what this is?" he asked, handing it over to her.

Lynn turned the heavy coin over in her hand. The gold was cool to the touch and, of course, she recognized it immediately. "It's an American-minted gold double eagle, circa 1891. Value in today's gold market at about nine hundred fifty dollars, give or take ten dollars. If memory serves me correctly, the twenty-dollar gold piece weighs approximately .9675 ounces of pure gold."

"I am astounded at your knowledge of such mundane things as gold, Ms. Simpson, truly amazed."

"We have to be up on the markets for terrorism purposes, that fact shouldn't surprise you that much."

"Nonetheless, you are correct. And somewhere out there is two wagons full of them and we are now here to find those wagons' resting place."

Lynn could sense the lie coming from Sagli's mouth. At first, she thought he was telling the truth, but it was in the way he quickly turned away from her that undid him. She was trained to see the small of a lie, when a larger one would have been hidden the truth better. She had also noticed that among the copies Sagli was examining, there was one that stood out. It was a computer-generated letter that had English language written upon it, and she saw the header; it was from the NSA—the National Security Agency of her own country.

"And no one since this Lattimer guy has ever looked for it?" she asked, trying to keep him talking and eyeing the papers, trying to see more of the NSA printout he held.

Sagli turned back to face her; at the same time he reached out and took the heavy double eagle from her hand and replaced it in the plastic case.

"As a matter of fact, this coin was found nearby back in 1968."

"And all of this stems from a Russian diary from 1918?"

"Yes, that was the starting point for Lattimer, when he found the rotting diary along this very point of the river, possibly at this very spot."

Lynn couldn't help but smile. "And you, being the wealthiest man in Russia, you decide to throw it all away for a treasure hunt, one that wouldn't even be a decimal point in advantage to that wealth? No, Mr. Sagli, I don't buy it, just like my agency won't swallow that load of bull. What are you really looking for?"

Sagli smiled. This time the humor went all the way to his eyes, which was far more unsettling to Lynn than when it hadn't.

"We are looking for the gold, and it is a far more valuable commodity than you or your agency is aware of."

Lynn watched Sagli walk away and then stride into the large tent. She followed at a slower pace as to not attract the attention of the men she knew had been assigned to watch her. As she stepped to the side of the unzippered flap, she leaned in and saw that Sagli was listening to the right side of a headset, and as he held the radio link up, he absentmindedly tossed the coin onto the large table that held the radio. As she examined that table, she saw small pieces of twisted metal lying next to even more of the gold coins. Before she could see the twisted shards of black painted metal closer, a large hand grabbed her arm and turned her around. She came face to face with Gregori Deonovich. He was wild haired and dirty. Several of the camps men were pulling the Zodiac he had arrived in up the bank of the river. Deonovich roughly pushed Lynn into the tent.

Sagli lowered the headphones, and saw his partner and the angry expression he had on his filthy face. Deonovich raised a hand and then brought it down across the face of the American woman. Lynn fell to the nylon floor of the tent and then received a kick from the much larger man.

"Brother, brother, what is the matter with you, we were just trying to contact your team, what happened?" Sagli said, grabbing Deonovich and staying the next kick he had already drawn back to deliver to Lynn.

"Someone is tracking this woman. An aircraft we thought was nothing more than fishermen opened fire on us from the air." He turned to face Sagli. "They took out my entire team." He suddenly stopped and then pulled Sagli to the back of the tent, angrily ordering some of the technicians away.

Lynn wiped blood from her mouth and then rubbed her ribs where the big boot had landed squarely. Then she saw the animated way Deonovich was talking to Sagli. Lynn could see by the large man's body language that it wasn't just the reverse ambush of his men, it was something else. Sagli turned away and closed his eyes. Then he turned back angrily.

"Was he killed?" he asked.

Deonovich looked from his partner to Lynn, then he stepped forward and once more removed Sagli from earshot. He whispered something and then let go of his arm.

"Still, would it not have been more prudent to allow the aircraft to land before opening fire on it? That way you would have at least known who was on it. Now we have lost men we cannot replace and you have also left a now obvious enemy in our rear."

"They have no radio, and that gives us at least two or three days to find what we came for," Deonovich said by way of making things right with his partner for his failed ambush and the planned murders of the fishing camp family. "That means they either have to go downriver for help, in which case when they return with help we will be gone from this place, or they will come after us. And that will be to our advantage because they will be bringing our . . ." He stopped talking and looked at Lynn. "Get this woman out of here," Deonovich shouted at the men lining the front of the tent. After Lynn was picked up and moved out, Deonovich continued. "These intruders obviously do not realize who it is they have brought with them."

"Still, the chances of our success have now been diminished at the very least." Sagli turned away in deep thought. He turned back to face Deonovich. "Do you have any idea who these people were?"

"I have no idea, they were expert marksmen I can tell you that, my friend. But the means in which they arrived should rule out the possibility of a government resource, even a Canadian one."

"Your meaning?" Sagli asked.

"The aircraft they arrived in looked as if it had been taken from a museum."

Sagli was confused as to who these intruders at the fishing camp could be. Especially if they had who Deonovich described as their partner on the same plane as themselves.

"Well," he said with a shrug. "The stakes are too high for us to concern ourselves with such a small force. We will watch and wait and continue our search, and when these men arrive, if they arrive, we will kill them all."

As both men stepped aside and allowed the technicians to continue adjusting their equipment, Sagli stopped at the tents flap and saw Lynn facing north across the river. Then he noticed a few of his own men looking in that direction. Before he could order all of them back to work, he heard what it was that had stopped everyone in their tracks. The hammering of wood on wood had started again from deep in the forest across the river. Sagli stepped from the tent and cocked his head to the right side, trying to figure area and distance of the irritating, strange sound. As he did, several more of the distinctive slapping of wood commenced in other parts of the forested wilderness. Some sounded as if they were on their side of the river. Unnerved, Sagli turned to Deonovich.

"I want a fifty percent alert status on watch tonight. I suspect we have Indians indigenous to this area out there trying desperately to get our attention, and I don't know what they have planned, but I want to be ready for whatever it is."

The noise grew in volume and continued for three hours until the sun set behind the western mountains, and then all became horribly still; even the constant buzzing of insects ceased as the moon slowly rose over the Stikine River and its nervous visitors.

The Chulimantan were starting to move south from the small plateau and into the valley of the Stikine.

SIXTY-FIVE MILES SOUTH ON THE STIKINE RIVER

Will Mendenhall had been placed in the bow of the fifteen-foot Zodiac boat. The old river craft had been reinforced at the bow and stern with slabs of plywood, and there was a small cockpit complete with a windshield and an ice-chest stool for the river pilot. Marla's father had built in coolers and the control panel with throttles for the twin Evenrude mo-

tors, complete with depth finders and fish locators. As Will looked back
at the cockpit where Carl Everett sat, his eyes moved to the colonel. Jack
had placed Will in the bow as a lookout, and then had placed Henri Farbeaux and Punchy Alexander at the sides for the same purpose, while he
sat next to Everett, cleaning one of the hunting rifles: an old-fashioned
.30-.30 Winchester.

Jack had talked nonstop for the past hour, sharing something with
Everett. Will wondered what it could be that made the captain sit as still
as he had while he listened, being as the colonel had placed the Frenchman and Alexander as far away as possible in the boat so he could talk to
the captain. Doc Ellenshaw was constantly writing in an open journal,
looking up from his words for a minute of reflection, then delving back
into his writing.

As they approached a large bend in the Stikine, Will turned and saw
that Collins had changed his position and had come up to the bow without him noticing.

"Colonel," Will said as he lowered the binoculars, and then turned
over from where he had been laying against the tall rubber and plywood
bow, "you shouldn't sneak up on me like that."

"Getting spooked in your old age, Lieutenant?" Jack said as he slid
down beside his security officer.

Mendenhall looked around at the passing scenery of the Stikine and
its surrounding woods. The sun was now so low as to set the trees and
even the water on fire with its bright orange illusion. The sun was dying
and Will could see hope doing the same in Jack's face; this would be a
long night of waiting on shore instead of going ahead upriver.

"To tell you the truth, Colonel, I've never been big on camping." Will
looked back at Jack with an embarrassing smile that started and then
failed to materialize. "I don't know, I guess it's become more acute since
we left the fishing camp, but I swear for the past fifty miles . . ."

Collins watched Will as he failed to say what he was thinking. He
glanced back as he felt the eyes of Farbeaux on him from behind. Henri
raised his brows, smiling. It was if he knew Will was distressed about his
surroundings and wanted to let Jack know that he knew. Collins gave him
no indication that he cared one way or another as he turned back to the
young black lieutenant.

"It's not like you to not finish a thought, Will, so give: What's on your
mind?"

"We're being watched, Colonel," Mendenhall said as he again attempted the smile, and then shook his head at his failure. He turned back to face the front of the boat and the river beyond.

"We just may have something watching us, although I believe we won't run into our Russian friends for another fifty or so miles."

"It's not that," Will said without turning back to face Jack. "It's more instinctual—like walking down a street in Compton, just knowing that there is someone lying in wait for you around the next corner."

"Are images and memories of growing up in L.A. coming back to spook you?"

"No, that I could deal with, now as then. This is something else, like a memory, a very old memory or something. A thing from the past; hell, I don't know what I'm trying to say."

"What you're feeling is the state of loneliness in this part of the world," Collins said as he relaxed and lay against the large rubber wall of the Zodiac, placing the blue, seventy-year-old baseball cap that the old woman had given him before they left at a lazy angle covering his eyes. "I don't know if men . . . people like you and me that is . . . were ever meant to be here. Hell, maybe no one was ever meant to be in a place like this." Jack lifted the old Brooklyn ball cap and looked squinty eyed at Will. "And, Lieutenant, in the wilderness there is *always* something out there."

"Yes, sir," Will said, but was not satisfied as he turned back and looked into the dark woods that slid by the large boat as it moved upriver.

As the boat with its six-man crew moved along the river, the sun began to set and the woods surrounding them began to come alive with the animals that used darkness to hunt. As Mendenhall nervously glanced behind him, he saw Punchy Alexander watching the left side with all the determination of a man truly seeking out the bad things that could harm them. Farbeaux, on the other hand, was looking right at Will, his smile still there. Henri then winked at him. It was if the Frenchman were conveying once more that he had a secret that only he knew. Will figured it was only Henri being the total ass that he was.

Mendenhall finally relaxed when Carl turned the Zodiac in toward shore. All eyes except for the colonel watched as a small clear area presented itself, and the roving band of rescuers had a spot in which to wait anxiously for the rising sun that would signal them another day closer to finding Jack's sister—one way or the other.

RUSSIAN BASE CAMP
NORTHERN STIKINE

The tent that had been set aside for half of the camp to eat in was still crowded as Lynn was given a plastic plate, and then watched as something resembling beets and a mystery meat was plopped into it. She was given a plastic fork but no knife. She turned away from the surly brute with the filthy apron and looked about the tent. She saw several places she could have sit down to eat, but decided that she would forgo the splendid company of men that grumbled and shoveled food down their throats and move to the outdoors. She chose a place by the small fire about halfway between the tents and river. The sun was now but a memory as the last of it dipped below the tree line to the west, signaling the true beginning of night.

As she sat down on a large rock worn smooth over a millennium worth of river water running over it, she saw that the guard had been set around the camp for the first of many shifts. They didn't care about her as she watched most of them as they in turn watched the surrounding woods. They were still on edge after the demonstration of noise had ceased about an hour before. The beating of wood on wood had set everyone's nerves on edge and the men didn't mind the reassuring feel of the large caliber weapons each of them held as they watched the darkness envelop the camp.

As Lynn nervously tasted the concoction of red sugar beets and beef, she saw Sagli and the freshly washed and cleaned Deonovich as they stood at the river's edge. They were talking with one of the technicians from the tent that held the lab and mechanical equipment she had seen earlier. Sagli seemed to be doing most of the talking. The ponytailed Russian was gesturing at the far shore of the Stikine, indicating with his hand certain areas she could not see from her place at the fire. She made a face when the beets and meat touched her tongue and then she placed the plate beside her and watched the animated exchange.

Sagli turned and saw her twenty yards away, and then pointed at the smaller Russian technician and then at Deonovich. Both of them turned abruptly and started for the tent brimming with electronic equipment. She noticed that both of the men had shoulder holsters as they passed by her. Deonovich glared at the small American woman and then growled something she couldn't understand as he eventually disappeared into the tent followed by the smaller man.

"We have possibly located something across the river by electronic means."

Lynn turned as the sound of Sagli's voice surprised her. He was standing by the fire looking down at her, but not really looking at her at all. The man was a thinker, and that was when she realized that all of her field reports were not quite telling her the truth; Sagli didn't really have a true partner in Deonovich, he was the man in charge and the other was just his lackey. To her, that could mean some sort of an advantage she could utilize down the road—but how? She didn't know just yet.

"Then why don't you wade across the river and get what you came for?" she asked, watching the man for his reaction.

When he didn't answer, she knew she had touched a nerve, one that he was trying to hide from her, for what reason she didn't know. Instead of answering the American's enquiry, he lowered his hands from the warming fire and then faced her.

"These woods," he said, gesturing around him to the dark tree line and even the flowing river, "what do you know of their history?"

"In case you haven't noticed, Sagli, I'm an American, and this"—she mocked him by gesturing around her, just as he had—"is Canada. I'm a city girl by nature."

Sagli actually looked disappointed that Lynn had not only mocked him, she had also not answered his question. He actually had the look of a man surprised that she hated his guts. He just looked at the fire and acted as though he was warming his hands on a not-so-cold night.

"My men, men who served with me in Georgia and Afghanistan, Spetsnaz all of them, are acting like schoolgirls. The noises emanating from the forest has them"—he finally looked at her as he searched for the right word—"on edge."

Lynn wanted to smile at the killer that stood nervously over the fire, but she thought mocking him again would be a dangerous proposition at best. So she looked toward the river instead.

"I suspect that it may be elk, or deer, maybe it's some kind of mating signal, you know, striking their antlers against trees, deadfalls, things like that. Look, I'm not up to date on *Animal Planet;* I've been a little busy with work and all."

"It does no good to mock me. And in case you haven't noticed, Ms. Simpson, you are sitting here in camp with us, and whatever is making that noise is growing close to you, as well as to me and my men."

Sagli abruptly turned and started walking toward the technical tent to join his so-called partner. As he disappeared inside, Lynn actually heard a call of an elk somewhere far to the north of them. A far different noise from what she had led the Russian to believe as she did know the difference between what an elk and deer sound like in the woods, and whatever that strange noise was that was plaguing the inner thoughts of everyone in camp. She knew that nothing she had ever read about in all of her education made the noises they had heard earlier. She was also aware that Sagli had been right—the sounds were drawing nearer every time they heard them.

For the first time since her abduction, Lynn wasn't so sure that having Russian commandos standing guard around her wasn't so bad after all.

SOUTH OF THE RUSSIAN BASE CAMP

As soon as they had brought the boat up and out of the water and staked it to the beach after their sixty-five-mile trip up the river, they set up a small fireless camp with no tents, Charlie Ellenshaw wandered off into the surrounding woods, necessitating that Everett go out to find him and admonish the curious side of the crazed professor for being careless.

As for Henri Farbeaux, the Frenchman tossed his sleeping bag onto the ground underneath a large tree, and then sat and watched the others. He placed his hands behind his head and watched Collins most of all. When Jack caught him looking, Henri didn't shy away, he just smiled that knowing smile of his.

"I don't know why you tolerate that man," Punchy said as Jack walked by. "The damn French, you can't trust them."

"Come on, Punchy, you're in charge of the only French-speaking province on the North American continent. Don't tell me Quebec and France still has their problems?" Collins looked from Alexander toward the reclining Farbeaux, who watched the two with interest.

"They have always treated not only Quebec as an ugly little sister, but the whole of Canada. They constantly interfere with our inner workings and still have one of the largest intelligence infrastructures outside of Moscow, and for what? To watch little Quebec?"

"Take it easy, old buddy. I didn't think you were that passionate about the ills of your relationship with France."

Alexander didn't say anything else, he just tossed his sleeping bag on the ground and with a last look at the Frenchman, sat down and started removing his boots.

Collins reluctantly looked away from Punchy and his sudden outburst, and looked at Henri. The man wasn't smiling, he didn't even move. Jack knew the Frenchman had heard the exchange between him and Alexander, but instead of joining the small debate, he just turned over and closed his eyes. Jack then threw his own unrolled sleeping bag down on the ground not far from the anchored and beached boat. Everett soon approached him with one of the Russian AK-47s slung around his shoulder.

"What are our orders for tomorrow, Jack?" Carl asked.

"I want to head upriver about an hour before sunrise, if that map and Charlie and the old woman's guesswork is accurate at all, we'll pull into shore around 0930 and we'll hoof it from there."

"And what makes you think they haven't heard us coming already?" Mendenhall asked, stepping up to the two men out of the darkness.

"Because we haven't been ambushed yet—with these killers, they wouldn't hesitate to kill us all if they knew we were close."

Mendenhall nodded his head and bowed to Jack's and Carl's experience in the field because between the two of them they had more combat and black operations experience than any two men in the country. He turned and went over and unslung his weapon, gently laid it down, and then he followed suit. His eyes were heavy and he knew that tomorrow there would be absolutely no rest.

Charlie Ellenshaw had watched the exchange between Collins, Everett, and Mendenhall and he waited until after Will had settled in to lean over Mendenhall to get his attention. Will had already closed his eyes without unzipping his sleeping bag.

"They wouldn't attack us in the dark, would they?" Charlie asked, startling the lieutenant.

"Jesus, Doc, don't do that!" Mendenhall said as he rolled over.

"Well, they wouldn't, would they?"

"Doc, if they knew we were here, yes, they would hit us in the dark. This isn't the old westerns you saw on television. Regardless of what you've heard, Indians, and Russians commandos, do attack at night."

Charlie looked around at the deep woods surrounding their small landing spot. "That's a comforting thought." As he settled into his sleeping bag, the stillness of the night calmed him. There were no beating of sticks against trees, a sound that had kept him terrified and intrigued since 1968. But for now the only sound was that of the light wind as it passed through the upper reaches of the trees.

"I take it we're not going to eat this evening?" Charlie asked, once more drawing the ire of Mendenhall.

Will removed his bush hat and then glanced over at the professor. "No, Doc, we're running a cold camp tonight, no hot grub, we'll eat some MREs in the morning when we hit the river again."

"Lovely" was all Charlie said as he lay down. "Lieutenant?"

"Good God, Doc, what is it?" Will asked opening his tired eyes for the third time since laying down. "I have the guard in just three hours."

"Oh . . . uh . . . I just wanted to say good night."

Will shook his head in the dark, feeling somewhat bad for snapping at the old professor. He knew he was just a little excited, and maybe even scared of being in these woods again. And after the story Ellenshaw told them, Will couldn't really blame him for reaching out. He smiled to himself and relaxed.

"Good night, Doc. Don't forget to take off your glasses before you go to sleep."

As Charlie lay down once more he stared at the mass of stars in the sky above. He knew that the others in the Group considered him a nerd, a man more prone to wet himself in a bad situation than to assist, but he knew things to be different for himself. He was far more excited about being back than men like Will Mendenhall would ever believe. He talked through his excitement just to calm the feelings he had about the Stikine and its wildlife.

As he lay on his sleeping bag, he looked over at the now still Mendenhall. He really liked Will, but he knew the lieutenant saw him as an old fool who filled his days with dreams of long-dead monsters and crazy ideas, but Charlie knew himself to be quite sufficient in the field, even though everyone thought him a lab rat. As he thought these things he slowly reached under his sleeping bag and made sure the safety was on the old-fashioned Smith & Wesson .38. Then he felt for the six-inch switchblade knife he always carried for luck. As he felt the two weapons he smiled; no, the old lab rat knew he could take care of himself when called upon—after all, he had been north of the Stikine before, and he knew it may take nerves of steel to face what's waiting for them across the river.

RUSSIAN BASE CAMP

As the rest of the force lay down in their tents, the few technicians still working had set up a powerful metal detector just a few feet from the water's edge. They made sure the connections were made and then they sighted the conical-shaped stand at a spot they had determined would show the best results. Two of the first shift guards watched them from a distance. There were at least fifteen men on watch around the camp.

"Do you think they have an idea where the gold is already?" one of them asked his shift partner.

The larger of the two Spetsnaz watched the technicians return to the largest of all the tents. "It's not the gold I would like to get my hands on, but the sister to that diamond the bosses have, that's what I would like to see."

The smaller guard was a late addition to the team, a man who had just received his discharge from the red army and one of the only men there that wasn't a true old-camp Spetsnaz. He looked at the tall man beside him, as if he were sizing him up. Then he looked around the camp and picked out six other teams of guards as they walked a perimeter. They were far enough away from their river position not to hear their voices.

"How deep do you think the river is at the point right across from us?" the man asked, watching the Spetsnaz for a reaction.

"Too deep to cross you fool, and don't think I don't know what it is you are thinking." He looked down at the man with steely blue eyes. "Even if you made it across, the boss would gut you and leave you for the wolves when you returned."

The small man turned away and saw the American woman who had chosen to sleep outside of her tent. She lay by the dwindling fire and he couldn't tell if she was awake or asleep. Then he turned back to look at the taller man.

"The boss wouldn't know if one of us stayed behind while the other had a look-see. I could be across and back in half an hour, with nobody suspecting I had even crossed."

"You fool, you don't even know what it is you're looking for. You could step right on something over there and not know it. Besides," the man looked across the river, "don't you feel it?"

"Feel what?" the small weasel of a man asked.

"I don't know. It's like when I was stationed in Afghanistan the last months of the war. I was a kid back then, but I remember I used to gaze into the mountains and know my killers were there." He looked back at the small man. "I get that same feeling looking out there, across the river. And I'll ask you this, we are being led by men who have taken on the new Russian government and beat them at every turn, so why are these very same men who are not afraid of anything, keeping south of the river. If what we seek is on the other side, why not camp there?"

The man didn't say anything. He just glanced over at the tent that held Sagli and Deonovich, and watched the line guard stationed at the front of their large enclosure.

"Because they know something we don't, my friend—they sense danger just as I do and they would prefer not to face whatever it is in the darkness. They are old-guard KGB and they know danger when they smell it."

The small man made a grunting sound and then shrugged his shoulders as if the explanation hadn't fazed him one bit.

"I think you Spetsnaz have been brainwashed to the point of paranoia. That story is proof that they just want to keep you in the dark about how much gold is really over there."

The tall commando just shook his head, and then turned and continued walking his post along the river.

The small man was regular army, one of only six others the team had been forced to take when others had been stopped and questioned coming into Canada. The Spetsnaz liked to joke about the regular army, saying "they didn't have the sense God gave to geese."

As the guard watched the far shore past the luminous passing of the river in the moonlight, he saw something that made him lean down and try to focus upon. It looked as if one of the trees had moved. He caught shadow moving against shadow, and that movement was betrayed by the bright moon as it shone down upon the far northern bank of the Stikine.

The man thought about calling his guard partner back over to inform him that someone had braved the river and crossed, and were now more than likely searching for the gold, just as they should be. However, something held him back as he glared into the night. He quickly unsnapped the small pouch on his belt and removed the night-vision goggles and placed them over his eyes. The movement on the far shore had ceased.

The darkness was still there beside one of the larger trees in the distant tree line and it hadn't moved since he froze and watched it. In the green filtered ambient light of the goggles, he could tell whatever it was it was huge, standing at least nine feet beside the tree. The guard raised the goggles and then shook his head and rubbed his eyes. When he focused the ambient light goggles again on the same spot on the far bank, the shadow he had been watching seemed to have blended in with the tree—or trees, as now he didn't see any discernable difference in any of the shadows as one bled into the other.

The guard knew that the Spetsnaz had tried to fool him with a spook story on how their bosses were frightened of the dark across the river, but he knew better. There was something over there all right, but it had nothing to do with spooks and goblins. There was gold, and what was the harm in finding out, especially if no one knew?

The guard smiled as he looked around and then caught up with his partner. After their shift was over, he would make his excuse to wander away to do his private latrine business, and then investigate on his own the far shore—danger be damned.

Twenty minutes later, the guard had waded across the same exact spot in the river that Professor Ellenshaw had crossed in 1968. The man turned just before exiting the water and watched the camp across the river. No alarm had been sounded as the change of watch was going about its business. The man smirked at the expertise of the old-guard Spetsnaz. They may have been good once, but those days were long past.

The man made his way out of the river and watched the woods. They were silent and unmoving. With the moon almost down, the ominous shadows had vanished and with it, the nervousness he had felt before crossing the Stikine.

As he made his way up the rocky slope, his foot struck something that sounded like metal. He stopped and reached for the object. He stayed on one knee and rolled the piece of black aluminum around in his hand. He was curious as to its misshapen state as he rose. At that split second of realization that he was no longer alone on the shore of the river, the guard slowly looked up. Instead of seeing the faint outline of the forest ahead, he saw nothing but blackness blocking his view. As his head continued to move upward, he dropped the aluminum he had been looking at and it tumbled to the rocks. As his eyes rose to the sky, he whimpered in his throat when he saw the eyes looking down at him.

The giant beast tilted its enormous head as it studied the small man before it. The eyes were a dull green and seemed to be illuminated from the inside. The man tried to take a step back and the beast grunted its displeasure at the movement. Then the guard made a move to unholster his weapon from his side. The great beast saw the movement and in a split second had reached out and grabbed the man's wrist, snapping the thick bone in two. The man was shocked at the speed of movement and really didn't realize his wrist had been snapped like a dry twig.

The animal grunted again and then its luminous eyes came up and it studied the camp across the river. When he felt the man start to pull away, the animal returned all of its attention to him. As the beast moved its head, the man was amazed to see that some of the thick, foul-smelling hair of its head had been braided. It was sloppily done, but braided nonetheless. The guard pulled harder at the restraining hand of the animal and that was when the great beast took the man into the air by grabbing his neck. It shook him like a rag doll, snapping not only his neck, but three places in his spine as well.

The animal held the man closer to its face and sniffed the body. It growled deep in its throat and shook the guard one last time, and when it stopped it glanced across the river once more toward the Russian encampment. It growled again, this time deeper in its chest until it finally escaped its apelike mouth.

The beast sniffed the air and then lowered the man in its grasp. Then it raised the body by its neck and tossed it into the Stikine as if it were nothing more than a stone. With one last look at the men across the river, the beast turned and walked into the dark woods.

Fifty-six miles downriver, Professor Charles Hindershot Ellenshaw III awoke so suddenly from dreaming of that long-ago summer of 1968 that he at first failed to realize where he was. He grimaced and then rolled over on the sleeping bag after tossing the top half off of his body, knowing that Mendenhall must have covered him after he had fallen asleep. He felt around and then raised the bottom half of the bag and pulled out a large rock that was jabbing painfully into his backside. He hefted the large stone and was just drawing back to toss it into the river, when a hand reached out and took his wrist. Charlie almost let out a wail of fright until he looked up and even without his glasses he realized it was the Frenchman, Farbeaux, who had stopped his rock toss. Standing beside him was Colonel Collins, who held his right index finger up to his lips. The stone fell from Charlie's grasp and it clinked onto the ground.

"What is it?" Charlie whispered when he saw their worried faces.

Instead of answering, Jack used hand signals to someone in the rear of their cold camp; Charlie then watched Carl Everett and Punchy Alexander emerge from the tree line. Then he placed a hand on Charlie's shoulder.

"Something came across the river about five minutes ago," Collins said, looking from a scared Ellenshaw to Will Mendenhall, who came in from the forest side of the camp. He stopped and shook his head in the negative at Collins. "Take a whiff with your nose, Doc. Have you ever smelled anything like that before?"

Ellenshaw turned his nose to the slight wind coming from the north. He did smell something on the air—it was an even deeper forest smell than what was naturally given on a regular wind. Earthy, most people would call it. Wetness, much like a waterlogged dog or other animal, mixed with the rich earth of the woods. He indeed had smelled that odor before.

"I have, once, many years ago." Charlie slowly stood and looked around. The moon was setting and he felt the small amount of wind that had been present a moment before, slowly subside. "They are close by."

Collins and Farbeaux were feeling something that the others besides Everett had yet to catch onto. They took a step toward the river, watching as they went. Then they stopped and one head turned the opposite of the other, slowly circling the area around them, finally settling on the trees behind their camp where Everett and Mendenhall had searched a moment before.

"Not even the Russians can be that brazen, or that stealthy," Will said as he looked around in the direction he had just come from with the old-fashioned Colt .45 Peacemaker six-shot revolver he had removed from his pack. The old woman had passed it to him back at the fishing camp saying, he looked more the fast-draw type than the others.

"I think the Russians are fast asleep many miles upriver, young Lieutenant; this is something else," Farbeaux said as he shook his head. "Whatever it was is gone now, Colonel."

"I told you, it's *them*," Charlie said, acting excited. "They are close."

Jack nodded his head, knowing Henri was right—whatever had come across the river was now gone. He was also taking Charlie a little more seriously than he had before. Their stealthy visitors were either gone, or went to ground. He looked at his watch and sighed. "Well, it's 0440, let's break out the Sterno and get some coffee going."

"Is that wise? The smell of coffee travels a long way," Charlie asked as he started rolling up his sleeping bag and then he looked up at Mendenhall. "And that I did see in a western."

Jack continued to look around the camp. "Wind is picking up again and coming from the north, Doc, the Russians are in the opposite direction," he said as if speaking to himself.

As the others watched the colonel slowly walk away, it was Henri who caught up with Jack at the river's edge. Collins turned and saw the Frenchman looking at a spot directly across from them on the northern riverbank.

"I'm glad you were alert during your watch, Colonel," Jack said turning back to face the river.

"Let's be honest here, you were as awake as I. No sleeping man has those kinds of reactions."

Collins gave a false smile, but didn't turn to face Farbeaux. "Whatever came across that river was fast and large as hell, it would have awoken a dead man."

"If you say so," Henri replied. "Now, what do we do about whatever it was, now that it is obviously over on this side of the river?"

"Nothing."

"That doesn't sound like you, Colonel."

"Whatever it was, all it did was join the others of its kind that were already following us, Henri." Jack finally faced Farbeaux. "In case you haven't noticed, we've been surrounded by whatever is out there every foot upriver we've traveled."

The Frenchman watched Jack turn and walk away. "Are you always so cheerful in the mornings, Colonel?"

WAHACHAPEE FISHING CAMP
THE STIKINE RIVER

Sarah McIntire and Jason Ryan had been so exhausted that they just rolled two sleeping bags out by the Bell Ranger where they had worked at tearing into the battered engine compartment most of the day and into the night. They had discovered that the only part that needed attention outside of a few rubber hoses was the fuel injector. It lay in several pieces on a blanket next to the skid of the Ranger. Jason said that he would be able to repair the minute holes in the complicated fuel delivery system with some melted lead or solder.

Finally, Sarah and Jason had called it quits and lowered the gas flow on the lanterns and went right to sleep without claiming the offer made by Marla and her grandmother of a hot meal. At 4:50 A.M., it was Marla who shook them awake.

"You have to come up to the porch—now," the girl said as she pulled a shawl tightly around her shoulders. Sarah saw that when the words came, the girl's eyes were not watching them but were on the woods to her right.

"What is it?" Sarah asked as her and Ryan sat up.

The girl didn't explain; she stood and started walking back to the general store. Sarah watched her go and then her eyes traveled to the porch. There she saw in the darkness the girl's grandmother standing with arms crossed, watching them.

"I think we better do what she says," Sarah said as she started shaking out of the sleeping bag.

"What? Is there a deer stampede headed our way or something?" Ryan asked, shaking his head and trying desperately to get the kinks in his muscles stretched out.

Suddenly, they both sensed the change that came over the fishing camp. The utter silence told them something was happening that they couldn't see, but could sense. Sarah looked at Ryan, and without hesitation stood and started for the grocery store and didn't look back until they had joined the old woman and Marla on the steps of the porch. When they turned, Sarah watched the woods, her eyes eventually moving to the river, which was now in total darkness since the setting of the moon. She could barely make out the helicopter as it sat before them only fifty yards away.

"What is it?" Ryan asked the old woman, who was watching the same area as Sarah.

"We've had visitors in the night," Helena Petrovich said as her eyes moved from the trees to the open area before the store. "I'm surprised you didn't wake up when they were rummagin' around that whirly chopper you were working on."

"When who was rummaging around?" Ryan asked, not liking the fact that something was so close to them and they never knew it.

The old woman didn't answer. She pulled her granddaughter closer to her and placed a protective arm around her.

"Are you saying that the local Indians steal things during the night?" Jason persisted.

Helena finally spared Ryan a look. "The Indians here 'bouts don't steal, navy man. And before you ask, we don't, either."

"He wasn't inferring—"

"Let's just say it would be better if you stretch out on the porch till the sun comes up."

In the distance, two gunshots rang out. They waited, but there was only one other that followed. Then silence once more took hold.

"Who in the hell's out there?" Sarah asked when the echoes stopped.

"Don't know," the old woman said looking toward the sound of the gunfire. "Maybe we should try for some sleep; Marla and I have a workday tomorrow."

"I think I can safely say, I'm done sleeping for the night," Ryan said, taking a step off the porch and walking toward the helicopter.

"Well, why don't we eat some breakfast then," Marla said hurriedly as she took three quick steps down the wooden stairs and quickly took Jason by the arm. "By that time, the sun'll be up."

Sarah could see that the girl was frightened and didn't want Ryan to return to the chopper.

"That's a good idea; we missed dinner last night," Sarah said, looking Ryan in the eyes and then using her head to get him to return to the porch.

"You know, it's not polite to keep secrets from strangers," Ryan said, relenting to Sarah's silent request and taking a step back as the girl pulled on his arm.

The old woman watched all three enter the store, then she called out: "Secrets are how privacy is kept, Lieutenant Ryan."

Two hours later the sun had crested over the small hills that hid the warmth of the new day till the last moment before it actually appeared over the closest of the giant trees.

Ryan stepped out onto the porch and was feeling better about the early morning wakeup call than he had before he ate a full stomach's worth of a breakfast that he knew was going to shorten his life by at least three years. He had never eaten so many eggs, sausage, biscuits and gravy in one setting. He patted his stomach and then made his way down the porch.

As he approached the Bell Ranger, he immediately saw that things were not as they were left when he and Sarah ceased working the night before. The blanket he had laid the fuel injector on was hanging from one of the rotor blades and even their sleeping bags had been tossed about like they were discarded rags. That meant that someone had been there after they had returned to the store early this morning.

"Damn it!" Ryan said angrily as Sarah stepped out onto the porch and saw him jogging toward the helicopter. She quickly followed.

As he approached, he started scanning the ground for the fuel injector. As he looked he saw the old tool box that the Petrov's had given him turned over and the old rusty tools were spread all over the rocky soil.

"What happened?" Sarah asked as she caught up with Ryan.

"Someone is screwing around with us," Jason said as he kicked the tool box upright. "The damn fuel injector is gone."

"Maybe it's on the ground somewhere," she said hopefully.

"All the other parts are here, but the injector is gone. It's large enough where you could spot it right off. Look, here are the hoses, even the housing screws."

"They took the one part that would get us into the air," Sarah said, deflating, as suspects started flashing through her mind.

"Was the part in need of repair shiny—you know, bright?"

They both turned to see Marla standing just behind them. She was fully dressed in her work clothes and had bundles of paper-wrapped bait fish piled in her arms.

"Yes, it was shiny aluminum," Ryan answered with hands on hips. "Why, do Indians like shiny things?"

"Grandmother said it wasn't Indians." Marla looked around, and then looked at the river. "As a matter of fact, they don't seem to be showing up this morning for their bait."

Sarah watched the girl as she scanned the river. Then she took a step toward Marla.

"Who took the part?" she asked, not trying to push the young girl too hard.

Marla laid the bundles of fish down on the stony ground. "I think if we look real hard, we may find it out there," she said pointing into the trees. "They usually get bored pretty quickly with things that they steal."

"Who gets bored with the shiny things?" Sarah asked.

"They mean no harm and just as I said, I bet we can find the thing you're looking for. They like shiny things is all," she repeated, scared that Sarah and Ryan were mad at her.

"It's the Indians, Sarah, come on," Ryan said, looking from McIntire to the girl. "Look, Marla, they won't be in trouble, but we need that part. We can't leave our friends out there with no way back. They'll need us, I guarantee you that."

"I'm sorry, I'll help you look. I bet it's not that far away," she said biting her lip and looking nervously about the woods.

"Oh, this is ridiculous," Ryan said as he reached down and retrieved the M-16 from where he had laid it the night before, thinking about why the Indians didn't take the weapon when they took the part.

"Lieutenant, the Tlingit are not thieves. They are the most honest people in the world, if they are guilty of anything, it's pride in what they do—living out here all alone. They live here where no man can survive without assistance from the outside world, they always have."

"Except for your family," Sarah reminded her.

"But that's just it, without the Tlingit, none of my ancestors could have made it here." Her eyes softened. "They did not take your part."

Ryan let out a loud breath, reached down and tossed Sarah her AK-47, and then started for the tree line.

Sarah watched him leave and then looked and made sure there was a round in the chamber of the Russian-made weapon. With a sad look at Marla—feeling she was being far less than honest with them—she turned and followed Ryan into the tree line. The girl quickly followed.

RUSSIAN BASE CAMP

Lynn had managed losing her tag-team guards for a few minutes, just long enough to relieve herself in the woods surrounding the camp. She could smell something that may be breakfast, or something akin to it. As she started toward the sounds and smells of the camp, that was when she saw it—or more accurate—them. There were a series of large footprints, the size of which were enormous, leading from the thick grove of trees to about the spot where Lynn had entered the woods to seek relief. As she bent over and looked closer at the footprints, she saw that they were almost human in appearance, with the exception of the size, as they were at least twenty-four inches in length and twelve inches wide. She swallowed as she turned her head back to where she had been moments before and saw that there were two differing sets, one coming, and one leaving the area. Whatever had made the prints had been watching the camp on the south side of the river.

Lynn stood, her eyes retuning to the giant impression at her feet. With total trepidation she laid her own size six shoe next to it. She closed her eyes when she realized that her small foot only covered the large toe of whatever creature made the print. Every legend and myth about the dark woods of the northwest came flooding back into her memory from childhood. When she found that she had actually stopped breathing, she opened her eyes and allowed the intrusion of the real world to flood back into her senses once more.

As Lynn took another deep breath, she first heard, and then saw several men running toward the large electronics tent. There were shouts and angry sounding orders being given, and then Sagli stepped out and looked around until he saw Lynn standing at the edge of the tree line. He quickly walked up to her, his hair hanging free and wild.

"Where have you been?" he asked stepping up menacingly.

"I assume I am allowed to use nature's facilities?" she asked, raising her brows, trying to get her emotions under control. She shuffled her feet across the closest foot impression as she stepped forward.

"You will ask for escort next time."

"I think I'll pass on presenting your men with a peep show so early in the morning."

Sagli looked as if he wanted to say something, but turned on his heels instead. Lynn watched as he started shouting orders. With one look back at the path she had just taken, she wondered if something was nearby—a thing that could not possibly exist, but evidently had escaped from the annals of B-Moviedom.

Deonovich soon joined the men as they started looking around the entire camp. It was as if they were searching for something. Lynn decided she would risk a backhanded strike from the large Russian and approached him.

"What happened, you lose something?" she asked.

Deonovich turned and saw Lynn and then grimaced. He started to turn away but stopped and then looked back at her.

"You slept out by the fire last night, am I correct?"

"Yes, I figured the tent was a little restrictive for a prisoner."

"Being a smart-ass American is not as endearing as you would believe. If we did not need you, I would throw your very mutilated body into the river."

Lynn didn't respond to the angry glare and threat as much as she wanted to.

"We are missing a man. Did you see anything out of the ordinary last night?" he asked.

"You mean outside of a bunch of Russian commandos out camping in the Canadian wilderness? No, not at all."

Deonovich raised his large hand to strike Lynn and actually managed to start it forward, when a shout stayed his punishment once again. Sagli was walking up, using a leather string to tie his hair back.

"Join the men in the search." He stared at Deonovich until the large man moved angrily away.

"Ms. Simpson, we have not only lost a man, but also the signal from our metal detectors from across the river. Do you have any idea how this could be?"

"Some of your men don't look to be the brightest, so—" Lynn started but stopped. She could see in the dark eyes of Sagli that he wouldn't brook another of her insults. "No, I don't."

Suddenly, several of the remaining twenty-five men started shouting from the edge of the river. Sagli turned and quickly left. Lynn, for her part, slowly followed as if only casually interested.

When they arrived, the men had calmed down. Sagli, expecting the worse—a drowned soldier—saw what they had been shouting about and the curious look on his face told Lynn that what he was seeing was something he had not expected. Lined along the rippling shoreline of the fast-moving Stikine, were arrayed four of the small round devices she had seen the large soldier shoot across the river the day before. From the look of them, they were still operating as lights flashed on and off. She saw Sagli look around and then down again at the metal detectors. Then he turned to the small technician who quickly leaned down and retrieved one on the small objects.

"Well, do you still have a pinpoint location to start the search? We no longer need these, am I correct?"

The small bespectacled man looked up. "Yes, sir, we triangulated a starting point last night from the devices. The radia—"

Sagli waved the man into sudden silence before he could complete his answer. He looked around him at the other soldiers who had started to wander away, continuing their search for the missing guard. Satisfied they hadn't heard anything, he looked at Lynn, but she had been smart enough to turn her back on the conversation soon after hearing the technician's slipup.

"Good, now how did these get over on this side of the river?" he asked, looking from the technician to once more eye Lynn. "It doesn't matter. You men"—he shouted out—"prepare the camp; we are moving across the river."

The men started splitting up as Lynn watched them move away. Deonovich waited and then waved Sagli over to the where he was standing with one foot in the river. Lynn stood her ground and watched, and they didn't seem to care that she was there. Sagli stood in front of his partner, and then looked down when Deonovich indicated something down upon the riverbank. The ponytailed Sagli bent to one knee and then reached and felt the wet soil. Then he stood and gestured for Lynn to come over.

"Tell me, have you ever seen anything like this before? Being American, you watch far more television than I or my friend here."

Lynn looked at him curiously, and then lowered her eyes to a spot indicated by the wet boot of Deonovich. Her eyes widened in pretend shock at seeing what she was looking at.

"No, I must say I haven't."

It was only half there, as the missing part disappeared into the clear waters of the Stikine, but she could clearly see the large toes and instep of the creature that had made the same prints inside the tree line. Like the one she had examined a few minutes before, this print dwarfed the boot of the giant Deonovich as he stood beside it. Sagli quickly reached out and scraped his own smaller boot across it, destroying the evidence. The other prints farther up the shoreline hadn't been as defined as they were laid into the larger stones that made up the riverbank.

"Look around and make sure that there no more of these about; check the sandier soil, these rocks would hide anything distinctive," he said to Deonovich. He then turned to Lynn. "You will remain quiet about this discovery, or I will be forced to deal with you."

Lynn didn't respond, she only looked at the disturbed sand where the print had once been. As Sagli started to walk away, she caught up with him.

"Maybe you haven't noticed, but I may not be your only problem. It seems like there may be something out there you didn't account for on this little safari. I think they call whatever is stalking us a Sasquatch, or that little funny name most people laugh at, Bigfoot. Maybe you should have listened and accounted for some of the stories about this area."

Sagli stopped and smiled at Lynn.

"We have accounted for everything, Ms. Simpson—everything."

9

Mendenhall slowly made his way back to the rear of the Zodiac, stepping easily past Captain Everett as he slowed the large boat down and threw the engine into idle to ease to silence their approach around a blind corner as they entered into another bend in the Stikine. Will squeezed in beside the food packs and eyed Jack.

"Colonel, how long have you known the Canadian?" he asked, looking away when Collins looked over at him.

"Punchy and I trained together once upon a time in the UK. He was with MI-5 at the time and I was assisting our DELTA teams. We were their garnering some training from the British SAS. Old Punchy never was much of a field man," Jack said as his eyes went from Will to the large form of Alexander sitting in the bow with Henri, who seemed to have developed a strange attachment to the Canadian, because of late he hadn't been ten feet away from him. "He and Doc Ellenshaw have that in common—they don't like bugs or things that go bump in the night. But he is the best intelligence officer I have ever run across"—he again looked at the black lieutenant—"with the exception of my baby sister. His main thing is computer espionage. He can break into most intelligence agencies and steal whatever he wants."

"Anything else, Colonel? I mean I've seen it before, like with Captain Everett: There's a closeness with people who have lived and almost died together. You and Alexander have that."

Collins eyed his young lieutenant and was proud of the way Will had progressed; he was starting to develop the leadership skills that he knew he had all along. What's more, Mendenhall was becoming an observer of human nature.

"In 1989, Punchy and I were dispatched on a recon mission just north of Vancouver to recover something of importance, that's how we met. There's nothing more than that."

"You're proud of what she's achieved, huh, Colonel?" Will asked, taking the colonel by surprise.

Mendenhall knew he was treading dangerous ground with the man he had known for three years now. Jack Collins was probably the most secretive person he had ever known—his private life was off limits.

Jack smiled as he thought about Will's question. "Yes, I am proud of Lynn. Oh, we've had our differences: She's a crusader, one that will bash her head against the wall to do the right thing."

"Sounds like someone we know, doesn't it, Lieutenant?" Carl Everett said from his place behind the wheel of the boat as he placed the throttle of the motor to almost full speed as they came to a straight stretch of river.

Mendenhall didn't say yes or no; he did however smile when he saw the look on Jack's face—a look that said he didn't know what Everett was talking about.

"Slow the boat, we have something in the water up here," Punchy called out as he and Henri traded places in the bow.

Carl eased the throttles back as Punchy Alexander looked at the Frenchman and told him to hold his belt as he leaned far over the side of the rubber craft. He yanked and pulled at something in the water until he finally lifted a body halfway out.

"Goodness," Professor Ellenshaw said, laying his notebook down and frowning.

The man was pale white, but they could see from the facial features that he hadn't been in the water that long. The head was twisted almost backward and looked as if his jaw and both cheek bones were smashed.

"Damn, his body is all busted up," Punchy called back.

"Check his arm," Jack ordered from behind Farbeaux and Alexander.

Henri reached out and ripped the sleeve away from the shoulder. There was no tattoo.

"Okay, so we now know all of the mercs aren't Spetsnaz," Collins said. "Let him go, Henri, we don't have time for any burials."

Alexander and Farbeaux let the body go and allowed the river to take him. Ellenshaw leaned over and watched the body slide by.

"I think I would have liked to determine the cause of death, Colonel," Charlie said as he watched until the river swallowed the young Russian soldier, not knowing if he really wanted to examine it or not, but feeling he should at least say he wanted to.

"I believe you could say his neck was broken, his back snapped in more than one place, and his face crushed, Doctor," Farbeaux said as he reached over and washed his hands in the Stikine.

"Poor man," Charlie said as he leaned back into the boat.

"Just remember, Doc, it was a bunch of those good men that tried to ambush us," Punchy said as he resumed his place in the bow of the boat. "The mercenary bastard looks like he may have gotten a taste of his own medicine."

Jack watched the exchange between Ellenshaw and Alexander with mild curiosity. Punchy slammed his hands into the bow wake of the Zodiac and washed his hands. Collins saw that his features were stretched with disgust, or was it something else about the body that disturbed him more than just the death stiffness of the soldier?

"He probably drowned and the rocky bottom of the river did the damage to his body, huh, Colonel?" Mendenhall asked.

Jack looked at Will but said nothing. He eased himself beside Everett.

"I think we can probably only risk about another two miles, then I think our little navy has to get out of this thing and start hoofing it—or as we say, do the Jack Collins two-step."

"Is that what they say?" Jack asked. "Yeah, I suspect we may be running into trouble soon enough if we stay on the water, these bends and curves are a perfect place to set up a river ambush."

"Oh good, are we going to walk now?" Charlie asked, actually looking excited to be off the water and into the woods.

"So now we can walk into a land ambush. Is that right, Colonel?" Henri said with his always present smile etched onto his face.

"You can always get out and swim back, Henri," Collins said, this time with his own smile.

"No, I'll try for the Twin diamonds, but looking at that Russian soldier, I would say that our chances on land may not be as good as we initially hoped they would be."

This time the smile on Jack's face widened as he was actually amused by the Frenchman.

"No one ever said you were dumb, Henri."

WAHACHAPEE FISHING CAMP

Jason pushed through the prickly bushes that covered the forest floor, having endured over a hundred scratches on his face for his efforts. He hadn't seen Sarah in the past hour, but heard her cuss loudly about fifteen minutes earlier, so he knew she was faring no better than himself in the tangled undergrowth searching for the fuel injector. Of Marla Petrov, he hadn't seen or heard a thing since their makeshift search party began.

Jason broke through a particular harsh section of undergrowth with pieces of bushes and thorns sticking to his face and Levis shirt, and into a small clearing of which a rippling creek ran through. He took a deep breath as a small fresh breeze sprang up. He instantly felt the clear air that greeted him after the harsh, closed in and fetid air of the thick tangle foot of the forest. He placed his hands on his knees and saw a million of the small thorns had also penetrated his jeans. He shook his head as he went to the clear creek. He washed his face, feeling the pleasant sting of the water hitting his sweat-filled scratches.

Feeling half human again, he looked into the water after drinking a few cupped handfuls. He instantly saw it and stood so fast that he dropped the M-16 he had rested on his bent knees. When he examined the fuel injector closely, he saw it had been wadded up like a piece of discarded paper. He looked around as the woods surrounding the creek became still. He slowly bent over, still watching the trees and retrieved the four-pound injector and the M-16 from the water.

"Damn it," he said under his breath. "Why in the hell would someone do that?"

When a crashing noise sounded behind him, Jason thought a bear was coming to claim his small person. He dropped the smashed fuel injector into the water and turned with the M-16 just as he saw Sarah trip and stumble into the clearing.

"You okay?" Jason asked as he reached to steady her.

"Water—oh that looks good," she said as she walked the few feet to the creek and then sank to her knees. She pushed her head into the cool stream and washed her face, and then she cupped her hands and drank. She took a breath and then turned to face Ryan. "We're not very good at this wilderness thing, are we?"

Ryan walked to within a few feet of Sarah and then reached into the water and pulled up the battered injector.

"So much for shiny things, huh?" he said as he let the fuel injector slide from his hand and into Sarah's.

"What the hell, did they take a rock to it?" she angrily asked as she stood up.

"They probably didn't even know they damaged it."

They both turned and saw Marla standing just out of the woods. She looked fresh as a daisy and didn't have a scratch on her.

"Okay, who in the hell are *they*?" Ryan asked, his temper starting to rise. "And don't give me any of this mystical bullshit."

The girl looked from Ryan to Sarah; instead of answering, she walked to the creek and took a drink of water from her cupped hand.

"It doesn't matter about the damaged part, Mr. Ryan," she said as she finally looked up. "You don't need it."

"What do you mean?"

"Jason, let her finish," Sarah said, eyeing the young woman closely.

The girl straightened and then pointed. "About a hundred yards in that direction." She stepped into the water and then across the creek and vanished into the woods.

"Jesus, can that girl ever give a straight answer to anything?" Ryan said angrily as he watched Sarah quickly follow Marla.

In extreme exasperation, Ryan followed. The woods were thinner here and for that he was grateful. He saw Sarah's back as she dipped and then straightened to come through the thinning trees. Suddenly, he ran into her backside as she came to an abrupt halt.

"What the—"

Sarah was just standing there, amazed at the sight she was looking at in the large clearing. Jason stepped around her and his mouth wanted to drop open. There, sitting pristine and shining in the bright sunlight were four, brand-spanking-new Sikorsky helicopters. They were the newest top of the line S-76 turbojet models. Their four bladed rotors drooped and swayed in the light breeze. Ryan brought up the M-16 and Sarah followed suit with the AK-47. Marla turned in front of them and shook her head.

"There's no one here. I came upon them just before I found you. These are the same ones those Russians arrived in."

"The pilots must have gone with them," Ryan said as he started to step out from the tree line, but Marla was quick to grab his arm.

"No, the pilots were ordered to stay, I heard that head Russian myself. I just assumed they went back to Juneau or someplace."

Ryan listened, but still couldn't grasp any danger. "Okay, we spare one and disable the others."

"You're not hearing me, Mr. Ryan, the pilots are missing," Marla persisted.

"Okay, young lady, you have our full attention, so I think it's about time you shed a little light on what's happening around here."

Marla looked at Sarah, dropping the restraining arm from Ryan.

"Okay, I fear those pilots may have run into the same thing you and Sarah did last night." Her eyes stayed on Ryan.

"Those gunshots, you mean?" Sarah asked.

Marla just nodded her head once while examining the makeshift landing area where the giant Sikorsky choppers sat. Sarah thought the scene was unreal. The empty helicopters, the wind whistling by the swaying rotors and the open staircases of the four aircraft lent an air of ghostliness to the scene that gave her cold chills.

"Look, Marla, what is happening here?" Sarah persisted with her earlier question.

"You wouldn't believe me if I told you."

"Try me," Sarah said still looking around, the AK-47 turning as she did.

"You don't look like the type to believe in myths and legends," Marla said looking from Sarah to Ryan.

Both of them exchanged looks but didn't smile at the foolish statement made by the girl. How could she know what they did for a living or the things that they have been witness to?

"We protect one of those legends here, or maybe they protect us, I don't know. But there are animals in these woods that belong here even more than the Indians that inhabit this area. They were here thousands of years before everyone, and this is their home. I'm afraid those Russians may have done something stupid last night and have paid dearly for it, or soon will. *They* protect their own."

Suddenly, there was a crackling sound coming from one of the choppers. It was loud in the stillness that now held sway over the clearing. Sarah looked at Ryan and she could tell he was feeling the same creepiness that overwhelmed her on this bright, clear, sun-filled day. Before she had a chance to ask what the crackling sound was, it came again, and then what seemed like a voice.

"Oh, God," Sarah said with a loud exhale, "it's a radio."

Ryan eased his way past the last of the trees and made his way to the first chopper in line. Sarah and Marla slowly followed. Jason leaned into the first of the well-equipped helicopters and saw that at first sight all looked normal. The plastic-covered interior was immaculate compared to the sparseness of the Bell Ranger they had been working on the night before. The windows sparkled and the carpeting on the floor smelled of its newness. As Ryan tilted his head, he heard the radio in the front cockpit come to life with a crackle and then a Russian voice come out of the speakers. It became insistent when there was no return answer.

As Ryan braced his feet to enter the Sikorsky, he felt a crunch under his right foot. He stepped away from the opening of the helicopter and looked at what he had stepped on. He looked from the object on the ground to Marla. The anger was etched in his features and his eyes were blazing. He kicked the smashed microphone from the choppers radio toward the spot Sarah and Marla stood.

"I suppose you didn't destroy the only way we had for calling for help?" Jason asked.

Marla held Ryan's gaze and gave back some of her own.

"I said before, Mr. Ryan, we will not allow the outside world to destroy what we have here. All of the invaders of the high country are on their own. If they're good, or bad, it makes no difference—you or the ones you are looking for don't belong here."

Sarah didn't know what to say, she was dumbfounded that Marla would go to those lengths knowing what the Russian assault team had done to the Mounties and to themselves.

"We have friends out there, and now it's time you let us in on your big secret. Jason, pick one of the helicopters, it's time we go and find Jack and the others."

RUSSIAN BASE CAMP

Lynn was watching the men as they lowered the tents and started placing the expensive equipment into their waterproof cases. The soldiers started placing heavy packs onto their backs as they made ready to cross over. The boats were filled and Sagli and Deonovich looked satisfied that their goal was within sight.

The search for the missing man had lasted all of five minutes as Sagli declared that he would eventually show up, and that seemed to satisfy most of the men, especially the Spetsnaz who weren't too interested in searching for the man at any rate. The others looked surprised that more of an effort wasn't forthcoming and wondered if the same effort would be in place for them if they disappeared. There were a few grumblings, but Lynn knew the men would never show it to Sagli or to the brute Deonovich and their group of hard nosed commandos.

A Spetsnaz came over to where she was sitting on a large stone. His weapon was slung across his shoulder as his dark eyes peered into her own.

"You are now my responsibly and I have orders to break something on your body once we have crossed the river if there is any troubling from you, are we understandings each other?" he asked in poor English.

"Nyet," Lynn said as she stood.

The man looked confused for a moment, and then he saw that the woman was toying with him.

"Good, then I will enjoy the tasking of my duty to breaking your arm sever-ling times."

"Okay, just kidding, pea brain. Shall we go boating?"

The man stepped aside, deciding instantly that he did not like the American and how it would be a pleasure to break her bones.

The last of the larger tents still stood and inside Dmitri Sagli threw the microphone down and it struck the radio operator.

"You mean to tell me they didn't check in last night and you felt it did not warrant informing me?"

The small operator cowered away from the demented eyes of the ponytailed Russian.

"Did it occur to you that we left those helicopters there to be safe, out of harm's way in case we had company arrive here in the form of the Canadian federal authorities? And now they do not answer their radios at all—four pilots and not one of them is monitoring their radio? Gregori, this man is no longer needed: Dispose of him, we do not need fools from here on out."

Deonovich stepped forward and pulled the radio operator from his chair. The other technicians in the room stood.

"You wish to comment on my order?" Sagli asked, eyeing each of the soft-skinned men one at a time. "Very well, let him go. If any of you fail in his duty again, and think that I do not need to be informed of any and every development, small or large, you will remain in this godforsaken place, is that understood?"

Not one man spoke as Deonovich let go of the radio technician.

"Now, get to the boats with that radio and the last of the detection gear, and place them with the rest of the equipment. Once we arrive at the area you have designated, and if we do not find what it is we came for, I will shoot every one of you. Now move, we may have a problem that was totally unforeseen, thanks to you fools."

Sagli pulled Deonovich aside once out of earshot of the others.

"You are sure the helicopters were hidden and the pilots were given orders not to leave them until they were contacted?"

"I am positive, I gave the orders myself."

"Then we must assume that whoever dealt you that blow at the camp has initiated further hostilities toward us. They will be coming, I am now positive of that. And the only thing that eases my mind is the fact that they have company with them that will forestall any attack on us. And our friend undoubtedly has what we need with him."

Fifteen minutes later, the seven Zodiacs, brimming full to capacity with men and equipment, shoved off from the southern shore of the Stikine. The current caught them and took them south for the briefest of moments, but the powerful outboards caught hold and pushed them back to their crossing point.

Lynn watched the men around her. Some seemed calm and anticipatory of what they would find across the river, while others looked around nervously. The day was turning hot, but Lynn got the chills as she watched some of the more veteran soldiers among the Russians. They were the ones that were nervously watching the far shoreline, hands on weapons as they grew near to their destination.

Lynn half turned and saw Sagli watching her. Although she hadn't heard about them not being able to contact their transport at the fishing camp, she knew for a fact that something had changed, and it wasn't to their benefit, and most assuredly wasn't to hers.

The first of the large Zodiacs pulled onto the rocky shore, and as Lynn watched technicians and soldiers start unloading their equipment, she knew they may be crossing into a place they shouldn't be going. It was just a feeling, but like her brother Jack, she was in tune to what those feelings held, and that you should always acknowledge them, for the good, or for the bad.

Jack was leading the group of six men through the woods. Collins and Everett had instructed the rest on how to use the natural elements around them to camouflage their faces and bodies after the loss of their field equipment in the Grumman. Mud was utilized heavily and if it wasn't for the appearance of Charlie Ellenshaw, the whole process would have been mundane and miserable. As it was, Mendenhall and Everett could hardly hide their smiles behind their hands. To cover most of the professor's white hair, Jack had encrusted it with twigs and grass, and that conglomeration was held in place by handfuls of drying mud. Everett thought that the colonel had applied everything a tad too liberally.

Farbeaux followed close behind and Punchy was told to follow the Frenchman. Then came Charlie, stumbling every few steps through the tangled undergrowth, and finally Will and Carl. They had been on foot for the past three hours.

Collins suddenly stopped and held up his right hand with spread fingers, then he quickly gestured to the right and then to the left. As Punchy and Charlie stayed in line, Farbeaux went to the left, and as Will quickly turned to cover the rear, Everett went right. As Henri and Everett covered their flanks, only Alexander and Charlie were left to watch Collins as he became perfectly still and watched the area immediately to their front.

Jack heard what sounded like talking and knew they were close to where the Russians could be. The plateau had risen in their view since they started making their way north on foot and Charlie had confirmed it was remarkably like his memory said it would be. The main landmark described in the Lattimer entry in the journal indicated that they had arrived.

As he listened, the voices ceased and boat motors started. Jack, running bent over at the waist, moved silently through the woods, easily stepping over and around the tangle-foot that would trip up most men with the practiced art of stepping, and then sliding the foot back and inch or two in case the toe of his boot had hooked on an obstacle. Collins moved until he could see the river through the trees. He saw the last Zodiac shove off from the south shore of the Stikine. His eyes clearly saw the other six boats as they fought the swift current and angled toward the far shore. He held his ground and waited. Then he saw what he was looking for when the third boat touched the far rocky shore. A large Russian manhandled Lynn out of the rubber boat and shoved her toward a group of men standing and looking into the woods. Lynn shrugged the man's hand from her and moved forward.

Jack closed his eyes for only a moment to give into the relief he felt upon seeing his sister. He took a breath and then removed the filthy ball cap the old woman had given him.

"That's her, huh?"

Collins turned and saw Charlie Ellenshaw kneeling behind him looking across the river. Jack angrily looked back at Punchy, who in turn looked at him and shrugged his shoulders, as if saying he tried to stop him.

"Doc, from now on, you don't move unless you're told to do so, is that clear?" Jack whispered.

"Oh, uh, yes, I just . . ."

"Don't worry about it, Doc. Get back with Punchy; we're going back into the woods about two hundred yards and wait until well after dark before we cross."

"Oh, we're going to swim the river?"

"You can swim, can't you?" Collins asked, worried about what the professor's answer was going to be.

"Oh, yes, I was on my high school—"

"Fine, Doc, that's fine. Now come on, we better rest up."

"But if my memory serves, there is a spot just to the left of their camp that is shallow, and even has a sandbar at its midpoint."

"Good, we need to hear things like that, Doc. Now go back with Mr. Alexander."

Jack watched Charlie go and then turned back and watched the men standing next to his baby sister. He hated to see her in the position she was in, but for now there was nothing he could do about it. Even after they crossed, he knew they were outgunned twenty to one. He replaced the baseball cap and then used his hand signals to order the others to fall back. As he did, he was thinking about why the Russians were keeping her alive and now it would be an eternity until Jack could cross the river and get his sister back from these men who murdered as easily as asking for a cup of coffee.

RUSSIAN BASE CAMP
NORTH OF THE STIKINE

The magnetometers started maxing out as soon as they were uncased and turned on. The technicians buzzed with excitement as they pointed northeast and held steady.

"From the signal strength, Mr. Sagli, I would say what we seek is but one mile that way," the small Russian tech said as he held his hands cupped around the LED-lighted gauge to stop the glare of the setting sun.

Sagli smiled and then looked at Deonovich. He then turned and looked at the small plateau rising ahead of them. He knew that the readings would place their goal at the base of the small climb or at its summit. In either case, it was going to be theirs.

"Now, the other detectors. What is their reading?"

Another of the field technicians walked up, almost anxious to deliver the news his employer wanted the most.

"The M-224 detectors are picking up elevated levels, far more than can be accounted for naturally. We suspect that it is near the other denser metals we are detecting."

Sagli felt his knees bend, wanting to fold in on themselves as he heard the greatly anticipated news indicating that their partner had been right all along and they now had the justification for leaving behind albeit a dangerous world, but a rich and fulfilling one. The item they wanted was near, and they would have it in the next few hours.

Deonovich started organizing ten of his best men to start the trek into the bush, he felt they had wasted enough time in setting up a camp that they might never have used if they had gone straight to setting up Sagli's expensive equipment.

"Gregori, we must hold our place here. Our discovery has waited a very long time, so it can wait a while longer; we have instructions we must follow."

Deonovich stopped in his tracks and slowly turned to face his partner. The anger was clearly shown on his features. "It is right there; we can retrieve it and still be following orders. He can examine our find at his leisure."

"That is not following instructions, my friend, because there is a reason for waiting. Someone is coming who can verify our find; until that man arrives, she is not to be touched."

Deonovich turned away from Sagli and saw one of the pinpoints of his continuing ire—Lynn. He raised a hand and slapped her onto the ground and was about to bring his tree trunk of a leg back to kick her, when suddenly Lynn had had enough. She kicked out with her own booted foot and struck the large Russian directly to the side of the knee. Deonovich grunted in pain and went to his back, immediately reaching for his throbbing leg. Lynn pounced as if she were part cat, landing on his chest, and then brought up a stick she had found on the ground and took it straight to the side of the Russian's throat.

Sagli watched from a distance and a smile stretched across his face. He saw the men Deonovich had been organizing to go into the tree line start forward to take the angry American off their boss, but he held up a hand, indicating he wanted to see how this played out.

Lynn placed pressure on the small stick and held it in place just over the pulsing throb of the Russians jugular vein. She pressed even harder when he made a move to try and dislodge her. With black hair hanging in her face, and her cheekbone throbbing where she had been struck, Lynn Simpson was at a point where she didn't care what the outcome would be, but knew she would make sure this bastard never touched her again.

"That is the last time you'll take out your inadequacies on me. If you ever raise a hand or one of those fucking hooves to me again, I swear to God the last thing you will ever see is me punching a hole in your throat." For emphasis, Lynn pressed the dull point of the stick into the thin layers of skin at Deonovich's throat until she had a nice flow of blood.

"Someone kill this goddamn bitch!" Deonovich hissed as he froze under the onslaught of the smaller woman and her stick.

Without removing the pressure she was exerting on the stick, and without moving her face from the angry eyes of Deonovich, Lynn flicked her own green eyes over to where the smiling Sagli still held his commandos at bay with a raised hand. Sagli just tilted his head, as if he were awaiting Lynn's decision.

Lynn angrily poked the stick one more time and at the same moment removed her small amount of weight from Deonovich. The man grabbed for his neck and rose as if shot from a cannon. He started reaching for his holstered weapon.

"No. That will not do, old friend. Too noisy and far too premature. We still need her."

Deonovich still went as far as to pull the weapon. Lynn braced for the bullet that was surely coming her way, still holding the stick as if it were a magic talisman that would ward off the giant ogre. As Deonovich turned and started to raise the weapon, the sound hit them with a force of a hundred loudspeakers.

Sagli turned, forgetting all about the humorous confrontation he was witnessing. The other men bent low as if they had been ambushed for real, other than just audibly assaulted.

The roar of an animal reverberated against the tree line as far away as the southern shore of the river. The sound bounced back and sounded as if the entire camp was surrounded by a herd of whatever it was that made that horrendous sound. The animal cry was unlike any of the men from Russia had ever heard before. Some of the Spetsnaz hailed from the cold and hearty region of the Urals and it seemed to affect these men the most. Unable to think clearly with the continuing echo of the cry coming from the plateau to the north, the technicians, although armed with handguns, backed away from where they had been setting up tripods with motorized metal detectors on them. They watched the bright sunlit woods ahead of them, but still backed away nonetheless.

"What in God's name is that?" Sagli asked as he turned away from the trees. His eyes fell on Lynn, who was just standing there stiff, just watching the sun-dappled tress before them, her antagonist Deonovich no longer a concern. The small stick she used as a weapon slowly slid from her fingers. The look in her eyes told Sagli she had been taken as far off guard by the roar as they had been.

The men had gone silent with every set of eyes turned toward the tree line. Deonovich forgot all about the assault on his neck and used hand gestures to get his commando team to move. He gestured right and left and then used both hands to point straight ahead, the blood still dripping from his fingers. The Spetsnaz immediately broke into two-man teams and entered the woods at a trot. Deonovich clearly understood at that moment the reason for restraint before entering an area that they basically knew nothing about.

Sagli broke the spell by walking over and taking the American woman by the arm and pushing her toward her small tent.

"From here on out, you are to remain inside. You have now become far more important than you would ever believe."

Lynn was shoved ahead of the Russian and she decided that she had no desire to be outside with the sun falling lower and lower in the sky.

Sagli turned to Deonovich.

"I should have let that woman cut your throat. You are never to question my authority again or threaten the American. You could allow this whole operation to fail if you continue your unthinking ways. It will not be tolerated by me, or by our partner, I assure you. Is that clearly understood?"

Deonovich holstered his weapon, but made no move to voice an answer. Sagli decided not to push the larger man at this time because he had sustained enough embarrassment delivered by the very much smaller woman.

"Now, we will press into the woods a hundred yards before dark, no farther. We cannot afford to stumble upon our quest in the twilight as that could be fatal. Do you understand?"

Deonovich tuned once more to face his old friend. This time he nodded once and turned to join his men on the perimeter of the camp with the camps doctor walking beside him, trying in vain to place a bandage on his neck.

"Gregori?" Sagli said, looking down at his feet.

Deonovich stopped walking, slapping the hands of the doctor away, and then he turned to look back. Sagli finally looked up at him.

"You are originally from the Urals, as are some of the men. Have you ever heard anything like that before—that animal cry?"

Deonovich looked around him slowly. He knew Sagli was never more than three miles away from Moscow growing up as a child, so he had never before heard the sounds that emanate from the forests. The way they can play tricks on your brain, the direction could be totally opposite of where you thought the roar came from, or the sound itself could have been any number of animals. Instead of saying this, he decided to let Sagli stew in his own confidence of being master of his domain and a slave to his false bravery.

"No, comrade, I have never heard such an animal cry before. It was if a thousand lions roared at the same moment."

As Sagli watched Deonovich turn and walk away, hiding his knowing smile, he turned and watched the sway at the top of the large pine trees as the wind sprang up. The blow was coming from the north and it brought a sour, primitive smell with it; but of the horrific sound, they heard no more.

"Holly shit, what in the hell was that?" Will Mendenhall asked as he held the cold MRE dinner out to a stunned and staring Charlie Ellenshaw. The beef stew was cold and since a moment before when the sound of the animal reached them across the river, was much anticipated by the cryptozoologist.

Charlie finally lowered his eyes from the trees surrounding their once-again cold camp. He swallowed and turned and looked at the offered freeze-dried ration as if it were a cow patty being held out by Mendenhall, who finally lowered the Meals-Ready-to-Eat package, and then looked into Ellenshaw's eyes.

"I assure you, Lieutenant, I never really witnessed the animal that lives in these woods, so that noise was as mysterious to me as you. As much as my natural inquisitiveness compels me to investigate, my common sense says to wait until a fresh sun has risen."

"Doc, do you know what could have possibly made that sound?" Everett asked as he stepped back into the small clearing they were calling camp for the evening with Farbeaux in tow.

Ellenshaw was about to answer, when Jack and Punchy Alexander entered the clearing from the opposite direction as Everett.

"Okay, we need to talk," Jack said as he took the cold meal from Will's hand and started eating.

"I would think we would talk about what made that cry across the river, Colonel," Farbeaux said as he knelt and rummaged through the small box of MREs looking for something palatable.

Jack tossed the bag of cold stew over to Mendenhall, who caught it on the fly, but not before spilling some of it on his green plaid hunting shirt. He shook off some of it by shaking his hand, and then looked at the colonel who acted as though he didn't even notice what he had done.

"That's what the doc is along for; I'm sure he'll come up with something to put in his report," Jack said, watching the others, his eyes finally falling on Punchy Alexander and then moving on. "You will all be staying on this side of the river tonight." Jack held up his hand as Will and Everett started to protest. "At ease. This is my thing, my sister, my mission."

"And if you fail to bring her back?" Everett said as he stepped toward Jack, "We're supposed to pull up stakes and go home?"

Collins smiled. "No, I want you to kill every one of the sons-a-bitches—but not until I and my sister are dead. After that, you do what you want. Personally, I would avenge your colonel's death."

Everett shook his head and Mendenhall looked away.

"I can't accept that, Jack. I was there when your sister was taken by these bastards and I want in on going after her. I've come too far for you to take that from me," Punchy said, finally speaking up. "Besides, this is all happening on Canadian soil. It's my bailiwick."

Jack eyed the large Canadian without saying anything. He then tossed Everett a small chunk of something.

"What do you make of that, Captain?" he asked.

Carl caught the lightweight material in his large hand. It was crumpled and looked as if it had sat in the sun for years. The aluminum was once painted black, faded now to a dark gray.

"Could be anything," he said.

"May I?" Farbeaux asked standing with his MRE in his hand. He caught the piece of metal when Everett tossed it.

"Aircraft aluminum," Henri said as he looked it over. "I found several more pieces myself; it's not gold, and so I didn't care to report it."

Jack watched Farbeaux and saw that he didn't meet his eyes, which meant in Collins's opinion the man was lying, but ignoring it for the moment, nodded his head and then looked at his watch. "Punchy, in answer to your request—denied, you'll stay on this side of the river with my people."

Alexander didn't say anything, he just shook his head.

"May I presume, since I am not under your command, I may accompany you in the pursuit of my payment?" Farbeaux asked as he opened his plastic MRE and poured a small amount of water inside to mesh the dehydrated food into the mashed conglomerate that it was.

"If you attempt to come across that river before I return with my sister, Colonel, Mr. Everett will shoot you in your head until you are convinced to stay put."

Farbeaux looked at Carl as he mashed the contents of the MRE together as Everett just nodded his head as if to say Jack was not lying.

"I'm sure that would break the captain's heart," Henri said, finally opening his meal.

The sun had about fifteen minutes until it disappeared over the western edge of the plateau above them. Sagli was pleased so far with the artifacts they were finding. Small pieces of metal that his non-Spetsnaz men had yet to notice were gathered and placed inside of a pack so the rest of his men couldn't see. As most of the trusted commandos stood guard around the perimeter of their search area, Deonovich kept regaling the mercenaries from the regular army about the tales of gold and diamonds to be found. The Spetsnaz pretended not to listen, even though they would prefer the stories of gold over what they knew to be the real truth. To Sagli, none of it mattered as he looked through the direction finder at the next signal that the detector had picked up.

"We keep picking up these trace amounts of aluminum and steel, nothing of a major volume. Have you thought that maybe the trace amounts of uranium we are picking up is just residual, and that what we are looking for may not be intact?" the radiological technician said as he looked at the LED readout as Sagli looked through the directional scope.

"My concerns are that you keep within your parameters of expertise. Do not go into territory that is none of your business." He finally looked up at the tech. "You are being paid handsomely either way." He watched the man until he returned to his clipboard. Satisfied, he returned his right eye to the scope. As he refocused the lens that shot a laser across the hundred yards ahead of him, he caught what looked like a shadow through the scope mounted above the laser. The darkness was large and seemed to disappear into the shade of the giant trees. "What?" he said as he tried to find the strange shadow once more.

As Sagli was searching for his phantom shadow, a Spetsnaz standing near a technician's small field table looked up just as a warning beep was heard. He watched the technician move the laser he controlled left, and then right.

"What is it?" the former Spetsnaz asked.

"I don't know; our passive motion detectors have picked up movement, about a thousand yards ahead."

"Where exactly?" the commando asked as he waved Deonovich over.

"I'm not sure—everywhere I think," the technician said anxiously.

"What do you have?" Deonovich asked.

"Possible movement ahead of us, we don't have an intruder count yet."

"Silence that weapon and take a man forward, only a hundred yards, take our little friend here with you," Deonovich said, slapping the tech on the shoulder and tossing a silencer to the Spetsnaz.

The experienced soldier smiled as a look of apprehension came across the tech's face. He removed his handgun from a shoulder holster and then started screwing the silencer onto it. The man next to him did the same, and then the first man reached out and took the tech by the arm and made him rise from the small field desk.

"Gather your sensors and let's go."

The movement caught the attention of Sagli who had failed to see the shadow again. He nodded his head at Deonovich in approval of his action. Once he saw the three men walk forward of their line, he leaned back to the scope. After all, if they ran into something, it would give them far more knowledge than they had at that moment.

Ten minutes later, the technician had not recorded the same motion as he did earlier. The trees ahead were still and the area totally silent as he swept the area with his handheld detector. He shook his head at the nearest man. The sun was now gone and twilight had set in.

Just as the lead Spetsnaz was going to motion them back to the rest of the group, he caught wind of something on the breeze. It was a pungent odor, an earthy smell that came from all around them. Then he strained his eyes as he caught sight of a large tree ahead of them. He had sensed it more than actually seeing movement. He raised a hand and caught the attention of the other commando on the far side of the technician. He waved him forward. As he approached the large pine, the shadow broke free of its cover. It moved so fast that the Russian couldn't react. He brought the automatic up and shot three times, but he knew his silenced bullets struck nothing but the tree and the air. The shadow shot back into the trees in a frenzy of dark motion.

The commando eased forward and then leaned against the same tree where he had seen the strange shadow. He saw a bullet hole where one of his rounds had struck, and then he looked down. His eyes widened when he saw the soft sand around the base of the giant tree. The footprint was larger than two of his feet, in width and length. He kept the pistol's aim outward as he kneeled down to examine the impression. The toes were distinct and the heel had been planted hard enough to leave a depression eight inches deep in the soft earth and had actually crushed one of the thick, exposed roots of the giant pine tree. He looked up in more wonder than fear. Whatever had made the print had to weigh in access of a five hundred kilos. He straightened, and then he saw a darker area on the tree where he had seen the shadow. He touched a finger to the spot and it came away with rich, copper-smelling blood. The soldier wiped the redness onto his pants and then motioned the others back toward the camp. His weapon never wavered from the area to their rear as they moved south toward the very welcoming sounds of men.

The forest was silent as the men moved. The breeze didn't seem to penetrate the woods on this side of the river as much as it had on the south side. The absence of wind made the forest seem depressive.

As the three men finally turned away and made their retreat faster than before, twenty more of the shadows broke free of their cover and went north. The forms were large, twice the size of most men, and they moved with an upright gate that made them swift and confident in their long strides.

The forest north of the Stikine River was coming to life.

10

Sarah had convinced Ryan that he would only kill them if he attempted to lift the large Sikorsky helicopter off the ground with only an hour of light left to them. So Marla had started to lead them back to the general store with the promise that whatever had disturbed them the night before would not return to cause further harm to the remaining helicopters. Even more skeptical than before, Ryan relented.

As they walked through the trees, Jason watched as Sarah confronted the girl.

"Now, are you going to tell us what's out there, and how you can guarantee the safety of the helicopters?"

"Because, I think they left here. I believe they started north last night. I just don't know for sure."

"There it is again—*they*," Ryan said, slapping at a low hanging branch. "Come on, who are *they?*"

Marla smiled as Ryan caught up with her and Sarah.

"You are not the believing kind, Lieutenant, but I'll tell you. We are relative newcomers to this land. There were animals of every sort here many thousands of years before us. I've studied it as much as I could in the classes I have taken since I was a small child. I also have the stories passed down by my parents, grandparents, and great-grandparents. Even the Tlingit have told me the stories of the old ones who live here."

"You've hinted at that already," Ryan said as he again moved a branch that Sarah and Marla had easily avoided.

"I never told you I am taking anthropology at school in Seattle, with my major being zoology, did I?" Marla asked.

Sarah smiled. "You know, Professor Ellenshaw is the tops in his field. You two should have hooked up."

"I didn't want to say anything to the professor at the time, but I have read every one of his published works. He's really a brilliant man. Too bad his beliefs got him run out of three universities. That shows how the world looks upon certain theories as being heretic in many ways."

"Doc Ellenshaw believes in a lot of things, but we're not as closed-minded as you would believe," Sarah said, reminding the girl of what she told her before.

Marla looked as though she were thinking something over, and then she stopped and faced Sarah and Ryan.

"We have something in the northern reaches that need to be left alone. They are ancient, far older than the men who have followed in their evolutionary slowness. They are animals, and then again they are not." She held a hand up when Jason angrily rolled his eyes and started to speak. "You wanted the truth, so I am going to give it to you the only way I can."

"Go ahead, Marla," Sarah said, looking back at Ryan and shaking her head, indicating that he should keep his personality in check.

"The truth of what's up here has been told since the time of early man, passed down by northern tribes, and even picked up by southern Indians as far south as the United States. They have been witness to the real truth of the Chulimantan for centuries upon centuries."

"Chulimantan," Sarah repeated.

Marla smiled and then relaxed, knowing she had at least one attentive person.

"Yes, Chulimantan, the old folk and Indians around these parts call them *They Who Follow*. The reasons why they were called this has been lost for millennia, but all the indigenous people take their legends as fact, and they don't apologize for it. *They Who Follow* once inhabited the great northwest from the Arctic Circle to Washington, Idaho, Oregon, California, and Nevada. They were soon forced out by the growing American population." Marla took a breath. "They have started to decline in their narrow lands now. Nature is weeding them out and, of course, they don't understand their diminishing family state, and lately, at least the last hundred years or so, they have become far more aggressive in their behavior."

"Can you tell me just what in the hell you're talking about?" Ryan asked.

It was Sarah's turn to smile as she finally understood without Marla naming her legend.

"She's talking about Sasquatch, or as we think of it, Bigfoot."

Ryan didn't say anything, he just looked from Sarah and then to

Marla. A slow, ever-growing smile crossed his lips and expanded until he raised his right index finger at both of the women.

"Okay, you had me going there for minute," he chuckled. "Bigfoot—now that makes sense."

"Remember the Amazon, Jason. Why is this so much harder to believe?"

Ryan did remember the Amazon, although he never saw the legendary creature, half man and half fish, that roamed in that dark, hidden lagoon. The colonel said it was there, so he himself never questioned the sanity of everyone who had seen it—but still, Bigfoot?

"No . . . fucking . . . way." Ryan laughed out loud.

Marla smiled. "That is the attitude we hope the rest of the world takes, Mr. Ryan. With that widespread disbelief it will keep people out and far away from the Stikine."

Before Ryan could comment again, the pounding of wood on wood sounded from miles away.

"You see, they are communicating. That's their way."

"Do you understand what they are trying to say?" Sarah asked.

"Don't have to understand, they only do that when they feel they are threatened. The striking of wood means they are gathering."

"Jack." Sarah only said the one word.

"It would seem the Russians and your friends have attracted some unwanted attention," Marla said as she turned to finish the walk back to the store. "And when pushed into a corner, the beast that legend, your own Professor Ellenshaw, and my family know as a possible link to a prehistoric ape called Giganticus Pythicus, they will prove what a survivor they truly are."

"Will they attack?" Sarah asked as she hurriedly followed, wanting an answer.

Marla stopped and turned.

"Giganticus Pythicus had supposedly died off during one of the most tumultuous and dangerous times in all of history—the last ice age. They are survivors; they have adapted to a violent world, so in defense of their home, Sarah, they will plan and execute, and they will kill anything they deem a threat to their family." Marla wanted to smile at the irony, but didn't. "Almost like a human would react, wouldn't you say? Maybe they have learned very well from watching our species."

NORTH SHORE OF THE STIKINE RIVER

Lynn watched the camp as it settled in for the night. Her attention was focused on a large tent that two guards stood in front of. Deonovich and Sagli had gone inside around sunset and had not left. Earlier, she had seen several boxes of articles moved inside, followed closely by the two Russian criminals.

She once more looked around and was about to exit her small tent when a pair of boots came into view. It was the large man who had threatened her small and fragile bones that morning. He raised his boot and not too gently shoved Lynn back inside.

"We's will be bringing your supper sooner, until then I do not wanting to see your face."

"Hey, I heard you guys had a scare this afternoon?" she said, hoping for a reaction.

She didn't see the large man frown, but she did see him abruptly turn away.

"I guess I will be wanting to seeing your face later," she said mocking his terrible English.

Lynn took a deep breath and was about to turn to lay down on her sleeping bag when she saw ten men gathering at the small fire in the center of the camp. They had darkened their faces and were in the process of checking some equipment. One of those pieces she saw were night-vision goggles. While she watched, Sagli finally made an appearance and approached the men. He spoke to them in Russian and Lynn could not follow what was being said. While she watched, she also took note that the men were all Spetsnaz. The other members of the team were standing guard or eating in their oversized mess tent.

Sagli said his final words and then looked at his watch. He nodded and the ten men left the fire, and disappeared toward the river where Lynn could no longer see them. She had a feeling that the commandos were leaving camp for a purpose that would not benefit her or anyone who may be following. The men she had seen were the most impressive of the Spetsnaz.

She only hoped if someone was out there they were alert, because she thought they were about to have company.

———

Jack was sitting alone. He looked at his watch three times in the last few minutes. The camp was fireless and they had finally forced some of the cold MREs down their throats with Henri Farbeaux complaining every bite of the way and constantly complaining about American military cuisine.

Jack watched as Professor Ellenshaw moved away from his sleeping bag where he had been sitting and watching the others. Collins knew something was on Charlie's mind, but was unwilling to ask him about it moments before he himself was due to cross the river. Charlie approached Jack, rubbing his hands on his pants leg as if he was nervous about what he had to say.

"Hi," Charlie said, not really knowing how to approach a man who still intimidated him even after years of knowing him.

"Hello, Doc. What's on your mind?" Jack said looking at his watch one more time and then pulling an old .45 Colt automatic from his side and checking the clip.

"Before you go, I wanted to say . . . well . . . thank you for bringing me along. I know it went against everything you believe me to be." The professor looked around; the others were busy doing this or that, things Ellenshaw had no idea about.

"Listen, Doc, I do pay attention to what you go through with the other sciences at the complex. A few of them snicker behind your back, but for the most part you've become a very valuable asset to the Group. After the things I've seen since being on this job, doing what you do probably makes more sense then what ten PhDs from other fields command."

"Thank you, Colonel. Outside of Niles, and even though you're a military man in the purest sense of the words, and being as I avoided the duty during my formative years, I respect you more than most for what you have achieved."

Jack looked the professor over, and then gave him a small smile and a short shake of the head.

"Thanks, Doc. You know, after the story you told about this place and the detail in which you delivered it, I could see you weren't scared like the others may have thought they saw. What I saw in your eyes wasn't fear, it was excitement. So telling you that you couldn't come on this trip would be like telling Mr. Everett tonight he couldn't go with me on a combat mission. My job is to protect field personnel, Doc; that's why you're here, to do your job and see what you can find out about what kind of animal life we have up here. That's all. You're here for differing reasons than us, but that doesn't make you any less important to this mission." Collins holstered the .45. "You belong here, Doc."

"I don't know what to say, I want—"

Jack stood and slapped Ellenshaw on the shoulder. "Save it, I have to go."

"Colonel?"

Collins stopped and turned to face the cryptozoologist.

"It's real, you know. It's not just a legend, and surely not a myth, but a scientific fact."

Jack rechecked the load in the AK-47 he was carrying, not wanting to look Ellenshaw in the face.

"What is real, Doc?" He finally looked up into the professor's thick lenses. "Can you say it? Believe me, out here in this place, no one's going to laugh."

"The animal is an offshoot of Giganticus Pythicus—the great ape. After many years of thought on the matter, that's the only thing it could be. It's here, Colonel, and very much a viable force."

Collins reinserted the magazine inside the Russian weapon and charged a round into the breach.

"Doc, what is its name? Until you say it, it really isn't real, is it?" Jack persisted.

"Bigfoot . . . it's . . . the legend of Bigfoot that's out there, Colonel."

"There, that wasn't so hard was it, Doc?"

Ellenshaw smiled and nodded. The colonel was right; it was far more comfortable once the name was out in the open.

Jack turned to leave as Everett approached.

"You're a damn fool, Jack. You need help."

"A long time ago when a woman was stolen by Indians, rescuers never launched a raid into their midst, they always snuck in at night and stole them back."

"Those men out there aren't Indians, Jack," Everett started to say, but saw something behind Jack that made him stop.

Collins turned and saw Punchy Alexander step into their small clearing. He nodded a greeting as he approached the two men.

"Where is Will?" Everett asked as he heard Jack click the selector switch on his weapon from its safe position. Carl wasn't wary until that moment. He had left his M-16 on his sleeping bag.

Alexander didn't answer. He went to one knee and then looked at the two men before him. Then he saw Ellenshaw, and just as quickly dismissed him. He found Henri Farbeaux lying on his sleeping bag, watching what was happening.

"Colonel Farbeaux, if you would remove your hand from that Colt at your side, you may live through this," Alexander said.

Henri sat up and held up two empty hands.

"What in the hell is this?" Everett asked, wondering why Jack remained silent.

"Professor Ellenshaw, please sit on your sleeping bag and make no silly movements." Punchy then turned and waved to the darkness behind him. "I'm afraid we have company," he said as he looked Jack in the eyes. "Sorry Jack, the bastards snuck up on me after they took the young lieutenant."

There was a grunt and then a man was thrust into the clearing. In the darkness, both Everett and Jack saw it was Will Mendenhall. He landed with a thud not far from them and Carl reached down to assist him to his feet. Mendenhall was bloodied somewhere in his scalp and his nose was broken.

"Sorry, Colonel . . . Captain," Will moaned, wiping blood from his nose. "This fucker cold-cocked me," Will said as one of the largest soldiers any of them had ever seen stepped into the clearing with his weapon leveled at Mendenhall's back. Then the Russian pointed his automatic at Alexander and gestured for him to join the others.

"I guess I'm getting too old for field work. I'm sorry, Jack." Alexander raised his hands as he stood next to Collins.

The large Russian waved his right hand and then the clearing became crowded with Russian commandos. They stood far back from the Americans, the Canadian, and lone Frenchman, but their weapons were well equipped and they were all aimed at preselected targets. Collins eyed the men surrounding them and then looked at Alexander.

"Will, do you think you're going to live?" Jack asked Mendenhall as he looked over the situation.

Will nodded his head, not liking the way it made him dizzy, but he didn't want the Russians to see how bad he was hurt. "I've been hit harder by my sister, Colonel," he said as he tried his best to stand straight, but kept most of his weight leaning against Everett.

"It's my fault, I was at point, I should have seen—"

"It's time to quit playing the good guy, Punchy."

Everett looked over at Alexander and saw a small smile appear as he lowered his hands.

Punchy turned and walked over to the largest of the Russians, the one that had slammed his rifle butt into Will's face, and reached out and took the holstered automatic from the man's side. Then he turned and faced Jack and the others. He clicked off the safety and then raised the weapon toward his one-time friend with the smile still on his face.

"Nice friends you have, Jack," Everett said as he reached out and steadied Will as he swayed, almost falling down.

Collins remained silent as he looked into the eyes of Alexander.

"I told you, Jack, you shouldn't cross the river tonight. My friends knew we were here and would have been waiting, and for the moment I can't have you hurt. You're far too valuable. However, everyone else here, including young Lynn across the way, are now expendable. Your sister has done quite well at luring you into the open, Jack . . . let's not waste that."

Charlie Ellenshaw, without warning, reached out and tried to grab a weapon that was in the firm hands of the Russian closest to him while at the same time pulling out the switchblade he kept in his back pocket. Jack and Everett tried to move, but for the first time in their professional lives, found they couldn't.

"Doc, no!" Collins finally shouted out.

Ellenshaw actually did manage to take the Spetsnaz off guard. He grabbed the barrel of the man's Kalashnikov, while at the same time slamming home the small knife into the man's arm, but that was as far as he got. While the Russian soldier screamed at the insult of the knife entering his arm, Punchy Alexander raised the automatic and shot Ellenshaw in the back. The professor, still holding the barrel of the weapon felt the bullet strike. He stumbled forward and fell, the bloody knife still clutched in his hand. The commando, ignoring the small wound to his arm, moved his feet out of the way and Charlie hit the dirt and lay still. The Spetsnaz watched the body go still and then spit on Ellenshaw's back.

Everett lunged but was stopped by Jack. Mendenhall turned and shouted something that was incoherent.

Collins gently shoved Carl back and then tossed the AK-47 to the ground. Then he looked up into Punchy's face.

"I'll kill you for that."

Alexander stood and shoved the still-smoking weapon into his waistband as he motioned for the Russians to take control of their new prisoners.

"The days of you making good on threats are over, Jack," he said as he stepped up and whispered into Collins's ear. "Tell me, as little as five years ago, could I have maneuvered you out of wherever you were hiding in the thick recesses of your black world and trick you into following your sister's kidnappers without you suspecting something was wrong?"

"What in the hell is he talking about, Jack?" Everett asked as he was shoved to the ground by a Russian and frisked.

"It was a setup from the beginning," Collins said as he, too, was shoved to the ground and roughly checked for more weapons. His pistol was tossed away and then for good measure, the large Spetsnaz shoved Jack's face into the dirt.

"Now, now, we'll have none of that. Our friend here is about to do us a great service. Let's move them across the river to meet the men they came here to meet?"

"Let me check the professor," Mendenhall said as Farbeaux was shoved into him.

"I'm afraid there is no use, Lieutenant, he cannot be saved," the Frenchman said. "And for that, I am sorry. I was becoming enamored with that quirky little man."

"Professor Ellenshaw is where he wanted to be, surrounded by the very forest that occupied his mind for so many years."

The four men were pushed toward the river. Collins passed close by Alexander and looked at him, but Jack said nothing—his statement on Punchy's future had been made and there was nothing left to add.

Charlie Ellenshaw moaned when he finally came to. His shoulder and the bones beneath hurt in such a way that he knew he had been paralyzed by his stupid action earlier. His line of thinking was a confused one in the moments leading up to his dreadful mistake—what could he do to save the others? Well, he managed to get himself shot and it hadn't made one ounce of difference to his friends, they were now captive and he was as good as dead. He had thought about what the colonel would do, or Captain Everett, if given an opening like he had been given and everything went well until he had decided to act upon his ridiculous thoughts.

Charlie tried to spit dirt and sand from his mouth, but found even that feeble effort too much for his overly taxed system. As his thoughts swirled around the fact that he was dying, his mind eased somewhat at the prospect. As he lay there he could hear the river and the voices of his killers as they moved about by the water's edge. The sound of a boat motor and then more shouted orders. Ellenshaw took a deep breath and wondered how long it would take to die. His pain had eased somewhat as his mind came to grips with the small factoid that here is where he would stay. At that moment, Ellenshaw realized he was no longer alone in the small clearing. It wasn't so much that he sensed it, but actually felt a heavy thud next to his head. Then he smelled that same gamey odor they had caught on the shifting winds coming from north of the Stikine.

Charles Hindershot Ellenshaw III smiled. Then he thought back to a time when he wasn't in pain, when he still thought the world made some sort of sense, and in his mind he was almost an immortal that summer of '68. His memory came into play and he started in a low and halting voice to sing "Crimson and Clover" by Tommy James and the Shondells. When the words became too much to force out of his mouth, he hummed the verses, thinking he was doing it in his head.

When he finally ran out of breath, trying to hang on to a good memory from his youth, the song continued to be hummed. The sound was deep, harsh, but it *was* humming, and had all the nuances of the song from the sixties. He realized that something was mimicking his own version of a moment before. Then the humming stopped and silence permeated the empty camp.

"I'm ready," Charlie whispered.

As he said those two words, he felt the ground actually shake and then something touched his tousled hair. As his eyes fluttered open, he felt something tapping on the right lens of his thick glasses. He tried to focus on the large finger and thick black nail as it almost pushed his glasses into his face with the force of the tapping. He heard a grunt and then felt pressure on his back where he thought he had been shot. Something probed his wound, and then the feeling disappeared. Then he heard a smacking sound as if something were tasting him.

Ellenshaw, repulsed at the idea of being eaten before he had actually passed over to the great beyond, or the last great adventure he had always told his students, tried to turn his head and look up. He managed with a tremendous amount of shaking to get a few inches off the ground. That was when he realized he was looking at the largest foot he had ever seen. As his eyes traveled upward he saw a set of knees as whatever was about to eat him was squatting next to his prone body. He finally managed a few inches more, and then he saw the face that slowly surveyed him from far above, seemingly a mile or so to Charlie's wounded mind.

"Oh . . . my," he said as the last vision he thought he would ever see faded to black.

The great beast rose to its full height of eleven and a half feet. It stood perfectly erect and raised its head and sniffed the air. It grunted deep in its chest and then looked back down at Professor Ellenshaw. The animal held a large wooden club about eight inches in circumference and six feet long. It raised it into the air with its muscled and powerful arm and then savagely swung it at the large tree three feet away, the long arms easily connecting through the distance. The beast struck out six times and then stopped and listened, its long brown and black hair blowing in the breeze that had started a few minutes before. Far off to the north the giant heard a response. It seemed satisfied, sniffing at the air once more. It grunted as it surveyed the area around its massive frame.

When Charlie moaned, that drew the animal's attention back to the wounded man. With its large self-illuminated brown eyes still watching the woods around it and its small ears listening to the sound of men and their boats leaving the south shore, the great beast reached down and took Ellenshaw by the right leg and lifted him free of the ground as easily as a man would pick up one of his child's toys. With a last grunt the animal turned and left the clearing with Professor Ellenshaw dangling from its grip.

As the Zodiac pulled onto the north shore of the Stikine, Jack, Everett, Mendenhall, and Farbeaux watched as Alexander was the first one out of the boat. He was met by two men, one of average size and one large and brutish looking.

"Sagli and Deonovich, I presume," Everett whispered, and then he received a sharp poke in the back by an AK-47 from a Russian seated behind him.

"No talk," the Spetsnaz said in the slow drawl of a man who knew only enough of the Americans language to get by.

Everett turned and looked at the man as the others started to rise from the boat.

"No fucky talky English? You piece of shit."

Everett quickly found out that the man spoke enough to understand the insult and he received a slam of the gun barrel into his kidneys for confirmation.

Jack grabbed Everett and assisted him out of the boat. Mendenhall was a little slower moving, and that worried Collins somewhat.

Will felt a set of hands take his arm; it was Farbeaux.

"In case you didn't know it, Lieutenant, you have a severe concussion."

"Is that your professional opinion, Colonel?" Will asked as he stepped over the high wall of the rubber boat.

Jack watched the greeting ahead of them as Punchy shook hands with first Sagli, and then when Deonovich extended his hand, Punchy instead of taking it, raised his .38 again and pointed it right at the face of the large Russian.

"I think I'll kill you right now for being far too great a fool. You almost killed me twice—as it is you got a very expensive team of my men killed at the fishing camp, and not only that you failed in your mission."

"How was I to know you were on that aircraft?" Deonovich asked, as his partner Sagli watched the confrontation with interest. We should have been contacted and warned that you were arriving with the enemy to our cause."

With that, Punchy lowered the weapon. "The only reason you are going to live is the fact that I have accomplished all I set out to do, and as luck would have it I have secured the one man that can finalize our plans." Punchy turned and gestured the Americans' way, eyeing Jack Collins as he did. "Now, have we found what we are looking for?"

Sagli stepped up and smiled. "Indeed we have, about a mile ahead, either at the plateau or in it. We have waited as per your instructions before claiming it."

"Not bad. I believe we can salvage this mess for the better." He looked at the large Deonovich and then the three men walked a few steps away.

"Have you sent in another team to take care of that damnable fishing camp? We cannot have them sitting in our rear."

Sagli looked nervous for the first time since their new partner in crime had arrived. He shifted his weight from foot to foot and then looked into the Canadian's eyes.

"I sent another attack element back downriver to finalize our exit area."

"That was very intuitive, comrade," Punchy mocked.

"I'm afraid there was a reason for doing so other than my intuition, Mr. Alexander. It seems we have lost contact with our helicopter pilots."

Alexander closed his eyes and then he opened them. "Well, I can fly us out of here if the need arises." He looked around the camp. "However, we may need to lighten the load somewhat," he said looking at his commandos.

Sagli finally smiled, feeling far better than a moment before.

"That should not be a problem. When and if that situation comes to pass, Gregori and I will arrange for"—he lowered his voice and smiled—"some accidents to befall some of our current personnel—adjusting for aircraft space, of course."

Collins watched as the Russians and Alexander spoke and laughed, and then turned back and watched as Jack, Everett, Will, and Farbeaux were escorted up the riverbank under heavy guard. It was Sagli who approached.

"I would have thought you might be somewhat more formidable than your sister, Colonel." Sagli watched the larger Collins as he released the quickly recovering Everett. Jack tilted his head in thought as he took in the man before him. He was small and thin, but Jack knew the eyes of a killer when he saw them and he saw that this man was a survivor—having almost the same look to him as Farbeaux.

"Is my sister still alive?" Collins asked, never letting the Russian know his very life hung in the balance, because if Sagli informed Jack that Lynn was indeed dead, Collins had decided to reach out and slowly tear the man's throat out.

"Yes, she is, Colonel. For how long is now totally in your hands. Do as we say, and she may survive her small side trip to Canada. If you do not do as we say, or fail in your instructions and reason for your being here, you will both be buried in this very lonely place, along with your men, and then everyone you left behind at the fishing camp."

Sagli was about to turn back toward the spot where Punchy Alexander and Deonovich waited, when they heard the sound of wood on wood start again. This time it came from the exact area where his men had captured Collins and his men across the river. Sagli watched and listened as the drumming was answered on their side of the river, and by more than one drummer.

When Sagli looked at Jack, he saw that the colonel was smiling at him, and for reasons he didn't understand, that smile made him look away.

"Did you catch what was said, Jack? Everett asked.

"It seems we have company out there in the woods," Collins said as he took Mendenhall by the arm, relieving Henri of the duty.

All together they were led into the Russian camp.

WAHACHAPEE FISHING CAMP

Ryan was restless. With his M-16 slung around his shoulder, he paced in front of the store. From just inside the store, Sarah watched him and shook her head. She knew the navy pilot was chomping at the bit to get airborne and to find Jack and his friends. She decided that she had to placate Ryan to get him to settle down, even though it went against Jack's orders. She eased the front door open and stepped out into the cool night air.

Ryan stopped and turned. He saw that it was Sarah and then he visibly relaxed.

"Good, it's you; I don't think I could take one more bullshit explanation about what's happening here from either that very strange girl or her whacked-out grandmother."

Sarah smiled and walked down the wooden steps. She looked down at her shoes and then looked up at Ryan. His face was framed by the most brilliant veil of stars Sarah had ever seen. Even with the rising of the three-quarter moon, the stars shone as they never could have down below the border.

"You know, Jack never does anything blindly."

Ryan didn't say anything, but he did stop his pacing.

"Oh, this time he really didn't have a plan, because he really didn't expect his sister to be in the bind she is in. But Jack knows what he's doing. We have to be patient and wait."

"Wait for what, Sarah? For their bodies to come floating down the damn river?" Ryan didn't flinch away from Sarah's look.

"Look, Jason, all I know is—"

That was as far as Sarah's explanation went as a line of bullets thumped into the rocky soil just to their front. Then another line stitched the store-front, shattering the window glass in the doors and the lone surviving plate-glass window next to them. Sarah dove and hit the ground, bloody-ing her lips as her face hit the rocks. Ryan removed the M-16 from his shoulder and then reached for Sarah as more bullets struck around him, one clipping his sleeve as he reached down.

"Get into the store!" Ryan shouted as the silenced rounds continued striking the ground, the store and the surrounding trees. They both re-alized this was a murder raid; the Russians had finally returned to see what had happened to their pilots, an argument Ryan now wished he had used to leave the camp earlier rather than later.

Suddenly, shotgun blasts started flaring from the upper windows of the store. Either Marla or Helena had begun to give Ryan and Sarah cov-ering fire to get into the store. Ryan seized the chance and pulled Sarah up the stairs. He got as far as the top step and then he felt something bite his right calf, he stumbled but stayed upright, and it was Sarah who was now pulling him up the stairs.

As they reached the door, a small hand reached out and pulled them inside. Marla slammed the front door closed and then hit the floor as more bullets streamed inside, striking canned goods and a line of fishing poles on a rack on the wall. Wood chips flew everywhere.

"Well, I guess we have to do exactly what Jack said not to do," Sarah shouted. "Let's get to the damn helicopter!"

Ryan placed a hand to his calf and felt from front to back, realizing that the bullet that had hit him went through the muscle without hitting anything vital and then exiting the other side.

"I'm for that!" he said as he rose up and let loose a ten-round burst through the smashed window, knowing he wouldn't strike anything but sky.

"Get to the back door, I have to get my grandmother," Marla said as she crawled on hands and knees to the middle of the floor. She hit the stairs running just as two more shotgun blasts sounded from upstairs. More automatic-weapons fire hit the store, sending wood and plaster in all directions. It seemed the attackers were now concentrating their fire on the upper floor.

"Well, what are we waiting for?" Sarah yelled. "I don't think these assholes will accept us waving a white flag here!"

"Get to the back door. I have to get the girl and the old lady!" he shouted over the din of the one way gun battle.

Sarah flinched as more rounds struck around them. She saw that Ryan would no more leave anyone behind than he would run away from anything. She nodded and started using her hands and knees to crawl toward the back.

As Ryan limped toward the stairs, he stumbled and fell onto the first step. He was attempting to stand when Marla's small hands took his arm.

"Come on, I hope you can still fly with that leg."

"Wait, wait!" Ryan said as he hopped around on his good leg. "What about your grandmother?"

Marla pulled at Ryan as they made their way toward the back door.

"She's dead, and it won't do any good for me to fall apart about it now. I have no intention of dying here. Now come on!" she shouted with tears spilling from her eyes. Ryan quickly got over the shock of what he had just heard about Helena, and then grabbed the girl's arm.

As they made it to the door, the shooting stopped and silence filled the night.

The first of the two-man teams of Russians to show themselves had arrived only minutes before Sarah had stepped out onto the porch. They had been sent out early that morning by Sagli to discover the problem with communicating with their air support. They had made good time coming down the river at full throttle and made it to the camp just before the sun had set. They didn't hesitate when they came upon the two Americans standing in front of the camp store. Now the first two started forward as they received no more fire from the inside. The second team made their way around the back of the store and icehouse.

As the first man knelt by a tree and waited for the second to cover the ground ahead, he saw a flash of movement and then the man he had been watching vanished in a split second of brutal motion. His eyes widened as a darkness, unlike anything he had ever seen before came from the surrounding trees and struck his partner, lifting him like a child and running back the way it had come. The wind had come up and that was when he was hit with a fine mist. The Spetsnaz swiped at his face and was shocked to see that his hand was covered with blood. Whatever had struck the man had done it so hard that blood had been forced out of the man's body.

The commando was so shocked that by the time he realized what was happening, he was late in raising his AK-47. He tried to fire, but the blur of motion was gone. And that was when the screaming started. He stood and ran toward where the man and his giant abductor vanished and went headlong into the brush of the tree line.

The soldier that had been taken sounded as if he was being torn limb from limb. The second Spetsnaz was quickly losing his nerve, and just as soon as the thought struck that he should return for the other two-man team, he ran into a dark object that stopped him cold. He rebounded with a bloody nose and lips, and fell and struck the ground. He shook his head to try and clear it, thinking he had stupidly struck a tree in the darkness of the forest, and then he saw the animal standing over him. The man's eyes widened in terror as the features of the beast became apparent in the three-quarter moon glow filtering though the trees. The face was like that of a man, but far hairier. The lips were wide and thick, the brows were large, and the eyes glowed a fierce yellowish-green that was brighter than anything the man had ever seen before. The beast growled from deep within its massive chest. The man saw the giant's left hand flexing at its side, and in the right he saw a club that had to weigh at least fifty pounds. As the trained Spetsnaz fought to bring up the AK-47, the beast easily lifted its left foot and brought it down on the weapon, slamming it into the man's leg, snapping the thigh bone in two.

The commando screamed in agony hearing the loud snap of his own leg. He reached for his leg, crying out in Russian. "Please, please," the soldier whimpered, trying to say the words and at the same moment trying to catch his hitching breath. The beast tilted its large head as if it was listening to the smaller man's plea. It grunted and then raised its head to the night sky and roared. It raised the club and struck its chest, a blow that would have caved a normal man's ribs in. It struck its chest three times and then roared again, this time even louder. It then looked down and fixed the man with its burning eyes. The thick brows arched and then it growled that low, menacing, and bone-chilling sound. The soldier could see the teeth that were flanked by the six-inch canines. The animal roared again, raising its head back to the sky, spreading the sound about the forest in triumph. Suddenly, the beast stopped and looked for a final time down at the struggling human before it. Then it raised the club and ended the man's pain with a sudden and vicious blow, burying the head and the yell for help a foot into the ground, so the only thing left twitching in the moonlight were the man's torso and legs.

Sarah and Ryan, flanked by Marla heard the roar of the animal. Ryan suddenly realized that the shooting had stopped. He looked around as the cry of the beast subsided. As he did, Marla screamed as something flew through the night to strike the rear of the store with a loud wet sound. Sarah turned away as she ran, realizing it was a man's body that hit and then fell over feet first from the wall of the store.

"Run, Ryan, run! They're here!"

Ryan didn't care a whole lot for that "they're here" remark. He knew the girl wasn't talking about the Russians. "Oh, shit," he said as he limped along, finally helped by Sarah. "I think I owe the girl an apology!" he screamed out of breath as they finally made it to the trees.

As the bruised and battered Sarah, Marla, and Ryan made the tree line, the forest became alive with movement and they were seeing for the first time the landlords and founders of the great northwest.

The Chulimantan was no longer a mere legend.

RUSSIAN BASE CAMP
NORTH OF THE STIKINE RIVER

Jack, Carl, Will, and Farbeaux had their hands wire-tied behind their backs. The commandos joked as they followed their orders, with Jack and Henri the only ones to pick up most of what they said. They joked on how easy it had been to capture the highly regarded Collins and his men. Jack kept his temper in check as his eyes roamed the camp, looking for any sign of Lynn.

As he looked around, the four men were unceremoniously pushed to the ground. Will still being weak from Alexander's blow to his head, fell completely over onto his side.

"Damn it," Everett hissed. "Will, are you still with us?" Carl frowned when he saw a small trickle of blood coming from Mendenhall's right ear. "You hang in there, Lieutenant; we've been in worse situations."

"We have?" Will hissed through clenched teeth as he struggled to sit up.

"Stay down," Collins ordered. "We'll be here for a while."

As Jack spoke, he saw a small tent just at the back of the clearing. There was a rather large guard watching it, standing only a few paces in front of its zippered flap. His eyes moved on, but kept coming back to the small blue tent.

"Are you seeing the same thing I am seeing, Colonel?" Henri asked as he tried to make himself more comfortable and failing miserably.

Before Jack could answer that he noticed the lone blue tent, the zipper of the very same enclosure lowered slowly and then the face Jack had been waiting to see appeared in the glow of the fire light. Lynn nodded her head quickly, letting Collins know she was alright. Before she could duck her head back inside after delivering her silent message, the large Spetsnaz in the front of the tent turned quickly and delivered a savage blow with his combat boot directly into Lynn's face, throwing her three feet backward.

Farbeaux and Everett knew what was going to happen a moment before it did. They tried to catch Jack in between their large frames, squeezing as hard as they could, trying to keep Collins wedged between them. Jack would have none of it. He was standing in a flash of movement; one minute he was sitting, the next he was on his feet and moving the thirty-five feet toward the tent where his sister had just been brutally assaulted.

The guard, smiling after making sure his charge wasn't getting up for a while, turned and saw a split second too late the American colonel as he approached. He tried to get his weapon unslung but Jack was much too fast for him. He struck out with his own boot, first knocking the AK-47 away and then with a second hop and kick, caught the guard squarely on the chin. The motion took a split second to happen, freezing the other commandos who had been totally caught off guard. They started moving in force toward Collins.

"Look out, Jack!" Everett called out, starting to stand but being knocked flat by others who contained the situation before they had to shoot the three men Collins had left behind.

Sagli, Deonovich, and Alexander stepped from the technician's tent.

They saw what was happening and then saw the fifteen men heading toward the lone American.

"Stop them," Alexander ordered Sagli.

The Russian stepped forward and held his men at bay. "Nyet!" he shouted.

"It's time your mercenaries find out just who it is they are dealing with," Punchy said as he watched the large guard gain his feet.

The Spetsnaz spit blood from his mouth and then felt the cracked chin bone where Jack's boot had connected with it. The man slowly grinned through his pain, putting it aside as he glanced at Sagli. It seemed his boss was going to let him dispose of the American regardless of his importance.

Collins looked behind him at the fifteen others who stood watching and not advancing on him, then took a quick glance at Alexander, who stood silhouetted in the light streaming from the tent he stood in front of.

"Don't let me down, Jack, I'm risking a lot here," the Canadian said.

The Spetsnaz slowly reached to his web belt and removed a large hunting knife. Its edge gleamed in the light of the rising moon, and tinted red by the blazing fire at the center of the camp.

Collins watched the man's feet first, then he raised his eyes to the arm holding the pointed and very sharp weapon. As his eyes climbed higher, he saw the man's eyes. They were dull and expressionless, and Jack knew immediately the man was far too confident of the kill. With his hands tied behind his back, Collins slowly turned in a wide circle, his eyes never wavering from the large brute before him.

The guard—standing at least six foot six inches—towered over Jack even though he was slightly bent at the waist. He smiled through his blood-stained teeth and spit again.

Farbeaux watched Jack closely like a future adversary that he needed to study. He admired the calm way Collins took on the man before him. He saw that Jack could have struck out at anytime he wanted, but he knew the colonel wanted to make this man suffer for his assault on his sister and knew the Spetsnaz would eventually make the move that could possibly get him killed.

The large guard lunged at Collins, who easily stepped away from the knife and the man's heavy body, then he brought his leg high into the air and the boot once more came down—this time on the man's arm, the one not holding the knife because that was the arm Jack knew the man used for balance. Everyone in camp heard the forearm snap as the large Spetsnaz fell to the ground, immediately rolling and regaining his feet. The useless left arm dangled before him. The man became enraged as he charged again; this time Jack stood his ground and at almost four feet away he once more jumped and kicked out with his foot. This time the blow caught the Russian squarely on the side of his face, the roughness of Jack's boot ripping the man's right ear away and sending it into the night.

The Spetsnaz watching couldn't help it; they started laughing at their comrade's predicament as his ear took flight. They were acting like this was a prize fight put on for their amusement.

Jack tired of the game. He thought quickly and knew that no matter what just happened to Lynn, he was not a sadist. As the large guard turned, grabbing the right side of his face as he did, Collins lashed out one last time, spinning horizontally in the air, the heel of his right boot catching the man solidly on the cheek bone, sending him flying to the left and down to the ground where he tried to rise, and then flopped into the sand and rock. For his part, Collins hit the ground, unable to balance himself with his hands tied behind his back. He slammed into the rock and sand, and then just lay there, face down, trying to get his thoughts and breathing under control once more.

Alexander started clapping, slow and loud from the tent, making sure everyone of the Spetsnaz mercenaries saw him do it.

"Damn, Jack, my money is still on you when things get tight." He looked from the downed man to the other Spetsnaz around him. "I hope the lesson here has been learned," he said, turning toward Sagli and Deonovich. It was Sagli who stepped away from the tent and interpreted what Alexander had just said. The commandos just watched and listened with their newfound respect for the American.

Punchy Alexander said something to Deonovich that the others could not hear. The large Russian raised a brow, but followed his orders. He pulled out a German-made Glock nine-millimeter automatic and quickly stepped up to the man Jack had so ruthlessly put down. Just as Collins rolled onto his side, finally under control, he watched as Deonovich aimed and placed a bullet into the back of the Russian's head, slamming him back to the ground from where he was attempting to rise.

At that moment all inside the camp heard the drumming of wood on wood. It was quick and sporadic across the Stikine and just to the north. Alexander chose to ignore the strange sound, not wanting to lend credence to it.

"Stupidity will not be tolerated," Alexander said loudly and waited while his words were delivered in Russian. "This is not a game and you are not dealing with fools." He turned and watched Sagli say his words. Then he said something to the smaller Russian and watched as he went to the tent and checked on Lynn. He stepped out and nodded to Alexander that the woman was okay. "Allow the colonel five minutes with his sister, then return him to his men."

Sagli started to reach for Jack to help him to his feet, and then he thought better of it. He nodded toward the tent and Jack, for his part, rolled and sat up. He watched Sagli as he waved some men over to remove the body of their fallen comrade. With one more respectful look at the restrained Collins, Sagli smiled and moved away; as he did, a sudden flash of lightning streaked across the sky and that was soon followed by a massive thunderclap.

Alexander looked over at Everett and Farbeaux and smiled, and then he looked up at the sky where fast-moving black clouds blotted out the moonlight, and then he finally turned away and reentered the large tent.

Jack didn't stand up, he just tried to get his breathing under control. Hands were on him, around him, and he could smell his sister. It was the same smell she had always had since childhood: one of roses in late summer. Even through the sweat and grime of captivity and the strong odor of antiseptic, he knew it was her, and he buried his head into her body as she hugged him. For the briefest of moments, that hug was enough and they stayed that way for a full minute as the first of the raindrops started falling from a sky that was fast becoming angry.

"You have never ceased to amaze me as to how you can get into so much trouble. How are you doing, little sister?" Jack asked as he finally looked into the bruised face of Lynn.

Both lips were swollen and her left eye was closing from the kick to the face she had just received, compliments of the late Spetsnaz guard just now being tossed out near the river.

Lynn smiled back down at her brother and placed a hand on his cheek.

Jack saw the bandage covering her missing finger, but he chose not to dwell on it because of his anger being so close to the surface.

"It's good to see you, Jack," she said, shaking her head. "By the way, this is one hell of a rescue."

"Hey, we have our moments, although this isn't the best advertisement for us," he said as he sat up with some effort.

Jack again wiggled toward the front of the tent and made himself as comfortable as possible. He once more took in the appearance of his sister. She was in rough shape, but he knew it could have been far worse with the bunch that had taken her.

"Sorry about Punchy Jack. I knew you two were close."

"I should have acted on my instincts, sis, the stupid bastard gave himself away in Los Angeles, but I just couldn't get myself to believe it. You were right all along. Now, if the rest of what you and your bosses think is happening is true, we may have a mess on our hands."

"Okay, everything we believed about Alexander back at the Farm is true. The trail he left in his computerespionage led us right to him. But what in the hell is he doing out here, Jack?"

"I had a feeling I had screwed up at some point and blown my cover, Jack, where was it?" Punchy asked. He had caught them off guard as he eased himself behind them while they spoke.

"Well, Lynn figured you for one of the bad guys over a year ago. When she told me I was alerted, as one of your closest friends, of course, to watch for Providence that you were as she said: a lying, dirty, treasonous son of a bitch. But to answer your question, confirmation of you going rogue came in L.A. It was the vest. You refused wearing bulletproof vests for fifteen years, swore you would never wear a safety net, that if agents were dumb enough to get shot, they deserved the consequences." Jack looked up and eyed the larger man. "Personally, I think it was because it made you look fatter than you are." The words were delivered slow and cold, as was Jack's way.

"Damn, I should have remembered that you had a memory to beat all hell." Alexander raised his coat collar as he examined the sky. Then he looked down at Lynn, who wanted to be sick with him standing so close to her and Jack.

"Why the murder in Seattle, Punchy? I know it wasn't for a damned diamond, or wagons full of gold. Hell, in your position you could steal half the treasury of the Canadian government and get away with it, so why?" Collins asked.

"It's called covering our tracks—black operations class 101 at MI-5, Jack, you know that. We didn't need anyone out there who could lead your intelligence apparatus or Canada's to us before we had our prize."

"What about Doc Ellenshaw?"

Punchy Alexander laughed as he leaned down and slapped Jack on the back, then he looked over at Lynn.

"Can you imagine my consternation when Jack's little girlfriend, Sarah, walked in with the one man we couldn't find for ten whole years, Professor Ellenshaw? Just who in the hell do you work for, Jack, that you would know a crazy, far-out bastard as that?"

"My new friends are far better than my old ones. By the way, Punchy, you know I'm going to kill you for what you did to the doc, don't you?" Jack said as the rain started falling in earnest.

Alexander became silent, the laughing had ceased and the humor had gone out of the situation.

"Let me guess at your interest in covering your tracks and why the doc was so prominent in your plans to cover them."

"Give it a try, Jack," Alexander said, his smile completely gone.

"Ellenshaw filed a report with the Washington State authorities, or hell, even with Stanford upon his return from Canada in '68, and you got a hold of that report through computer espionage, which my baby sister here uncovered over a year ago and traced it back to you. With the reports the doc filed he became an interest to you. You tried to find him so he could lead you here without the maps and the journal because of his relationship with L. T. Lattimer, but he was with me in a place you could never imagine, lost to everyone but a select few." He looked up into the rain at Punchy. "Just what in the hell are you after, Punchy, that would compel you to commit treason and murder innocent people?"

"It took me years and years, Jack, my boy. Using every avenue I could find, any generated report coming from Canada and Alaska. Every word laid down on paper—until I came across an obscure mention of L. T. Lattimer and a gold find back in 1968." A powerful lightning bolt made Alexander flinch and duck, but both Lynn and Jack saw the smile spread on his lips. "Then my keyword was hit. . . . Keyword—computers made my life so much easier, Jack. One small little word placed into a far-fetched report by a hippy grad student from Stanford University—your

Professor Ellenshaw. A guilt-fed report on a missing man in the Canadian wilderness, a man who left behind a description of a place where not only one treasure resided, but possibly two. And tomorrow, I will recover the second item and be off, and you, Jack, will play a large part in the happily-ever-after part of my story. By the way, if that little girlfriend is still at the fishing camp, I'll tell you, Jack, I wouldn't mind getting some of that." Alexander smiled, then that turned into a laugh, and then he turned and made his way out of the heavy rain.

Jack watched Alexander trudge through the rain. Then he saw him turn and face him once more.

"Brainteaser, Jack. Remember our first mission together in 1989, our little foray into the Vancouver wilderness?"

Collins didn't say anything as the memory of that nighttime HALO drop into Canada back when he was a captain came back to him. The search for the prize was a wild goose chase, as the hundred other missions before that had been. That particular search had been on since October 1962, and now Jack finally realized that his worst fears were confirmed, and that Lynn's and her bosses at CIA had been on the right track all along, with only one of their theories about Alexander falling far short of the mark.

Punchy saw the concern spread across Jack's face. He laughed out loud and then turned away, slapping his thighs in laughter.

"Doesn't sound like he's speaking about gold, does it?" Lynn asked.

"The son of a bitch has found it, baby sister. You were right; I should have hit the alarm when you first broached Alexander's actions about the upper Stikine, I just didn't put it all together."

"What's he going to do with what he finds?" Lynn asked.

"If he's doing what I believe he's capable of, there could be a civil war brewing, and we're bound to be caught up in it."

"Jack, when we saw that Punchy had turned bad at the agency, we only thought he was involved in the separatist movement in Quebec. If it's not financing he wants, what in the hell is he here for?"

"Your boss at CIA should have let you in on something that used to be above your pay grade, baby sis. He's after Solar Flare."

Lynn knew the code name. She always thought it was a military myth, something that was used to make agents have sleepless nights during training.

"What does Alexander need you for?"

Collins knew that everyone being held by Alexander, Sagli, and Deonovich were now pawns in a game that Jack knew he couldn't win—at least until he knew the rules of that game. They would kill every one of them, and Collins knew there wasn't anything he could do but cooperate.

"The item he's looking for, the one the president, your boss and mine, only suspected he was after . . . well, he needs me to use the damnable thing. Jesus, that bomb is here somewhere."

"You and he were on a joint mission to recover it years ago? He knows you have something he needs."

"Yes, he needs me, but he doesn't need you, or them"—he nodded toward his friends—"anymore."

Lynn became silent as she thought about the trouble she had gotten her brother into just because she happened upon Alexander hacking NSA communications two years before. She shook her head in the pouring rain.

Jack leaned against Lynn and just took her in. He was happy she was alive and that was a good starting point.

"Hey, Jack?" Lynn asked through the pouring rain, and hoping to make the situation somewhat lighter.

"What?" he asked as the Russians arrived to take him back to Everett and the others.

"You have a girlfriend?"

Collins rolled his eyes as he was roughly lifted from the wet ground by the angry Spetsnaz and Jack looked down upon Lynn just as she looked up.

"Go back into your tent, at least you have one, brat!"

WAHACHAPEE FISHING CAMP

Marla and Sarah, with Jason limping along in the middle and being supported by the two women broke into the small clearing and saw the first of the four large Sikorsky helicopters. They ran toward the nearest one, stumbling and tripping until Jason literally bounced off one of the main landing gear and then rebounded to the ground out of breath.

"Now's not the time, Jason," Sarah said, out of breath herself, but pulling at Ryan nonetheless. Marla was looking around the clearing, not liking the absolute stillness of it as the far-off lightning illuminated the clearing and cast eerie shadows in all directions.

"We have to hurry, they're here," Marla said reaching up and pulling down the staircase.

That was all Ryan had to be reminded of as he pulled himself up and stumbled over to the folding steps. He crawled inside and then rose in the middle of the tight aisle, using the seats to help support him. Marla followed Sarah, and that was when she stopped and looked back out of the chopper, then she tried to exit the Sikorsky.

"The weapons, I dropped them by the door," she shouted back at Marla.

Marla continued to block her way.

"Leave them, the animals won't differentiate between us and the attackers anymore. They have their blood up."

"Jesus, are they animals or humans?" Sarah asked as she turned away angry.

"They're both," Marla said as she started to get frustrated. Tears were starting to form in her eyes. "They fall back on instinct in violent situations. My father and grandfather have seen them tear a grizzly to pieces."

"Great," Sarah said as she gave up and turned toward the cockpit of the expensive helicopter.

Ryan had managed to squeeze himself into the pilot's left seat. He was studying the control panel when Sarah entered and pulled herself into the copilot's seat.

"Just like old times, huh?" Sarah asked just to take her mind off of grizzly bears getting torn to pieces.

Ryan looked over at McIntire and shook his head. "Attempting to fly a Blackhawk was easy. Look at this thing, it's an executive model Sikorsky that assumes the pilot's an expert. This is fucking nuts . . . I never have the time to study anything before some idiot asks me to fly it!"

Sarah understood where Ryan was coming from as she looked at the thousand gauges and switches that lined not only the front console but the overhead as well. Still, she was shocked when Ryan reached out and flipped two switches, which produced a loud whine.

"There, at least I got the preheaters online. Okay, we're in the red, turbines are coming up."

"Are you sure?" Sarah asked as everything on the main-control panel started flashing, blue, green, and red.

"No, for all I know I could have selected auto-destruct in that sequence of switches."

Sarah relaxed when she saw through the windscreen that the four bladed rotors slowly start to turn.

"Well, evidently you hit something!"

Marla squeezed between the pilots seats and pointed out of the window to the left.

"Look!"

When Ryan and Sarah both turned their attention on the tree line, they saw one of their Russian assailants break free at a dead run. He was waving his arms wildly trying to get the crew of the helicopter's attention. Then their eyes widened when something stopped just short of entering the clearing. The animal was huge and blended almost perfectly with its surroundings. They would never have seen it had they not been looking at the blank space behind the Russian at that precise moment.

"Should we let him in?" Sarah asked, unsnapping her seatbelt.

"No!" Marla said defiantly. "He may have been the one that shot my grandmother," she coldly said as she pushed Sarah back into her seat. "He may have injured one of the animals by shooting wildly; besides, he'll never make it. Look."

As they watched, another animal bolted from the trees to the man's left. Another streak of lightning brightened the clearing and Ryan and Sarah saw the legend for the first time.

The Russian commando saw the burst of motion from his peripheral vision and tried to veer away from the collision that was imminent, but he was far too slow. The massive beast struck the man and sent him flying, but before he could strike the ground, another of the massive creatures, moving at unbelievable speed, came from nowhere and struck the Spetsnaz again, pinwheeling him back into the sky. Then the one that they had seen standing at the tree line burst from cover and caught the man in its long and muscular arms, and angrily threw him toward the Sikorsky. The three occupants in the cockpit flinched when the man hit the slowly turning rotor blades and caromed off onto the ground.

"Oh, god," Sarah said, "we can't leave him like that!"

Marla again restrained her from rising.

"Leave him, he's our only chance of getting out of here. They are in a blood frenzy, one of them must have been hurt by these murdering bastards!"

Sarah turned away as the first creature slowly ambled into the clearing. Ryan watched in amazement as the engines of the Sikorsky ramped up to idle power. The beast was almost invisible as it advanced with its long strides. The head was large and the torso long and powerfully built. The arms were long and massive, the muscles bristling under the coat of dark hair. The legs were not as short as a normal ape would have been, they were long and well proportioned. The muscles in the legs were that of a well-built man. The Sasquatch walked completely upright and had no slouch at all. The giant's hands and arms swung easily at its sides and the gait was tremendous. It covered the seventy yards in just twenty strides.

"Look at its hair," Sarah said, turning toward the scientist inside of her, more for protection against the fear she was feeling than because of her studies. "It shimmers, like it's taking on the contours of its surroundings."

Ryan was flabbergasted as he watched the beast approach. The hair was thicker in some places more than others. The hair was light in areas, dark in some, and with these natural colors, it took on light and shadow and made it difficult to see against any backdrop—a natural camouflage that any military would have been envious of. If it weren't for the growing light show in the sky, they would be hard-pressed to follow its progress toward them and the downed man.

"That's why they are never seen; they are masters at camouflaging themselves with their environment—the muscle movement below their fur, or hair, ripples at a simple suggestion from its brain, and the shadows created by those differing movements of muscles are able to increase and decrease, creating shadows and valleys, making their outline almost impossible to see."

"I hate to break up this *National Geographic* moment here, but that thing is coming right for us," Ryan said as he tried desperately to find the collective handle that allowed the helicopter to rise into the air.

"This model doesn't have a collective; the throttle is on the stick!" Marla said as she pointed. "The Mounties told me a little about them a long time ago."

Ryan found the throttle on the stick in front of him and twisted it. With no collective like older models, Ryan tried to apply power. The helicopter started to rise, but he pushed the stick forward too soon and the nose dipped, almost sending the spinning rotors into the hard ground in front of them.

"Oh, shit," he said as he pulled back just as the beast ducked and barely avoided the blades. "Sorry, I didn't try to do that!" Ryan said almost apologetically to the great beast now standing and looking through the glass at the three people in the helicopter.

The Sasquatch roared and then bent down and retrieved the Russian by the leg and lifted the bleeding man off the ground. The animal tossed it into the tree line as easily as a rag doll and then watched as the Sikorsky finally started gaining altitude, rising above the trees.

"Okay, I'm an asshole for not believing you. Later I'll hold still for you and you can kick my ass!" Ryan shouted, getting the cold chills from the closeness of their encounter.

"I'm so glad I could convince you," Marla said as she turned away from the cockpit and sat in the first row of seats.

Sarah looked over at Ryan and patted his arm, and then looked back through the opening and watched as the death of her grandmother finally caught up with the young girl. She was looking out of the window to her left at the retreating fishing camp below, crying into the glass.

11

RUSSIAN BASE CAMP
NORTH OF THE STIKINE RIVER

Jack and the others watched the comings and goings of Sagli, Deonovich, and their newest partner in crime, Punchy Alexander, as they entered and exited the technician's tent. The Spetsnaz, while paying particular attention to the American captives, made ready their weapons and other equipment for their planned foray into the upper reaches of the Stikine Valley from their tents, while some of the more unseasoned regular army misfits walked the perimeter around the camp.

They were all still bound with their hands behind their backs, but at least the Russians had placed a tarp over them that kept all but their butts dry. Will Mendenhall had regained some of his senses, but was in a foul mood because of the refreshed memory of Doc Ellenshaw's meaningless death, and Jack could see it in the black man's eyes. That was the one failing of the young lieutenant—he found it hard at times to place his personal feelings aside and concentrate on what was at hand. Jack knew this trait because he had the same problem at times, as he had demonstrated earlier.

"Will, are you with us or someplace else?" Collins asked, trying to get Mendenhall awake and back to work mentally.

The lieutenant looked up from the fire that was only a few yards away, and fixed Jack with his eyes. Then he broke eye contact and looked at the falling rain.

"I'm here, Colonel," he said and then looked back down at the fire.

There was a tremendous bolt of lightning that struck the ground directly across the river. The flash lit up the entire area around them.

Jack finally decided he had had enough. He wanted to end the cat-and-mouse game that had been going on between himself and Henri Farbeaux, who was obviously dodging the truth behind why he was so adamant about coming along.

"Colonel, when are you going to let us in on why it is you chose to come with us on this little outing, and please don't tell me it's for the Twins of Peter the Great."

Farbeaux turned, the mud beneath him making the maneuver extremely uncomfortable. He smiled at Jack and then looked away.

"Colonel Collins, when have you known me to do anything other than for profit? I am still what you would call, 'the bad guy,' here."

"I have no doubt of that."

"As proof, I advance to you the small fact that I was afraid that when you confronted that rather large Spetsnaz gentleman, you would deprive me of the death I have planned for you when all of this is finished, a death that I have dreamed of for going on a full year. But alas, I should have known you would prevail. I am beginning to call it the 'Collins luck.'"

"Don't worry, Henri, I'll figure it out. You have another scheme going here and I will . . ."

Jack didn't finish his statement. Overhead, through the thick cloud cover they all heard it at the same time. It was the sound of a helicopter—a large one, much larger than the Bell Ranger that he had left Ryan behind at the fishing camp to repair. As they listened the sound grew louder.

Lightning flashed again and they saw Russians running from their tents. Whoever was dropping in on them, it looked as if they wouldn't be welcomed all that warmly.

"Jesus," Everett said shaking his head. "Don't tell me . . ."

"Ryan and Sarah," Jack said as they heard the distress of the helicopter as it raised and lowered in the wind.

"Yeah, I can tell Ryan's flying anywhere," Mendenhall added.

As they watched in dawning knowledge and the horror of that fact, one of the Spetsnaz went to the center of the camp and while being assisted by another, raised a long tube into the air and aimed.

Pointed directly into the lightning-streaked sky and at the sound created by the misguided Sikorsky was a heat-seeking anti-aircraft missile.

The wind had picked up by thirty knots and Ryan, since sliding the Sikorsky down toward the river so he could follow the terrain, had a difficult time keeping the sharp nose of the helicopter trained in the right direction. The stiff wind was forcing the tail both right and left, which was a usual state for Ryan flying machines he hadn't formally trained in before.

"We're going to have to set this thing down before I kill all of us," he said looking straight ahead.

"We may as well," Sarah said as she held on tight to the side window frame as the large helicopter swung sharply to the right, sliding dangerously close to the trees lining the river. "We'll never see either camp from this low, anyway."

"Okay, see if we can find a clearing, one not too far from the river, I don't want to slam these rotors into the top of any trees. Maybe if we—"

At that moment a streak of fire passed by three feet in front of the windscreen. Ryan, his reactions a split second too late threw the stick to the right, dipping the rotors only fifty feet from the now raging Stikine.

"Jesus, was that a missile?" Sarah shouted.

"I saw when it was fired at us," Marla said as she suddenly appeared between Ryan and Sarah. "The Russian camp must be about a thousand yards ahead!"

"Get back to your seat and strap in," Ryan shouted as he brought the

Sikorsky back up into the air. The wipers had a hard time keeping up with the battering rain slamming into the speeding helicopter.

"Here comes another one!" Marla shouted from her seat in the back.

Ryan couldn't see in what direction he should turn—so he quickly took a chance and headed north and climbed. The steepness of the ascent pressed Sarah into her seat and that was when she started praying. Just as Ryan thought maybe they had evaded the missile, the warhead exploded just outside of the rear rotor. Two of the four blades were sheared away in a split second and Ryan felt the Sikorsky veer sharply to the left. He tried to compensate by slamming the control stick as far right as possible while at the same time slamming his wounded leg onto the right pedal.

"That's it, kids, we heading down," he called out just as the Sikorsky started to spin, heading for the trees far below.

As a large streak of lightning flashed across the forest, it illuminated the death plunge of Ryan, Sarah, and Marla as they fell from the sky north of the Stikine.

RUSSIAN BASE CAMP
THE STIKINE RIVER

Everett stamped his feet, willing the missile to miss the poor bastards flying into the makeshift ambush. As the flare of the missile exhaust lit up the camp and the driving rain pummeling it, they watched as the heat-seeking missile streaked toward the shiny new helicopter.

Collins stepped in front of the others and, like Carl, willed the missile to miss. He knew that the projectile was a heat seeker, and he also knew that it would have a hard time locking onto to the exhaust because of the cold rain. The mistake for the Russians was not having radar-guided stingers. As he watched, his eyes never left the exhaust trail of the small warhead.

"Damn, he doesn't even see it!" Collins shouted.

With the luck of a drunken sailor, Ryan caught a break as a strong gust of wind, reaching sixty miles an hour, pushed the missile far ahead of its target, and as luck would also have it, it didn't lock onto the heated engine at all. The missile streaked by the front nose of the Sikorsky, missing it by mere feet.

"Is that your Mr. Ryan?" Henri asked.

"It was," Mendenhall said as he joined the others.

"Turn away, Ryan, turn away," Jack hissed as his eyes went to the fire team as they brought out a fresh weapon from an elongated box.

"He's too close, they won't miss this time," Everett said as he too turned toward the shooters.

Collins and Everett had the same thought at exactly the same time. They both sprinted for the team just now bringing the helicopter into their sights. With hands still tied behind them, they didn't stand a chance in hitting the shooters in time. What they did do was make the Russian aiming the weapon flinch when he heard his comrades shouting a warning. The man assisting the shooter turned and was only able to tackle Collins, but Everett continued on. Several shots rang out through the noise of the storm, but all the bullets missed the large SEAL as he leaped. Just before his shoulder connected solidly with the shooter, the missile left the tube. Carl slammed into the man and they rolled over into the mud.

Alexander, Sagli, and Deonovich ran out into the rain. Deonovich threw himself onto Everett and brought the brief struggle to a stop, and Alexander ran to Jack and gave the colonel a sharp kick into his kidneys. He drew back to kick again, but was stopped by the brief flash of an explosion as the missile hit the Sikorsky at the very tip of the tail boom.

"Damn you, Jack, you're going to force me to kill every one of you. Stop interfering!" Alexander screamed, water and spittle running down his chin.

Deonovich had stood and was also using his boots to explain to Everett the price of interference. The captain was trying his best to roll away from the brutal kicks, but he just couldn't in the deepening mud.

Mendenhall and even Farbeaux started forward to assist Everett, but were stopped cold by four men who quickly showed them the price of foolishness. Will was struck in the stomach and Farbeaux in the back by butts of automatic weapons. They both went down into the mud to join Jack and Everett.

Sagli reached Deonovich before he could deliver his fifth kick into the back and stomach of Everett. He reached both arms around the larger man and held him in place. Deonovich was about to reach back and pull his smaller partner off when the sound from the sky stilled him.

As all looked skyward, the gleaming Sikorsky streaked overhead, barely missing the tree line at the back of the camp. Most of the men ducked and hit the ground, fearing an explosion when the Sikorsky hit. However, the pilot fought the torque created by the sheared-off tail rotors and managed to get the huge aircraft to hop over the initial assault of large pines until he plunged deeper into the woods. Expecting the giant aircraft to strike the trees at any moment, the chaotic assault on the Americans ceased as all eyes watched through the storm the death plunge of the foolish people who tried to come upriver at night and in a powerful storm.

"Your people brought this on themselves, Jack."

Collins rolled over and looked with killing eyes at his old friend. Alexander saw the look just as they all heard the Sikorsky slam into the forest no more than half a mile away.

"Do what's asked of you, Colonel, and those may be the last people you lose."

Collins didn't say anything, his eyes just moved away from Alexander to the smoke and flames now rising up through the falling rain.

Jack didn't know exactly who had been on the helicopter, but knew anyone who was, was now burning inside the crumpled hulk.

As Ryan fought the helicopter for control, the spin increased as the failed tail rotor could not stop the torque placed on the airframe as the four bladed main rotors turned the craft to the right at fantastic speed. Jason gritted his teeth to the point of shearing them off as he saw the trees coming at them in a spiraling nightmare. Beside him, Sarah was being pressed to the side window from the fantastic g-forces being placed on the Sikorsky. She could only close her eyes as the spin increased and pray.

In the passenger compartment, Marla hadn't had time to fasten the seatbelt upon returning. She was thrown hard against the opposite row of seats and was pinned there as the helicopter started settling for the trees.

The S-76 clipped the first tree, sending a spray of water outward and then Ryan felt the fuselage strike, bounce, and then hit again. The second time the main rotors caught in the treetops, sheering them away from the transmission hub. The spin stopped suddenly as the tail boom struck the trees in earnest, shearing it away in a microsecond. Air, water, and the smell of fuel coursed through the doomed Sikorsky as Ryan finally gave up and threw his arms over his face. Sarah bent at the waist as soon as the centrifugal force ceased, holding her against the bulkhead. She bent as low as her harness would allow. The move was just in time as a fifteen-foot piece of the main rotor slammed into the windscreen, passing between Jason and Sarah, and exiting the space where the tail boom had been seconds before.

The helicopter slammed into a large tree and then started its fall with ear-shattering noise. It hung for a moment on the thick upper branches of a huge pine and then started down again. Ryan was inundated with water, pine needles, and fuel as the lines under the engine cowling ruptured. The airframe hit another set of branches that were interlocked between two trees and the fall from the sky had stopped fifty feet from the ground.

At the sudden realization their fall had been arrested, Sarah reached over and tried to find Ryan with just her hands. She was disoriented and finally realized they were almost turned completely upside down. As she finally felt Ryan's head, she heard him moan. At that moment, time froze as Sarah heard a whump from somewhere below them and that was when she again realized the engine was now under them as they hung upside down. As the cockpit lit up with the bright flames, Sarah saw the reason Jason wasn't moving and why he was moaning. A large branch had been launched through the shattered windscreen and had embedded itself in Ryan's shoulder. Sarah reached out and pulled on the limb and Jason closed his eyes in pain. Sarah saw she didn't have enough power to pull it out from her position, so she unsnapped the seat harness that was holding her in place.

The movement of Sarah and the weight of the airframe was still trying to push the bird into the ground—it fell another ten feet and Sarah closed her eyes, thinking they would hit and the rest of the fuel would go up with them in it. Suddenly, the movement stopped as they hung up again, this time on their side. Sarah fought to climb over the center console and found she was stuck. As she screamed in frustration, small hands poked through and into the cockpit. It was Marla.

"Get out on your side. It's a long fall, but you should make it. I'll get Mr. Ryan!" she shouted as she pulled out a large knife and started sawing into the branch pinning Jason.

Sarah watched as she never felt more helpless in her life. The flames were now opposite of where they had been and they were now licking up the side of the cockpit where Jason was trapped.

"Go!" Marla shouted again as she tossed the knife away and started pulling on the branch for all she was worth. All the while, Ryan was silent as he fought back the sheer agony he was feeling.

Sarah raised up and pushed on the crumpled door on the copilot's side, sending the lightweight aluminum up and over. She squirmed until she found a handhold and then pulled herself up. Once out she felt the heat of the flames as they grew. She immediately saw the trunk of the tree they had hung up on. Not hesitating, Sarah jumped down the three feet and grabbed for all she was worth, but she missed. She hit the trunk and tried desperately to dig her nails in but the force of the jump only made her bounce off and then fall to the ground thirty feet below. She hit feet first on the soft forest floor but immediately fell on her back, knocking the wind out of her lungs. As she fought for breath she saw the burning Sikorsky thirty feet over her head.

Suddenly, there was a blur at the pilot's door opened and Jason Ryan fell from the cockpit. Sarah rolled out of the way as Ryan hit with a thud and a snap as his arm broke. While Sarah finally caught her breath, Marla jumped free of the helicopter, hitting with both feet planted firmly. Still, Sarah heard the girl scream as her ankles rolled and she fell.

Sarah rose up and started pulling on Ryan. The helicopter made a loud screeching sound and they all heard the snapping of branches as the flaming Sikorsky started its final plunge for the forest floor. Sarah knew they were had. She pulled but Ryan had passed out and he was far heavier than she thought. In another flash of motion, Marla dove for both of them and pushed them hard. They all fell six feet back into the trees as the helicopter hit. Fuel was forced though the ruptured tank and the woods around them lit up with a small explosion.

With rain pummeling them and their prone bodies illuminated by the roaring flames, Marla, Sarah, and Ryan lay where they had fallen. Sarah finally placed a hand on Ryan, using his shirt to pull herself up. She looked at his shoulder wound and saw that it was bad. Blood was oozing out at a good clip. She leaned over him and placed both hands onto the wound and pressed down as hard as she could. Marla, her ankles swelling, rolled over and tried to focus on Sarah's attempts at saving Ryan. Tears had sprung up in her eyes as she realized Jason was close to bleeding out.

The woods around them were being protected from the fire by the fierce storm that was passing through the Stikine Valley. The heat produced by the fuel-fed fire felt odd in the downpour. Marla leaned over and started lightly slapping Ryan on the face.

"Please, oh, please, don't die, Mr. Ryan. Come on."

"I promise not to die, if one, you stop slapping me, and two, you get off of my broken arm."

Sarah couldn't help it, she smiled. Ryan looked up at her. She had a broken nose, a severe cut over her left eye, and a long scrape down the side of her face. She lifted her hands and saw that Ryan's flow of blood had slowed—not stopped, but she thought if she could get the wound plugged, he would make it.

Marla swiped at the tears that coursed down her face and moved away from Ryan and Sarah. She was so happy that Ryan was talking that she started to get the shakes. She backed away until her sprained ankles came into contact with something large and hard. She tripped backward and again landed on her back. As she rolled over she came face to face with a grinning skull. She screamed and tried to stand. She backed away as Sarah came to see what she had run into. McIntire saw the old ejection seat and the skeletal remains still strapped in it. As she held Marla, who was close to collapsing, a bolt of lightning flashed across the sky, and in that brief moment of illumination, that was when both Marla and Sarah saw it. The thunder roared as if announcing their find and then another zigzag pattern of light creased the sky above them. Sarah, dripping wet and bleeding, held Marla tighter.

The darkened mouth of a giant cave bid the two women welcome as they stared into what looked like a darkened maw of a huge animal.

The ancient home of the Chulimantan had been found once again.

Alexander turned away from Jack as the whump of the explosion flashed across the tree-riddled landscape. With one look back at Collins and his murderous glare, Punchy waved over his partners to the communications tent. The guards allowed a bruised Everett, Farbeaux, and Mendenhall to assist Collins to his feet, and they were unceremoniously shoved back underneath their tarpaulin.

Jack spit blood out of his mouth as he stared at the Spetsnaz until they smiled at him and turned away. He winced as he tried to get comfortable with at least one broken rib.

"For my part, Colonel, if indeed little Sarah was on that helicopter, I . . ."

"Now's not a good time," Everett said, cutting short Farbeaux's sympathy for Jack's loss.

Instead of being angry at the Frenchman, Collins leaned into Mendenhall to support his rib cage and after he felt he could take a deep breath, he looked over at Farbeaux.

"Henri, tell me the French government has a backup plan to your incursion into Canada."

Farbeaux was silent after Jack had asked the question. He slowly turned his head as lightning flashed, illuminating the stunned look on his face. He shook his head and then caught the looks on the faces of Everett and Mendenhall.

"I think it's time you come clean with us, Henri. We've lost too much to continue to keep secrets."

Henri looked up at the black sky and the pouring rain, he waited until a thick roll of thunder echoed in the valley and then he turned and nodded his head at the American.

"Your perception and intelligence is something that I failed to get my friends at DGSE to take into account. I knew my charade would only last so long."

Everett twisted his head and looked at the drenched Frenchman. He knew the bastard had been up to something but leave it to Jack to have confirmed it somewhere along the way.

"The DGSE?" Mendenhall asked.

"Direction Générale de la Sécurité Extérieure—The Directorate-General for External Security," Collins said.

"Are you saying that you're back in the spying business, Henri?" Carl asked, amazed and confounded that anyone could talk Farbeaux out of his lucrative retirement.

Another flash of lightning lit up the sky, and Jack could see Alexander looking at them from the large tent across the clearing. He was giving Sagli and Deonovich instructions about something and through the downpour Jack could see that the new orders made Deonovich smile while looking their way. It wasn't good.

"I'm afraid I had little choice in the matter, Captain. It seems my recent activities attracted the wrong sort of attention, and with pressure from your president, and with endorsements I'm sure from your little bald boss at the Event Group, I was . . . let's say, drafted."

"Niles Compton thought you were dead, Henri, lost at sea. Remember?" Jack reminded him.

"Regardless, here I am," he said as he noticed Deonovich gathering a few of his men together. "I must explain to you, time, I fear, is growing short for some of us."

Everett and Mendenhall saw what was coming as the guards made ready their pistols.

"The DGSE has uncovered an extreme terrorist cell operating in Montreal. They know it was being operated by someone immune to discovery because there was just too much information not being passed back through DGSE contacts. Many agents were found murdered, indicating someone was getting identifications out to the cell. Either we had a traitor in our midst, or the Canadian government had one in theirs. Obviously, being French, my superiors ruled out any DGSE failures, so they concentrated on the Canadian side."

Jack watched as Alexander looked his way and then turned back inside of the tent. Sagli gave the group of captives one last look and then he also turned away. Deonovich was explaining something to the three Spetsnaz he had pulled aside. They all looked their way as he explained something to them.

"Cut to the chase, Henri, our time is running out," Jack said as he took a shallow breath.

"DGSE suspected someone at the top of the Canadian food chain, but soon it was confirmed by the traitor himself. Back in 1962, during your governments' little spat with the Kremlin over the Cuban inclusion into the world of Soviet nuclear weapons, something went wrong. I know this will disturb you to no end, being Americans are thought of as the good guys, but I'm afraid your government was looking at the darker outcome of that battle of wills. Your President Kennedy had issued orders for a preemptive strike against the high command of the civilian and military heads of the Soviet regime. The mission was called Operation Solar Flare. Alexander was caught snooping where he shouldn't have been. However, my former superiors didn't know how far Alexander's treason went, thus, when they learned of this assault in Los Angeles, they sent me."

"Another coincidence, Henri?" Jack persisted.

"Not at all. I know of the importance of the Lattimer Notes and the journal, that's why I had them stolen. It is, as you say, a small world. My associates leaked this information to waiting ears, thus, I was volunteered by my old employers to find out what your Mr. Alexander was up to. I guess my government credentials had yet to expire."

"I don't believe it," Everett said. "If that had been an actual plan, our Group, above anyone in the country, would have the information—secret information to be sure—but we would have access to it."

"You still insist that your nation is morally superior to everyone else, Captain Everett; that is not being a true historian. Oh, Operation Solar Flare was approved by France, Great Britain, and Germany, so you weren't alone in hiding your heads in the sand. But my government made the dropping of the most powerful weapon in human history possible by disclosing the secret location where the hierarchy of the Soviet government would be bunkered. Thus, Operation Solar Flare was taken from fantasy to reality."

"What happened? I mean the mission was obviously canceled since history doesn't show any mushroom-cloud footage springing up in Moscow," Mendenhall said, not believing what he and his commanding officers were hearing.

"Now, Colonel Collins, it's your turn to come clean."

Will looked at Jack, but Everett knew what his boss was about to say as the memory of that brief moment on the boat came back to Mendenhall. The long talk Collins had with the captain.

"Punchy and I were on one of the last attempts to recover the downed weapon. The F-4 Phantom carrying Solar Flare went down somewhere north of the border. The air force never found its transponder beacon back in '62. The mission was a bust; we never found it. Higher-ups then figured that somehow the mission terminated over water."

"I'm afraid the Western democracies don't get let off the hook that easy, Colonel. The aircraft failed to even reach its fail-safe point. It went down either in Canada or in Alaska, and as the colonel just said, they never found the wreckage even though the most massive recovery operation the world had ever seen took place for close to fifty years."

"What was the megatonnage of the weapon and its type?" Mendenhall asked.

"That was a secret your government kept well. But the DGSE suspected it was what's known as a doomsday device, for lack of a better term, maybe as much as five hundred megatons—powerful enough to destroy any bunker in the world, no matter its depth in the earth. The fact that it was an advanced cruise missile designed for supersonic flight in a straight nose-down attitude, and equipped with a solid tungsten nose cone, it would bury itself so deep into the ground that no bunker ever made could survive."

"Jesus, the world really had gone mad," Will said.

"So, Alexander is after the weapon—and now he's found it, so what now?" Everett asked.

"I suspect he has found the Hyper Glide, as the weapon was known, or Solar Flare," Henri said. "The gold and diamonds was actually a ruse. Your Professor Ellenshaw, without knowing it, of course, pinpointed the location for Mr. Alexander in his report to Stanford University and to the next of kin of L. T. Lattimer."

"What are the DGSE's suspicions on why that asshole wants it? To sell it?" Everett asked as he saw the three Spetsnaz coming toward their group.

"No, he wants it for blackmail."

Farbeaux looked over at Collins, their eyes met and they both knew the reasons why blackmail was the obvious choice.

"Correct, Colonel, blackmail."

"The ballsy bastard is trying for a coup in Quebec, that's why Sagli and Deonovich were so quick to give up what they had going in Russia; a safe haven and their own country with Punchy at its head."

"My country believes the weapon in question can be broken up into twenty devices and would all be the equivalent of any high-yield weapon in the modern arsenals of the world—"

"An instant superpower armed with nuclear weapons only a hundred miles from the American border. A power that would be able to dictate terms to Ottawa and to London," Collins explained as he closed his eyes.

"Well, that may not happen. It is my understanding that this weapon can only be armed by a code particular to the Hyper Glide, and this code remains one of the most guarded secrets of your government. Only a few men in the world know how to activate it and disarm it, and these men are more of a secret than the code itself," Henri said trying to make the others see a brighter side to their predicament.

As the guard detail were only feet away, Everett, Farbeaux, and Mendenhall looked to Jack. His silence told them that something was wrong. He was deep in thought and his lips were actually moving with the effort.

"Colonel?" Will said, trying to get him to say something.

"Please don't tell me—"

Farbeaux knew in his heart and when Jack cut his question off in mid-sentence, he lowered his head and closed his eyes.

"The men who know the codes to the Hyper Guide weaponry may not be as guarded a secret as you think," Collins said as they all instantly realized why Jack was led to the Canadian wilderness.

"Jack, is there something we should know before these assholes shoot us?" Everett asked as the three Spetsnaz stopped in front of their make-shift tarp.

"Punchy knows I can arm or disarm the weapon. That's why as a captain I was a team leader in the search in '89."

"You see, what did I tell you? Everyone has these damn weapons just sitting on their back porch, and if I ever go on a field mission and not run into one, I wouldn't know what to do with myself!" Mendenhall said as he slammed his booted feet on the ground as if he were throwing a fit.

Farbeaux leaned over as far as he could toward Jack as the first guard reached down to pull him off the ground.

"As I said, Colonel Collins, you never cease to amaze me."

Jack knew he had to act and do so without getting everyone shot before he had a chance to say what he had to say to Alexander. Mendenhall, Farbeaux, and Everett were stood up and moved out into the falling rain. They were lined up by the three Spetsnaz and while they were occupied, Jack made a break for the large communications tent. Just three feet from the flap, he was caught and knocked to the ground by Deonovich. He stood over Collins, smiling. His one mistake was straddling Jack as he lay on his back. Evidently the man hadn't learned about Jack's very quick feet. Collins reared his right leg up and brought it up toward the large Russians crotch—that was when Jack found out that, yes indeedy, the big man had learned—he caught Jack's foot and twisted, throwing Collins over onto his stomach.

"I told you to execute his men, not torture the colonel!"

Deonovich looked up at the man standing just inside the tent. Alexander had a murderous scowl on his face. Even Sagli shook his head from the dryness of the tent.

"Punchy, you better listen to what I have to say!" Jack called out through the rain.

Deonovich, ignoring the warning from Alexander, raised his own right foot and slowly smashed Jack's face into the rocky mud. The pressure was tremendous as the colonel's features became totally submerged as he struggled to free his neck.

Alexander looked at Sagli and nodded his head angrily. The Russian stepped out and shoved his partner from Collins. Jack's head popped up and he took a deep breath, shaking his head to free some of the mud. As lightning streaked across the sky, Alexander, without moving from the tent watched as Sagli moved the insane Deonovich away and tried to get him back to the executions he was ordered to perform.

"You have one minute, Jack."

Jack rolled over onto his back and sat up. He looked up into the rain to wash some of the mud away and then he looked at Alexander.

"You kill them, and my sister and myself be damned. I know what you want me for, and I will never free up the weapon with the codes you need."

Alexander was stunned. He stepped into the downpour and stood over Collins. He knelt beside Jack and looked him in the eyes. His large frame didn't move as if he were searching for the lie in his old friend's eye.

"How did you know?" was all he asked.

"Your treasonous game is up, Alexander. At least one intelligence service knows all about your plan to find the bomb and use it to stage a coup in Quebec."

Alexander suddenly stood and shouted at the three Spetsnaz, "Shoot them all now!"

"You know me, Punchy, I'll never give you the codes—so stop this from happening," Jack hissed as he struggled to stand.

"Goddamn you, Jack!"

"No! Goddamn *you*, you son of a bitch! You won't get a damn thing from me if one more of my people die!" The last words were the first Alexander had ever heard Collins scream out loud.

A hundred feet away, the three Spetsnaz took aim.

"Stop!" Alexander shouted through the storm just as lightning and its accompanying thunder came from overhead.

Jack flinched, thinking his friends were behind him lying in the mud, shot to death by a man he once claimed as a pal.

Sagli and Deonovich were stunned. Still, Sagli reached out and pushed down on the barrel of the weapon of the first man in line. The other two saw this and lowered their own AK-47s. Deonovich looked up and was furious that the American had said something to their new partner and changed his mind all in a few seconds. He turned and stormed away, his heavy boots splashing water and mud as he went.

Mendenhall felt weak in his knees, but remained upright, not giving the mercenaries in front of him the pleasure of seeing him afraid. He just thanked God that the heavy rain camouflaged the tear that rolled down his face.

"It seems I will owe your colonel after this," Farbeaux said in relief.

"Don't be in such a hurry, Farbeaux. Jack just may have bought us time by trading you for us," Everett joked, as he himself still had his heart in his throat.

"In any case, it was worth it to see the expression on that bastard's face when he was foiled from shooting us."

"It was worth me almost crapping my pants for at that," Everett quipped.

Alexander lifted Jack up and shook him.

"Listen to me!" he shouted into the face of Collins. "I have spent over twenty-five years in shit holes around the world; I have planned this for half as many of those years. I will not allow to you to fuck it up for me, Jack! If you don't do as I ask and enter those codes on that weapon, I will not kill your friends, I will skin them alive right in front of you. Then you will watch Lynn as she's taken by every mercenary in this camp, and then you will watch as she's cut to pieces! Am I clear, Jack?"

"Clear, Punchy." The voice was cool and the words said as if he had just been given an order by the president. "One question?"

Alexander had turned away, but stopped. He refused to face Jack again.

"What?" he shouted over the rain.

"Do you think the United States, or Canada will allow this to happen?"

This time Alexander decided to deliver the news himself; it was his turn to shock Collins with knowledge.

"Yes, I do expect them to allow the separation of Quebec from Ottawa, Jack," he said as he slowly turned. Collins could see the insanity coursing through his features, "Because the first weapons derived from this one warhead will be delivered to Toronto, New York, Washington, London, and Paris. Yes, they will welcome a new Quebec, and its new head of state, maybe not with open arms, but they will welcome it, if only publicly. Stranger alliances have happened in history, Jack, you should know that."

Collins saw Punchy turn and walk away. Then he stopped as a sudden shout and angry voices sounded from the camp. Jack turned and saw fifteen of the commandos running for the back of camp, toward the line of tents, in particular, Lynn's tent. His eyes widened when he saw the tent flap open and then his eyes flicked to the line of trees just as Lynn disappeared into the forest.

"Stop, let her go," Punchy shouted. The looked at Sagli and Deonovich, who were standing dumbfounded at opposite ends of the camp. "Gather up your prisoners, get the men to their weapons and the techs out of their tents; we move in tonight. This ends here, now!"

Alexander walked over to the larger Deonovich and grabbed him by the jacket he was wearing and as Sagli watched in shock, the big man actually cowered away from the smaller Canadian.

"You take what you have on you and get the woman back—*now!*"

Deonovich was released and he cowered even farther away from the insanely bright eyes of Alexander. Then he turned on his heels and ran in the same direction as Lynn.

The maniacal sound of the Canadian's voice startled everyone who heard it. It blasted over the thunder and rain, and it seemed to center on each individual. As Collins watched, men made for their tents and packs, weapons and equipment. The Spetsnaz was going to secure the doomsday weapon, and all Jack could do was watch.

The group would follow Lynn into the northern woods of the Stikine, and two different species of man would meet head-on after a million years of living separately.

The outcome might just decide the inheritors of the new world.

PART THREE
THE FOREST PRIMEVAL

12

Charles Hindershot Ellenshaw III was hearing droning once more from deep in his mind. He tried to focus on the dream but it kept fluttering tantalizing close and then vanishing; it was constantly in and out of hearing range. The song was the same one he was singing before he had passed out: "Crystal Blue Persuasion" was being hummed with a deepness to it that made it seem it was coming from a deep and darkened well. The humming was not good, but continuous. Finally, the pain in his shoulder brought Charlie to the brink of wakefulness.

The smell of mildew and earth was the first thing to enter his waking mind as his eyes fluttered open. Or did they, he wondered. The blackness told him he was dreaming yet again as he tried to move his head. That was when he realized he was awake and that wherever he was, the sun never reached. Then it hit him like a comet: the cave and that old familiar smell from 1968—he was inside of Lattimer's cave.

Charlie tried to sit up, but the pain in his shoulder told him that was definitely not a good idea. He lay back down and that was when he realized the humming had stopped. With his shoulder screaming, Charlie moved his right hand to his front pants pocket and removed a small lighter. That was when his memory came back and he knew that the Russians had shot him—for what? Then it struck him: because he tried to be a hero, and he knew then for the first time in his life he had to admit that he just wasn't the hero type.

"Foolish old man," he said to himself, not realizing he had spoken out loud. That was when he heard movement to his right. Something large had scurried from where he lay to someplace farther down the cave's long and dark passage. Charlie swallowed, and still lying on his back, he used the lighter in his hand.

He kept his eyes closed for the longest time, afraid to open them for fear of what his vision would behold. Finally, gathering up his courage, he opened one eye and saw the cave's ceiling some thirty-five feet above his prone body. The ancient stalactites hung down like teeth in a nightmare mouth. He swallowed and opened his other eye, and then he turned his head. He saw that he was lying on a bed of leaves and moss. The smell of rotting vegetation was atrocious and he crinkled his nose. He smelled urine and feces, but the rotting bed mat was the worst.

As his eyes roamed the cave, he saw cave drawings, not unlike the ones he remembered from his first encounter back in 1968. As he tried to sit up, he was amazed at how deep the colors used on the paintings were. They looked powerful in their renderings of deer, elk, and other forest animals, and unlike the cave paintings of Paleolithic man in European paintings, these were depictions of hunts, or the killing of game; these were like a naturalist's view of the wild world. Charlie saw whole herds of beasts, running through the woods, grazing, and doing the everyday things that these animals would do.

Charlie managed to push the throbbing pain in his shoulder to the back of his mind, absentmindedly reaching for his left arm. With the lighter so close to his wound, Charlie was astounded to see that the bullet hole had been packed with what looked to be mud and small shavings of bark and grass. It smelled like someone had placed animal droppings in there for good measure. He shook his head and shied away from looking at the disgusting mess. He concentrated on standing up, one movement at a time, inches at most. Finally he managed to gain his feet, which he noticed were bare. Someone had removed his boots. When he looked around he could see them a few feet away. His eyes widened when he realized they looked as if they had been virtually stripped from his feet like a banana peel—the tongues were completely torn free and the laces were missing.

Ellenshaw shook his head, letting the lighter go out to give his thumb a rest. He stepped forward from the bed of leaves and grass until he felt dirt beneath his feet. Using his good right arm, he felt the coldness of the cave wall. His fingers felt the dampness and he rubbed them together. Overhead through the rock strata of the cave, Charlie heard the soft rumble of thunder and knew that the humidity he was feeling was caused by the deepness of the cave. He was far beneath the earth and that was when he realized that he was far away from the opening he had been in those many years ago. He almost became ill with the thought of being buried so far from the surface of the world.

He shook his head when he discovered that he was acting like a schoolgirl. He had a chance here to possibly see something that no man in history had ever been witness to: an actual living entity that hadn't changed in millions of years. With that thought Charlie struck the lighter once more. The flame illuminated the cave wall and Ellenshaw saw a large painting of what looked to be a bird—it almost resembled the phoenix of southern Maya and Inca origins. It looked like it was rising in flames from the earth, but no, Charlie thought to himself, it wasn't rising at all—it was falling. And never once had he seen any historical depiction of the phoenix with a man riding on the back of the giant bird.

"Amazing detail for a prehistoric rendering, I must say," Charlie said to himself.

Ellenshaw shook his head and stepped to his right. There were more depictions of animals and of the surrounding woods. He turned and looked behind him at the rear wall of the giant cave—there were more paintings there. As he stepped up, his eyes widened. There were straight horizontal lines drawn over a wavy surface, almost looking like a zigzag pattern against the stone wall. On these horizontal lines were what Charlie realized immediately were representations of men. They were stick men, but he could see that these men were on what had to be boats, the straight lines riding over a rippling surface. *The Stikine River!* he thought to himself.

Ellenshaw, placing the lighter as close to the painting as he could, reached out and with his finger touched the red (blood, he was thinking) and green pigment, then he brought the finger away and moaned deep in his chest. The water-based colors were still wet. Charlie's eyes widened as a sudden gust of breeze blew the lighter out. He cursed and struck the small wheel again, flicking the lighter and trying to get it to catch. Every time the flint was struck, the wall and interior of the cave illuminated around him, and that was when he failed to realize in those momentary flashes of light, that he wasn't alone.

He cursed one more time and struck the flint wheel of the lighter; this time the flame came up and stayed lit and as he turned, still in shock that the painting he had just touched was still wet to the touch, he came face to face with the artist.

Ellenshaw's mouth fell open as the vision of a million years penetrated his soul. Standing five feet over Charlie's head was Giganticus Pythicus, an ape that was supposedly extinct for the past ten thousand years. The eyes were that of no ape, and the face was not covered in fur or hair. The skin was clean and the lines of age were clearly seen. The nose was actually very similar to a man's, not flat like a modern ape, not large like a humans, either—it was somewhere in between. The mouth was large and as it opened its maw, Ellenshaw could see that the teeth were still that of an animal that could use its canines for very adequate defense.

Charlie's hand holding the lighter remained steady as he realized his life's dream was standing before him. An amazing discovery in the human experience was staring at him right in the face, justifying everything he had ever believed about the world. The animal's brown eyes bore into Ellenshaw's and he could see the brows rise up in a curious maneuver of facial muscles. The great beast tilted its head as it looked Charlie over in the flickering flame of the small lighter.

"He . . . hello," Ellenshaw mumbled.

The giant ape—Sasquatch, Bigfoot, a legend and myth of the new world—looked at Charlie with its expressive eyes, and then slowly leaned over the small man and gently blew out the lighter.

"Oh, crap."

Lynn crashed through the undergrowth as if the devil himself were chasing her. She knew that if she could take the threat of her own imminent death out of the equation, Jack just may have a fighting chance at thwarting whatever it was Punchy had in mind for him.

The lightning was striking the ground up and down the Stikine in a display of power Lynn had never seen south of the Canadian border. She knew that this had to be one of the largest electrical storms she had ever been witness to. The rain was so thick and the raindrops so large that she felt she was in danger of drowning as she tried for her escape.

Lynn tried in vain to look behind her as she ran, thinking the Russians had to be close behind, but seeing nothing. In that split second of turning her head back, she ran into a brick wall. She rebounded so hard that her breath was knocked from her lungs as she flew backward five feet. When she hit the noise she made as she tried to force air back into her throat sounded like a water pipe with air in its system. As she looked up through the falling rain, her eyes widened when she realized she could see clearly. She saw why almost immediately: She was only thirty feet away from what was left of the giant Sikorsky helicopter as it lay in pieces before her. The flames illuminated the area that, in her haste to escape, she hadn't even noticed.

When she finally rolled onto her stomach, she managed to draw a breath, still wondering what it was she had ran headlong into. She tried to stand. She went to her knees, knowing that if she didn't get moving soon she would have the mercenaries catching her and undoubtedly returning her for use against Jack. As she finally gained her feet, she turned toward the still-flaming helicopter. That was when she saw what she had slammed into at a full run. It towered over her small frame. Her eyes traveled up- ward and locked on the fierce eyes of an animal that could not possibly be standing there.

"What the . . . ?"

Lynn saw the giant apelike creature as it opened its mouth, clearly vis- ible in its outline in front of the fire; the beast let out a grunt and then showed its teeth. In its massive human-looking hands was a club, which seemed to be adorned with marks of some sort that she couldn't make out. The large weapon looked as if it had been through hell and back again, scared and chipped, as if the animal had forever used it as a tool, a killing weapon. Before she knew it, the giant was gone. It just vanished before her shocked eyes, blending into the trees that surrounded the downed heli- copter.

Suddenly she heard the crashing of underbrush coming from behind her, and before she could react after being stunned by the beast she had stumbled into, Lynn saw the angry face of Gregory Deonovich as he ran headlong into the small clearing where she stood. Before she realized what happened, she was grabbed by the large Russian just as Alexander had grabbed him only minutes before. He raised a hand and hit Lynn across the face. Then he repeated the assault, this time from the opposite direction. He threw her down to the wet forest floor and stood over her.

"You have caused me embarrassment for the last time. You will never be found and that will be my excuse for not bringing you back."

Lynn, dazed from the two successive blows to her face, started to sit up, the rain washing the blood from her features. As she rose, she saw Deonovich reach for the shoulder holster at his chest and remove the Glock nine-millimeter he carried there. The look on his face was calm and collected. He knew he would face the wrath of the Canadian, but it would be worth it. He figured to shoot the American and then drag her body off and hide it, claiming he could not catch her.

Lynn watched as the gun was aimed at her face. She defiantly looked at the muzzle and then her eyes widened as something behind Deonovich separated itself from the large tree it was hiding against. The animal had blended perfectly with its surroundings. She couldn't tell where the tree began and the beast ended. Only in the firelight did she see the true nature of the animal as it grabbed Deonovich by the shoulders.

The Russian's eyes widened as he felt his large frame lifted free of the earth. The pistol swung up and around, and fired two shots, both missing the animal as it raised the man completely over its head. Before Lynn could even flinch or Deonovich could realize he was about to die, the great animal smashed the Russian against the tree, snapping his back and almost bending him in two. The branch Deonovich was pushed into caught him twenty feet off the ground and the large man grunted as the wood penetrated through his chest cavity. The animal roared and watched as Deonovich took his last breath. The beast admired what it had just done, tilting its large head first left, and then right. Then with a satisfied grunt, the beast leaned over and recovered something from the ground, and then turned on Lynn.

"Oh, shit," she said under her breath.

The giant ape took two long strides and it was suddenly standing over the small woman. It looked her in the eyes, and then it suddenly shook its entire body, releasing a torrent of water. For some reason, Lynn could see the animal far more clearly than she had before. Somehow, the beast had used not only its differing colors and thickness of its hair, but also the rain to hide itself. She was even more amazed to see some of the hair along the left side of its massive head had braids in it. Collected through those braids were what looked like colored stones, and to her amazement there were at least two of the gold American double eagles Sagli had shown her only the day before.

The animal looked down at her and grunted, raising the club, and then jabbing the blunt end into her ribs.

"Ow!" she cried out before she even realized she did it.

Another grunt, and then the beast looked up and seemed to see or sense something. It rose again to its full height of over ten feet, grunted once again, and then turned and ran for the deep woods off to the right, vanishing among the trees in mere seconds.

Lynn slowly collapsed until her head was resting on the soft carpet of wet pine needles. She shook her head for the reason she didn't fully understand her miraculous escape from the hands of the killer, Deonovich. She sat back up and looked at the still hanging body of the large Russian. The firelight caught the steady stream of blood as it flowed from his body. Lynn shook her head again and knew she was nearing the state of shock as cold chills overtook her system. She lay back down and closed her eyes.

"Jesus," was all she could say.

When she heard someone say something to her, she didn't move. She did, however, open her eyes and look into a set of green eyes. In the firelight she could see that it was a woman who was kneeling beside her and trying to get her attention.

"Who are you?" Lynn croaked through the taste of blood in her mouth.

"My name is Sarah, and I think we'd better get back to the cave before your knight in shining armor returns, don't you?"

"You bet," Lynn said as Sarah and the girl Lynn knew from the fishing camp helped her. She was grateful to the two women and was about to thank them, when a realization struck Lynn Simpson. "Hey, you're Jack's girlfriend!"

With that and before Sarah had a chance to respond, Lynn passed out and slumped against the two women.

"Yes, I'm Jack's girlfriend, and you must be his sister Lynn."

"It really is a small world, isn't it," Marla said as she took most of the American woman's weight on her own.

"Yeah, well, we'd better get back to Jason before we have company other than our animal friend."

Sarah, Marla, and their newest friend, Lynn, stepped through the fire and then walked fifteen feet to the cave opening.

All three suspected they were in the realm of something they didn't understand, and little did they realize they had entered the forest home of the fiercest creatures that had ever lived on the North American continent.

The ancient brother of man was no longer a myth.

Alexander and his tech team were just twenty feet behind the advance recon team. Altogether the Russians were heading into the bush with fifteen Spetsnaz, five mercenaries, and seven technicians. Alexander had five of the commandos watching Collins and the three additional captives with strict orders to keep Jack alive.

One of the technicians reached out and stopped Alexander, who was intent on following his point team as quickly as possible through the woods. With the rain lessening somewhat, Punchy turned and saw his main technicians hold up the visual metal detector. As he took in the small LED screen, he could see that they were in the middle of a dense minefield of metal. He quickly looked around his feet and spied one of the objects they were chasing. He bent over and picked it up and smiled. It was a two-foot-by-eleven-inch piece of aircraft aluminum. Punchy tossed it away and they continued through the trees, trying to get to their goal as quickly as possible.

As Jack, Carl, Will, and Farbeaux were pushed and pulled through the dense undergrowth beneath the thick canopy of trees, Everett quickly stepped up to Jack.

"Okay, boss, this little trip of ours has turned into something extraspecial, so it would be helpful if you said your baby sister was great in the field."

"She couldn't tell you a walnut from a rock, buddy," Collins said as he tried to keep Alexander in his sights through the falling rain.

"So, she won't be bringing any cavalry this time out."

Jack looked over at Everett and just raised his brows, and Carl took his meaning.

"You, get back in the line," a voice said and pulled Everett backward by his wire-tie. Carl eyed the mercenary and tried not to let on to the fact that he felt the plastic strap break. He followed orders after being released and fell into line just in front of Henri.

"You seem to have injured your wrist, Captain Everett. I hope you understand the severity of that cut," Farbeaux said as he saw the snapped plastic around Carl's bloody wrist.

"Yeah, Henri, it's not as severe as it looks. I'll hold off getting attention for it until the colonel says to."

"A wise decision," the Frenchman said believing that they might have a shot if Everett moved at just the right time.

Suddenly, they were stopped abruptly. Men were ahead of them and they were brightly silhouetted in the flash of a flare being lit. The red tinted glow made the scene eerie at best as Jack tried to see what was happening as many thoughts swirled through his mind; Deonovich and Lynn, the worst-case scenario was Lynn, of course. Was she lying up ahead where the large Russian had caught her? Or was it their prize that they were examining? As he thought this, they were pushed to the ground by the guards and made to sit still.

"Ow!" Mendenhall said as he sat. He wiggled free of something and then literally bent over backward to see what it was. His fingers curled around a small object and he twisted around to see it, bringing his arms up close to his left hip. As soon as saw it, he dropped it in disgust. "Jesus!" he said out loud.

Jack turned back to see what was wrong with Will when in the red glow of the flare up ahead he saw what it was as Mendenhall leaned away from it. It was a skeletal hand. As Collins squirmed over he saw that something was wrapped around the terminated wrist bone—it was silverfish in color and rusted almost through.

"Lieutenant, pick it up," Jack whispered.

Will got a sick look on his face, but knowing the colonel, he had a reason for the macabre request. So he once again went through the maneuvering involved to pick the human hand up once again. When he twisted back around, Jack had turned his back to him and then removed the still attached bones from his grasp. Collins twisted in his restraints to look at the hand and what was wrapped around it. He grasped the small object and saw the band momentarily expand and then the years of rust did its job—it snapped. Jack held the wristwatch in his palm and looked it over. It was a simple Timex watch and he could see the small hands through the fog-clouded crystal: they were frozen at 1:58 and ten seconds. He didn't know if it were A.M. or P.M.

"What have you got there, Jack?" Everett whispered.

"A watch; its hands are frozen at almost the exact same time as right now."

"That's interesting, Colonel, but does it have a particular significance to our current situation?" Farbeaux asked as he tried to huddle closer to the others without getting hit with the butt of a weapon or getting shot.

Collins turned the watch over and looked at the back. The inscription etched by a jeweler many years before was hard to make out, but Jack managed to turn the watch toward the bright light from the trail ahead. His eyes betrayed his surprise to the others. He looked up, and when they saw their curious faces, he examined the writing once more and then read the inscription.

"'Commander John C. Phillips, USN, with admiration—your mates (CVN) 62, VF-13, 1960—Best of Luck!'"

Collins looked up at Carl who was deep in thought.

"Does that remind you of something, Captain?" Henri asked.

"CVN 62, I think that was the USS *Independence*. VF -13, I believe, was a fighter squadron."

"Are you thinking what I am, Colonel?" Farbeaux asked.

"It looks like our long-lost naval aviator there had volunteered for a particularly dangerous mission back in October of 1962."

"I agree, coincidence in this very strange affair has to end sometime," Henri said as he spied one of the Spetsnaz coming over from the area where the flare was glowing.

"Jack, we have company," Everett said. "Just to let you know, I'm loose."

Collins just nodded his head as the large commando reached down and pulled him to his feet.

"I'll keep that in mind, Captain; for now, just take it easy and enjoy your surroundings."

Jack was pulled along until he was met by Alexander. As the colonel looked around in the light of the flare, he saw Sagli squatting by a large tree and he had a look of sadness on his face as he stared at his hands.

"I'm going to ask you something, Jack, and be straightforward with your answer, because I believe your life, as well as mine and my men, may be at stake."

Collins didn't say anything. He looked up through the thick branches of the trees as the rain had almost stopped. He then looked back down into the face of the Canadian.

"I know Lynn has no field prowess to speak of. Is there another of your men that you had along that has yet to be accounted for?"

Collins was almost amused. He gave Alexander a curious look but remained noncommittal.

"That's what I thought. No, if you had a man that wasn't accounted for, he would have made some sort of move by now." He raised his eyebrows at Jack. "You see, I know you train your people to be aggressive."

Alexander was out of patience with the silent Collins as he grabbed him by the collar and pulled him over into the bright light cast by the dying flare.

"Did one of your people do this?" he shouted as he thrust Jack forward, almost making him lose his balance.

As Collins caught himself, he finally looked around, and then up until his eyes saw the body of Gregory Deonovich impaled on the tree branch. The body was slammed into the tree in a prone position with the limb traveling through his rib cage until it poked out the opposite side. The eyes were wide and staring. Jack could also see that the body had been impaled with such brutal force that the man's back had been shattered to the point where the entire large frame of the Russian bent far enough to create a an upside-down U shape.

"Either Little Sis has been working out, or I would say you have a problem on your hands, and by the look of it, I would say, a rather large one."

Collins was suddenly attacked from the rear and tackled. Alexander moved fast, but was slow in pulling Dmitri Sagli off. The man had actually gotten as far as to pull his large knife from its sheath and raise it, ready to bring it down into Jack's chest before he was kicked off by Alexander.

"Is there something wrong with the English phrase, *I need him alive*, that you idiots don't understand?" Punchy yelled angrily. "You know how stupid Deonovich was; he undoubtedly deserved what he got. You yourself watched him be humiliated earlier by a small woman and you would have allowed her to kill him. It's a little late for sympathies about how you and he fought in Afghanistan together."

Sagli lay where he had fallen, then he slowly picked himself up out of the wet loam of the forest floor. He sheathed his knife and then looked at Alexander.

"It's the manner in which my old comrade was killed, not the justification of it."

"You cannot account for fools, my friend, just grieve for them," Alexander said, making Jack's stomach lurch at the falsity of the sentiment.

Sagli just dipped his head once. Yes, he knew his partner was a fool, but one he could always control and order about. He knew he may have regret that Deonovich is gone after dealing with their new partner. He may have had a use for him down the road that Alexander would not have understood.

Jack watched the exchange. As he did, he felt something under him that he had fallen on, just like Mendenhall had only minutes before. He knew what it was immediately as he had handled the same weapon a hundred times in his career: a Glock nine-millimeter automatic. The weapon must have fallen from the hand of Deonovich as he was being killed.

Punchy Alexander strode over and lifted Jack in one strong sweep of his arms. Then he roughly turned him over and removed the handgun from his grasp. He angrily turned and tossed the automatic toward Sagli, who flinched and let it fall to the wet ground.

"Don't get into the habit of disappointing me," he said to the Russian. "Now let's go."

Alexander pushed Jack back toward the commandos and started walking. Sagli went to his dead friend and reached up, calling for assistance from someone taller to help remove Deonovich from the tree.

"Leave him," Alexander said as he had stopped and turned around. "Let the men see the price of not being vigilant in this place." He turned back and headed for the plateau that was rising before them.

Sagli angrily motioned the men away as he reached up and touched the face of his oldest friend. He glared at Jack and then abruptly turned and followed Alexander—*his* new boss.

"What did we miss?" Everett asked as he and Will, and then finally Farbeaux, were led into the light of the flare.

"I take it we missed this," Farbeaux said as he nodded toward the tree with Deonovich hanging from it.

"What in the hell did that?" Will asked as he backed away from the gruesome sight.

"Jack, are you starting to consider that either your sister hasn't told you about her current strength-and-conditioning program, or that we may have more than these assholes to worry about in these woods?"

Collins just looked at Everett and was about to say something when all around them, close and far, the pounding of clubs on trees started, far louder and closer than they had ever heard before. Inside of the light of the flare, Collins saw the Russians as they turned every which way, in anticipation of something unexpected. Jack saw the look of fright on most of the battle-hardened faces and the sheer terror in the eyes of the regularly trained troops. All twenty-seven of the technicians and soldiers had the look that must have crossed the faces of Custer and his men when they realized the jig was up at the Little Bighorn.

"I have a feeling we're about to find out just who it is we pissed off by being here," Mendenhall said as he backed into Collins, all the while his eyes never leaving the woods around him.

"I believe I must concur with the lieutenant's assessment; these sounds are far angrier than before."

Farbeaux didn't have the words out of his mouth when the first flash of dark movement took the two men bringing up the rear of their small group. They were gone in an instant without as much as a shout.

Mendenhall just turned to face Collins with his eyes wide as the drumming continued.

"It . . . it . . . it was . . . was big!" he finally said.

The rain had stopped but the clubbing of the trees continued. Suddenly, a shot was fired, and that led to another, then another, and then someone opened up an AK-47 on full automatic.

Collins and the others cringed as bullets started ricocheting off of trees, and tracers lit up the night. He looked around as fast as he could and saw that no one was watching them. The lone guard was terrified and watching the woods to the rear where the two men had vanished.

"Mr. Everett, I think now would be a good time."

Carl didn't hesitate once given the order, he simply moved his hands from his back to his front and then as quick as the earlier lightning streaking across the night sky, he reached out and twisted the soldier's neck, snapping it, and then catching the AK-47 before it fell to the ground. He quickly aimed at one of the men as he turned at the sudden movement behind him. A single shot by Everett brought the man down. The single discharge wasn't even noticed in the din of gunfire.

"May I suggest egress from this area?" Farbeaux yelled as he ran past the others and then turned suddenly to his left and jumped into thick woods. Jack and the others quickly followed the man who had made a living out of surviving when he should have died.

All around the trail of men and equipment, clubs sang out and the dwellers of the forest primeval attacked in earnest.

———————

As the rain slowed, Jason Ryan was trying with his wounded shoulder pounding in pain to get the ejection seat inside the cave opening. He slipped and fell several times while dragging the heavy piece of safety equipment and attached body to cover. He had decided to do something when Marla and Sarah had abandoned him when they went out after hearing noise in the brush.

After ten minutes of struggle, Ryan fell in backward through the cave's opening. The ejection seat was now secured inside with him. As he moved his hand to his right shoulder, he felt the stickiness of his own blood. *Great*, he thought, *Sarah's going to be furious with me for opening my wound again.* He lay back and tried to get his breathing under control. When he thought he had achieved a modicum of control after so much exertion, Ryan sat up and looked over the skeletal remains of the pilot as the ejection seat lay on its side. He couldn't see much in the dark, but he could make out the basic outline of the remains. The left hand was missing and the fibula was sticking out of the rotting flight suit. The crash helmet was still in place but Jason could see that it had done this poor bastard no good at all. From all the evidence he could see from the time outside in the illumination of the lightning storm, this man had died of a high-impact crash.

Ryan reached out, felt around the left shoulder of the decaying flight suit, and lifted a small flap and felt underneath. There should have been a patch indicating this pilot's flight group, or at least a flag of his country, but the space was empty. He felt around the sickening remains again in the dark. He came upon a rotting piece of leather and allowed his hand to travel down farther. It was a shoulder holster that all military combat pilots carry. As he unsnapped the strap that held the weapon in place, it came off in his hands and then the entire holster fell free. He lifted it to his face and saw that is was a snub-nosed Smith & Wesson .38 Special. He opened the cylinder and felt the rounds there—six.

"Sorry, buddy, but I may have need of this."

Suddenly, he heard noise from outside the cave and he pointed the .38 into the dark. He didn't even know if the gun would work as he pulled back the hammer. He swallowed as whatever it was had not one concern for the noise it was making. He hoped the damn weapon would fire and was about to find out when the voice came through the opening.

"Jason, is that you?"

Ryan rolled his eyes and released the hammer on the small handgun. He let out a deep breath and then laid the weapon in his lap.

"No, it's Mary Jane Rotten Crotch. Who else would it be? Do you guys think you can make any more noise?" he asked angrily.

"Sorry, we picked up a hitchhiker," Sarah said as three people came crashing into the cave.

All Jason could see was dark hair and a shapely butt; his anger immediately vanished.

"Jason Ryan, meet Lynn Simpson, Jack's sister."

Sarah could see Ryan as he cringed when he heard it was the colonel's sister. He soon got over it and then picked up the small .38.

"Nice to meet you," Ryan said sarcastically.

"I'm sure," Lynn said as she stepped around the skeleton and the ejection seat.

"Don't mind him; he's being a baby because he got speared by a tree branch. He's been in a bad mood ever since he crashed our helicopter," Sarah said as she kneeled over and checked Ryan's wound.

"*I* crashed! You mean, when *we* got shot down?"

"So, that was you?" Lynn asked as she looked around the darkened cave. "Your flying drew enough attention from the Russians to give me time to escape."

"So glad I could be of assistance."

"Damn it, you're bleeding again!" Sarah said as she once more applied pressure to his wounded shoulder. "You did it dragging that thing in here, didn't you? You stupid idiot."

"Yeah, does this look stupid?" he asked thrusting the pilot's handgun into her hand.

Sarah still kept one hand on the wound but felt the reassuring feel of a gun in her other.

Lynn looked around her. "Hey, where did the girl go?" she asked.

Sarah looked up and saw nothing. She couldn't tell if Marla was standing right next to her.

"Marla," Sarah called out. "Marla, get back here with us, right—"

The sound of wood striking wood filled the cave. Then the sound of automatic-weapons fire erupted not far from the caves opening. Ryan saw tracers flying everywhere and that was when he decided.

"I think we better find a back door to this place; that doesn't sound good at all."

"I think you're right," Sarah said as she lifted the pilot to his feet, her small frame far stronger than Ryan realized.

With Lynn and Sarah flanking Jason, they entered the cave.

"By the way Mr. Ryan, who is Mary Jane Rotten Crotch? An associate of yours?" Lynn asked, knowing full well the name was one of those many foul-sounding delicacies the military used for describing the not-so-virtuous women hounding servicemen. "Maybe an old girlfriend?"

"Yeah, most definitely an old flame of mine."

As they went farther into the cave it wasn't long before long-sought-for items became visible in the bleak darkness and as Ryan fell over one of these Lynn realized they had found what Alexander was looking for: the Hyper Glide.

Lynn knew it by its real name: It was the weapon of choice for a mission known to the military as Operation Solar Flare.

Punchy Alexander couldn't see anything other than the Spetsnaz taking aim at nothing and firing. He aimed his own Beretta nine-millimeter into the dark, but all he could see was the smoldering remains of one of his Sikorsky helicopters and smoke rising from the men doing the shooting. He tried to get them under control by shouting out orders, but through the explosive reports bouncing off of trees and rocks he didn't stand a chance at being heard.

He finally reached out and grabbed Sagli who was just as frightened as his men. He turned him toward the north and pushed him forward. They were soon joined by three of the Spetsnaz.

As Alexander turned to look behind him, he saw something that froze his blood. A dark shape jumped from the trees and clubbed one of the soldiers to the ground. The beast struck the man three times in quick succession and then vanished before the men next to him could react.

"Jesus, what are these things?" he yelled as the beating of the clubs continued in its deafening cadence.

The men he left behind started to fight in earnest, laying down a dense cover fire in all direction. Then, one of the Spetsnaz who had gone to ground in a prone position was struck by a huge rock that was thrown from the darkness of the trees. That was followed by a roar that chilled the blood of every man who heard it. As the prone man was quickly checked by one of the electronic technicians, another rock was thrown, this one even larger that the first. The tech didn't have a chance as the stone hit him square in the face. That was what broke the other techs' will to stay and fight. They all ran for the trail that Alexander had just disappeared down and that was when the animals hit with force. At least twenty of the great beasts broke free of their camouflage against the trees and started swinging their clubs. The sounds of wood striking flesh overpowered the screams of men as they were taken down one by one.

Giganticus Pythicus had evolved over the last twenty thousand years, enough to gain the knowledge that led them to the use of tools and they were using them now and winning against the advanced firepower of mankind. The camouflage and striking capability coupled with the knowledge of when to attack caught the Spetsnaz, the technicians and the regular soldiers off guard, and when the last one fell, he died never knowing what it was that attacked and killed them.

The battle for the Stikine River was over in three minutes.

Jack stopped long enough for Everett to snap the wire-ties with a sharp stone. It took them far too long as they heard the battle in the back of them. The shooting was getting lighter and the drumming louder. The screams of animals no one in their small group ever wanted to see in person tore through the trees and assaulted their hearing. The primal fear they all felt growing inside of them was surreal in the fact that they sensed this was something that their ancestors may have feared as they went about their daily lives, in that Jack remembered Mendenhall's brief description of what he was feeling on the river.

"Damn, Jack, whatever we're dealing with here is kicking the hell out of Alexander's men," Everett said as he finally freed Mendenhall and turned to work on Farbeaux.

"May I suggest now that we have a weapon that we continue north and see if we can't thwart that old friend of yours?" Henri said as Everett cut through the thick plastic of his restraint.

As they all looked up, Jack Collins made sure the Russian-made weapon had a full clip and then he turned and ran for the trail where he knew his old buddy, Punchy, was heading.

"I think the colonel's way ahead of you," Mendenhall said as he didn't wait for Everett or Farbeaux as he hurriedly dove into the brush and followed Jack.

When Henri and Everett started running after Will and Jack, they saw something pacing with them through the woods beside them, just on the other side of a line of trees. It dwarfed them as they ran. They would speed up and the shadow in the darkness would speed up. They would turn following Jack's lead, and then the shadow would mimic the maneuver.

"We have another one directly behind us, Captain," Henri said with as much grace as he could muster in the circumstance of that terrifying moment.

"Oh, shit, look," Everett called out as another of the giants was seen to their right, running just far enough away to be seen. "Jack!" Everett shouted as loud as he could. "We have some very large company!"

Everett saw that Collins was too far ahead to hear, but Mendenhall wasn't. The lieutenant half turned and saw the giant shadows as they raced along beside them and he yelled out an incoherency and doubled his efforts to catch up with the colonel, or more to the point, the only man with a weapon.

"May I suggest we give the colonel the time he needs?" Farbeaux shouted and then turned into the trees to his right.

Everett couldn't believe Henri was about to give himself up like that. His bosses in France really must have threatened him. In any case, the SEAL captain wasn't about to let the Frenchman show him up, he also peeled off, only to the left.

As Will chanced a glace backward, he was shocked to see an empty trail where Everett and Farbeaux had been. He shook his head knowing the captain and Henri must have met a fate that he was trying desperately to avoid.

Sarah, Ryan, and Lynn had only gone fifteen feet into the caves interior when they stumbled into the large, black object. Lynn let go of Ryan long enough to reach down and feel the thing they had stumbled into. She swallowed when she felt the condensation on the dark casing. She ran her hands along the surface and felt the heat just beneath. She moaned and that was when Ryan also touched it.

"Feels like a giant pocket warmer."

"Yeah," Lynn said straightening up. "You could call it that, about five hundred megatons worth."

Ryan straightened like a man shot from cannon. He swallowed and started wiping his hands on his pants.

"What?" Sarah asked, taking an involuntary step back.

"That's right, you've missed the discussions to date, this thing here, this massive nuclear device is what Mr. Alexander is looking for."

"Harrumph," Ryan said clearing his throat. "And his reason for that is . . . ?"

"Oh, I forgot, he's a traitor to Canada and wants to start his own country in Quebec," Lynn said as plainly and as simply as she could.

"Okay, that makes some sense—I guess," Ryan said.

"No, Mr. Ryan, it makes all the sense in the world."

Ryan looked around and saw that the cave had a wide-open shaft that was situated against the far wall. The opening was about ten feet in diameter and it looked deep, possibly hundreds of feet.

"Look, why don't we just push the weapon down this hole. Alexander would never find it down there."

"That wouldn't be very nice, Mr. Ryan."

A light suddenly clicked on, and standing only a few feet away was Punchy Alexander, bloodied and out of breath, and in the backlight they saw Dmitri Sagli and three of his commandos. Alexander had them covered with his automatic and Sagli looked to be enjoying the moment as he approached Lynn and slammed his fist into her stomach. Ryan reacted without thinking: he hurled himself into the smaller Russian, but after the death of his partner over the woman he had just slammed to the ground, Sagli saw Jason's move long before he tried it. He reached up and slammed the pistol he was holding into the head of Ryan and he went down hard onto the packed earth of the cave.

"Ms. McIntire, Jack will be so pleased to see you, almost as much as I. You and the colonel's sister will come in very handy when it comes time to complete our business here."

Sagli turned on Alexander and whispered something Sarah failed to catch.

"Have the men cover the cave's opening. If the animals try to gain access, shoot them all. They can do that, can't they?" he said sarcastically. "I mean, they are capable of covering a bottleneck?"

"You are missing the point here," Sagli said angrily. "We have to leave here at some point, you fool, and those things will be waiting."

Alexander smiled. "No, I think they'll go for whoever runs interference for us," he said as he stared at Sarah.

In three minutes in the light of four flashlights taken from the packs of the commandos, Alexander had the access port to the Hyper Glide device illuminated and opened. The warmth he felt from the outer casing told Punchy that the weapon was still viable and it had been contained since its violent end in 1962. He closed his eyes, feeling the power at his very fingertips. Soon this lone device, split into twenty smaller weapons would give *him* the power to make his own country, and with the radical element of the French-speaking population, it would be a simple transition.

"I can't believe that you actually think you can do this. This isn't a movie, Alexander; this is the real world, a coup in a civilized Western country?" "

Alexander looked up at Lynn, swiped some of the moisture from his face and smiled.

"A coup in a province that is awaiting a chance of a lifetime. They'll willingly threaten any nation for the chance to be their own country."

"Quebec? Do you think even the most ardent supporters of separation of state from country will follow you, or allow you to stay in power using threats to the security of their friends as persuasion?"

"Yes, I do. I know them and I know the element that they seek: power, my girl, it's always power. And in the right hands, it's such a liberating feeling. Yes, I will have almost total support. Even the United States will find it preferable to the rebellious nature of Canadian policy." Alexander had had just about enough of Lynn so he nodded toward Sagli who immediately reached out and slammed his fist into the side of her head. She fell and struck Ryan as he lay on the cave's floor.

"You bastard," Sarah said as she leaned over and checked both Lynn and Ryan.

Alexander waved Sagli over and then stood.

"My friend, knowing Colonel Collins as I do, and his tendency to be the hero, he should be very close to the opening of this cave. Please step forward with one of your commandos and ask him to join us. It's time he does his part."

Sagli gave Alexander a strange look, but shrugged his shoulders and pulled one of the Spetsnaz toward the mouth of the cave.

"There's no need, Punchy, I'm here."

Alexander quickly grabbed Sarah and brought her to his front, placing the nine-millimeter to her head.

"No need to do that, I have no weapon," Collins said from the darkness of the cave.

Sagli had stopped dead in his tracks as the man beside him went to one knee. The Russian mobster held a flashlight and he pointed it in the direction of the voice. In the light, Jack stood erect and his hands were held out in front of him, palms outward.

"I knew you would get away, Jack. One can always depend on you giving it your all," Alexander said as he forced the muzzle of the gun into Sarah's temple.

"Don't do that, Punchy" Collins said with cold intensity.

"Don't be so melodramatic, Jack, my boy. Now come on, let's finish up here. The access panel has been removed and we're ready for your expertise."

As Alexander finished speaking, there was a loud noise from behind as Mendenhall, Henri, and Everett burst through the opening, yelling and happily slapping each other on the back.

"They're big, but we're faster!" Carl shouted as he helped hold Farbeaux up from the exhausting run they had just endured.

Jack never turned around. He stepped back a foot as Sagli adjusted his light on the others.

"Oh," was all Mendenhall said, getting the attention of the Captain and Frenchman.

"I knew there would be a catch to this cave," Everett said looking over at Farbeaux.

He just shrugged and bent over and rested his hands on his knees. "Any port in a storm, Captain"—he managed to look back up at Carl— "it's not always a friendly port, however.

"Alright, we're all here. It's time, Jack."

Outside, Collins heard the drumming of clubs against the trees come to a sudden stop, it was if the animals knew that this thing would be over soon, for better or worse. Before he spoke he felt the hand of Everett slap him on the back, and then Carl saw the strap wrapped around Jack's shoulder and then he straightened quickly.

"You sneaky bastard—what makes you think they don't see what you have dangling from your back?" he hissed through his teeth.

"Because, I told you all along when you're dealing with these people, they're not soldiers, they're just stupid," Collins mumbled back at Everett.

"If you don't get over here and enter that damn code, Jack, whatever you just whispered will be the last thing this little lady ever hears from you. And, if you could, please hurry. The wildlife around here is beginning to make me a bit nervous."

"Punchy, I think it's time we talked," Jack said, keeping his backside as far from the light as possible.

"The time for talking is over," he said as he roughly shook Sarah and actually slammed the muzzle of the gun harder into her cheek.

"Sarah, look at me," Collins said as he was now flanked by Mendenhall on the right and Everett and Farbeaux on his left. They were all four covered by the three Spetsnaz to their front and Sagli, who looked anxious to shoot, someone, anyone. "Do you believe that everything is going to be alright?"

Sarah nodded her head, not doubting, just hoping Jack had a plan.

Collins looked down at the prone bodies of Ryan and Lynn.

"They needed persuading that I was in charge. Don't worry, Jack, they're alive, and they'll stay that way, just as long as you do what is asked."

"As I said, Punchy, we need to talk."

Letting out a deep breath, Alexander cocked the automatic, letting Jack know that any pressure whatsoever on the trigger would send a bullet into Sarah's head.

"Okay, let's get this over with. Talk."

"October 1962, the United States was in the process of trying to convince the Soviets that President Kennedy was dead serious about getting those missiles out of Cuba. The threat of a blockade didn't seem to be scaring the high command, or the leadership at the Kremlin that Kennedy meant business on this issue. So, Operation Solar Flare was devised, a top-secret scenario that would take the head of the chicken off at the neck, with a weapon so powerful that the war would be over before it ever started—what's known as a doomsday device."

"You are wasting time, Jack. I am growing bored with a story I know as well as you."

"Well, here's something you didn't know, Punchy, you stupid son of a bitch. It was a bluff. The Soviets were allowed to learn of Operation Solar Flare before it was launched in October of that year. They were allowed to see not one, but two aircraft take off that night. One from McCord Air Force Base in Washington State, the other from the carrier USS *Oriskany* in the Sea of Japan. The Soviet high command knew they had no defense against anything like the Hyper Glide device. A highly precise standoff weapon with such a huge punch was game over for them. They folded their hand, bluffed out of the game by a bold and well-planned lie. So you see, Punchy, what you have there is a small amount of active plutonium, placed there so their detectors, stationed in vans and trucks around all of our bases, knew they must be live weapons, when all it was is a case with enough plutonium in it to light up your bedside clock."

"You're lying!" Alexander shouted. "Why would the U.S. spend millions of dollars in a recovery effort?"

"No, Punchy, I'm not lying. The bluff continued for years after; we had to make the Soviets believe we weren't the kind of country to run a poker game on them. They had to know the threat was serious and would continue to be just in case their memories failed them at some point. Colonel Farbeaux?"

"Yes, Jack?" Henri said eyeing Punchy and then turning his eyes toward Collins.

"Explain the situation to the director of Internal Security for the province of Montreal, please."

"Sorry, Mr. Alexander, the colonel's story is a fact—or more to the point, the truth about a lie, which the Americans have become pretty adept at, of late." Henri looked at Jack and nodded; Jack remained still, focusing solely on Alexander.

"Kill the Frenchman!" Alexander shouted. As the three Spetsnaz and Sagli flinched at the order, Jack saw his opening.

As Mendenhall, Everett, and Farbeaux dove for cover, Jack used his hip to swing the AK-47 up and into his hands. The weapon had been hanging upside down across his shoulder waiting for Jack's chance to use it. The first of the weapon's bright flashes caught the three Spetsnaz totally unaware. By the time one of them turned in Jack's direction, rounds had stitched across the chests of all three. As they fell, Collins trained the weapon on Sagli, who immediately dropped his gun. Jack tilted his head and pursed his lips.

"Sorry," he said as he fired a single round into the Russian's head.

Alexander wasn't taking any chances. He backed away from Collins, screaming, "I'll kill her, Jack! You know that I will."

Collins held his hand up when Mendenhall and Everett stood and made to move forward. Farbeaux reached for one of the fallen flashlights and shone it on Alexander.

"You just don't know when to quit, Jack. Well, this time it's going to cost you."

To the surprise of Collins and everyone else, he didn't shoot Sarah, but quickly aimed the pistol at the prone, unconscious body of Lynn, lying next to Ryan. As he depressed the trigger, the light in Farbeaux's hand caught a sight that none of them would have ever believed. A giant hand reached out and caught the weapon in Punchy's hand just as the gun fired. His wrist was bent up and snapped in two. Alexander screamed just as Sarah was torn from his grasp. She fell to the ground and Jack rushed forward. The light still played on Alexander as the giant beast that had came up behind him grabbed the large Canadian by the neck and lifted him free of the cave floor.

"My God," Farbeaux said as the full view of the beast was illuminated in the bright light. Jack and Sarah looked at the giant towering over them and saw not only brawn, but intelligence.

The giant ape, the reason behind twenty thousand years of myth and legends, from the Arctic Circle to the Rocky Mountains, stood erect, and the intelligence in its eyes would forever be undeniable to all who looked into them. He held Punchy, gazing calmly at the humans before him for a moment, and then it *roared*. And every man in the cave knew he'd been challenged, been dared to try to take what was now his. When none of them moved—though Mendenhall began visibly shaking—it turned and stepped into the darkness beyond the power of the flashlight to see it.

Mendenhall stood and walked over and sat down upon the first thing he came across. It was the casing for the Hyper Glide bomb. He sat and was actually grateful for the warmth he felt penetrating through to his wet butt. He placed his head in his hands and tried to calm his heart. It was Jack who slowly stood and touched Will on the shoulder, and even Farbeaux gingerly reached out and touched him on the opposite side.

"Will, you may want to get off of the five hundred megaton nuclear weapon."

Mendenhall looked up, a sad look came across his face as he took in the colonel.

"Not a bluff?" was the simple question.

"No, not a bluff," Jack answered as he let go of Will's shoulder, and winked at his young lieutenant.

"Perhaps you could help me stand up, Colonel Farbeaux?"

"Yes, Lieutenant, I think that would be best."

Everett had gone over to Ryan and Lynn and found both just coming around. Jack kissed Sarah on the top of her head, but that didn't stop her from plopping to the ground as the last few moments caught up with her. Collins went to his sister and lifted her off the ground and Farbeaux shone the light on them both as Lynn's eyes fluttered open.

"When you were a kid, you always managed to fall asleep at the end of the good movies," Jack said, smiling, "or throw your hands across your face at the scary parts."

Lynn didn't say anything. She just placed her arms around her big brother and hugged him.

"Okay, I missed something again, didn't I?" Ryan said as he tried to gain his feet. Grimacing, he sat down again, leaning against the wall well away from the bomb.

As Sarah stood, watching Jack and his little sister, she heard someone behind her. She slowly turned fully expecting to see another animal, but instead she saw an older, slightly built man leaning against the cave wall. His hair was wild looking and his glasses were bent so badly that it was difficult to figure out how he was able to see. The cave wall was clearly all that was holding him up.

"Charlie!" Sarah said as she reached out to help him.

"I'll be damned," Everett said as he raced forward to help Sarah. "What in the hell have you been up to?" Carl asked when he smelled the odors coming off of Ellenshaw.

"I'm not going to dignify that with an answer." Charlie looked around. "I see my savior saved you nonbelievers as well."

Jack walked over after propping Lynn up next to Ryan. The lieutenant, who was really seeing her for the first time, suddenly leaned over and kissed her on the swollen lips. It happened so fast that she couldn't even get angry, but she could give him a shocked grin as she took stock of the wiry little navy aviator.

"Sorry," Ryan said. "Just thrilled to be alive."

Ellenshaw wearily sat down in the glorious light. His eyes had adjusted to the dark well enough to see what he was dealing with.

"I would say Giganticus Pythicus is a fact—to be taken out of the realm of myth and legend forever? Does anyone disagree with my theory?" Charlie looked at the faces turning toward him in the shadowy cave with a smug look on his face. When no one said anything, he was satisfied. "Good," he smiled through his obvious pain as Sarah patted him on the back. "Colonel Farbeaux?"

"No, you have no argument from me, Professor. What I saw here tonight—"

"No, Colonel, I was about to say you may want to look in the cave just a little farther back—you may find two wagons and the ornate box that this used to lay in." Charlie Ellenshaw tossed a small object toward Farbeaux and he caught it in midair. He shone the light on it and then smiled.

"So, are you going to accept such a large payment for doing your duty, Colonel?" Jack asked, already knowing the answer.

As Farbeaux looked at the second half of the Twins of Peter the Great, he returned Jack's smile.

"Bad guy, remember?"

Collins nodded his head, satisfied that Henri was still Henri.

"Hey, where is the girl?" Ryan said looking around with another flashlight he had picked up.

"I believe young Marla ran in that direction," Charlie said as he pointed toward the rear of the cave.

Before any of them could follow the trail back into the dark interior of the cave, they were shocked when one of the Sasquatch appeared from the front. It roared and then stepped into the light. Jack and the others watched as it angrily kicked at the bodies of Sagli and his commandos. The bodies were tossed as if they were nothing more that beanbags. The beast roared again. They all saw the small bones that were entwined in its long hair. The club it carried struck out at the rock wall, knocking free stone and dirt with the powerful blow.

"I thought they were on our side," Mendenhall said as he took in the giant, Bigfoot.

"Look at its side, it's been shot, and it looks to be a mortal wound," Charlie said, actually stepping forward until Jack halted him.

"Doc, I don't think it cares who shot it; it only sees us at the moment."

The beast roared for a third time. With its mouth wide they could see the blood as it coursed through the throat from another wound they couldn't see. The great animal kicked out once more, its large foot striking the Hyper Glide, sending it into the stone wall of the cave.

"Whoa!" Ryan said as he grabbed Lynn and retreated a few steps. The beast saw the movement and screamed once more, making all of them cringe.

"Don't move, the weapon can't be armed without the code," Collins said, gesturing for Ryan and Lynn to stop moving.

The beast saw the two stop and stare at it, and it obviously thought that was a threatening gesture. This time it swung the massive club and again it struck the large bomb on its outer casing. When it did, the outer primer popped free and that was when they saw the electronic display on the Hyper Glide come to life. The numbers were the old-fashioned kind seen at NASA in the early days before LED lights. The bright numbers started counting down from five minutes."

"Oh, shit," Farbeaux said. For the first time his cool was evaporating. "Colonel, you seem to be taking this current situation rather calmly."

Collins watched the device as it counted down, but at the moment he was more concerned with the enraged animal before him.

"The Hyper Glide can count down all it wants, it may be armed but it would be impossible for it to detonate."

The beast roared again when Jack spoke, silencing him. Then the animal wavered and leaned against the rock wall, finally getting weaker from its wounds.

"Now, why would it be impossible for this rather large weapon to explode?" Everett asked as he, too, watched the Sasquatch.

"Because it was designed to detonate at minus three hundred feet; it was a giant bunker-Buster. For safety of the local surface population the bomb had to bury itself in three hundred feet of earth before it went off."

The beast was breathing its last. The animal let out a cry, not unlike a human would when death was close. Then the beast laid its head to the side and rolled over to the floor.

The men and women in the cave visibly relaxed as Jack moved toward the bomb.

"I don't mean to be a stickler, Colonel, but you were wrong about the weapon not being able to be armed without the codes; so what if you're wrong about this?" Henri asked, joining him as Jack looked the bomb over.

"I'm not wrong. The device must have rotted through its wiring and disabled the sequencing of the installed code. Now look here," he said, pointing to a set of smaller numbers below that of the larger countdown digits ticking off. "That is plus or minus altitude, the numbers from the countdown have to match in sequence with the minus numbers in altitude, in this case, three hundred feet minus zero altitude, in other words, three hundred feet below ground."

Farbeaux breathed easier as he saw that Collins was right, at least he hoped so.

"Well, I guess we'll find out in four minutes, but may I suggest we use that time to—"

They were all caught off guard when the beast half rose and roared once more. In its death throes it lashed out with its large club and barely missed the Frenchman and Jack as they dove away from the strike. Instead of hitting them, the club struck the Hyper Glide one last time. The powerful blow sent the weapon sailing against the wall one more time. Only this created the bounce that would kill them all. It struck the floor and then the giant weapon teetered on the edge of the large shaft that Ryan had found earlier. As Jack jumped for the weapon to steady it, it tilted and went down. They all were stunned. They heard the Hyper Glide collide with the bottom of the shaft far below them just as the animal lay its head down and died.

Collins rolled over onto his side and stared at the ceiling of the cave in frustration. "Mr. Ryan, how deep would you say that shaft is?"

Jason swallowed and leaned over the hole in the cave's floor. He grimaced and then looked at the people around him.

"Uh, real deep, Colonel, maybe even three hundred feet."

"Oh this is a fun time, thanks, Jack," Lynn said as she sat in frustration.

They all heard the grunt before they turned and saw the giant animal that had absconded with Alexander. It was sanding erect and watching them. It grunted once more and then its eyes fell on the fallen Sasquatch. Its angry eyes went from its fallen family member to those humans standing and sitting in the cave.

It was Ellenshaw that moved first when he recognized that the beast was the artist that had saved his life after he was shot. He quickly reached out and after closing his eyes, grabbed the animal by its massive arm. The beast grunted and then shook Charlie's arm loose as it continued to stare at the fallen Bigfoot before it. Charlie tried again, this time the animal looked down at him and its mouth opened, showing its massive incisors it leaned over and breathed heavily into Ellenshaw's face.

"For God's sake, Charlie, what are you doing? We have another situation here that requires attention," Everett called out.

"I think I know what I'm doing," he answered. He then pulled on the hairy arm until the beast allowed itself to be pulled along. The animal barely cleared the twelve-foot ceiling as Charlie led it toward the hole. The others quickly scrambled out of the way. Once in front of the hole Ellenshaw pointed down. The beast grunted and then it growled once again, this time it was far more menacing than the grunt before it.

"We don't have the time, Charlie," Jack said as he came to his feet. He approached the hole, all the while watching the animal in case it attacked, which would matter very much if the Hyper Glide went off. Jack eyed the creature and then stepped around it. The dark brown eyes of the beast followed Jack's every move, its lips curling over sharp teeth as it did so. Collins bent at the waist and then looked down into the shaft. He saw nothing but darkness.

"Jack, what are you thinking? You won't have the time," Sarah said as she gingerly joined him at the hole, all the while also watching the giant animal before them.

Jack looked up at Sarah and then Bigfoot; he shook his head and smiled. "What the hell, I've got to try."

Collins started to place his feet into the hole and was about to turn and start his way down the shaft. Then the dawning of understanding came to the giant's eyes. It reached down and picked Jack up by the scruff of the collar and roughly hoisted him to its back, Then without warning the great beast turned and jumped into the hole, its strong arms grabbing handholds to arrest its descent. They were all shocked at the suddenness of Jack's capture and disappearance.

Farbeaux ran to the hole and tossed down a flashlight; he heard the distinct sound of it hitting something.

"That didn't help the situation," Jack called back up through the blackness.

Henri looked up at the others who were staring at him.

"I thought the colonel may need that—if we're lucky."

As they waited, there was no sound coming from the shaft. Henri looked at his watch and frowned. He didn't need to announce that they were only three minutes away from a quick but horrible death. Interested in his fate, Farbeaux looked down the dark shaft one last time.

"How long has it been now? Sarah asked as she held Ryan upright with Lynn on the other side of him.

"We only have two minutes now," Everett said as he placed a hand on Mendenhall's back.

Suddenly, there was a roar from far below in the shaft.

"That didn't sound good," Ryan said as he relieved Lynn and Sarah of their burden as he slowly sat down and waited for the melting heat that would signal their death.

They all heard it at the same time, a rumbling coming from below. Farbeaux looked into the shaft and barely had the time to jump out of the way as the beast sprang from the hole. They all yelled at the sudden appearance of the animal as it landed with bent knees; then it shook its back, shaking Jack free from where he was holding on. The beast immediately went to its fallen brethren as the men and women stared on in shock as Collins picked himself up from the floor and came to his knees.

There was silence as they looked Jack over. He had his hands on his knees and he was bloody from head to ripped pants. He was breathing heavy, as heavy as Will, Ryan, and Mendenhall had ever seen him.

"Now that was one express elevator to hell," he said finally.

"I don't mean to be the pushy one in the group, Colonel, but can you tell us what happened. I mean, is our death immanent or not?" Henri said as his eyes never left the beast kneeling beside him. Finally, he chanced a look at Collins when he realized the giant animal was mourning and wasn't hostile.

Jack took a deep breath and then finally looked up at the others. He found Lynn and Sarah and then a smile slowly crept across his bloody face. Then he cleared his throat and then held out his right hand, in it, cupped solidly against his palm was what looked like a circuit breaker that had wires dangling off of it.

"It wasn't even close, it only reached one minute and three seconds."

Most wanted to fall to the cave floor at Jack's remark.

"That animal is amazing; it took me right to the Hyper Glide. It was if the damn thing knew what we wanted. Charlie, if anyone ever gives you crap about what it is you do, you send them to see me."

Jack finally stood with the help of Sarah and Lynn, making a very sore and tired Ryan jealous that he had lost his two nurses. They all stopped when the great beast stood erect with the fallen Bigfoot in its arms. It grunted and then quickly moved down the far end of the cave.

"Let's follow," Jack said placing his arms around his sister and Sarah. "Marla is back there, let's get her and go home."

"There could be a hundred of those . . . those animals back there, Jack," Lynn said.

"Giganticus Pythicus, my dear," Charlie corrected, thinking he was helping out.

"Whatever . . . there could be—"

"There are. Not just hundreds, but thousands. They live here, in each and every single plateau in this area. There is a cave system that must stretch from the Stikine to the Alaskan border." Charlie smiled wide. "Oh, yes, there is indeed something back there young lady."

Jack looked at Everett and he shrugged. Then he took a flashlight and Everett another. They had to see if they could find the girl.

"Should we take this?" Carl asked, holding up the AK-47.

"No," was the fast and simple answer from Jack.

"Okay, but I'm going with you," Sarah said. "You owe me Jack, for that trust you asked for."

"And how do you figure that, Short Stuff?"

"Because, what made you think Alexander wouldn't pull that trigger if he thought all was lost."

Jack smiled. "Because Punchy is the kind that always thinks he can luck his way out of trouble. I knew different."

"Yeah, well, I'm still coming."

Collins nodded, not really wanting to leave Sarah behind anyway. "The rest of you stay put," He gestured at Sarah with her arm around his battered body she started forward.

Charlie Ellenshaw smiled and nodded his head. If the people around him could learn to live without guns and take a chance on nature, and live with it for what it is, or very possibly could be, there was hope indeed.

They saw a bend in the wall of the cave as they slowly advanced. Jack was in the lead with Sarah in the middle and Everett taking up their rear. As Collins neared the wall and the bend, he saw something that looked vaguely familiar. Then he recognized it: It was a steering bar for a horse-drawn wagon. As Jack drew nearer, he could see something on the ground. He shone the light on it and then turned to Sarah and Everett.

"Well, someone lost their lunch money," he said, smiling and showing both Sarah and Carl the lost treasure of L. T. Lattimer as it glimmered even through the hundred years of dust.

On the ground were spilled bags, and even some stacked gold double eagles. Lattimer must have done the stacking before he vanished into Ellenshaw's past.

"Now that's impressive," Carl said as he stared at the millions just sitting, spilled on the ground.

Jack shook his head and moved on, shining the light left and then right. He was looking for any trail the girl may have left in the soft earth of the cave's floor, but as it was they only had the giant prints of the beast as it had went this way with its sorrowful load. As he approached the second wagon, he flashed his light on its tarp-covered bed and squeezed by. Close behind him, Sarah stumbled into the wagon's wooden side. It was Carl who heard the sound of cracking wood and ran to push Sarah out of the way. As they cleared the side of the wagon, Jack pulled them out the rest of the way just as bags upon bags of gold double eagles fell free. It was Sarah who saw it first.

"Wow," Everett said and that was followed by a whistle.

Lying among the bags of gold was the skeletal remains of a man dressed in a plaid shirt with suspenders. The skull looked as if it had been crushed as its blank eyes stared out at nothing. Jack saw that the skeletons arms seemed to wrap around two of the large bags of coins and to him it looked as if the skull were grinning.

"The late Mr. Lattimer I presume," Sarah said, staring at the remains.

"Well, he got what he came for," Jack said as he pulled on Sarah's arm. They left the two wagons behind and allowed L. T. Lattimer to have his gold.

As they advanced, the cave became more humid. They saw where several tunnels branched off the main cave. Jack was starting to think it would be an impossible task to find Marla. That was when he heard a sound that sent chills down his back. It was the cry of a baby, or more precisely, several babies.

Everett pointed toward one of the shafts of the cave that bent to the right. Collins shone the light in that direction and then he looked back at Carl and Sarah. He shook his head.

"I wouldn't want anyone barging in on my children, and Charlie's beasts seem to take things the way humans would."

"I am in total agreement," Everett said.

"Look," Sarah whispered.

As Carl and Jack followed Sarah's eyes, they saw the small footprints that led up a small incline and into another shaft fifty feet above their heads.

"At least the tracks don't lead through the nursery," Jack said as he started up in that direction.

As they moved upward from the cave floor, the paintings on the cave walls became more numerous. There were scenes of family life, not of humans or even ancient man, but of the animals that they had encountered that night. The gathering of vegetables and berries, even the killing of small animals were shown in stark detail in a rainbow of colors. Jack was amazed at the differing views that the artist had, a very steady and talented hand was at work here and they all knew by looking at the paintings they were dealing with an advancement of a mammal that went far beyond that of mere evolution. It was like they were looking at themselves a millions years before.

"Jack, look at this," Sarah said as she examined a larger than normal drawing. Collins shone the light and was amazed to see an articulate and colorful painting of a large bird: an eagle.

"Why does it have two heads?" Sarah asked.

As Collins examined the painting, a sense a familiarity came into his mind. The eagle was displayed with wings spread and the heads were facing opposite of one another. The colors were red and yellow. What plants were used to make this he didn't know, the colors were so bright.

"I don't know why it has two heads, but why would that seem strange in a place like this?"

"Point taken," Sarah said as she moved along behind Jack.

As they climbed, they all could smell a change in the air. It was cooler and there was more of a freshness to it after the oppressiveness of the lower cave system. Suddenly, Collins stopped and shut off the flashlight.

Sarah saw it, too. There was light up ahead.

"It must be dawn outside," Everett said standing next to Sarah.

"Listen," Jack said, tilting his head toward the dull light coming through the passage ahead.

"It sounds like crying, or moaning," Sarah said in wonder. She reached for Jack as he started forward, suddenly realizing there were limits to her natural curiosity.

Jack climbed toward the diffused light ahead. Sarah and Everett followed, while Carl was wishing he would have brought the AK-47 along—just for comfort. Jack saw the opening up ahead. The noise coming from outside was sorrowful and again he got the cold chills. It reminded him of a time in Mogadishu and the funeral rites for forty-seven children murdered by a warlord. The sound was that of mothers mourning their young—or a lost husband.

As they came to the large opening that led out onto the top of the plateau, Jack held Sarah close by. When they looked out of the opening, they froze. It was if they were looking at a scene that would have been described by some ancient architect of primordial recordings. Collins had seen pictures and read books about the American Indian tribes and how they respected their dead. The scene spread out before them was one of the most fantastic sights they had ever seen. The trees were the first thing they saw. Among the branches of these trees were placed the bodies of the giant apes that had been killed that night by the Russian mercenaries. Jack counted three of the large animals that were raised to the highest branches of the trees.

"Look," Sarah said pointing from their high vantage point.

The animals, from what Jack could quickly count, numbered in the hundreds as they stood around and watched as some of the larger beasts lifted the bodies of the dead upward into the thick trees. Jack quickly saw their savior as it lifted the body of the beast from the cave. It was as though he was witnessing a father morning his son.

"Is this where the Indians got their burial traditions?" Sarah asked no one in particular.

The moaning and crying was being done by most of the animals on the ground. Some sat on the ground, other stood, but all had the look of bereavement that everyone in the world has felt at one time or another.

When the three bodies were situated in the top branches, Jack could see the large animals remove long straps of what looked like leather, or rawhide. They wrapped these around the dead to secure them to the branches. It was amazing that these giant beasts were smart enough to have a ceremony for the dead and actually grieve, which placed them at the head of the entire animal kingdom and just below the intelligence level of man. They actually knew and understood the concept of death.

"Oh my God," came a voice behind them.

They all turned and saw Charlie Ellenshaw as he took in the scene before him.

"I would give my right arm to have a camera," he said, swiping at a tear that coursed its way down his old cheek.

"Jack, you won't believe this," Carl said as he started shaking his head.

Off in the distance, covering at least ten miles of trees at the upper-most portion of the plateau, were the raised remains of thousands of creatures. Some were old, others ancient, and some looked as if they had died recently. They covered the tops of trees for miles around.

"How long have they been here?" Sarah asked.

Collins could only shake his head.

The ceremony was finished. They saw the larger of the animals drop from the lower branches of the trees after securing the dead. Then the Sasquatch moved off in small groups, in what looked like family units. Then they vanished before their eyes, blending in with the trees and shrubs of the mountain. Jack, Sarah, Charlie, and Carl were silent. To be a witness to what modern man brought with them to the nature of their own world was quite unsettling.

When Jack looked back down onto the plateau, he saw a sight that froze his heart.

"I'll be damned," Jack mumbled.

Sarah, Charlie, and Everett looked down and saw what Jack was seeing. There, huddled where a hundred giant beasts had been a moment earlier, was Marla. She was on her knees and she was praying over a body.

"Oh my God," Sarah said. "It's Helena, her grandmother."

Twenty minutes later, Jack, Sarah, Ellenshaw, and Everett reached Marla from the ledge, and joined her on the top of the plateau. The girl had stopped praying and was just looking straight ahead. When Sarah touched her on the shoulder, Marla didn't do anything other than place her own hand on top of Sarah's.

"Honey, how did your grandmother get here?" Sarah asked.

Marla patted Sarah's hand and then half turned. "*They Who Follow* brought her from home."

"*They Who Follow?*" Carl asked.

Marla finally stood. She had been crying heavily, just as the giant apes had been. She wiped at her dirty face and looked at Everett.

"That's what the old ones called them. *They Who Follow.* They say they got their name by coming across from Asia thousands of years ago—the last time when man was forced to this continent by drought and ice. Legend has it that they followed the clans of men. They have been here ever since."

"Marla, why would they bring your grandmother here?" Jack asked.

The young girl looked curiously at Jack for a long moment, and then she turned to face the rising sun.

"I'm happy you escaped alive from those men—those Russians."

Jack didn't ask why she didn't answer his question, he just looked at Carl and Sarah and waited while the girl figured something out. It had been the way she had looked at them a moment ago that told Jack to be patient.

"The others—" She looked at Jack for a split second. "Your sister, is she alright?"

Collins dipped his head in answer, silent because of the unvoiced sympathy the girl had been prepared to deliver if Lynn hadn't been safe. He could now see that this young woman had been around death all of her life, and she understood it more than being afraid of it.

Marla reached out and took Jack by the hand. Then she started walking. Sarah looked at Carl and Charlie, and they slowly followed along. They walked for about a quarter mile when Marla took them into a copse of young trees encircled by far more ancient pines. She led them into a clearing where Jack stopped and allowed Marla to go on alone. She stopped and then turned. Jack waited for Sarah, the Doc, and Carl; they all slowly approached. Marla was standing in front of five objects that were half buried in the ground and covered by small bushes that had sprung up in front of them.

"My grandmother didn't allow me to come out here by myself. She was always wary of *They Who Follow*. She said that no matter how smart we thought they were, they were still animals in their own right." Marla turned and smiled at the three people who stood silently, waiting for her to say what it was she brought them here to tell them. "My grandmother will be buried here along with my mother, my father, and the rest of our family."

"Marla," Sarah said, removing Jack's hand that tried to stay her from talking. "Why are they buried all the way out here, and not close to your home?"

"They need to be safe—safe from people like those men that came here. There will always be men like that; men that seek to take what is not theirs to have."

As they watched, Marla uncover the first of the headstones that had been carved by a Tlingit Indian, year after year, every time there was one of her family to be buried. The secret had been kept close to the hearts of the inhabitants inside the Stikine Valley, and known only to a few.

Jack stepped forward and saw the first two names on the first two stones. It was the names of Marla's parents. She ran a loving hand over the cool stone, and then stood and moved to the far right of her parents' burial spot.

"Sarah had said you and yours have run into things that would amaze and astound the rest of the world, so maybe you *can* keep a secret. That is the least I can do for stopping you men; share what has only been known to my family for almost a hundred years."

She started pulling the small bushes standing guard in front of the last three headstones. Marla looked as if this was something she had wanted to do since she had been born, maybe as a way of explaining herself—her very existence.

As the first carved name was uncovered, Jack stepped forward and his mouth fell open as he read the headstone.

"Colonel Iosovich Petrov, beloved husband and servant to Tsar Nicholas, died 25 September 1955," Jack said aloud. He looked back at Everett; Ellenshaw, and Sarah, all of whom stood dumbfounded.

When Marla had removed the bushes from the last two stones, the entire story behind the fishing camp, the gold and the Twins of Peter the Great came into sharp focus and understanding dawned in Jack's eyes. The words were clear and they were literally earth-shaking.

Grand Duchess Anastasia Nicolaievna Romanov
Beloved wife of Iosovich
Born 5 June 1901 Died 18 February 1956

Tsarevich Alexei Nikolayevich Romanov
Beloved son of Nicholas II and Alexandria
Born 12 August 1904 Died 3 March 1919

Marla finally turned and faced Jack, the professor, Sarah, and Everett. She smiled, almost embarrassed at what she had shown them.

"They didn't deserve to be separated from their mother, father, and sisters, no matter what the outcome. My great-great-grandfather Nicholas should have understood that, without family, there is nothing."

Jack swallowed; he was speechless as to what he was witness to. Sarah swiped at a tear as she looked at the words on the tombstone. Charlie was amazed to the point of grieving for the girl and her long-lost ancestors. Everett, for his part, placed his arm around the girl.

"My family, since being here, has taken on the responsibility of something just as great, or even greater: the protection of the wildlife that live here. You see, they used to roam the open spaces from Canada to Mexico—now they have only this place," Marla said as she gestured around her. "We lost our home once, for reasons that were brought on by arrogance and class, something we will never attain again."

"The Crown Prince Alexei and Anastasia, your great-uncle and your great-grandmother," Sarah said as she couldn't take her eyes from the stones in front of her.

"You once said your people were good at keeping secrets—I hope this is true," Marla said as she smiled sadly, and moved off to bury her grandmother alongside a family lost to history.

Jack swore that this was one secret that would be kept.

EPILOGUE

13

Lynn Simpson sat at the rear of the office. Her arm was in a sling from the twelve-hour surgery she underwent for the infection in her hand after the crude amputation by Sagli. She waited patiently staring at the back of her boss's head.

Nancy Grogan would turn around and smile every few minutes as she waited with Lynn and the director of CIA, Harlan Easterbrook, for a day of judgment that was long in coming. The director sat silently waiting for the visit they all were expecting.

A buzz sounded and the director hit his intercom. It was his male secretary.

"Mr. Rosen is here, sir."

"Send the boy right in and also give the order I gave to you earlier."

"It's already in the works, sir."

Easterbrook sat back in his chair and waited. Soon, a knock sounded and the door opened. Stan Rosen, the assistant director for operations stood smiling at the door.

"You wanted to see me?"

"Stanley, come in, please."

Rosen entered, closing the door without turning around. He nodded his head toward Nancy Grogan and then he noticed the seated figure in the back of the office. Recognition came to his eyes and he smiled once again.

"Ms. Simpson, I had heard you were making a return to your desk, but I thought you would take more time to heal up?"

Lynn returned the smile. "Usually I would have, but my brother convinced me to come back early. He said I would want to be in on the final disposition of my case."

"Your brother?" he asked finally sitting down, but keeping his eyes on Lynn. "Oh, yes, Colonel Collins, the big mystery man."

"Not as big a mystery as you were led to believe, Stan," Easterbrook said. "Actually, Colonel Collins turned up and did a little work for us; he would like a chance to explain to you what he found."

"Me? Why would he have to explain anything to me?" Rosen said becoming slightly concerned.

"Colonel Collins, are you there, sir?" Easterbrook said aloud so the speakerphone could be utilized.

"Indeed, Mr. Director. Mr. Rosen, how are you today?" Jack Collins asked from his own director's office in Nevada.

"Fine, Colonel, I'm afraid I haven't had the pleasure."

"Indeed, you haven't, you lucky son of a bitch. I just wanted to hear your voice, memorize it, with that I will always know that your plans were thwarted by my baby sister. Now, I think she has something to say to you. Lynn, I'll see you at Thanksgiving."

"Thanks, Jack, and by the way, I expect you to bring Sarah with you when you come."

"You bet. Mr. Rosen, enjoy it."

The connection to the Event group was terminated.

"Enjoy what?" Stanley Rosen asked as he became most uncomfortable. "And I don't like the fact that an assistant director of CIA can be talked to like that by a colonel in the U.S. army."

"Oh, believe it, you traitorous bastard," Lynn said as she stood and paced to Rosen's chair. She deftly tossed a photo onto his lap. "Recognize those?" she asked.

Rosen looked the photos over and then up at Lynn. "Yes, they are the photos of Sagli and Deonovich when they came through the Seattle airport."

"Yes, the same pictures you passed on to Nancy Grogan. Is that correct, Nancy?"

"Yes. Actually they came from Sagli himself and sent through your private computer at home. A computer you thought was so secure that the CIA could never break in. Well, luckily, Lynn's brother is somewhat a genius at doing just that. Or maybe it's someone who works for him, I don't know. When the pictures were forwarded to me, it sounded like a gorgeous assistant, almost sounding like Marilyn Monroe who offered them to me. You bastard, Stan."

"I want my lawyer," he said standing.

"Sit down, Stanley. You'll get your lawyer," Easterbrook said as he looked the small man over.

"You worked directly with Punchy Alexander and notified him when I left for Montreal the morning of the ambush. And then you supplied him with access codes to the NSA archives that led indirectly to information about a project known as Solar Flare."

"You are nuts, and you better be prepared to prove it. I know nothing about anything titled Solar Flare."

"Ms. Grogan, Ms. Simpson, did you hear this man utter the words 'Solar Flare'?" Easterbrook asked.

"Yes, I did," both women said at the same time.

"What does that matter?"

"Mr. President, are you there?" the director asked.

"Yes, I am." His voice came through the intercom.

"Did you hear Mr. Rosen say the name of a top secret project called Solar Flare?"

"Yes, Mr. Director, I did indeed."

"Mr. Rosen, you are hereby under arrest for the act of treason against the United States."

"For what?" he said to Lynn in shock. "You can't prove a damn thing. A computer can lie as well as a human and would be beat in a court of law, especially with the business we're in."

"Oh, you're not under arrest for what you did to me in Montreal, Mr. Rosen. You're under arrest for the act of espionage. You see, only ten people this side of the White House knew the name Solar Flare, therefore you had to have been inside of classified presidential documents, since President Kennedy placed the top secret cover on Solar Flare, a name you magically just said aloud with the commander-in-chief as a witness; ergo, you're a traitor." Lynn smiled as she leaned over the shaken Rosen. "Our little white lie, sir, is compliments of the president of the United States and my big brother, Jack."

EVENT GROUP COMPLEX
NELLIS AIR FORCE BASE, NEVADA

The report delivered by Professor Charles Hindershot Ellenshaw III was one of those few times that the sixteen department heads of the Event Group were taken back. They had sat enraptured by the cryptozoology details that outlined the newly discovered and documented life-form known as Giganticus Pythicus—Bigfoot.

Jack, Sarah, and Carl had sat and listened and felt for Charlie as he finally received the respect of those doubters in the conference room who always had a snide remark waiting for when the wild-haired professor walked by. They would never talk behind his back again.

Director Niles Compton was the first to stand and applaud Ellenshaw's report, stating in closing that he was sure he would have received the Nobel Prize, if only the rest of the world could know about it.

"Charlie, thank you. Would everyone but Colonel Collins and Captain Everett please excuse us?"

As the department heads rose to leave, more than a few of Ellenshaw's previous doubters of him and his entire department came up to him and shook his hand, all of them playing the humbled colleague to the hilt. Sarah smiled as she left the conference room. She was about to go to her classroom when she saw Will Mendenhall sitting at the desk of Alice Hamilton doing paperwork and waiting for his bosses. She stood before him and smiled.

"What are you doing here?" she asked.

Mendenhall looked up angrily. "Filling out insurance claims—what else?"

"On what?" she asked sitting on the edge of Alice Hamilton's old desk.

"For Alice's damned crashed seaplane—boy, was she hot!"

"Why isn't Ryan doing that?"

Will put down the stack of papers in exasperation. "Because, Lieutenant McIntire, she has him over at her place working for the senator as he transcribes his memoirs."

"Oh, that's rich; if you can't do the time, don't do the crime."

"Yeah, whatever. Just what did I do to have to do all of this paper-work? I didn't crash the plane or burn down Alice's kitchen."

"What?" Sarah asked, trying hard not to laugh.

"That's what these second set of insurance papers are for: While Alice was flying us to L.A., the senator set fire to their kitchen; seems he forgot all about a casserole in the oven or something. God, is she pissed!"

Several of the department heads had to stop and look at Sarah McIntire as she broke into laughter, and then watch as Will Mendenhall glared at her.

Niles looked at Jack's report and placed it in his own personal file. Then he looked up at Everett and Jack.

"I'm glad you got your sister back, Jack. The president sends his—well, he's happy, too."

"What about declaring Punchy Alexander for what he was, a traitor? That may assist with the French-speaking problem Canada is facing."

Jack understood. The event never happened. Punchy Alexander would be listed as a missing agent by the Canadian government and that would be that. A Nest team had been dispatched clandestinely to the area north of the Wahachapee Fishing Camp where they discovered by accident a downed aircraft. The pilot and his payload were recovered and the pilot's family, Commander John Charles Phillips, was returned with honors after being missing for forty-eight years to his family who could finally stop grieving for a son, a father, and a husband that was lost in a war that never went hot—thanks to men and women like him. As for the animals, after Jack and the others had taken the Hyper Glide from the cave and hidden it along the Stikine, they were never seen again.

"Director," Everett said, after clearing his throat. "What about that area north of the Stikine River? What can we do to protect it from outsiders?"

Niles pursed his lips and looked from Everett to Jack.

"Nothing."

"But—"

"Captain Everett, if we push the Canadian government for protection of that area, I guarantee you that word of the creatures will get out, and then what? It will be their extinction. I left that question up to Charlie Ellenshaw and he said to leave it be. Giganticus Pythicus has survived for thousands of years without our assistance and he thinks they can survive even longer with no help from us."

Niles stood and placed his glasses on his face, walked around the table, and put his hand on Everett's shoulder. "Don't worry, Captain, I won't hold it against you for caring. Now, Jack, I must ask, whatever became of our old friend, Colonel Farbeaux?"

Collins shook his head. "That son of a bitch ran out on us after getting his hands on not only the second diamond, but also the first that he tore through the Russian camp to find. He stole one of the boats we needed, and then took one of the helicopters, so as I figure it, he not only got away again, he stole about a billion dollars' worth of stones and equipment."

"I guess we have to give him a pass this time around, especially since he's now wanted again by his own government for not turning over his final report on what was recovered and what wasn't."

"Why are they so hot about that?" Jack asked.

"Because he called them and said they can have his confidential report for fifty million francs, or he would go public with it."

Jack laughed as did Everett.

"Your sister, is she back at work?" Niles asked as he went over to his seat and activated the large-screen monitor at the front of the conference room.

"Yes, sir, she has a new desk at Langley, of her own choosing—she's handling the International Crimes Division, basically assisting Interpol in their manhunts."

"Don't tell me?"

"Uh-huh, she says that Colonel Henri Farbeaux intrigues her, so she's going after him."

"Well, she may save us some heartache down the road then," Niles said, adjusting the large monitor while Jack and Everett stood.

"She just might do that. . . . If that's all, Niles, we have some work to catch up on."

"Just a second, Jack. I thought you may find this interesting."

Collins stopped and turned to face the large monitor. There was a test pattern on it and then a screen came up. Europa, the supercomputer, was shanghaiing a signal from the Central Pacific that was generated by the CBS Nightly News. Soon, the picture cleared and there was a woman reporter standing in front of a camera with pieces of construction equipment in the background. There were American and Japanese flags flying from that equipment.

"Late this afternoon, professor of historical studies, Eileen Santos of Colorado State University, in a joint announcement with the Imperial Japanese Historical Society has released data that confirms the identity of the famous aviatrix, Amelia Earhart, whose body was discovered in the early-morning hours of August first by the Colorado State forensic search team five days ago. The body, by all accounts was covered in an American flag along with the remains of her navigator, Fred Noonan, as they were pulled from long-forgotten sands on this small island, ending the mystery of her disappearance more than—"

Niles turned the monitor off and then sat down. He watched Jack for a moment and then cleared his throat.

"She's on her way home, Jack. After all of these years she's about to get her just due, and now you can look at yourself in the mirror and know for a fact all of this is meant to do something, even if it's as small as bringing a little girl, or a woman, home again."

Jack stood and was deep in thought. Then he slowly looked up and nodded his head.

"As in the case of the Romanov children, I guess you could say they're at home, also," Niles said as he walked around and opened the conference doors for Jack and Carl.

"Yes," Collins said as he turned to leave.

"And that's where our history will leave them." Niles smiled. "Some things need to be kept secret."

As Jack and Everett left, Niles closed the door and then walked to his chair and opened the file that was marked EVENT FILE 19908757. He looked at the picture stapled to the inside jacket. He couldn't help it—he smiled at the image of Marla Petrovich and then looked at the picture opposite of hers. It was of Anastasia Romanov. The two young women were almost twins of each other. Niles shook his head and then closed the file. The real beauty was not the Twins of Peter the Great, but another set of twins that were far more precious.

"Indeed, some history is good right where it's at."

Outside the conference room on level seven, the Event Group prepared for the return of full operational status as their condition was reported to the president of the United States.

Yes, life would go on, and some secrets would be kept forever deep beneath the Nevada desert.